"Being a soldier was the only thing I ever wanted to do."

"Why?" She had to know why Hawk had chosen to be a ranger. "Why do you guys feel so committed to the army?"

"Because I fight for what I believe in. I love this country. I want to do my part." Not defensive, just powerful. Poignant. "Although it comes at a cost. I'm still single."

"Why haven't you gotten married?"

"Why get involved with someone when I knew I had to leave?"

"And yet being alone is the reason you stayed in the army?"

"It's a circular argument. Don't think I don't know that." He shrugged a shoulder, as if dismissing it, but something that looked like sadness clung to his features. "You're alone too, September. I don't have to ask to know the answer. You aren't dating."

"No. I don't have the heart left." She couldn't give voice to the loneliness of the past two years and the fear that she had been broken beyond repair. Beyond hope. Beyond God.

"We are two of a kind."

New York Times bestselling author **Jillian Hart** grew up on her family's homestead, where she helped raise cattle, rode horses and scribbled stories in her spare time. After earning her English degree from Whitman College, she worked in travel and advertising before selling her first novel. When Jillian isn't working on her next story, she can be found puttering in her rose garden, curled up with a good book or spending quiet evenings at home with her family.

Kat Brookes is an award-winning author and past Romance Writers of America Golden Heart® Award finalist. She is married to her childhood sweetheart and has been blessed with two beautiful daughters. She loves writing stories that can both make you smile and touch your heart. Kat is represented by Michelle Grajkowski with 3 Seas Literary Agency. Read more about Kat and her upcoming releases at katbrookes.com. Email her at katbrookes@comcast.net. Facebook: Kat Brookes.

The Soldier's Holiday Vow

New York Times Bestselling Author

Jillian Hart

&

His Holiday Matchmaker

Kat Brookes

LOVE INSPIRED
INSPIRATIONAL ROMANCE

Recycling programs for this product may not exist in your area.

LOVE INSPIRED®
INSPIRATIONAL ROMANCE

ISBN-13: 978-1-335-42499-0

The Soldier's Holiday Vow and His Holiday Matchmaker

Copyright © 2021 by Harlequin Books S.A.

The Soldier's Holiday Vow
First published in 2009. This edition published in 2021.
Copyright © 2009 by Jill Strickler

His Holiday Matchmaker
First published in 2016. This edition published in 2021.
Copyright © 2016 by Kimberly Duffy

This edition published by arrangement with Harlequin Books S.A.

For questions and comments about the quality of this book, please contact us at CustomerService@Harlequin.com.

Love Inspired
22 Adelaide St. West, 40th Floor
Toronto, Ontario M5H 4E3, Canada
www.Harlequin.com

Printed in U.S.A.

CONTENTS

THE SOLDIER'S HOLIDAY VOW

Jillian Hart

So let us come boldly to the throne of our gracious God. There we will receive his mercy, and we will find grace to help us when we need it most.
—*Hebrews* 4:16

Chapter One

September Stevens fought despair. Not an easy thing to do. The cold damp earth surrounded her like a grave. The jagged, crumbling walls of the mine shaft lifted above her and drank up the faint starlight. She and little Crystal Toppins had been down here for a good twelve hours. Sunset came early, near to four-thirty this time of year. That meant enough time had passed for it to be nearly midnight. If the sky wasn't partly overcast, typical for the Pacific Northwest in winter, the rising moon might have offered some relief from the suffocating dark and fear.

Maybe then it would have been easier to hold on to hope.

"They aren't coming, are they?" The ten-year-old girl gulped down a sob. It was too dark in the belly of the shaft to see more than a shadow of the child lying on her back on the earthen floor. Terror made the girl's voice thin and raw. "Are we going to d-die?"

"No, of course not." September leaned back against the hard-packed dirt wall and stretched her legs out as far as they would go. She had to believe that was the truth, but privately, she wasn't so sure. Crystal had been seriously hurt. September's injuries weren't as severe, but her left forearm had a compound fracture. With no antiseptic wipes, no sterile bandages and no first-aid kit—all of which were still packed safely in her saddle pack on her horse—she had done all she could.

She couldn't let her fear win. The horses would have returned to the stable, although it was miles away down Bear Mountain. Comanche was well trained and fond of his molasses snacks. He would have gone straight home and that meant Colleen, her boss, knew they were missing. Search parties would have gone out immediately—probably ten hours ago or so.

"They know where we were headed, so everyone knows where to look," she reasoned, putting as much reassurance as she could in her voice. Crystal's condition could be fragile, and she had to give the girl strength. "They are coming. They will be here as soon as they can."

"What if they can't find us? What if they stop looking?"

"They won't do that, sweetie." September pressed her arm against the girl's gently, comfortingly. "Do you think your mom would let that happen?"

"No." Crystal had to almost be smiling. "Mom's a little intense."

"Yes, she is, and that's a great thing. A fantastic thing. She will mow this mountain down to find you. I'm absolutely sure about that, so no more worrying. Got it?"

"Got it." Crystal sighed, a desolate sound in the dark. A nearly absolute dark. September looked up through the ragged hole in the earth above to the disappearing stars. A cloud layer was moving in from the coast, blotting out the twinkling lights one by one. The dank chill of the ground crept into her bones, and it was a cold that gripped with talons. She would never be warm again.

Where was their search party? It was the question she had been asking since their horses balked, probably feeling the earth shift beneath their hooves. It was a good hour's ride back to the stable. That meant a search party should have been passing by within an hour, maybe two. Although she had listened diligently and watched carefully, there had been no sign of anyone riding the trail hunting for them. Did that mean no one would be coming? How long could they last, injured and without food or water or even a blanket for warmth? Was it possible they would die in this thirty-foot grave?

If so, this wasn't how she wanted to go, afraid and wishing she could change so much of her life. Her mess of a life. She drew in a rattling breath, leaned back against the cold earthen wall and closed her eyes against the thrum of pain inside her head. No one twenty-three years old should die with regrets. It wasn't right that she had so many of them.

If she had one do-over, it would be to go back in time exactly two years, two months and ten days and force Tim out of the army. To have made her fiancé realize that he had done his part in serving several tours of duty overseas. That he didn't have to stay in the military.

If she had been adamant, if she had stood her ground, then he would still be alive today and she wouldn't be in this abandoned shaft with an injured child weakening by the hour, bits of earth crumbling down on top of them.

Please, Lord. Send somebody before it's too late for Crystal. She sent the prayer heavenward, but feared it was not strong enough to escape this dark hole. Her faith was not exactly rock solid these days. She feared God had given up on her. She didn't blame Him one bit.

"I'm c-cold."

"Here, lean closer to me." She lifted her arm, carefully scooching closer to the injured girl. It was all she could offer.

The little girl leaned against her with another sigh, and September held her. She felt the fine chills of Crystal's body and feared she was slipping into shock. She could do nothing more for the child, who she feared was bleeding internally. Before the sun had gone down, there had been just enough light to see the growing bruise on the girl's abdomen. There was only so much basic first aid could do.

"September?" Crystal's voice sounded feeble, as if she were fading away. "What is it like to die?"

"I don't know." She felt the strike of the past, as if she was being pulled back to the cold, lifeless shock two years, two months and ten days ago. She had just turned into her driveway after coming home from the grocery store and seen the army chaplain and Tim's commanding officer at her front door.

She shut off her feelings to block the pain. After all this time, she still battled the overwhelming wave of grief. What had death been like for Tim? Had he known it was coming or was it so sudden, he didn't know? Had he suffered? Was his last thought of her? She hated how time had begun to dim his memory. She could no longer pull his image up in her mind as clearly. It felt doubly cruel.

"Jesus is supposed to be in heaven waiting for us, but what if I don't go there?" Crystal's voice wobbled. "What if I'm not good enough?"

"Jesus loves you, Crystal." She didn't feel equipped to be reassuring anyone's faith. "Please stop worrying and relax. You need to rest."

"Okay." The girl sounded all wrong—as if her condition were worsening, as if she were fading away.

Please, Lord, don't let that happen. It wasn't fair that Crystal had been so wounded when she had not been. She adjusted her broken arm carefully, where it rested on her thigh, and ignored the searing pain. *Take anything from me, Lord, and give it to Crystal. Please use it to save her life.*

No answer came. The last stars winked out. The little girl beside her gave a sob, as if she were running out of hope, too. September's stomach clamped tight with prickly fear for the girl. The truth was, she felt as if God could not see them and suspected He didn't care.

And wasn't that a sad way to feel? Her breath hitched in her lungs with a sharp pain. What happened to the woman she used to be? She dug deep, past the hard, suffocating shell of grief, and tried to see her old self, the one she had lost along with Tim and their dreams. *That* September would not be on the edge of despair. She would be certain God would see her to safety.

She'd had such perfect faith back then and doubt

would never have crept in. Nor the certainty that she was forgotten in this grave deep in the earth.

How had she come to this place in her spiritual life? She felt blood trickling down her forehead—the cut must have started bleeding again—and gingerly blotted it with her T-shirt hem. The two years were a blur as she'd fought to put one foot in front of the other and make it through each minute, each hour, each day. Now she found herself here, trapped in the earth, more lost than she knew how to say.

"I feel real bad, September." Crystal sobbed once, just once.

"Hang in there, sweetie." She adored her little riding student; she felt useless to help her now. She tightened her hold on the girl. "Close your eyes and rest."

A snapping branch shattered the vast silence. Hope flared to life. She eased her arm around the girl and sat up, not daring to say anything or to even think the words. After all, it could be a wild animal passing by and not a rescue party. But still, it *could* be. She carefully rose upward, laying her good hand on the damp clay wall for support. Bright spots flashed in front of her eyes and the pounding in her head felt like the worst of thunderstorms. She kept her thoughts clear and strained for the tiniest sign that anyone was nearby.

"Hi, there." A man's rough baritone preceded the shine of a halogen flashlight.

There was something about that voice, both familiar and startling. Her thumping brain couldn't make sense of it right off. He took a moment to look away, as if signaling to more people out of her sight. Her double vision made it hard at first to recognize the striking, chiseled lines of his face, the high, proud forehead and straight bridge of his nose.

"You two are a welcome sight." He grinned down at her with an easy friendliness that spun her back in time.

"Hawk." Tim's best friend. Her blood went cold. Seeing his shadowed face sent her into another shock wave. Tremors quaked through her as she stared, open-mouthed. The last time she'd seen him it had been dark, too, as dark as this mine shaft, the night full of loss and sorrow where no light could reach.

Why did it have to be him? Couldn't their rescuer be someone—anyone—other than Mark Hawkins?

"September Stevens, you look worse for the wear. Contusion. Concussion, maybe? Your arm's broken?"

She nodded, struggling to think past her shock. "Crystal's hurt. I think she needs a helicopter."

"Got it." Their gazes met and the force of it was like a punch. She knew without asking that he understood what she couldn't say, not without panicking the girl. He turned toward the child. "Crystal, hello there. Can you see me?"

"Ye-ah." She sounded weak. Too weak.

"Good, 'cause I'm comin' down to fetch you. You are the prettiest girl I've ever rescued." Unruffled, that was Hawk, and beyond the tough-as-bedrock Army Ranger was the heart of a truly kind man. He climbed into a harness and tied off. "Everything's gonna be fine now. You hear me?"

"Ye-ah." Even in terrible pain, the girl managed a small, brief smile.

September's knees were watery, so she sank back down beside the girl, watching as Hawk tested the rope and nodded to the other rescuers somewhere out of her sight. Good to go, he rappelled through the darkness, the rasp of the rope the only sound between them. Their ordeal was over, and they were found. That ought to bring her sheer relief. It didn't. Knowing their rescue came at the price of seeing Hawk again was no comfort. She winced when his feet hit ground. His presence seemed to draw every particle of air from the underground cave.

"We'll get Crystal up first," he murmured, leaning close. She could feel the heat radiating off his skin and smell the mix of mountain air, leather and exhaust clinging to his clothes. "We've got a chopper coming…" He paused to catch the gurney being lowered on a rope. "And Crystal's mom knows she's been found."

"Good." What a relief. She thought of Patty Toppins, a concerned, caring mom who had to be frantic with terror. Dully, she realized Hawk was kneeling next to Crystal. She cleared her throat. "Let me help."

"No need." His gloved hand caught hers and sent a shock through her system.

Alarmed, she wrenched her hand away, bumping into the earthen barrier. Her breathing came raggedly, her pulse thudded too loudly in her ears. Why had she reacted so strongly to Hawk's touch? Why had he unsettled her? She blinked, realizing another man was circling around to assist Hawk. Someone else roped down without her noticing. Too much was happening, and she couldn't seem to focus. It must be because of the concussion.

Hawk had already turned back to business, the wide set of his shoulders visible in the eerie shaft of light from above. It was good to see him. It was horrible to see him. She felt useless as the men started an IV for the girl and strapped her into the gurney. The second man hooked in. She caught a glimpse of Crystal's face, ashen in the harsh lighting, before the ground team hoisted her swiftly upward into waiting hands. The *whop-whop* of a helicopter told her help had arrived just in time.

"Let me take a look at you, September." Hawk's voice, gentle with concern. "You're hurt."

"Nothing like Crystal." It was too hard to look him in the eye, tougher still to see the shadows of the life and the dreams, which were gone. He reminded her of what was lost. Of the determined, competitive, patriotic man she had wanted to marry. A part of her had died right along with Tim. She wished she could step farther away from him, but there wasn't room enough to escape him. Stuck against the earth with nowhere to go, she was forced to stand while he inched closer. The cold damp seeped through her shirt and she shivered.

"Look up." Hawk shone a light into her eyes and flicked it away. He did it a second time, frowning.

She wanted to pretend he was a stranger, a man she did not know. It felt as if parts of her cracked again after she'd worked so hard to keep together. Panic crept through her and she pushed away. "I'm fine, Hawk. I just need to get out of here, that's all."

"I don't think you're fine. You're going to need stitches." His gaze raked across her face like a touch. "You've got quite a concussion. And what about that arm? That's going to need surgery."

"I'm alive. That's fine in my book." Maybe she sounded a little harsh, but it had been a terrible day and a worse night. Seeing him suddenly like this was the last thing she could deal with. She couldn't risk going back to that dark, broken place. "All I need is one of those harness things. Can you call up for one?"

"Better yet, you can ride with me." He sounded calm and unwavering. He was a fine soldier; seeing her again and remembering what had happened to Tim wasn't likely to throw him.

Unlike her. She caught sight of the extra harness hooked into his, and her knees wobbled. His hand shot out, steadying her by the elbow, the strength and heat of his touch seared like a burn. She didn't want to go up with him. "Maybe someone else—"

"We have to hurry, September." His gaze turned grim, the only hint at what he might be feeling. His shadowed face became a hard mask, impossible to read. "We don't want to keep the bird waiting."

"I don't need the helicopter."

"It's the best way." He had been calm on the night after they had buried Tim, too, a steady rock in the darkness. "I don't call the shots."

"But I don't want—" She couldn't finish. Her skull felt ready to explode from pain. Her stomach cramped with light nausea. She couldn't keep arguing with him, but how could she let him take her into his arms? She fisted her hands. She was not strong enough.

"You don't want to cost Crystal valuable time." Gentleness blended with cold-hard steel. He wrapped the harness around her hips and secured the strap, so close she could see the whorl of dark hair at his crown and smell the clean scent of his shampoo. His gaze latched on to hers with the force of the earth on the moon. "Put your arms around me."

If Crystal hadn't been waiting on her, she never

would have done it. One thought of the girl had her wrapping her arms around Hawk's wide, muscled chest. She laid her cheek against his shirt pocket and squeezed her eyes shut, remembering the night she had refused his sympathy and the kind embrace of Tim's best friend. His heart walloped beneath her ear. The fabric of his BDUs roughly caressed her cheek as the iron band of his arms embraced her. The rope tugged, lifting them off the ground.

She had to will away the memories whispering at the edges of her mind and force them into silence again. Looking back wouldn't change the truth. It wouldn't make her whole and strong again. It wouldn't return Tim to her. Would Hawk understand that? They began to sway, oddly buoyant as the rope drew them upward.

"You doin' okay?"

She nodded.

"You're not gonna pass out on me, are you?"

Choosing silence again, she shook her head. Hands were reaching out for her.

"Careful of her left arm," Hawk called out.

She felt someone grab her good arm to hoist her to her feet. She opened her eyes to see the gloomy bowl of the sky and the brightly lit wooded area. A dozen search-and-rescue team members were busy at work, manning the ropes, running the lights or talking on squawking radios. A search dog barked at his handler, excited by her arrival, as if he had been worried, too. She looked everywhere but at the man with one arm still around her. Even on solid ground, she felt as if she were swaying in midair.

Hawk was talking, rattling off her injuries, unhooking the carabineer connecting them, and her harness fell away. Other soldiers helped her onto a gurney. She didn't want to, but her head was spinning. She realized the volunteers were from nearby Fort Lewis, where the Ranger battalion Tim had belonged to was stationed. She'd been introduced to some of the men at one time or another, men who were faceless now in the shadowy dark. She let them strap her down and check her vitals.

"You did great." He knelt at her side, his hair slick with sweat, and his granite face compassionate. "You saved that girl's life. You knew what to do and you did it."

"I didn't do much. I raised her feet. I kept her quiet. I gave her my sweatshirt."

"It's the simple stuff that can make the most difference. You kept her as stable as you could until help came." The gurney bounced as the men lifted her. He stayed by her, carrying his share of her weight. "You did good."

"I know what you're doing. You're distracting me from my injuries so they don't seem as bad."

"Someone will splint that arm for you in the chopper. I'm glad you're okay, September. I'm glad I found you." He kept his voice casual and easy.

"Thank you, Hawk."

"Sure thing." He kept his footing, not easy on the rocky edge of the steep trail. They were closer to the bird now, the engine noise making it too loud to say much. He had enough light to see her better, the silk of her cinnamon-brown hair, her smooth creamy complexion and her lovely, oval face. She was not the same woman he remembered. Gone was her sparkle, her quick, easy manner that twinkled like summer stars. Sure enough, Tim's loss had been hard on her.

She wasn't alone with that.

Strange how God worked, he thought, as he ducked against the draft from the blades. While he hadn't seen her in years, time and the rigors of active duty hadn't obliterated her from his memory.

Why was it so easy to remember the good times? They flashed through his mind unbidden and unwanted. Seeing her picture for the first time when Tim had dug it out of his wallet after joining their battalion. Meeting her at a bowling party when their scheduled picnic had been rained out—typical Seattle-Tacoma weather. Hearing about her in the letters Tim read when they'd been sharing a tent and griping good-naturedly about their time in the desert. Those were innocent times, before he'd lost one of his lifelong friends. Before he'd had to deal with the harsh realities of war.

"On three," their sergeant barked, and they lifted her into the chopper. Hawk hopped in after, glancing at Crystal, stabilized and prepped, before his gaze lingered on September's face. Even in the harsh light, she was beautiful.

"You want me to call anyone?" he asked her, taking her good hand, careful of the IV. "Your mom?"

"Don't trouble her. I can take care of myself." That was it, no more explanation. She didn't meet his gaze.

He could feel the wall she put up between them like a concrete barrier. Was she mad because he had missed Tim's funeral? His plane had come in late. He'd flown halfway around the world, and military transports weren't the most on-time birds in the sky.

Had she been alone? Tim's brother, Pierce, had been there, but he couldn't remember the details, like if her family lived nearby. Anyway, he and Pierce had flown out that night, leaving her desolated in the cold rain.

"Anyone else I can contact?"

"There's no one." She turned her head away and swallowed hard, as if she were in emotional pain. The shadows hid her, but he could feel her sadness.

The captain tapped him on the shoulder. Time to go. He hated that he couldn't say goodbye; she didn't want to hear it. He hated what his presence was doing to her. Some memories were best left buried. He knew how that was.

His boots hit the ground, and he got clear. Dirt rose up in clouds as the bird took off, hovering off the ground for a moment as if battling gravity, then turning tail and lifting purposefully into the starless black.

"Was that September Stevens, Tim's former fiancée?" Reno asked as they watched the taillights grow distant.

"Yep." That was all he could say. Something sat in his throat, refusing to let him say more. He, Tim and Pierce had all been buddies since they were kids. They'd been neighbors back home in Wyoming, running wild in the foothills of the Rockies. They'd called themselves the dynamic trio back then, naive kids in a different world. War had changed that. War changed a lot of things.

He thought of September and her broken heart. There was some serious pain there. He felt for her, but it was why he kept clear of relationships. His life as a Ranger wasn't conducive to long-term commitment. It was his experience that love didn't necessarily grow fonder half a world apart. What he did was dangerous. Tim hadn't been the only soldier buried over the recent conflicts defending this country's freedom. He couldn't justify putting a woman through that, waiting and wondering, fearing with every phone call or knock on the door that he was dead. Seeing September was all the proof he ever needed of that.

He couldn't say why, but she stayed on his mind, a sad and beautiful image he could not forget.

Chapter Two

"How are you feeling today?" The hospital volunteer flashed a sunny smile as she set the bouquet of flowers onto September's bedside table.

"Better." In some ways, but not in others. She smoothed the wrinkles out of her hospital gown. For one thing, this had to go. She felt vulnerable in it. She carefully adjusted her casted forearm on the pillow. "I get to go home."

"Great news." The volunteer stepped back to admire the small collection of flowers. "I'm going to come by the riding stable you work for. I've always wanted to take lessons. I don't suppose you teach beginners. I don't even have a horse."

"You can rent one along with your lesson. It's done all the time." September reached for the pen and notepad on the bedside table, ignored the twinge of pain in her skull and the bite beneath her cast. She scribbled down the stable's phone number. "When you call, ask for me. I'll give your first lesson free, although you will have to spring for the horse rental."

"That would be fantastic. Thank you." The volunteer brightened and looked younger than September had first guessed. Maybe in her early thirties or late twenties. It reminded her that everyone went through tough times. Everyone had a challenging road to walk. The volunteer padded to the door. "Oh, it looks like you have a visitor. A *totally* handsome one."

That could only mean one man—Hawk. She didn't know anyone else who could be described as *totally* handsome. She expected dread to build inside her like a river dam, but it didn't.

"Hey there." Hawk waited for the volunteer to clear the room before he leaned one brawny shoulder against the doorjamb. He clutched a small vase of gardenias in one capable hand. "Thought I would swing by and check on you. See how you're doing."

"Good, considering." She hugged the bedcovers to her, aware that they were practically alone together. The nurses at the station a few doors down felt very far away.

"You look much better than the last time I saw you. Trust me." A hint of a grin tugged at the spare corners of his mouth, but his gaze remained serious and kind. "I hear they're springing you today."

"Yes, they're releasing me on my own recognizance." She wanted to keep things light and on the surface, to hide the fact that she was numb inside, like winter's frozen ground. It was better that way. This was how she had survived Tim's burial and moved on. Today was simply another day, like so many had been, one she needed to get through one step at a time, one breath, one moment. Seeing Hawk didn't change a thing.

"I meant to come by sooner, but you know how it is. Duty calls." He strode into the room like some

kind of action hero, confident and athletically powerful and mild mannered all at once. "I didn't know if
you wanted to see me again, but I had to look at you
and know for myself that you are going to be all right."

It hurt to look at him. Not only because of Tim—but
also because of the hardship etched on Hawk's face.
She studied him as he set the vase on the night table
with the several other arrangements, the sweet garde-
nia scent mixing pleasantly with the roses and carna-
tion bouquets. Her skin prickled at his nearness like
a warning buzzer going off to announce that he was
too near. She could smell the sunshine on his T-shirt
and the faint scent of motor oil on his faded denims.

This close, she could see the lines etched at the corners of his eyes, ones that hadn't been there the last
time she'd seen him. She wrapped her arm around her
middle like a shield. He'd had his losses, his trials and
his sorrows. She was not looking at the same man she'd
once known as Hawk, in those long-ago-seeming days
before Tim's death. War and loss had changed him, too.

"You have family coming for you?" The sunlight
from the window spilled over him, gilding him. With
his muscled frame straight and strong, he resembled
the noble warrior he was.

And exactly why was she noticing that? She had
no interest in love anymore. She would never fall for
another soldier. It was that simple. She stared hard at
a fraying thread in the hem of the blanket covering
her instead of meeting his gaze. "My sister is running
late. She's taking me home."

"You still have an apartment near the post?"

"No." She was surprised he had remembered her little one-bedroom place in a pretty gray building along

a greenbelt. He'd attended Tim's birthday party, the only one Tim had been home for through their entire relationship. "I've got a town house now, not far from where I work."

He didn't say the obvious, that both she and Tim had been saving up to buy a house after they were married. She had invested her savings in a place of her own instead.

"Look, September. I never thought we'd meet again." He squared those impressive shoulders of his. "I thought about looking you up and seeing how you were. But I was afraid it would be too painful for you. I can see it is."

"It's okay." She wasn't the only one hurting. She might not have known him well—he'd been one of Tim's best friends, not hers—but she could see he had walked a hard road, too. "I've thought about finding you or Tim's brother, on and off. I wanted to, but I could never make myself do it."

"You wanted to see me?"

She nodded. He and Tim had been together at those last moments. Hawk held the answers to the questions that had kept her wondering. But would asking them bring up as much sadness for him as it did for her? "You missed his funeral."

"Not my idea, but I made it for the wake. I didn't get a chance to talk to you." His brows knit together and he leaned back against the wall, pensive and dark. "You could have asked me then, but you refused to speak to me."

"I was hurting too much. I wasn't ready to hear about what happened over there. I had lost my one true love. I was torn apart. I couldn't stand to know the details."

"Don't blame you there."

"But I had questions later. After the first shock of loss faded, I thought of all the things I should have asked, things that I needed to know. And you were far away and unreachable."

"I'm sorry about that." He felt helpless. He should have looked her up. He should have made sure she was all right.

"There's a part of me that doesn't want to know the answers." Her confession came as softly as a hymn, resonating deep within him.

Ranger School had taught him how to lead, how to fight and how to accomplish his goal the right way, no excuses allowed. He might have led missions in the most dangerous places in the world, but facing the pretty brunette in front of him, he was at a loss. He was well trained and fearless, but right now all his training meant little. He did not know how to ease her grief. She had loved Tim deeply.

"You let me know which side wins out." It was all he could do for her. "If you want answers, I will give you what I can."

"Thanks, Hawk, and the flowers are lovely. My favorite." Although she sat straight and sweetly, the corners of her mouth fought to hold steady. Shadows dimmed the bronze depths of her eyes, which had once sparkled and twinkled with abundant joy.

It was hard seeing the change in her. She looked like a woman who no longer laughed or who no longer knew how to live. Sympathy squeezed his hard heart. "I picked up a few things hanging out with the Granger brothers. Tim was always sending you gardenias. I figured there had to be a reason."

"A slight one." She didn't need to say how much she had appreciated that about her man.

Hawk could see it. He felt drawn to her in a way that was beyond sympathy. The tightness in his chest was much more than a man's concern over a woman he had rescued. The past connected them like a bridge across a river, taut and undeniable. He'd been a fool to come; it had been the right thing, but foolish. In the end, he couldn't stay away. "I made a mistake with the flowers. They've reminded you of Tim."

"Yes, but it was thoughtful." She tried to put a bandage on her pain with a tentative smile, but he wasn't fooled.

"I didn't think. I just remembered—"

"I know," she interrupted, saving him from feeling in the wrong. She was gentle and kind that way. Lovely, not just on the outside but inside, where it truly counted. "I haven't received flowers in a long time. Now look at all of this. Fall down an old mine shaft and I get all this attention."

She was trying to steer away from talk of the past and of everything that hurt, too. Relieved, he went with it and put on a grin. Maybe it was best to leave sad things in the shadows. "How did you get down there, anyway?"

"You don't want to know." She played with the blanket hem, her long, sensitive fingers working a blue thread. Her sleek brown hair fell around her face like a shield. "I made a mistake."

"Who hasn't at one time or another?"

"I should have been more strict with Crystal, but she's one of my favorite students."

"Plus, you are a pushover. At least, that's my best impression of you."

"I've been called worse." She twirled a loose thread around her fingers, hating the way her hand trembled. She fought to stay numb, keeping the broken pieces safely frozen as if they were nothing, nothing at all. "Crystal's mare was sidestepping and acting weird."

"In my opinion, horses always act weird."

"That's because they aren't always predictable. Even the best-trained horse will surprise a good rider."

"Even you?" He arched one dark brow. "I've heard you are quite the horsewoman."

"Believe me, I know plenty who are better riders than I will ever be. Especially when Crystal refused to get back on the trail. When her horse balked, I should have insisted she dismount immediately. I already had, and I was reaching for her mare's bridle."

"You must have trouble with wildlife on that mountainside."

"Yes, and if a horse sees a predator, there's no guarantee you can hold them. Crystal is a strong-minded girl, I adore her, but she was testing my patience by not listening. Then the ground gave out. Her mare must have sensed the earth wasn't steady. She took off, threw Crystal. I hit a back hoof on the way down. We fell a long way. My horse had already taken a few steps off the trail and had calmed down."

"Both horses wound up back home okay."

"Yes, and I'm grateful. Comanche is a good boy. He's the reason you found us."

"Yes. It's the reason we knew where to start looking. At first they thought Crystal's dad might have abducted her. That threw everyone off for a bit."

"Oh." She hadn't considered that. She knew a little of her students' private lives, but not too much. She was aware the family had been through a bitter divorce. "I can't imagine how terrified Patty must have been."

"We were called in around chow time to help with the search." Hawk pushed away from the wall and grabbed a hard-backed chair by the top. He swung it toward the bed, seating himself on it like a motorcycle.

"I should have realized they would have called over to Fort Lewis for help with search and rescue."

"Then, what, you would have been better prepared to see me?" Kindness warmed his intense blue gaze. "You couldn't have known I would be on post at all. Just like I couldn't have known when I took a look at who we were searching for that they would hand me your picture."

"No." She swallowed hard, as if not pleased they had circled back around to the past, which was an impossible river between them.

"It's going to be all right, September." He reached out, his warm callused hand settling on her forearm. "We don't have to talk or think about it. We'll chalk it up to divine providence and go on from here."

"Good plan." She tried to think straight, but the sunlight blazed strangely bright until she could not see. Maybe it had something to do with her concussion. When the sun faded to its usual midmorning glow, Hawk gazed with concern at her, appearing as solid and as unyielding as a granite mountain. She swallowed hard, trying to act normal. "You must be up for deployment soon."

"I'll be Stateside for a while, but you know that can change at a drop of a hat."

"I do. You've been a Ranger for a long time. You like the lifestyle."

"Seven years." He shook his head, scattering what there was of his short dark hair. "You're doing well for yourself. I hear you have a reputation at what you do."

"A good one, I hope."

"Very good, from what everyone at the stables told me. You've done an admirable job, September. I wish I could say I've got my life together the way you have yours."

"Why do you say that? I thought you loved your job."

"Now, I never said that exactly. I love being a Ranger, but it comes at a high cost. I almost opted out. Losing my best friend was hard on me. In the end I feel committed to what I do. I don't think I will ever give up the military. Although you have a nice peaceful life here. Spending your days doing what you love. It's got to be a good gig."

"I like it." She tried to resist the pull of his kindness. "It's not saving the world."

"There are many ways to save the world. Teaching kids to ride and show their horses, that's a good way for them to spend their time. Instead of some alternatives."

"I've never thought of it that way. There are a lot of good life lessons in caring for a horse and establishing a trusting relationship."

"Maybe that's where I went wrong in life. I didn't have a horse." He winked at her, but she got the feeling he was covering up something that saddened him. He rose from the chair and swung it back into its original place. "Well, I don't want to take up more of your time. I'm glad you're doing well, that's what I had to know."

"Thanks to you." Her throat tightened, and if she didn't say it now, then she never would. "It was easier seeing you again this time, when I expected it."

"You knew I would drop by?"

"Yes. It's something a man like you would do." She blushed at the compliment she paid him, feeling uncomfortable and vulnerable when she didn't want to feel anything at all. "When we were in the mine and I first saw your face, I knew everything was going to be all right."

"That has to do with you, September, the woman you are. I did my job, that's all."

How she wished she could turn back time and work it so her life and Tim's could have turned out differently. She would give anything to fix what had been broken, both in her and for Hawk, as well. He'd lost one of his best friends, a friend he hadn't been able to protect.

She didn't know what to say to him as he crossed toward the door. A knock startled her. Her sister hurried into the room with a duffel bag slung over her shoulder and gave Hawk a narrow look.

"And here I thought you would be bored waiting for me." Chessie backtracked. "I didn't know you had a visitor. I can come back. I'm dying for a cup of tea."

A seed of panic took root between September's ribs. Panic, because her sister had jumped to the wrong conclusion—that she and Hawk were interested in each other. Even the thought of opening herself up like that again terrified her. "No, stay."

A little too abrupt, September, she told herself. Hawk had to have heard the sharpness in her tone. What was he thinking?

"No need." His rich, buttery baritone rang reassuringly. "I'm on my way out. September, you take care now."

"You, too, Hawk." The words squeaked out of her throat.

His gaze fastened on hers, making the room and her sister's presence fade away. She saw something akin to her own wounds shadowed there, hiding in his eyes. Her pulse skyrocketed over the fact that she wanted something she no longer believed in.

"I hope you find that happy ending you always wanted. You deserve it, September." His voice resonated with sincerity. Saying nothing more, he nodded in acknowledgment to her sister and strode from the room. The pad of his boots on the tile faded to silence, but his presence somehow remained.

"Good-looking guy." Chessie poked her head around the door frame to get another look. "Who is he?"

"One of the Rangers from Fort Lewis who found Crystal and me." She breathed a sigh of relief, troubled by the man and his shadows. At least he understood. He had his wounds, deeper and more severe than hers could ever have been. War could do that to a man.

"There was road construction. Sorry. I should have remembered, but you know me, too much on my mind." Chessie plopped the duffel on the foot of the bed and unzipped it. "So, are you going to date him?"

"Date Hawk?" There was a picture she couldn't quite bring into focus. "Hardly."

"I had to ask. You never know. Time heals all wounds. I know it doesn't seem like it now, but one day things will be better."

"I'm sure you're right." She didn't believe it, but she didn't want to drag her sister down. "Did you remember to bring shoes?"

"Are you kidding? There's nothing more important than shoes." Chessie pulled a pair of snazzy boots from the bottom of the bag. "Ta-da. See, your big sister won't ever let you down."

"You're one blessing I'm grateful for." She smiled, trying too hard to find the normalcy her life had once been. It didn't work, but she hoped she looked as if it did. She feared she would always feel out of sync, as if she were looking at her own life through a foggy mirror. She thought of Hawk and wondered what he was doing with his day off. She wondered how he managed to walk in the light with so many wounds in his soul.

Hawk strode through the automatic doors and into the blinding sunlight. The cool kiss of the mid-December breeze felt pleasant against his skin. He'd stopped by to see the little girl, Crystal, but she was in ICU and not taking any visitors. He'd met her mom, though, and learned that they expected to move her out onto a floor that afternoon. Things were looking up. He'd left a balloon bouquet with Patty, and that was that. He had no more reason to think about September Stevens. So, why was she on his mind?

It was a mystery. Loose ends, maybe, or just the fact that their paths had crossed. He hauled his bike key from his pocket, fiddling with it as he hiked toward the parking lot. If only he could have stayed away. Seeing her again tied him up in knots, and he was afraid to look at those tangled threads too closely.

He straddled his Harley and plugged in the key. While the engine rumbled, he hauled his helmet off the backrest and that's when he saw her. His gaze drew to her like fate. September, in a mandatory wheelchair, emerged from the automatic doors onto the concrete walkway, with his gardenias in her arms.

How pretty she looked. She wore a light pink T-shirt that said Ride for the Cure, jeans and black riding boots. Her softly bouncy hair shone like cinnamon in the sunshine. She was still as sweet as ever. She'd always been delicate and kind, and not even life's hardships had changed that. He surely hoped that God had been watching over her specially, as he'd kept her in prayer. He would never forget seeing her after the funeral, an image of perfect grief. He'd been in awe of her. What would it be like to love so much? To have been loved like that?

He tugged on his helmet and yanked on the straps to secure them. Across the way, a light blue SUV crawled to a stop at the curb, and September's sister emerged from it. With a hurried gait, she started loading the flowers several hospital volunteers were carrying. They scolded September for standing and trying to help out. He spotted a few arrangements already in the back of the SUV.

He grabbed the grips and fed the engine. The bike gave a satisfying roar. Something kept him from leaving. Maybe it was the sight of September, pale and fragile with a bandage on her forehead and a pink cast on her left arm. Yep, that got to him. He couldn't hold back the pounding need to look after her. He wanted to be the one to take care of her. It wasn't a conscious choice. It simply came into being.

With one last look, he rolled the bike backward out of the parking space and released the clutch. The Harley shot forward, taking him away from September, but not from the thought of her.

Chapter Three

Chessie set the last vase of flowers in the middle of the breakfast bar and fussed with it, turning the vase to get it just right. "So, time to fess up. What's the deal?"

"About what?" September looked up from her position on the couch, sorting her mail. A surprising amount of junk had accumulated during the two days she'd been in the hospital.

"Not what. Who." Satisfied with the way the flowers looked, Chessie dropped into one of the bar chairs. "What was Mark Hawkins really doing in your hospital room?"

"The obvious. Bringing flowers. Seeing how I was."

"I didn't know you had anything to do with that life anymore."

She meant army life. September sighed, remembering the tough time her sister had given her over her decision to date a Ranger and then accept his marriage proposal. She tossed a handful of advertisements into the paper-recycling bin. "I haven't seen Hawk since the funeral."

"Talk about coincidences."

"You have no idea."

"Not a good coincidence."

"No." Her heart twisted hard, remembering how Hawk had changed. What had happened to him? "I'm trying to move on with my life, and it's not easy. Something always pops up to pull me back." Something forced her to remember when life had been bright and her dreams shiny and new.

"He should know that. He should have left you alone." Chessie, protective big sister, folded her arms across her chest. "Want me to talk to him?"

"No. He meant well. Besides, it's not like I'm going to see him again. As if. He will probably be TDY by the end of the week."

"You mean on a tour of duty?" Chessie relaxed and propped her chin on her fists. "All right, I won't hunt him down. But that doesn't mean you're okay. You didn't need a reminder of your losses."

"True." She tossed a few more envelopes thick with coupons she would never need. "He looks hardened. No longer the carefree guy I remember."

"War will do that, I suppose. It's his choice to do what he does, carrying a gun and shooting people with it." Chessie had a strong opinion on that. She had strong opinions on just about everything. "Don't worry, I will stay off my soapbox, but what kind of man does that year after year?"

The kind who cares about others more than himself. September kept quiet. She wasn't up to any kind of serious discussion about the rights and wrongs of war. Nor did she remind her sister that those words maligned Tim's memory. Tim who had died trying to save innocent embassy hostages. Hawk had been wounded on that mission, she remembered. The hows and whys were a mystery to her.

"I'm going to swing by and pick up some pizza. That ought to put a smile on your face." Chessie slid off the chair and hooked her purse strap over her shoulder. "I'll get a dessert pizza, too. The Stevens girls are going to totally carb out."

"Sounds just like what I need." Comfort food all the way. She flung the last junk mail envelope into the bin. There, done with that chore. Not that there weren't a dozen more needing to be done around here. Clutter was accumulating. She needed to give her family room and kitchen area a serious going-over. Keeping busy would keep her mind off her troubles, right?

"What are you doing?" Chessie scolded from the doorway. "I see you getting up. You're going to do housework, aren't you?"

"Why do you say that like an accusation?" September swiped a stack of books off the coffee table and tucked them into the crook of her good arm. "I have pizza coupons you can use."

"I have some in my car." Chessie closed the door and crossed through the living room. "That's it, I'm calling for delivery. Someone needs to keep an eye on you. Now lie down. Do it now, or I'll make you."

"This sounds exactly like my childhood," she quipped, reluctantly putting down the books. "No one can understand the hardship I went through as your sister."

"Ha, ha." Chessie tapped her foot, pointing to the arm of the couch where she'd propped two fluffy down pillows earlier. "Feet up. I mean it—"

The doorbell rang. She was saved. She kept her feet firmly on the hardwood floor. "Should I get that?"

"As if." Chessie huffed out a frustrated sigh as she pivoted on her Mary Janes and marched through the town house. "You stay right where you are, sister dear. You just got out of the hospital and you're going to take care of yourself even if I have to—"

She opened the door and fell silent. Curious, September leaned forward far enough on the cushions to see a uniformed delivery dude holding pizza boxes.

"Got a delivery for Hawkins," he announced.

"Hawkins?" That had her moving across the room. She was halfway to the door before she saw the black motorcycle pulling up to the curb out front. Hawk swung off his bike, unbuckling his helmet.

"I'll sign for it." He slung his helmet over the backrest while the delivery guy handed Chessie the pizzas. The look on her sister's face wasn't a good one.

What was Hawk up to now? Why was he here? She hadn't recovered from seeing him in the hospital. She hadn't recovered from seeing him at all. Why did he have to show up looking so alive and vital?

"What aren't you telling me?" Chessie asked as they watched Hawk sign the charge slip with an efficient scribble.

"Not one thing."

"I hope you're right. I'll take these to the kitchen." Chessie tapped away, her tone cool.

The sunlight graced him, but he was a man who walked as if he did not notice. He'd turned grim over the last hard years, and his strong, granite face, which had always been quick to grin, was serious.

She held the door for him, watching as he strode up

the walkway. She couldn't stop from caring. Well, not the serious kind of caring. What she felt was sympathy, she told herself, understanding for the man who had rescued her. Nothing more complicated than that.

"Hope you don't mind." He slipped the receipt into his wallet. "I figured you wouldn't be up to cooking and your sister might appreciate a little help."

"It was nice of you." She didn't need to wonder if there was a deeper motive or a hidden agenda. He was a straightforward guy. She liked Hawk; she had always liked him, and why wouldn't she? He had been a good friend to Tim. He was a good man. That's what she would concentrate on and not the past, not the hurt. She pulled open the door a little wider in welcome. "Why don't you come in and have lunch with us?"

"I don't mean to impose. I wondered if there was anything I could do for you. Run some errands or something." He crossed the threshold, towering over her. "I'm good at fetching."

"Are you sure you don't have anything better to do?"

"Positive." His humble grin reassured her.

He was merely being kind, the way Tim would have wanted. That realization made her heart squeeze shut. There was the past, yawning wide open, full of everything she had lost. Best to pretend it wasn't there, a void between them. Dully, she let him take charge of the door and close it.

"I didn't know what kind of pizza you like," he explained, "so I got a couple different combos."

"It smells delicious. When it comes to pizza, I'm not picky. As long as it has a crust and cheese, I'm happy. Thanks, Hawk."

"No problem. I'm glad to see you doing better." He jammed his hands into his jean pockets, matching his stride to hers as they crossed through the living room. "You gave me a good scare when I first saw you in that mine."

"I was pretty scared myself." She ignored the look her sister gave her and reached up into the kitchen cabinets for three plates. "But it was only a few stitches."

"Don't forget the surgery. What do you think you're doing?" Hawk sidled in behind her and took the plates before she could lift them from the shelf. "Go sit down. I'm thinking your sister will agree with me."

"That's right," Chessie answered curtly from across the room.

"I'm fine." Sure, her arm hurt, but she wasn't about to be waited on. She could take care of herself.

"You had best stay off your feet, September. You need to heal." His warm, caring baritone wrapped around her like a wool blanket, soothing and tender. Caring was in the layers of his voice, in the lines crinkling pleasantly at the corners of his eyes, in the space between them.

He really is a nice man, she thought. She simply had to be careful so the memories couldn't hurt her. So he couldn't hurt her. She slipped away from the counter and from him. "Nobody needs to worry about me. It was a hard fall, true, but I wasn't hurt like Crystal. Did you hear? She's doing better. I heard from her mom that she was already asking when she could go riding again."

"That's a good sign. She's a trooper. I hope she's back in the saddle before long."

"Me, too. You were great with her. I know all about

your training, of course, but to see it in action, it was impressive."

"Just your tax dollars at work." He opened the box tops for Chessie, so she didn't have to put down her plate to dish up, but his gaze remained firmly on September. "You kept the girl alive until help came. You made a real difference."

"I didn't do much, and you already said that earlier."

"That doesn't make it less true." He took the next plate, watching her carefully. "Ham and pineapple or the works?"

"A slice of both, please." She was ashen, all the color drained from her cheeks, her wide brown eyes too big for her face. Had his presence done that to her? Or her ordeal? She looked fragile with her casted arm in a sling.

"I'll dish you up. Go ahead and sit down," he told her. "Join your sister."

She nodded once in acknowledgment, watching him closely with appreciation or caution, he couldn't tell which. Maybe a little bit of both. He chose the largest slices and slid them onto her plate, aware of every step she took through the kitchen of granite counters and white cabinets to the seating arrangement in a sunny bay window nook. Her sister spoke to her in low tones, and the murmur of women's voices was a strange, musical sound he wasn't accustomed to. But he liked it. He was more used to the sound of plane engines, gunfire in the shooting range and barked orders rising above it all in a no-nonsense cadence.

He reached for the last plate and served himself two slices of the works. Why was he here? He couldn't quite say. He wanted to believe he'd come because

Tim would have wanted him to make sure September was well.

That wasn't the whole of it. He had to be honest. He closed the tops to the pizza boxes and crossed over to the women. His boots knelled as loud as a jackhammer on her wood floor, or at least it felt that way because when the women looked up, their conversation silenced. One studied him with suspicion, the other with a hint of care. That surprised him. Her caring couldn't be personal. He'd never had the chance to know September much, it was hard to get to know any civilian with his job, but he knew she was gentle and kind to all she met—even to a guy like him. Emotion tugged within him, distant and unfamiliar, and he dismissed it. He was simply glad for the luxury of her company, that's all.

"The motorcycle is new," she began after her sister said the blessing. "I didn't know you rode."

"Since high school, but I sold my Honda after I enlisted." He tried not to look at her. Maybe it would make the unaccustomed feelings within him fade instead of live. "Last year I realized I missed riding, so I got another bike. I figured why not?"

Small talk. That's what this was. It was uncomfortable. Maybe he shouldn't have stayed, he thought, as he took his first bite of pizza. The taste of spicy sauce, cheese, dough and pepperoni ought to overpower everything he was feeling, but it didn't come close. He cared about her. He hadn't planned on it, but his feelings were there just the same. The threads knotted up inside him tightened; he didn't dare look at those hidden feelings.

"I had forgotten." She set her pizza on her plate.

The tiniest bite had been taken from the end of the slice. "You, Tim and his brother, Pierce, had dirt bikes when you were kids."

"My mom didn't like the idea of me speeding around on the back of a motorized bike, as I was prone to getting hurt on the regular two-wheeled variety, but I didn't relent and she finally gave in. Tim, Pierce and me, we rode far and wide. I think at one point we knew every trail and old forgotten logging road in two national forests."

"It sounds similar to how we grew up, right, Chessie?" September glanced across the table at her sister, and her look said, *Play nice.*

He appreciated that. The table was a small round one, and that meant there wasn't much room between him and either lady. He could feel icy dislike radiating off September's sister like vapor off dry ice. The only thing worse was the awareness of September, how she was close, how he wanted her to be closer. He wanted to comfort her. Even he could see that she'd hit a rough patch.

"Instead of dirt bikes, we had horses." When she spoke of times past, the shadows in her eyes softened. The corners of her mouth upturned with a hint of a smile.

"Those had to be good times," he found himself saying, as if to urge her on. As if he wanted to hear more.

"They were. We had the sweetest little mare to learn on. Clyde was twenty-two years old. Our dad was worried about us getting hurt—we were in grade school—so he would only let us get a very old and even-tempered horse."

"Sounds like he was a good dad."

"The best." Dad was the reason she'd grown up living her childhood dream. He and Mom had sacrificed a lot so she could have Comanche. "He wanted us to live our dreams and he did all he could to help us work for them. Right, Chessie?"

She looked to her sister, maybe to include her in the conversation and also for an unspoken need for sisterly support. He had the distinct feeling she was uncomfortable with him. She kept avoiding direct eye contact. Maybe dropping by hadn't been his smartest idea ever.

"Dad is stellar. They don't make men like him anymore." The older, sterner sister's tone implied that Hawk fell short. Very short.

"There are plenty of good men," September said gently. "Chessie and I were fortunate enough to take riding lessons. When we were older, we both worked in the barn to earn board for our show horses. We were suburb girls, but Mom drove us the twenty-three-mile trip each way twice a day. Sometimes more."

"Sounds like a good mom." His mom had suffered from depression after his dad's passing, which was why he'd practically grown up with the neighboring Granger boys. He would have explained it all to September, but that would mean bringing up a past she shouldn't have to deal with. Instead, he kept it simple and in the moment. "She obviously loved you both."

"And we love her. After the divorce, she remarried and moved to San Francisco. We don't see her like we used to, but she's happy." Longing weighed down her voice. Clearly she was close to her mother.

"My dad died when I was in third grade." The words were out before he could draw them back. Once said, they couldn't be unspoken. So much for his decision not to mention the past. He shrugged a shoulder, as if that past couldn't hurt him anymore. "She never got over it."

"Sometimes a woman doesn't." The shadows in her beautiful eyes deepened, like twilight falling.

The human heart was a fragile thing, capable of great, indestructible love and yet able to infinitely break. He bit into his second slice of pizza, crunching on a few green peppers, thinking. He didn't believe in coincidence; he'd seen it too many times in the heat of battle and had felt God's swift hand. He had to consider that reuniting with September was God at work. Maybe she needed a little help. Maybe he was being given a mission to be that help.

"I always thought it was a great loss that Mom never learned to live or to love again." He kept out his experiences of growing up underneath that dark, hopeless cloud. When his father had died in a logging accident, it was as if he had lost both parents. Understandably, his mother was never the same. But she had never been a mother again. He'd grown up a lonely kid, taking care of his younger sister and finding belonging and acceptance in the neighboring Grangers' house. "I don't think Dad would have wanted her to be alone like she is. He would have wanted her to be happy."

"And you're telling me this because…?"

"We were on the topic. My mom would never have driven me anywhere once, let alone twice, every day of the week." His tone was indifferent, as if his past was something he'd learned to deal with long ago. "Sounds like you have an awfully nice mom."

"We do," Chessie answered, regarding Hawk with

a narrow, terse look, which she reserved for possible swindlers and fraudulent door-to-door salesmen. "What I don't get is why you're here. Sure, you were on the search-and-rescue team the base sent out. I get that. But you could have let this go."

"Perhaps I should have." He straightened his shoulders, sitting ramrod in the chair, looking as tough as nails and nobler than any man ever.

"Can't you see this is causing September more pain?" Chessie pushed away from the table and stood, protective older sister and something more. Her distrust was showing. "She shouldn't be reminded of—"

"Stop, Francesca." Her stomach tied up in knots and she took a deep, cleansing breath. "I'm glad Hawk is here. Please don't chase him off."

"I'm going to the grocery store, then." Chessie didn't look happy with her chin set and her mouth clamped into a firm line. "I won't be long. Hawk, I'm guessing you won't be here when I get back. Thank you for finding my sister. And for the pizza."

"Not a problem." He was the kind of man who showed respect, even to a woman being rude to him.

She had to admire him a little more for that. Hawk was a very good man. She simply had to think that and nothing else—the past, Tim or what could have been. She waited until the door had closed behind her sister before she turned back to him. "She's overprotective. I'm sorry."

"She loves her sister. Who can blame her for that?"

At his kindness, the tightness within her chest coiled tighter, cutting off her air. It made no sense why his kindness troubled her more.

"Is it true?" His voice dipped low and comforting. "Is it better for you if I go?"

This was her chance for safety. He was offering her a way out. She could say yes, walk him to the door, thank him for his thoughtfulness and never see him again. The past could remain buried, where it couldn't harm her.

But she had learned to survive. She had become good enough at it to fool everyone else and some days herself. Not today, but some days. Possibly, right now, she could cope instead of simply survive. "No, Hawk. I'm glad you're here. Remember I told you I had wanted to look you up?"

"Sure." He grabbed a napkin from the holder on the table and swiped his mouth and rubbed his hands, looking busy, as if the act was what held his attention, although she could feel his interest, sharp and focused.

"You're here, and this is my chance. I need closure." She thought of the prayers she had given up on and of her need for God's comfort that she had been too lost to feel. Maybe having Hawk here would help as much as anything could. "I'm stronger now than I was after Tim's funeral. Could you tell me what happened to him? Could you tell me how he died? You were there."

"Are you sure you want to hear this?" His hand covered hers, and everything within her stilled.

"Yes." It wasn't the whole truth. She was afraid that it would be better to stay in the dark, to leave the last moments of Tim's life a mystery. She didn't want to hurt again, yet how could she let this chance slip by? Finally she could lay to rest the broken shards of the questions that had troubled her. With the answers, maybe she could have closure.

"I want to know, even if it's difficult." She set her shoulders, braced for the truth. "I know you had been shot, too."

"Caught a ricochet. Nothing serious."

"Can you tell me what he said?"

He didn't answer right away. Moments ticked by and the heater clicked on, breezing warm air across her ankles and teasing the curtains at the window. Hawk sat like a seasoned warrior, his face set, his shadows deepening and his truth unmistakable. He was a man who fought for others and who protected them. He looked every inch of it.

She leaned forward, pulse fluttering, both dreading what he would say and hungering for it.

Chapter Four

"He didn't have a pulse when I got to him." Hawk sounded distant, as if that was the only way he could cope with the memory.

"He was already gone?"

"His brother was closer to him and got there first. He started CPR. The machine guns, the grenades, the shouting, it all faded to silence. Everything went slow motion. I pulled a corpsman over to help because he wasn't coming fast enough."

"You fought for Tim's life." She read the emotion twisting his face and saw what he could not say. This loss had been a turning point in his life, too. "You fought with everything you had."

"We all did." He swallowed hard, the tendons in his neck working with effort. It had to be torture remembering.

She was sorry to put him through that. Maybe she shouldn't have asked. "At least he didn't suffer. That's what I had to know. That he wasn't afraid."

"Tim? Never. We got him back for a minute or so, but the bullet caused too much damage." He reached across the distance separating them, both physical and emotional, to take her hand.

His touch alarmed her. Her spirit flickered and warmed, like dawn's first light. She withdrew her hand, and the brightness dimmed. She sat as if in shadow.

"He gave Pierce a message for his family," he went on as if nothing had happened. "That was all the time he had. He died in his brother's arms and in a circle of friends. The last thoughts he had were of you."

"How do you know?"

"His last breath was your name. Didn't you know?"

She shook her head. She wanted to stay unaffected, to gather the information logically and heal from it. Impossible. Tim's life had ended—all that he would be, all that he would do wiped away. That's what she wanted to change. "If God could give me one wish, I would go back in time and have forced Tim to get out. I would never have let him serve a second hitch in the army. He wouldn't have been sent overseas. He wouldn't have died."

"You don't know that. You can't torture yourself with that guilt."

"How do you know?" She stared at him in amazement, this big, capable man more wise than she had given him credit for.

"I know how you feel," he confessed. "I did everything I could. Everything I knew how. I couldn't save him, either."

Everything within her stilled. Their gazes collided and the force of it left her paralyzed. The honest sincerity of his gaze held a power she had never felt before, one strong enough to chip at the frozen tundra of her shielded heart. "How do you go on?"

"I struggled for a long time." Honesty softened the planes of his rugged face and revealed more of his character. One of strength and deep feeling. "I almost opted out and thought about finding a civilian job."

"You were soul-searching, too."

"Not that I want to admit it to anyone." He squared his shoulders. "I had to question what one life is worth, and what cost? I had a hole in my life as a reminder. I had to figure that Tim would want me to make good choices for me, so I turned down my uncle's offer to find me a job and signed for another two years."

"That was your idea of a good choice? Going back into danger?"

"I want to make a difference."

"There are a lot of ways to do that without risking your life."

"Are you questioning my decision?" Not defensive, but curious. He looked as if he wanted to take hold of her hand again.

She kept them tightly folded together. "I'm just asking, that's all."

"My sister is happily working in San Diego. She doesn't need me. My mom is safe and living her life the way she wants to in Wyoming. They are the only family I have, and neither of them really needs me. I'm not married. I don't have any strong calling to do charity work or anything like that. The military is what I believe in. Being a soldier was the only thing I ever wanted to be."

"Why?" It was Tim's decision she was asking about, not Hawk's. But she had to know why Hawk had chosen to be a Ranger. "Why do you guys feel so committed to the army?"

"Because I fight for what I believe in. I love this country. I want to do my part." Not defensive, just powerful. Poignant. "Although it comes at a cost. I'm still single."

"Why haven't you gotten married?"

"Why get involved with someone when I knew I had to leave?"

"And yet being alone is the reason you stayed in the army?"

"It's a circular argument. Don't think I don't know that." He shrugged a shoulder, as if dismissing it, but something that looked like sadness clung to his features. "You're alone, too, September. I don't have to ask to know the answer. You aren't dating."

"No. I don't have the heart left to." She couldn't give voice to the loneliness of the last two years and the fears that she had been broken beyond repair. Beyond hope. Beyond God.

"We are two of a kind."

"In some ways," she agreed.

He leaned closer, looking as if he wanted to comfort her and didn't know how.

She was grateful he didn't reach out. It was easier to stay frozen inside than to look toward the light. "Are you going to be here alone for the holidays? Or are you flying home?"

"I haven't decided. I might head down to Mom's. My sister will be there. It would be good to see them both."

"You haven't said it, but I can hear it. There's something holding you back."

"It's tough going down there. My mom never got over my dad's death. Nearly twenty years later, she lives like a hermit, closed off from what life has to offer." He shifted in his chair. "I love her, and it's hard for me to see. I couldn't save her, either."

"Don't give up on her, Hawk." Sunlight brightened, tumbling through the windows, finding her. The lemony brightness graced her, emphasizing an inner strength, a glimpse into the real September Stevens. "Everyone needs love in their life. Even you."

"Me? When did this conversation become about me?" Sure, he was uncomfortable with the *L* word. He was too tough for love. Too scarred. "I'll go visit my mom for Christmas. Fine. We were talking about you."

"Were we? I don't think it's necessary. I'm fine, too."

"Sure, you look it, bandaged and casted. Don't forget I found you in that hole in the earth. You can't fool me."

"Okay, fine. My arm hurts. My head hurts. I sat in what felt like a grave and worried about dying."

"I'm glad I found you."

"Me, too."

He would never forget the relief or how it had pounded through him with the force of a riptide, leaving him weak down to the quick. Like now, never had he seen a lovelier sight than her alive. The sunshine clung to her, as if it thought so, too. He was thankful to God for this mercy. "You are going to take care of yourself, right? Need me to get you anything? Do something for you?"

"In case you haven't noticed, I have my sister for that."

"Yeah, well, I was asking as a friend." Okay, so he cared for her. He was man enough to admit it. But it was caring on a nonromantic level. "Don't know about you, but that's something I could use."

"Me, too." She relaxed, as if a wall went down. When she stood, it didn't feel as if she were trying to keep him at a safe distance. "Any man who hauls me out of a mine is a friend for life."

"Glad to hear it." He kept pace with her through the kitchen. Nice and amiable, walking alongside her. "I noticed you have a gutter coming loose from your fascia."

"My what?"

"The board beneath the roofline."

"Oh. No idea. I haven't looked up in a while, but there are a few drips when it rains."

"This is the Pacific Northwest. It tends to rain a lot here. Hello." He was chuckling, knowing full well what she was doing. Downplaying the problem because she knew what was coming next. "There's no avoiding it. We're friends now. You have to accept my help."

"It's a law? Written into the Constitution?"

"I'm sure it is. I'll put it on my to-do list." She wasn't getting rid of him easily. He wasn't a man who walked away from a mission or regrets. He spotted a trio of cardboard boxes next to the big front window. Indentations in the carpet showed that a piece of furniture had been recently moved. "That would make a perfect spot for a Christmas tree."

"Which is why I moved the couch. Don't give me that look. I did it before the accident. Last weekend."

She shook her head. "I'm afraid to ask about that expression on your face. You are planning something."

"I'm a planner. It's who I am." He didn't deny it. Regrets could haunt a man when he was belly down in the sand, taking fire. That meant he couldn't afford to back off now. "Since we're friends and all, I have a few thoughts to help you out while you are down and out."

"In case you haven't noticed, I am getting around just fine. My arm is casted, that's all. The rest of me is good to go."

She tried to hide it, but he wasn't a fool. He knew how loss could strip you of your heart, breaking it off piece by piece until there was no light, no love and no hope left. Sometimes a person needed a hand up, that was all. More than anything he wanted to be that hand for her.

"Getting a tree. Putting up lights. Decorating." He had reached the door and turned, drawing out his time with her. "Seems like doing all that is going to be hard with that cast."

"Then it's a good thing I'm not going to go all-out for Christmas. I'm going to haul out my little plastic tree—"

"Plastic? Sorry. No. I can't allow that."

"The last time I looked, you were not in charge of me." She planted her good arm on her hip. "I'm used to you pushy alpha types. You don't intimidate me, Mark Hawkins."

"I'm not trying to intimidate you." He grinned, bringing out his dashing twin dimples. He had a smile that could charm glaciers into melting. "I'm helping out a friend. Remember, that's what we are?"

"I owe my life to you. How could I forget?" Yes, he

really was far too charming for his good—and hers. "I know what you're up to."

"Just trying to help spread Christmas cheer. Do unto others. Help the less fortunate." He sure *appeared* innocent.

"Sure you are." She could see right through him to the pure kindness beneath. Hard not to appreciate that. "If you really have nothing else to do with your free time."

"I'm on leave. The rest of the year is mine."

He didn't need to say the words, because she understood. He was lonely, too. One of his best friends was gone. She knew just what that was like.

"How about I drop by tomorrow?" He gave the knob a turn. Damp, chilly air puffed into the room. "We'll see if we can do something about your lack of Christmas spirit."

"I may need help." What she needed was a friend. She liked the idea that maybe he needed her.

"Then prepare yourself. I fully intend to put you in a festive mood. Consider it fair warning."

"Yes, Sergeant." She couldn't resist saluting him. He eased onto the front porch, reminding her of the man she'd once lost and the future she was still grappling to find. "You were shot on that mission, but you didn't say where."

"Nothing serious. I healed up okay."

She recognized that hollow sound, for it was the way her voice sounded when the past threatened to overtake her. "What happened? No one has told me."

"First I took a bullet to the shoulder and then shrapnel in my back. A grenade went off nearby and I covered Tim's body with mine to protect him." He waved off the importance, but emotion darkened his eyes. He was not a man to talk of his sacrifices. He had come to the wake, but he'd been more injured than she had realized.

Caring rolled through her, unbidden and impossible to stop.

"I'm glad you recovered, Hawk."

"Until tomorrow." He saluted her in return, pivoted on his heel and marched into the watery sunshine. She thought she caught a hint of hope on his handsome face, but she couldn't be sure.

Good, she thought, because that's how she felt, too. Hopeful because he was coming back, encouraged at the prospect of seeing him again. Maybe it was because he was familiar, an old acquaintance. She liked the idea of being friends with him. As he strode toward his bike, she remembered the few group outings they had been on together long ago: volleyball at the park, bowling at Tim's favorite rink, a barbecue on base. In all of those memories, Hawk had always been laughing, a dependable guy, a steadfast and loyal friend to the man she'd lost.

She closed the door, and the click echoed in the silent house. She leaned against the door, fighting against falling into the hole of grief she had spent years climbing out of. She could no longer feel God, but she had to believe He was somewhere close. *Lord, I'm trying to move on and let go. I've given my sorrow up to You so many times, too many to count. And yet I'm still holding this burden. It's like being trapped beneath a deep layer of ice. I can't see You to find my way out. A little help, please.*

No answer came, and she didn't expect one. She

only hoped her words had a chance of being heard. A motor roared to life outside, muffled by the sturdy walls, and she caught sight of a blur moving beyond the window—Hawk rocketing down the street. She moved to the sill, but he was already gone. Sunshine swept the steady branches of the rhododendrons outside, their green leaves held up toward the sky, as if with faith.

The back door opened and Chessie's shoes clicked on the hardwood. Sacks rustled as they came to rest on the kitchen counter.

"I see he's gone." Her voice echoed in the coved ceiling and bounced off the plain white walls. She clomped into sight. "Tell me why you aren't lying on the couch with your feet up."

"Because I'm bored of lying still. Let me help put away the groceries."

"Not on your life. Get on that couch or do I have to come over there and make you do it?" Chessie might be all bark, but it was concern that softened her dark eyes, worry that furrowed across her brow. "You are my only sister, don't forget. I could have lost you. So, are you going to do what I ask?"

"Yes, big sis." Tired and drained, she retreated to the couch. It felt good to lie back on the soft cushions and fluffy pillows and grab the remote.

After Chessie was done putting away the groceries, she plopped in the nearby chair. They spent the afternoon watching classic movies and humming along with Fred Astaire. But to her, Hawk wasn't forgotten. He was like those old songs, familiar and dear, the ones she wanted to sing over and over again.

* * *

The tree lot on the corner of two main roads sparkled with cheerful Christmas lights rimming their blocked-off portion of the grocery store parking lot. Through the rain speckling the windshield, she spotted an older man and his wife trying to stay dry under a small makeshift awning. It had to be a cold job. She empathized, as she often worked in the cold winter rain, too.

"Looks like we have plenty of choices." Hawk stopped the truck and killed the engine. The hot air from the heater sputtered out, and the windshield immediately began to fog. "We're the only customers here."

"I can't imagine why." She released her seat belt, turning toward him in the seat. Rain pinged on the glass, smearing the outside world like one big Christmas watercolor. "Don't most people shop for trees in the pouring rain?"

"I've been in monsoons that were drier than this," he quipped. "Wait a second. I'll grab an umbrella and come around for you."

"Umbrella? Who do you think I am? I'm a Seattle girl. I'm not afraid of a little rain." She opened her door and hopped down from the truck, lifting her face to the spattering rain.

Footsteps splashed on the wet blacktop, pounding in her direction. Hawk, glowering at her, as he rounded the front corner of the truck.

"You could have waited for me to help you down." He stared at the umbrella, folded and tied neatly in hand. "It's too late for this now. You're already dripping wet and loving it."

"After being cooped up indoors for so many days, I do love it." She swiped at the raindrops collecting on her lashes and breathed in the fresh-cut tree scent. "I'm feeling better already."

"You look better. There's color in your cheeks."

"See? I don't need to be pampered. Too bad my sister isn't here to see. I'm going stir-crazy." She waved to the couple huddled under their awning. "Good morning."

"Hello there," the husband greeted. "Are you two wanting anything in particular?"

"We'll browse around and let you know." Hawk stepped in, locking his arm through her good one. They must look like a couple out to buy their tree. "Where do you want to start? There's some good-looking spruce right here. Well shaped and full. That would look mighty pretty in your front window."

"I would rather shop around first. See what my options are."

"That's where we are different. I know what I want and when I see it, I grab it and go. Quick in and quick out."

"The Ranger way?" She shook her head, enjoying the pleasant squish of puddled water beneath her boots and the symphony of rainfall pattering around them. Holiday lights flashed cheerfully as she followed an aisle past the perfect trees. "I like to take a careful look. Sometimes you find a hidden treasure."

"I see what you mean." His tone was thoughtful, drawing her attention. Suddenly she didn't feel as if he was talking about the trees surrounding them.

Heat stained her face, and she looked away. With every step she took, she was deeply aware of him at her side. The force of his noble presence was as tangible as the ground beneath her feet.

"How about this one?" He paused to admire a noble fir, tall and proud and perfect.

"It is lovely." She bit her bottom lip, a habit when she was thinking. "I can't help but think this tree is gorgeous. Any number of people will want it. It will sell in a snap."

"Well, I don't know. It's still here, isn't it?"

"It's two weeks before Christmas. A lot of people haven't come by yet. I'm positive this tree will find a home."

"So that means we get it?" He wasn't exactly paying attention to her every word. He couldn't. She captivated him, looking like Christmas come early with her spun-sugar pink hat, scarf and mittens and matching coat.

"It means I feel confident leaving the tree right here."

"Right. Because we have to worry about the trees who won't find a home?" A total guess on his part, but he knew he was right when he was rewarded by her smile.

"Now you're getting it, Hawkins." She took the lead. "I'll take point. Follow me."

"You've picked up a few military terms." He jammed his fists into his coat pockets and trailed after her.

"Hard not to. C'mon, soldier. I see exactly what I'm looking for." She forged ahead, undaunted by the virtual forest surrounding them, sure of her mission.

"I know what you are up to." He hiked to keep up with her. "You are going for the pity tree."

"Pity tree? I don't think that's a very nice thing to say. Trees are God's creations and every one of them is beautiful." She tossed a grin over her shoulder, as if daring him to argue.

As if he could argue with the likes of her. Too pretty

and smart for a guy like him—besides, she made any arguments vanish. How could any guy argue with her? When she smiled, she made his heart skip three beats, but he didn't break stride as he caught up to her. He shook his head. "I should have known."

"This one is perfect." She touched a scrawny branch of the slightly lopsided Douglas fir. He'd never seen a sorrier tree—or at least not one that was still green.

"I'm not even going to try to talk you out of it." He might not be the smartest tool in the shed, but he knew happiness when he saw it. He wouldn't take that from her for the world. "You're sure this is the one you want? There might be a more sickly looking one on the other side of the lot."

"I've bonded with this one. Plus, it's a live tree." She pointed to the big brown planter, presumably of all natural material.

"Perfect."

"I'm glad you think so. You're more of a kindred spirit than I first thought." She beamed up at him, a moment of joy on a rainy gray day, and his heart did more than skip a few beats. Everything within him stilled, as if he would never be the same.

"Can I help you with that?" The owner appeared with a handcart.

Hawk hardly heard him. In the whimsical flash of the multicolored twinkle lights, September's gaze locked on his with appreciation, and guilt hit him like a cluster bomb.

Chapter Five

The cotton candy clouds slowly ripped apart, and the rain turned to a lazy drizzle as she let Hawk help her into the truck. His hand at her elbow was a comfort. She felt better today than she had in a long time. Maybe it had to do with getting out of the house and feeling the wonder of the outdoors, the rugged, snow-capped mountains rimming the horizon. Maybe—just maybe—it had to do with the man who pulled her seat belt for her and buckled her in snuggly.

"Tell me why you aren't married again?" He was a gentleman and a caretaker. She had a soft spot for the protective, caring type.

"No woman will have me." He grinned, flashing those gorgeous dimples of his as if he knew full well the effect they had on a girl. "Probably because I'm deployed all the time. Hard to know a girl long enough that she could see past my faults."

"Your *numerous* faults," she couldn't resist correcting.

"Hey! I'm not that bad. At least, I hope not." He winked, confident as always, and closed the door. Even through the blur of the wet windshield, he radiated integrity and good humor. Definitely hard not to like the guy.

The door wrenched open and he hopped behind the wheel. "I hope you're not keeping count of my faults."

"I've decided to make a list."

"That's bound to be one mighty long list." He laughed at that and started the truck.

A list. That might do it. She would need some way to keep from liking him too much. Hard to say why, but she felt more herself today. She could almost see the girl she used to be in the reflection of the shadowy windshield.

"Anything you need to get? Any place you need to go?" He put the truck in Reverse and laid his arm over the back of the bench seat dangerously close to her. "Maybe new decorations for your new tree?"

Sitting there, with the defroster blowing through his short, dark hair and happiness softening the striking planes of his masculine face, he represented everything noble and righteous in the world. His honor shone through, unmistakable. She saw friendship and kindness and a soldier's loyalty. She had the feeling that if she asked him, he would move the mountains stone by stone.

"There is somewhere I'm dying to go." She pointed to the right—away from the way home—after he turned the truck around. "I need to see my horse."

"I thought doctor's orders were to take it easy. You might not have been hurt the way Crystal was, but you're bruised up pretty good. I know. Back at the hospital, I sweet-talked the nurses into telling me the truth." Serious concern layered the deep notes of his voice and warmed the air between them. Not accusing, when he could be, and not controlling when he could simply drive her home. He probably had no idea how attractive that made him. His gaze fastened on hers, as if he were expecting nothing short of the whole truth. "Do you feel up to it?"

"Not exactly. I'm still fairly weak." His gaze intensified, or maybe it was her perception. She resisted the urge to tear away and break the intimacy. "I've heard the reports, I've spoken to my boss and the vet, but I have to see with my own eyes that Comanche is okay. He's been my best friend for the last ten years."

"Friendship means a lot to you."

"It's everything." Friendship was the kind of love she could depend on. She fingered her cast, fighting frustration. "I miss him. Whatever has gone wrong in my life, Comanche has always been there to make it easier. And now I can't drive because of the medication I'm on, so I can't see him."

"What about your sister? Won't she drive you?"

"Chessie tends to be a little overprotective."

"A big sister's prerogative." He hit the turn signal—right, not left toward home. "Here's the deal—no riding, no stress and strain, no exertion of any kind."

"*Thank* you, Hawk." Hard not to like him more than she already did. Joy sparkled through her, and it was because of him. "You never answered my question."

"Neatly evaded it, did I? Learned how to walk softly in Ranger School. It's saved me more than once."

"You can't tiptoe around this ambush. I have skills of my own. Being a riding instructor teaches you a lot of things. Perseverance. Focus. How to stick with a problem until you work out a solution." She liked how tiny lines crinkled at the corners of his eyes when he grinned.

"So you're saying I have met my match?"

"You have. No more glib phrases so you don't have to face the real issue."

"I'm in big trouble." He slowed to a stop at the intersection and let his eyes meet hers. "Okay, here's the scoop. I'm not looking for marriage right now for the same reason you haven't started dating again."

"Oh." She didn't want to look at the places iced over and wintry within her, but she understood. He didn't need to say more. "Tim."

"I don't want to leave someone behind to grieve me." He checked for traffic and concentrated overly hard on his driving, as if the simple task of making a right-hand turn took all of his mental capabilities.

Caring. That was the danger. She understood what he could not say. That when you took the initial small step in a relationship, you let that person through your first layer of defenses. When you cared, you opened your heart, leaving you vulnerable to the world, to life and to loss. Sometimes that was too much of a risk to take.

The swipe of the wiper against the windshield helped to fill the silence between them. Miles rolled by in many shades of green—the faded tones of the grass, the deeper hues of the evergreens, the sedate greens of bushes and shrubbery. Houses on acreage whisked by and within minutes she was pointing at the turnoff to the riding stables.

"Is this the same place where you learned to ride as a kid?" he asked as he parked in the gravel lot.

"Yes. When I was ten, I used to makes wishes on

the first star of the night that I would grow up to be just like Colleen. She owns the stables. I couldn't imagine spending my life working with horses and riding all day." She reached to release her seat belt, but he beat her to it.

"Just proves some dreams are meant to come true." He released the buckle, his hand catching hers. The calm of the contact shook her. It lasted only for a moment before he turned away. "This time you wait for me to come help you down. I know I don't look like it, but I can be a gentleman."

"I never doubted it." The door shut, leaving her alone in the compartment. He dominated her thoughts. He was all she could see as he circled around and opened her door. His hand took hers again, and she leaned into his touch, wanting more of the unyielding peace he brought to her. She wasn't sure the exact moment her feet touched the ground.

"Tell me what you do here besides private lessons." He beeped his truck locked and followed her across the gravel toward the main barn. "Did you used to show?"

"Now I train others who show. But don't get me wrong. I spend a lot of hours mucking stalls and hauling hay. Barn work is a part of owning a horse." She strode through the main doors, open to the blustery winds, and hiked down the aisle. Gladness radiated from her, and she raised her good hand to someone out of his sight and kept going. "I practically live here. I'm never home."

"I know what that's like." He loved his job, too, the challenge and the duty. This was a different world, one that smelled like fresh alfalfa and horse. A pleasant combination, one that drew up memories of his boyhood in Wyoming, racing through the fields of wild grasses, while across the way farmers cut their fields, the scent carrying on the summer breeze. On either side of him, horses poked their heads over their gates, full of curiosity. Everything was clean and shining, from the polished wood to the animals themselves.

"There's my boy." A horse whinnied, more anxious than the others at the sight of the woman in the aisle, and she went to him. Her good hand curled around his fancy purple halter. "Hey, Comanche. I've been missing you, big fella."

Hawk froze in the aisle, caught by the sight of the petite woman, diminutive compared to the giant gold horse. The animal strained against the gate, making it groan as he pressed his face into her hand. He nibbled the edge of her cast as if with great concern.

"It's all right. I can still ride." Her assurance was met with a doubting nicker.

He could watch the woman all day long. She was different with her horse, softer, more alive and less shadowed. Her hair hung in a straight curtain, framing her sweetheart's face, and she moved like a Christmas carol—with grace and spirit. She leaned her forehead against the horse's cheek, a moment of pure tenderness between two friends.

That was what it would be like to be close to her, he realized. Sugarcoated moments and quiet closeness. His heart warmed as feelings came to life, new and powerful and unlike anything he'd known before. Soft and tender emotions, ones he had no right to. He more than cared about her. He liked her. A lot. Guilt returned to pierce him like a blade.

"He's a good-looking horse." What he knew about

the creatures could fit into a boot, but it didn't take a horseman to see the quality of the animal. His face was finely shaped, his forehead high and intelligent, his eyes wise and kind. His coat gleamed like honey in sunshine, and his mane shimmered like white silk. Beneath the purple blanketlike garment he wore, the horse looked pleasingly built.

"Comanche has an impressive pedigree. A quality quarter horse isn't cheap. I think my parents took out a second mortgage on their house for him and the mare they bought my sister when we were in junior high."

"Good parents."

"The best." She readily agreed, and she had never looked lovelier or more wholesome, the kind of woman a man wanted to come home to. She could make a soldier like him wish for things that were out of his reach.

He winced, wanting to retreat. He had no right feeling this way. He was wrong to look at September and wish.

"My sister mostly grew out of her horse phase, but I never will." Her laughter rippled, the sound of gentle chiming joy, as the horse lapped at her coat pocket, trying to work it open. Gently, she focused her attention on Comanche. "Let me see what I have in here. I might be out of peppermint."

They were a pair, Hawk decided as he watched woman and horse. September bent to her task, her hair hiding her face as she searched in her pocket and came up with a single wrapped piece of candy. Best friends, she had said. He didn't doubt that the horse adored her. Being close to her had to be as sweet as walking in heaven.

"This is the only one, sorry, buddy." She unwrapped

the candy, while the horse tried to grab it with his whiskery lips. When he succeeded, she laughed again, a sound that wrapped around Hawk's heart, a memory he would never let go of.

His quiet, unspoken wish remained, right and wrong all at once. Torture. He cleared his throat, struggling to hide it. "I bet there isn't anything Comanche doesn't know about you."

"True. He is my closest confidant."

"So, if I want to learn your secrets, I would have to go to him. Get him to talk." He ambled closer and rubbed the gelding's nose. Comanche crunched happily on his candy.

"Why? Is there something you want to know about me?" She cast him a sideways glance, curiosity alight on her delicate features.

"Don't worry. Your secrets are safe. I don't speak horse."

"Lucky for me." She dipped her head, as if suddenly shy.

Maybe because he was studying her too boldly. He didn't mean to. She had hints of little dimples, and he missed seeing her real smile, the full-fledged, all-out one he remembered back when she had been dating Tim. What would it take to see that full-out grin again? Everything within him longed for the sight.

Guilt wedged again into his soul. What would Tim think? Was his buddy looking down from heaven right now with anger? Or would he understand? Hawk shifted his weight, stepping away, and the horse nickered in protest. Apparently Comanche was used to a lot of adoration.

September had turned to him, about to speak, when

someone called her name. She whipped around, her hair flying, calling out a howdy to the woman bouncing down the aisle.

"I knew you couldn't stay away!" A redhead wrapped September in a careful hug. "Everyone has been asking about you and wanting to know when you're coming back."

"As soon as the doctor says I can."

The two women fell into a lively conversation about people and horses. Hawk leaned against Comanche's stall and folded his arms. September was all he could see—the graceful, tall way she stood like a ballet dancer. Her warm manner, her concern for the other people she discussed with the redhead, her gentle voice that had the nearby horses turning their heads to listen to her. Could he blame them? Not one bit.

Face it, you like her, man. And not just a little, either. If only he knew how to bury his affection for her or to somehow erase his feelings. He had no right to them. None at all.

Peace. It seeped into her in an innocent warm rush that went straight to her heart. September took one last look at the stables—a comforting place where she truly belonged—before Hawk turned the truck around and headed down the drive. "At least the rain has stopped."

"I hadn't noticed."

"I was afraid of that." She rolled her eyes at the amusement in his voice. Of course she hadn't meant to stay so long. "You have gone numb with boredom, haven't you? Chessie is always quick to tell me how monotonous it is to wait when I'm in my horse zone."

"Trust me, I wasn't bored." A sheepish curve of his mouth did intriguing things to his dimples.

Not that she was noticing. "How could you not be? I shouldn't have yakked on like that. Once I get going, I can't seem to stop. It's like time isn't passing. I'm sorry. How can I make it up to you?"

"I'll think of something. After all, I *did* suffer."

"So now you change your story? When there's something to be gained?"

"Call it curiosity." He hit the turn signal and checked for traffic. "You can't fault me for being inquisitive."

"How does a homemade dinner sound?"

"I wouldn't turn that down. I'm not the typical bachelor. I can cook for myself. The trouble is that I don't like to cook for one. Something tells me you are a good cook."

"I'm fair to middling." She leaned back against the seat, already looking forward to it. "I should be up to it tomorrow. I suppose a handsome bachelor like you has plans for a Saturday night."

"Are you kidding? I'm as free as a bird."

"You say that with a grin. You don't have any solid plans at all?"

"I'm usually pretty scheduled. Since I'm on leave, I want to hang loose. Take it as it comes. See where the road takes me." He accelerated across the lanes of traffic and merged into the flow of the other cars. "I'm a free spirit."

"I've noticed." She tried to recall what she knew about Hawk. Somewhere in the recesses of her mind, she remembered Tim saying he always went for action sports. "You like skiing, right? Plan on doing any while you're a free spirit?"

"I've got a few trips planned. A buddy of mine and I are heading to Canada to do a climb."

"You mean as in scaling a mountain?"

"No, the glacier. Ice climbing."

"If I were you, I would head south. Find sunshine and a warm beach."

"Tempting, but I've decided to stick around here. Who says life isn't adventurous around you? I'm curious to see what happens next."

"Me, too." She laughed, deep and true, and it felt good. "I'm not sure I can compete with extreme skiing or inching up a glacier with an ice pick, but I make a great pot of spaghetti and meatballs."

"Are you kidding? I got a good view of you back at the stables."

"A good view of me?" She hardly noticed the yards and trees flashing by, or the fact that she was almost home. He intrigued her. His presence filled the truck's cab, overwhelming her. A smart girl would keep him at a distance.

"It's who you are, with your horse and your friends. It's a dream you had as a little girl, spending your time with your horse, learning all you could about riding. Your friends are there. Your life is there. You want your future there, exactly the same way it's been. You fit at that stable. You can be the woman you were meant to be."

"Yes. How did you know?" She felt her jaw drop. She stared at him, astonished.

"It fits with your beliefs. You wear your causes on your T-shirts."

"I am a fan of the ride and walkathons." She looked down at her blue shirt; the white lettering read Race for Childhood Diabetes. "Comanche and I like to do our part. Next week there's a ride for the local food bank. It's not ice climbing, but it might be fun."

"I'll do it, but I don't have a horse."

"No worries. I can find you a mount."

"I *knew* you were going to say that. I guess there's no way out now." He didn't look too broken up by it.

His gentle friendliness was hard to resist. Through the permanent layers of ice she had been buried in, he reached her. She was helpless to stop his gentle breach of her defenses. His grin, his dimples, his friendliness, his understanding, his willingness to ride along touched her deeply. A true caring took root within her, and she could not stop it.

"Count me in." He pulled into her driveway. The sun broke, piercing ragged gray clouds as if in victory. He cut the engine.

Like the sun, her feelings were too intense. She blinked against the brightness and unlatched her seat belt before he could do it. Overwhelmed, she struggled to keep him at a distance, but her emotions weren't cooperating. She had to stop the caring from taking firmer root in her heart.

"There you are." Her sister stormed down the walkway, mouth pursed, and anger flashing. "I've been worried about you. No note. Nothing. Your car in the garage. What was I supposed to think?"

"I didn't know you were coming over." She hopped down from the seat and spotted Chessie's sedan in the nearby guest parking spot. "I didn't mean to worry you."

"Too late." Chessie sent an accusing glance Hawk's way. "You. I should have known you had something to do with this. I suppose you let her talk you into going to the stables?"

"Guilty. She's hard to say no to." Hawk did look guilty as he unlatched the tailgate. "I didn't keep her out long."

"She has a concussion. She's had surgery. She can't be out running around with the likes of you." Chessie stopped herself, just in time. "I'm sorry. I'm grateful to you for finding her. I always will be. But she's fine now. She doesn't need another soldier messing up her life."

"Francesca." September's face burned. She took a step toward her sister, then realized how alone Hawk looked as he hauled the tree out of the truck bed. How miserable as he wrapped his arms around the planter and lifted. Tendons strained in his neck—it had to be heavy. "Hawk, let me get the door for you."

"You might want to find something to put under this. You don't want this on your pretty wood floor." He sounded strained, and the branches hid him effectively. It was hard to read the emotion on his face.

She didn't need to see him to know he'd been hurt. "Chessie, will you find something?"

Her sister gave her a long look, as if she were about to refuse, but decided better of it. She meant well, September thought as she followed her sister onto the porch, but Chessie's strong opinions had a way of always hurting someone. She was too much like their dad—a good soul, but so sure her way was the only one.

"You've done me a world of good today." September held the door for him and her perfectly imperfect Christmas tree. "Don't forget that. I'm grateful, Hawk."

"You did me a world of good, too." He ambled in on a ray of sunshine. He didn't meet her gaze. Something had changed. Maybe it was what Chessie said, or maybe he felt this, too—the growing closeness between them.

Perhaps he wasn't comfortable with that, either. She searched for something to say in the beats of silence between them. Chessie saved her, marching into the room like a field general with an extralarge serving platter she'd found in the kitchen.

"Right here?" Hawk asked, his voice hooking her attention.

"Yes. Perfect." She hardly noticed where her sister placed the platter and Hawk settled the tree. Sunshine tumbled through the window, growing brighter, and gracing the man who turned the planter to show off the fir.

Hawk was a thoughtful man. He had become a loner, too, just as she had. Somehow Chessie had left the room, she hadn't noticed that, either, leaving them alone. The pleasant afternoon, their conversation and closeness remained between them.

"If you've changed your mind about supper tomorrow, I would understand." He jammed his fists into his coat pockets, attempting to seem casual.

She wasn't fooled. It had to be an effort for him, as it was for her. Their wounded pasts stood between them, something that could not be erased or forgotten.

"No way, soldier. You are coming tomorrow. End of story." She owed him that much. She couldn't risk caring about him, but she wasn't about to toss him out in the cold, either. Hadn't he admitted today had helped him, too? Maybe there was a higher purpose at work—and that thought surprised her. She hadn't looked to her faith in a long time. She followed him to the door. "I'm going to need help with the tree. I can't decorate by myself."

His grin said he saw straight through her. He glanced toward the kitchen—must be where Chessie had retreated to—but he didn't point out the obvious, that she was hardly alone. Instead, he hesitated on the porch and peered up at the gutters. "I'll bring my toolbox and see if I can't get that patched for you."

"That would be nice of you, Hawk."

"Not nice, trust me." He looked like a man struggling as he lifted a hand. "See you tomorrow."

"Come anytime," she called after him. She wasn't sure if she caught a grim downturn to his mouth, or if it were simply a trick of the light. He bounded away, a powerful, substantial man.

What a relief. She eased into the house and closed the door. Through the window, she could see his truck door close and pale exhaust puff into the damp, cold air. Since he was leaving, she could return to her peaceful numbness, to let her feelings settle into nothingness. She could go back to the way she'd been.

"I don't like how he looks at you." Chessie returned with two steaming cups, tea bag tags dangling.

"What are you talking about? Hawk looks at me with respect."

"Exactly. You aren't going to get involved with him, are you?"

"How could you think such a thing?" As if. She

wasn't that girl, not anymore. "Nothing happened. Nothing's changed."

"Are you sure about that?"

Staying silent, September turned to the window in time to catch sight of Hawk's truck ambling down the road, and her spirit brightened. She was wrong—everything had changed. She had changed. Hawk had stirred her emotions to life and there was no going back.

Chapter Six

Why couldn't he get her out of his mind? He'd been home for hours, but the five-mile jog and the hour's worth of chores had not pushed her from his thoughts. She remained front and center and nothing he did could dislodge the sweet memories of how she had looked in that stable, her uninjured arm around her horse. Her girl-next-door beauty and gentle nature had caught him like a fish on a hook.

He dropped the laundry basket in front of the dryer and opened the door. No way could he deny how he felt about her. He knelt, reaching in for his fresh, warm laundry. As towels tumbled into the basket, he battled something that went beyond guilt. If Tim knew, what would he think? Should he walk away?

"What are you doing here, Hawk?" Reno, a fellow Ranger, plodded into the basement laundry room with a full basket in his arms. "I thought you were on leave?"

"Still have to do laundry regardless." He knew that wasn't what his buddy meant. He closed the dryer door, caught the basket with the side of his boot and scooted it over to the next dryer. "Haven't gotten around to heading out of town."

"What is it this time? Extreme skiing? Base jumping?" Reno set his burden on top of a washer. Typically, he was wearing an army T-shirt and battered jeans, just like Hawk. "I heard you and Granger were up to something."

"We've got a date with a mountain up north, and a backcountry trip in Wyoming." He tugged open the dryer. "That ought to keep me out of trouble."

"Or in it." Reno smirked and upended his basket into a washer. "Only two scheduled activities? I don't get Granger. Once you tie yourself up with a woman, your fun gets curtailed. That's why I'm a free man."

"That's not why you don't have a gorgeous fiancée." Hawk couldn't resist. Joking with one's buddies was the Ranger way. "It's your personality, man. No woman would have you."

"Hey, I could get a fiancée if I wanted one. Girls would line up to marry me."

"Right. I'll try not to trip over the long line on my way out." His basket full, he headed for the exit. "Dude, there's only one reason you and I are doing laundry on a Friday night."

"I've got a ten-mile run first thing in the morning." Reno boasted. "Got to keep in killer shape. The ladies can't resist that."

"You're a sad man, Reno." He shook his head with mock pity. "Destined to be a lonely bachelor."

"Hey, you're doing laundry, too." Reno's laughter filled the stairwell. "I'm not alone in the sad department."

No denying that. With a grin, Hawk took the

staircase, rounded the landing and kept climbing. His footsteps made a lonely sound. His buddy's good-natured banter stuck with him. They were two confirmed bachelors—at least in this stage of life—and since he wasn't one to hang out in bars or play dating games, he was doing chores on a Friday night. He used to hang out with Pierce, but Pierce was in Wyoming with his fiancée, the lucky dog.

That was one reason he had considered getting out. He didn't have the kind of faith in love that Pierce did. No way could he leave a woman behind over and over again, knowing what distance and constant separation could do to a relationship. He didn't want to take that chance. No, it was better to wait, at least that's what he told himself as he unlocked his door and dropped the laundry on his couch. He didn't want to admit his heart had ideas of its own.

September. The light floral scent of her shampoo and lotion had somehow gotten on his shirt, and he couldn't forget her. The image of her, tall and slim and graceful, trailed after him as he ambled into the kitchen. The music of her laughter, the warmth of her joy, the way she picked out Christmas trees and tried to save the world riding and walking for one cause after another. Emotions swelled within him, pure and honest tenderness.

He was in trouble. He opened the mayonnaise jar, knifed some on the bread lying on a plate and finished making his sandwich. A smart man would end it right here. He would never turn around and look back, but keep going forward without another thought of the woman.

You know that's the right thing, he told himself. He

slapped slice after slice of roast beef on the bread, then went for the cheese. The Lord knew he had enough to keep him busy. He didn't want any emotional entanglements, so he should stop these feelings. Do what it took to break the connection he felt with her.

He layered lettuce and tomato on his sandwich and reached for the mustard jar. That settled it. Tomorrow, he would help with September's decorations and do a few minor repairs around the house, but he would keep a tight rein on his feelings. Sure, it would be tough, but he was a Ranger. He was tougher.

Satisfied, he moved his sandwich to a plate, grabbed a bag of chips and headed to the couch.

September heard the knock over the sizzling meatballs. She turned down the heat, checked on the bubbling tomato sauce and grabbed a towel to wipe her fingers. She hurried to the door, feeling both anticipation and dread. The tree looked lonely without decorations as she passed by, but that would be soon remedied. She found him on her doorstep, looking dapper in a black leather jacket, matching T-shirt and jeans.

"I brought dessert." He held a baker's box in both hands, and on top lay a bouquet of baby pink roses. "Decided I ought to show up with something besides my tool chest."

"And the flowers?"

"Those are to make you smile."

"Is it working?"

"Prettiest smile I've ever seen. So, yes." He handed her the bouquet, carefully wrapped in florist's paper.

Why this man? Why did her heart flutter when their

fingers brushed? "Come in. I've got to get back to the stove."

"Fine. I'll make myself useful out here for a bit."

"Let me know if you need anything. I've got tea water simmering."

"I'll keep that in mind." He set the box on the entry table, a man on a mission. His red toolbox waited for him, and he seemed eager to get to it.

Since the meatballs needed a turn and the sauce a stir, she admired the flowers on her return route to the kitchen. The little pink rosebuds were perfect, not romantic, not casual, just right. She spotted a florist's card tucked into the paper and tugged it loose.

Ecclesiastes 11:7.

She couldn't place it. Since the meat was sizzling, she laid the flowers and card on the counter and grabbed a pair of tongs. Just in time—the meatballs were perfectly browned, and she turned them. Over the drone of the stove exhaust and the popping and crackling oil, she heard the rhythmic beat of a hammer.

Hawk. What was she going to do about him? Before he'd walked back into her life, she had been buried in the past, she believed she might never find her way out. But she had been wrong. He had shown her that.

After giving the sauce a stir, she went in search of her Bible, tucked in with her books on the table. She flipped through the thin, dog-eared pages until she found Ecclesiastes. The hammering stopped as she began to read. *Truly the light is sweet, and a pleasant thing it is for the eyes to behold the sun.*

The door squeaked open, and she didn't need to hear the pad of his boots on the hardwood to know he was coming. She felt his closeness like a touch to her soul. By the time he rounded the corner, she'd put her Bible away and was reaching with her good arm for the teakettle.

"Smells good in here." He took the kettle from her. "Are you sure you should be doing all this? I'm just about ready to take over and order you to the couch."

"Just try taking over my kitchen, soldier." She felt featherlight as she held up two tea boxes for him to choose. He pointed at the mint blend. "I don't relinquish my command easily."

"You could delegate." He filled the two waiting cups on the counter, not bothering to wait for the tea bags. "I've got a few domestic skills."

"We'll see about that." She plopped the bags in the steaming water, pretending to size him up. "I have an order for you. Are you ready?"

"Lay it on me. Whatever it is I can take it." He drew his shoulders back, military posture.

Show-off, September thought, and in the best possible way. He was exemplary and growing in her estimation with every passing moment. Not that she was letting it affect her, because that would be foolish. This was totally casual. She tried not to see anything but a friend standing in her kitchen. A friend. Tim's friend. Reminding herself of Tim ought to make the tension within her ease.

It didn't.

"The pot needs water, if you please. I can't lift it." She found a vase in a bottom cabinet.

"As you wish, pretty lady." He grabbed the pot off the counter next to the sink and hit the tap. Over the rush of water, he kept talking. "Have I told you how impressed I am? It takes a strong woman to rebuild her life."

"If that's how it looks, then I'm glad. It's what I've been trying to do. Go through the motions every day, put one foot in front of the other. Eventually life would get better. If I lived as if it were normal, then maybe one day it might be." She turned off the water for him. "You didn't come here to hear about this."

"Sure I did. We're friends, September. I care." His words grew tender, personal, everything she was afraid of. Her pulse lurched, but before she could move away, he was the one who broke the distance. He carried the pot to the stove and twisted on the burner. "You have a nice home, a job you love, friends who treasure you. I saw all those flowers at the hospital. When you were missing, a lot of people were really scared for you."

"I've done the best I could without my heart." Her throat closed, making it impossible to speak. *Until you,* she wanted to say, *I think you are bringing me back.*

How could she say something like that? It would sound romantic, as if she had a crush on him. She searched, but could not find the words to tell him the difference his friendship had already made for her.

"Your heart is still here." Hawk came to her and cupped her face in his calloused hands. Absolute certainty blazed in his intense gaze.

Feelings, powerful and overwhelming, winked to life. Her throat clogged tighter, making it impossible to breathe. She felt as if she were falling, but she stood on solid ground. The sauce still bubbled, the oven beeped that it had finished preheating, and the roses on the counter added a delicate fragrance to the air—those things remained the same.

Inside she felt as if the frost within her cracked apart one painful break at a time. The defenses had kept her safe after she lost Tim, and without them she felt as if she might crack apart with them. Except for Hawk's presence. His hands cradled her face with caring reverence, a link that held her together. Thank the Lord for the blessing of friendship.

"How did you do it?" Her voice sounded thin and raw. "You've lost close friends. You've seen suffering and war and terrible things. Yet you are centered and vital. Alive. It's as if none of that has touched you."

"Of course it has. I am a different man because of it." His thumbs stroked her jawline in small comforting circles. "I don't take the good moments for granted. I treasure friendships, respect the hardships other people go through and I'm grateful for every moment. I try to live my life in honor of the friends I have lost."

"How do you deal with the hurt?"

"The way anyone does. I face it and go on."

"With honor." She smiled a little, as if she didn't need to be told that was the Ranger way. "That's what I'm trying to do, but I feel as if I'm groping in the dark."

"That's the sure sign you're doing it right. The right path is never the easiest." He did his best to keep a barrier around his feelings. He was here to help her, nothing more, because it was the right thing. "No gain without pain. It's always darkest before the dawn."

"You're a fount of wisdom."

"Just repeating what I've heard. You're painting me to be someone I'm not. Someone better." He was like anyone else, with more hang-ups than he wanted, just trying to make good decisions and live right. "That doesn't mean I haven't questioned everything from God's motives to my role in the military."

"You mentioned leaving the military."

"I lost a lifelong friend. He died right in front of me. It was a loss that hit hard." He stopped to shore up his defenses and keep his emotions rock steady. "It took me a lot of soul-searching to figure out that I can't be less than who God meant me to be. Holding myself back because of grief, or choosing a path that might not be right for me because I don't want to hurt like that again, is not doing justice to the life God gave me."

"That's what troubles me most." She looked even prettier in her sincerity. She was vulnerable and exposed, and it was easy to see the real September Stevens. He winced. She tugged at every emotion in him, but he had to stand firm.

"I have been doing my best, but I've only been existing. Surviving." Her throat worked, as if she were struggling with emotions, too. "Until you."

"I've done nothing, September. Unless you count the gutter work."

"Go ahead and deny it, but what you have done for me is no joke." She resonated with gratitude and caring.

Easy to read the shine of emotion, for she was an open book to him. With her cinnamon-brown locks curling from the warm kitchen, and her cheeks pink from heightened emotion, it took all his reserve to release her and step away. Letting go of her was the last thing he wanted, but he did it. Instead of drawing her into his arms and holding her close, instead of lifting her chin and capturing her mouth with his, he backed away.

"The water is boiling, and my toolbox is waiting. I've got a few more things to fix. Are you okay?" He fisted his hands to keep from reaching for her.

"Better." She squared her slim shoulders, looking stronger than he had ever seen her.

It wasn't right, it wasn't what he wanted, but he couldn't stop from caring. From truly caring. Right now he would stop the earth from spinning if it would guarantee her happiness.

"I'll be back to dump that pot for you." He turned on his heel, retreating. A smart soldier knew when to head for high ground. "You had better give me a shout when the noodles are done."

"Yes, sir." She saluted him, a twinkle glimmering in her eyes. The hint of her dimples had the force of a grenade attack.

A bigger chunk of guilt dug like shrapnel in his chest, and he headed for safety. There was a lightbulb out in the entryway. He would concentrate on getting that problem solved and repair the damage to his defenses. The evening wasn't over yet.

Good thing Hawk kept the conversation light throughout the meal. Their honest encounter left her raw and vulnerable, as if a rift had been made in her defenses. She needed to regroup and get used to the change in her. He regaled her with funny stories of him and his buddies, from tent life to travel near disasters and tales of his friendship with other Rangers. He probably thought he was entertaining her—no doubt about it, he was hilarious.

But she got a thorough view of the real Mark Hawkins—loyal, devoted, ever resourceful. A man

who never let his friends down. She felt honored to
be one of his friends.

He insisted they put on a Christmas CD and sang in
harmony while they did the dishes. Bing Crosby ser-
enaded them as they took the bakery box of brownies into the living room and started stringing the tree
lights. She told him of her students and a typical day
at the stables. He asked about the trail rides she took
her students on and the upcoming benefit ride-a-thon.
She asked about his sister, who sold real estate, and he
asked her about her sister, who was unmarried also.

By the time the multicolor lights were strung around
the tree, she felt on stable ground again. Maybe this
was the way things between them should stay—on
the surface, casual, nothing too personal. Safer, she
opened one of the storage boxes to find a beautiful
wreath on top—she and Chessie had made it at a day
workshop at a local crafts store.

"Let me guess, you made that." Hawk grabbed another brownie from the box—his third—and took a
bite. "You are one of those talented people, aren't you?
You probably had never made a wreath before."

"Not a wreath, no." She held it up, deciding it did
have a certain festive flare. "This was my only decoration last year. I figured, why bother? My sister and
I flew down to Mom's for the whole week."

"Is that what you're doing this year?" Hawk took
a second bite of the brownie—gone—and took the
wreath.

"This year Mom's husband is taking her for a Medi-
terranean cruise. She's always wanted to go."

"What about you?"

"Dad and his wife live in Seattle, so we will celebrate up there with them." She removed a box of ornaments from the storage bin. Gold and silver winked in the light. "Work is light around Christmastime. Most people are busy with family and getting ready for the holidays."

"So you will have some time off?" He grabbed his hammer and a nail from his box. "Something tells me you will be at the stables anyway. I saw you yesterday. It's tough on you to stay away."

"My best friend lives there, remember?" She took out an ornament and approached the tree, studying it speculatively. She gave it some thought, as she apparently did everything, before hanging it. "When do you leave for your ice climbing trip?"

"Tomorrow." He didn't like to think about it. Usually he would be gung ho, itching to go and ready to roll. But heading up north meant he wouldn't be with September. Nope, he didn't like that one bit. He grimaced and drove a nail into the door.

"Most people are going Christmas shopping. Lighting Advent candles. Giving time or money to charity." She studied the tree again, another ornament in hand.

"That's how *you* do it." Didn't take a genius to see how candy-sweet her holidays were. With songs about white Christmases and angels on high, good causes and candlelight services, she had the kind of life he'd forgotten about. Eight of the last nine Christmases he'd spent either on a forward post, a camp out in the middle of nowhere or gearing up for a deployment. Sometimes it got easy to forget the details of what he was fighting for and what he wanted his life to be after he laid down his rifle.

Maybe it was the picture of this life and not the

woman that pulled at his heartstrings. Perhaps this glimpse of a dreamlike holiday would explain the well of emotion troubling him. He'd been jumping out of planes and fast-roping out of helicopters for most of his adult life. Sometimes a man wanted more.

And his gaze went right back to September. Sure enough, she was picture-perfect in a simple green sweater and jeans. He flipped off the switch, and the room fell into darkness. The flash and gleam of the jewel-colored twinkle lights shone like something off a Christmas card, adorning her with the sparkle of red, blue, yellow and green. With the colors burnishing September's hair and accenting her delicate profile, Hawk lost the argument with himself. He could try to logically explain away his soft spot for her with all kinds of reasons, but that didn't disguise the truth.

"The wreath looks great." She considered the ornament and moved it an inch to the left. The frail branch dipped down, swaying with the silvered ball. "Come help with the ornaments."

"I don't have the knack for it." That, and it would mean he would have to be near to her. Bad idea. "I'm a terrible ornament hanger."

"You did fine with the wreath." She had no idea how appealing she was, like a carol. She flipped a lock of hair behind her shoulder and chose another ball from the box. "I'll take my chances. Come help me."

His feet moved him forward and he learned something new. It was impossible for him to say no to her. Impossible to keep the walls up and the defenses strong.

"Don't know how much help I'll be." Gone were the days of his boyhood, where he was the one in charge of the tree. Of his little sister wanting decorations and his mother, lost to depression, having left them to make what Christmas they could. He chose a blue ball from one of the boxes, liking the sprinkles of glitter that formed the star of Bethlehem, and slid a hook through the eye. "Don't say I didn't warn you."

"Get over here, Gloomy Gus." Gloomy was the last thing she could possibly be, wreathed by the richly colored lights and twice as radiant. "That would look perfect right here."

Good thing he had control of his heart. He stalked toward her, the perimeter around his feelings reinforced. He shouldered close to her, teeth gritted, ignoring the wish tempting him. Easy to see how it would be for the guy who landed her as his wife, Christmas seasons just like this, each one better than the next. He hung the ornament where she'd indicated, and the glistening blue orb made the twig bow dangerously.

"It's not going to hold," he warned her.

"Sure it is. Have a little faith."

"Faith, sure, but this is a matter of physics." He was captivated by the mystery in her expression. He shifted away and pretended interest in choosing another ornament, but in truth, it was to study her more. He grabbed a hook just as the limb slumped, the ornament tumbled and bounced down the tree.

He caught it before it crashed to the floor. "See, Galileo was—"

"Yeah, yeah, I know who Galileo was." She batted him in the arm, a light playful slap.

His perimeter shattered, his defenses fractured. There was nothing left of his will. He could not hold back the rising tide of his adoration. He was not that strong.

"Next you will bring up something about Ptolemy and the stars." She took the holy star from him and hung it on a bough.

He was staring again. Way to go, Hawkins. He tried to act casual and reached into the storage bin. Maybe there would be something in here he could hang on the front porch and get some fresh air and his head clear.

"What's that?" She swept close, luminous with the blinking lights. When he didn't answer, she bent to take a look, squinting in the dark. "It's plastic mistletoe. It's a family tradition to hang a sprig over the front door. When we were little, Dad would chase us for a raspberry kiss every time he came home."

"I can picture it." He brushed a lock of hair from her face. It wasn't really in her way, but he took the excuse to touch her. To close the bridge between them. He caught her hand in his and lifted it over her head. He didn't know what made him do it. It just happened. His lips fit over hers in one tender brush—that just happened, too.

Chapter Seven

❧

It was a perfect kiss. For an instant, September's eyes drifted shut and she let the sweetness sweep through her. It was something out of a dream. His mouth was patient and not demanding, and that made it easier to grasp his arm, hold on tight. Her mind stopped working. It took her a few long moments to realize this was no dream. Hawk was kissing her.

Kissing her! She broke away, watching the dance of light on his face. He seemed lost in a dream, too—the dream of Christmas, she told herself firmly. She uncurled her hand from his shirtsleeve and stepped away. The moment over, he bolted away, too, and together they stared at the mistletoe she held.

"Got to keep up the traditions." His glib remark told her that his hadn't been a serious kiss. "Want me to hang that for you?"

"Sure." She was shaken. Did it show in her voice? She couldn't tell. He looked pretty blasé as he scooped the plastic twig of mistletoe from her and ambled to the entryway. He scooted the ladder up and into place, quite as if their kiss hadn't happened.

She could not forget it. She fumbled with the hooks. They globbed together and she couldn't free a single one from the knot. When she did, two dozen of them tumbled to the floor.

"You okay over there?" His good-natured baritone held no hint as to what he was feeling.

"Just peachy." For a girl who didn't want to wake up from the dream. Who wouldn't have minded if the kiss lasted a few beats longer, because then she could have had time to absorb and process. To make sense out of why he had kissed her.

Get a grip, September. He kissed you. He didn't propose to you. She scooped up the last of the hooks, dumped them back into their original box and opened the next container of ornaments.

He didn't appear to be affected, but she was. Her hands continued to tremble, her knees stayed like jelly. Out of the corner of her eye, she watched him climb the ladder and drive a small white nail into the ceiling. She chose a hand-painted glass ball, careful not to drop it. She didn't trust her fingers. She didn't trust herself. All shields were down. How had Hawk gotten through her defenses?

"You were right." He startled her. Suddenly he came up behind her. "It's the perfect Christmas tree. You didn't need my help tonight, not really, but I'm glad to be here with you."

"You're a good friend." She wanted him to know she understood. It was only a friendly kiss. A holiday kiss. Nothing more. She wasn't one of those women who was prone to seeing romance everywhere—not anymore. "It wouldn't have been half so fun decorating this by myself, and I did need you. I could never have done the lights by myself."

"So you said, but your sister could have helped you." He reached out as if to brush her face, but his hand changed directions in midair and caught the length of her hair. He nudged it back behind her ear, although it hadn't been out of place.

Perhaps he felt more awkward than she'd guessed. That made two of them. Good thing she was a pro at covering up her true feelings. "You've packed up your toolbox."

"I can stay if you need me to, but your tree is nearly done. Unless there's anything else you want me to hang, fix or nail for you, I'd better be on my way." He didn't sound in a hurry to exit stage left.

Maybe she was reading too much into things. It was—she glanced at the wall clock—after nine. "You probably have an early day tomorrow."

"I'm picking up Pierce at Sea-Tac in the morning. We're driving to Canada." The only hint of tension was the tight line of his jaw. "We'll be gone for five days."

"You say that with such excitement, as if you're heading off on a Caribbean cruise." She hung another ornament, careful to keep her gaze on the tree. "Mountain glaciers have to be horribly cold this time of year. Are you staying at a lodge or a cabin or something?"

"A tent. We're roughing it."

"You'll freeze this time of year. Are you nuts?"

"Beyond a doubt." He laughed along with her. "This is fun for us. We get to test our mettle. We bundle up in goose down and build fire like cavemen. We eat beef jerky and complain about how cold we are. It's a blast."

"It certainly sounds appealing. Remind me to *never* go on a vacation with you."

"For you, I could make less challenging plans. I'm flexible." He hefted his toolbox, feeling as if he had not accomplished what he had set out to do, although he couldn't begin to explain what that was. Unsettled, wanting more and knowing he couldn't have it, he headed for the door. "When you head back to work, say hi to Comanche for me. I think he and I bonded."

"I'll be sure and mention you to him." She followed him to the door. "Want me to pick out a ride for you?"

"A ride? You mean, like a horse?" His hand lingered on the knob. One turn, and he would have to walk out the door. It was getting late, but did he want to go? No way.

"You agreed to go on the benefit ride. You promised, remember?" She could talk him into jumping to the moon, he figured.

"I'll be there." Probably not a good idea, because of his impulsive kiss. It stood between them right now. September wasn't as easygoing; there was something she held back just beneath the surface. She kept a few more paces between them than was necessary. When she smiled, her eyes didn't dance and sparkle.

Yep, the kiss was to blame. He opened the door, hooked one arm around the ladder and hauled it onto the porch. Rain speared under the porch roof, background music on a cold winter's eve.

"I'll call and leave the details on your answering machine." She hung in the doorway, probably not wanting to get wet or cold. Although it could be she was afraid he might plant another kiss on her.

Cool, Hawk. Real cool.

"You forgot your brownies. Let me go wrap them up for you—"

"No," he interrupted. "You keep 'em. I appreciate the meal. You're a good cook."

"You say that as if you were surprised."

"No. Maybe one day I'll cook for you."

"I would be brave enough to eat whatever you prepare."

"I'll hold you to it." His gaze slipped to her mouth. He couldn't help it. He thought of that kiss again, like peppermint and Christmas morning and a Sunday hymn all rolled together. "Good night, September."

"Good night, and thank you." She beamed up at him, quiet and shy, a wholesome combination. "I appreciated your help tonight. I appreciate you."

"Back at you, cutie." Call him an idiot, but he apparently hadn't learned his lesson. He leaned down to slant his mouth over hers. One soft brush was all he allowed himself before he pulled away. He had only one explanation for his rash action. "Mistletoe."

"It's not directly over the door." She sounded amused, not really protesting at all.

"Close enough." He grabbed his tools and his ladder and hoofed it down the steps. "I'll call you when I get back."

"Be careful on that glacier."

"Count on it."

"Better yet, I'll pray on it." She waved her good hand in goodbye. Night had fallen, and as he left, Hawk was a shadow against the dark curtain of rain, so it made no sense why she could see him clearly. Maybe she wasn't looking as much with her eyes as with her heart.

The big, strapping man striding confidently through the storm was no longer a reminder from the past, Tim's Ranger buddy or a passing acquaintance. He was her friend, the man who had chased away her shadows and brought color and light back into her life. The tree lights blinked as if in perfect agreement as she closed the door against the damp, chilly night and moved to the window to watch his truck drive away.

Beside her the tree stood in silent reminder of the evening. She raised her hand to wave again, not sure if he could see her, as his pickup ambled down the road. Hawk, a faint silhouette behind the wheel, waved in return. The first stirrings of deep emotion fluttered to existence in her heart—hope in the darkness.

"Earth to Hawk."

As the freeway north of Seattle swished by beneath the hood of his truck, Hawk heard a distant amused voice. Shaking his head to clear it—not that it worked—he attempted to stay in the here and now. His mind was stuck in a loop that took him straight back to last night. Two kisses. Correction—two mistletoe kisses, and she didn't seem sorry about it. He shook his head again, hit his turn signal to pass and moved into the far left lane. "Sorry, buddy. I've got a lot on my mind."

"Apparently. Whenever I have that much on my mind, it always has to do with Lexie." His fiancée. Smirking, Pierce waited for affirmation. He already knew he was right.

Why deny it? Hawk maneuvered past the semi, keeping his eyes on the road. "I ran into September Stevens, Tim's—"

"I know who she is," Pierce interrupted, surprised. "She could barely speak to my family at the funeral. I've never seen anyone so devastated."

"I have." He thought of his mom. He knew about loss. He'd lost not only his dad in a logging accident, but his mother, too. "She's doing better. I was over at her place last night. She bought a nice little town house south of the city. I did a few repairs and hauled in her Christmas tree for her. No biggie."

Except for those kisses. He couldn't get rid of the feeling that he shouldn't have done that. September was off-limits. Any decent man would think so. She was still recovering from a deep heartbreak. She had once been his best friend's girl. He might have tried explaining those kisses away using the mistletoe, but the truth was he would have kissed her without it. It wasn't right to care about her in any other way than friendship.

"No biggie, huh?" Pierce, fearless on the battlefield and smart tactically, was never easily fooled. "I understand, man. Don't sweat it. I've been there before. Fact is, I still am. Nearly killed me to leave Lexie behind. It doesn't get easier. Every time I go, it's leaving a piece of me."

"Hey, what kind of talk is that? This is your last outing as a free man." Not exactly your usual bachelor party. "Getting cold feet yet?"

"Not a chance, but Lexie keeps saying we should forget the expense and bother and head for Vegas. I know it's the stress of the preparations talking, but my mom would tan me for sure if she doesn't get a wedding. I'm the first of us to get married."

"I can see her really liking the wedding stuff."

"You're still going to be my best man, right?"

"*I* don't have cold feet." Although when it came to September, he should. Guilt tore through him. He couldn't bring himself to tell Pierce what had really happened last night. Maybe it was time to reevaluate this relationship with her. Since his normally impenetrable defenses and iron will had no effect around her, he ought to consider ending things.

"Take the next exit, would you?" Pierce gestured toward a freeway sign coming up on them pretty fast. "It's about chow time and I'm starving."

"Sure thing." Still troubled, Hawk tapped the turn signal and changed lanes just as the first drops of rain fell.

"I know you're getting antsy, handsome. You've been without a long ride for way too long." September gave the cinch a good tug and laid her casted hand against Comanche's stomach. "You aren't holding your breath, are you?"

Caught in the act, the palomino exhaled sheepishly.

"Every time," she told him. "That's how I know. You might as well not even try."

He shook his head, as if he had an opinion on that. He was the best horse in the entire world—okay, she was biased—but he tended to have a mind of his own. She buckled up, and they were ready to go.

"C'mon, boy." She caught his reins and led him down the aisle. "We can't take the trails up the mountain until they are all inspected. You don't mind, do you?"

Comanche lipped her ponytail, just glad to be with her. She knew, because that's how she felt. Grateful to be spending time with her best bud. Her riding boots gave a satisfying knell alongside her gelding's steeled shoes as they followed the cement pathway past the riding arena.

"I didn't know you were cleared to ride." Colleen, her boss, appeared in the office doorway. "Did your doctor give you clearance?"

"Not only that, but I can come back to work whenever, if you'll have me." She dug in her jacket pocket and handed over the doctor's memo. "I'm not sure how useful I'll be in the barns, but I can do my lessons."

"Excellent. I'll put you in the office on Monday instead of cleaning stalls until that's healed." Colleen studied the paper and folded it in precise half. "I heard from Mrs. Toppins. She says Crystal is home and recovering nicely. The girl is already begging to resume her lessons."

"Sounds like Crystal." She had a definite soft spot for her favorite student. "I meant to call her mom today. I'm glad she isn't afraid to ride. A lot of kids wouldn't want to get back on a horse after an experience like that."

"She's got grit," Colleen agreed. "Speaking of which, I'm glad to see you here, too. I was worried."

"About me? Don't be. I've had my share of falls and I've gotten back up every time." The horse tugged on her ponytail again, and she stroked Comanche's nose. "About working in the office. You have to know I won't have the best typing speed with this cast."

"Speed isn't everything. I hear the phone ringing. Have a good ride."

"Thanks, Colleen." As her boss hurried into the office to catch the call, September led her horse the rest of the way to the trailhead. The way north—to the mountain—was barricaded, but there were others to choose from. She grabbed the saddle horn, slid her toe into the stirrup and lifted herself into the saddle. The gelding stood patiently, ears pricked and scenting the wind. Yep, he was glad to be headed out, too.

She reined Comanche to the right, choosing the meadow path that looped around the grounds. The cold wind ruffled his platinum mane, and the gathering gray clouds above suggested the weathermen would soon be right. Green grass spread like emeralds for a mile, broken only by the white board fencing where horses grazed and riders practiced their pace changes. Voices from the covered arena carried faintly. Grade-school-aged girls sat astride their mounts in the beginners' class in the far paddock, and their excitement reminded her of being a little girl on a much younger Comanche, living her dream.

She'd always felt that God had led her here. Years had slipped by, time passed by well spent with friends and riding and working hard for competitions. He had known her heart and brought her to this wonderful place where she had always been happy. Even in her darkest times after she lost her beloved Tim, this place was the best refuge for her hurting soul.

Comanche nickered at a nearby buddy, who looked up from grazing and whinnied back. They continued on at a leisurely walk. Good to be in the saddle again. She breathed in fresh country air. Robins and sparrows soared and chattered, hurrying to get their work done before the rain. Mount Rainier's beautiful glaciered peak was lost in a crown of clouds. Hawk. She wondered how he was doing, if he had reached the mountain whose glacier he intended to scale or if he was still on the road.

Her thoughts kept circling back to him. He'd been a true helper fixing the leak, and her foyer hadn't been so bright in a while. As for his kisses—

You don't have to think about them, she reminded herself as rain pinged off her hat. She lifted her face and let the droplets bathe her. Nice and relaxing after an unsettled day. Tension eased, as if washed away by the rain, and she realized how worked up she'd been over Hawk. And why? She drew in a cleansing breath. After the benefit ride, it wasn't as if she were going to see him again. Likely as not he would be deployed by the new year and she would have worried for nothing.

Comanche extended his neck, asking for more rein, commanding her attention. He wanted to run. Well, she was up for it. She signaled him with her knees and leaned into his gait change. He dug in with all fours, from a smooth trot to a rolling cantor. She felt stronger, as she always did, racing the wind with her best bud. Everything came clear. Hawk's kisses were nothing she needed to worry about. As lovely as they were, he wasn't dating her. He had to know love was the last thing she would ever risk again.

The ground raced by in a blur as Comanche broke into a fast gallop, and she left her troubles behind.

Talk about cold. Hawk drove the stake into the ground and checked the anchor rope's tension. It ought to hold in all but the highest winds. They had driven as far as they could and had barely enough daylight left to set up camp. They would ski in to the climb come morning. For now, dark had fallen and the rain had turned to snow.

"Got the fire going." Pierce came around the corner of the tent. "Want me to break out the hot dogs or the Spam?"

"Hot dogs." He hiked through the accumulating snow and dropped the hammer with the rest of the gear. "Any chance you got some water hot yet?"

"You're gettin' soft." Pierce shook his head. "You should have bailed out of the Rangers when you got the chance. Don't know how you are gonna make it two more years."

"Hey, *I'm* not about to be an old married man." Not that he blamed Pierce one bit. Married life sounded just fine with him. Which was odd. He liked being a lone wolf. Thinking about it made him think of September, and that couldn't be a good sign, so he grabbed his collapsible cup and a tea bag and hunkered down on a rock to check on the heating water.

"Tell me more about what happened after you carried her out of the mine shaft." Pierce broke open a package of beef franks and impaled a couple of them on a skewer before handing it over.

"There's nothing to tell. I checked on her at the hospital. I dropped by to help her out. Figured Tim would have wanted me to make sure she was okay." He took the skewer and held it over the lively flame.

"So you did it for Tim?" Pierce nodded with understanding. "I was always deployed, never got to know September very well, but I recall she was pretty and kind. Tim was crazy about her."

"I know." Guilt with pinpoint accuracy. A top sniper

didn't have better aim. "Being crazy about her would be easy to do."

"Ah, I thought so." Pierce angled his meal over the cracking fire pit. "Tim would have expected her to go on with her life and find someone again. He would want a guy to take good care of her and treat her well. If you want my opinion, I think he would be glad if that man was you. Just something to think about."

Snow tapped on his parka and sizzled on the ring of rocks, and he gave his skewer a turn, watching the skins blacken as the meat cooked. Pierce thought he was helping, but it hadn't removed the bullet of guilt lodged in his chest.

"Catch." Pierce tossed a hot dog bun over the fire and smoke.

Hawk caught it in one hand, caught a second one and pulled the skewer from the heat. Dinner was served.

The afternoon's light rain had turned into what sounded like a monsoon by the time September finished wiping down her kitchen counters. There. The chores were done for the evening. Satisfied, she hit the start button and the dishwasher chugged to life. The marble gleamed, the cabinets shone, the appliances sparkled in the white twinkle lights she had strung around the top edge of the upper cabinets.

The phone rang. Chessie, checking up on her. She didn't have to look at caller ID as she grabbed the cordless and turned off the overhead lights. She left behind the soft glow of the twinkle lights and headed to the living room. The gas fireplace was going, chasing the winter's chill from the room. "No, I don't have my feet up, but as soon as the phone rang I headed for the couch."

"How did you know it was me calling?"

"My big-sister radar beeped." She stretched out on the couch and grabbed the remote. "And no, I didn't overdo it at the stables. I needed to get in some saddle time before next week's event."

"Excuses. As if you need more time on the back of a horse." Beneath Chessie's tough-girl facade ran true caring. "You sound better. More like yourself."

"It takes more than a fall into a big hole in the earth to keep me down," she quipped, hit the mute button and began to channel-surf.

"You know I wasn't talking about that. You haven't sounded this chipper since…" She paused, as if she didn't want to cause any pain by bringing up Tim's name.

"I had a good day." That was the simplest explanation. She didn't know why she felt better—she certainly didn't want to pin that on one man. She was not that needy or fragile; she was the kind of woman who stood on her own two feet. "How did your day at work go?"

"The same old thing. Not much changes at the library. People check out books, they bring them back." Librarian humor. "Have you heard from Dad yet?"

They passed the next thirty minutes catching up on family news and holiday plans. In the background, September's thoughts were way too preoccupied with a certain new friend. After she said goodbye to her sister, she punched in Hawk's home number. His machine came on and his rugged baritone across the line made her smile. She left him the information he needed for the ride—just businesslike stuff. Nothing personal.

Except for the small detail that she was grinning ear to ear by the time she hung up. So what? She was looking forward to seeing the guy. They were friends. That was a prerequisite for a friendship, right?

Right, and so were those kisses. She rolled her eyes. Best not to think about the kisses.

Luckily, *Jeopardy* came on. One of her faves. She turned up the volume, calling out answers along with the contestants.

But what was at the back of her mind?

Yes. Hawk. He had taken up permanent residence in her thoughts.

Chapter Eight

The rain had miraculously cleared after it had been pouring for hours. It's a sign, September decided as she guided Comanche around the last corner and onto the main trail of the park. Clusters of trees waved, shedding the morning's rain with plops and plinks. A half dozen squirrels peeked out from branches and boughs to get a good look at all the activity. The local trail riders' association had a booth set up at the starting line, where she had volunteered last year.

People and horses were everywhere. She waited for a break in the line before dismounting, unwrapped General's reins from the saddle horn and led both horses to the booth.

"I'm glad to see you back in the saddle." A friendly face smiled up at her from behind a table. Fred Adkins made a check on his clipboard. "We were all so worried when you and that little girl went missing."

"Thanks for joining the search party." She opened a saddlebag. She had already sent a thank-you note to the association, for many of the members had volunteered. "It means a lot."

"That's what friends are for. Here are your T-shirts." He piled a small and an extra large on the table.

"And here is my donation." She traded six cans and two boxes of mac and cheese for the shirts. "And my sponsor sheet."

"You are phenomenal, as always. This is going to help feed a lot of hungry kids in our town." Fred straightened his shoulders, almost as if he were trying to get her to notice him. But did it work?

Not in the slightest. She grabbed the T-shirts, thanked him again and felt the back of her neck tingle. Comanche nickered in recognition. Hawk. He ambled toward her. In his black jacket, black jeans, black boots, he looked like the Special Forces soldier he was. His gaze found hers, and her soul stirred.

Why does he affect me so strongly, Lord? She would have loved to hear God's answer, because she didn't have a clue. The man had magnetism.

"I see you made it off the glacier okay." She handed him one of the T-shirts.

"No worse for the wear." He shrugged off his jacket and pulled the T-shirt over his head. "We had a great time. Challenged the ice. Roughed it like real men. Got in our bro bonding before his big day."

"When is his wedding?"

"Two days before Christmas." He caught the collar of her coat, helping her out of it.

Oh, his manner was so appealing. She tried to hide her giddiness as she pulled her new T-shirt on over the March of Dimes shirt she already wore. Both horses stood obediently, although Comanche was shaking his head up and down, as if trying desperately to say something.

"I think he's saying hi." She slid her arms into her coat sleeves, dangerously close to Hawk. He settled the garment at her shoulders. It was nice, how old-fashioned he was. "The black gelding who is politely waiting is General. He's one of the horses we rent out. Gentle as a lamb and very imposing."

"I came prepared." Surprising her, he hauled something out of his pocket. The horses nickered, excited by whatever he held in his hand.

"Peppermints." She laughed. Leave it to Hawk to notice the details. "You saw me feed him one."

He nodded, and unwrapped two candies and offered one to each horse. Comanche dove for his. General politely lipped the treat from Hawk's palm.

"And one for you." He unwrapped a third candy and raised it to her lips.

Okay, she had never had a friend do this before, she thought as the peppermint melted on her tongue, but Hawk couldn't be anything more. They both knew it.

"Riders, welcome to our tenth annual Ride for Hunger." A voice aided by a bullhorn rose above the sounds of the milling crowd. September recognized the president of the riding club astride his handsome bay. "What a turnout. Thanks for being here. It might be a cold day, but we're a warm-hearted bunch. I'll see you at the finish line."

Cheers rose up from the crowd and the noise swelled as people mounted up. September couldn't resist sneaking a peek at Hawk. Through the president's little talk, he had been rubbing General's nose. The two struck an accord, and Hawk swiftly and competently adjusted the stirrup length.

"You thought I was new at this, huh?" He swung

neatly into the saddle. "My grandma kept a pony at her place. When she was alive I would visit her quite a bit. I didn't get a lot of horse time in, I was more of a tree-climbing, fort-building kind of kid, but I know enough to keep my seat."

"You are one surprise after another." She should have known, she thought, rolling her eyes. She eased into Comanche's saddle and gathered her reins, unable to take her gaze off the man. Was there anything Hawk couldn't do?

"I strong-armed my Ranger buddies to contribute to the cause." With a wink, he pulled a half dozen checks from his pocket. "Do I turn them in now?"

"You can. Here, we'll take them over." She pressed her gelding into a slow walk. She hadn't realized most of the crowd had taken off, following the course through the park. Odd. How had she not noticed?

Fred, however, was still at the stand, glad to take the offered checks. His smile dimmed when he caught sight of Hawk and didn't try to flirt.

"So, this is what you do when you aren't at the stable?" Hawk asked, after waiting until they were on their way. "You ride for benefits. Hang out with other horse enthusiasts. Make donations to the food bank."

"Guilty. I've also been known to teach Sunday school."

"I should have known." His voice dipped low, amused. "I can see you leading a class. Little kids?"

"First and second graders. They are so funny and I always learn something new." She chuckled at something she didn't share with him. Maybe she thought he wouldn't be interested in kids. She would be wrong.

"Any other hobbies?" he asked.

"With what time? Only a true horseman would understand. Comanche is my hobby. He's my life, too." She leaned forward with a slight creak of the saddle to pat the palomino's neck. Comanche tossed his head and nickered, as if to say, *Of course. I deserve all her time.*

Hard to argue with that.

"What about you? Besides the ice-climbing thing, which is nuts in my opinion—"

"That's because you don't do it," he quipped, teasing her just to make her laugh. "A true mountaineer would understand."

"Hey, I didn't talk down to you when I said that."

"I know, but I couldn't resist." Laughter felt good, almost as great as being with her again. "There's nothing like being pitted against nature and winning. Besides, at the end of a climb when you are sitting on top of that mountain, sometimes pretty precariously, you can feel very close to God."

"That's what I like about you, Hawk. You can be funny, and you know how to be real, too." She beamed at him.

She liked him. She said the word *like.* He sat straighter in the saddle, feeling mighty good. She had stayed on his mind through the last handful of days on the side of the mountain and throughout the return trip home. The guilt dogging him hadn't faded one whit, but something began to outshine it—the strength of his feelings for her.

"You have to be real when you do what I do for a living." It was that simple. "You become the job. It's something you love and feel commitment for. But you know all that. If I could have hobbies, aside from ski-ing and climbing, I would like to do a lot of things."

"You are one of those guys with a long list of things he wants to accomplish before he dies, right?"

"How did you know about the list?" He hadn't told anyone about his goals in life—except for God.

"Good guess."

The air had turned damp, the way it did before a good rain. He breathed in fresh air, scenting the nearby sound. He could hear the lap of the waves against the rocky shore between the *clomp, clomp* of the horse's hooves.

"So, what's at the top of your list?"

"That's awfully personal, isn't it?" He wanted to keep it casual, safely away from the crater in his heart. The one that she was bound to notice and fault him for. The Lord knew it had always been his Achilles' heel, the reason he might always be alone.

"Hey, we're friends. We are supposed to be personal."

Hard not to look at her, cute and expecting something from him, and not give it to her. He bit the bullet and admitted the truth. Easier to stare off at the blue-gray sound ebbing against the gravel beach than to let her see his vulnerability. "A family. That's at the top of my list."

She didn't say anything for a moment. He'd surprised her. Sure, that would surprise everyone. He cleared his throat. Since he had gone this far, he might as well say it all. "The free spirit thing is because it's easier. I don't want to make commitments."

"Being Special Forces comes with a cost." Her soft alto deepened with understanding. She had paid a price, too. They rode in silence for a moment, taking advantage of the calm of the water. The first drops pattered on the gray rock and the trail ahead of them. The low gray sky turned the sound pewter-gray, and the quiet reverence of the land and water felt as if God had sent the peaceful moment just for the two of them. A healing balm of sorts, to ease the memory of war and loss, of two futures without love.

"How many kids do you want?" she asked after a long while.

"I'd like at least two or three, but that wouldn't depend entirely on me." His future wife, whoever she might be, had always been an idea, a wish unformed. Maybe because he was never certain he could let any woman close enough to want to stick with him. Now, as the path ahead turned away from the water to cut through the greenbelt of the park, he saw September's face—his future. "I've always wanted enough kids so that we feel like a family, but not too many so that I'm outgunned."

"You want a nice balance. Understandable."

"I want what I didn't have growing up. I'm lucky I had next-door neighbors who included me. I was almost a part of the family, I was over at their house so much. It got so that Mrs. Granger would set a place for me at the table without even asking if I wanted to stay. It was just assumed."

"I'm glad you had them. How old were you when you lost your dad?"

"Eight." The suddenness had been the hardest part. One morning, life was normal. A happy mom, a caring dad and he was a content kid off to catch the school bus. By day's end, that life was gone for good. Not something he wanted to talk about. That wasn't why he'd come back. That wasn't why he'd been dying to see her. He swiped rain from his eyes. "How about you?"

"Me? No, I don't want kids." She tensed, shifting away from him.

"You don't want kids? That can't be." The words were out before he could think them through. The moment he heard what he had said, he would have given anything to be able to turn back time and keep the thought to himself.

"Of course I want kids, except I'll never get married." She tried to fake a smile, but there was no hiding her sadness. He could feel it on the air and in his soul.

"Maybe one day?" He gave General a little heel so he would catch up to Comanche. September didn't turn toward him. Her hair tumbled like a curtain, shielding her from his sight. Her silence hurt, and he felt his hopes slipping. "Down the road, I mean. There might come a day in the far future when you find you can love again."

"I won't do it." She sounded so sure—sad and sure, all at once. "Never again."

His heart cracked right open in two equal parts, leaving him vulnerable and defenseless. He didn't know what to say, so he stayed quiet. The rocking gait of the horse, the other riders up ahead, the trees singing in the rain, even the chilly damp were all memorable. A glorious day, sure, but it turned out to be one of his darkest.

"I'm impressed." September gave Comanche a final rub with the towel—he was fresh, dry, warm and clean—and took a similar towel Hawk was offering her. "Not many guys would volunteer to help with the horses. You did a great job, too."

"I even did a decent job with the hoof pick cleaner thing."

She laughed; she couldn't help it. Happiness bubbled out of her. She gave the towels a toss into the laundry barrel and took hold of Comanche's lead. "This way, cowboy. All we have left to do is to stable them, and we're done."

"Great. I'm starving."

"You are always starving." As the stops for ice cream, a hot dog and, less than an hour ago, an enormous pretzel at a kiosk near the benefit's booth attested. "I would hate to see your food budget."

"Daunting."

The man could make her laugh. She led the way down the main aisle. It was quiet this late in the day, the lessons done. Only the die-hard riders, considering the sounds of horse hooves coming from the arena. It had been forever since she'd been this happy. The day felt light, the world around her hopeful and her spirit brightening. Hawk's friendship was turning out to be a true blessing.

"Come home with me and I'll feed you." She opened General's gate. "It's the least I can do for making you ride for hours in the rain."

"The pouring rain," he corrected, leading the black gelding into his stall. "I'm wet to the skin. You might owe me two dinners. Better yet, maybe I should treat you."

"What do you have in mind?"

"You're worried, right?"

"Just a tad. More like curious."

"Nope, I'm not going to tell you. You will have to stay in suspense." General dove into his feed trough. Hawk unclipped the lead and closed the gate. "Fine. I'll give you one hint. Noodles."

"That isn't a help. A lot of foods have pasta in them."

"True." Trouble danced in his eyes. Definitely a man she was going to have to keep an eye on. He was too charming for his own good. She spoke to Comanche and led him two stalls down. "I could go for carbs."

"Awesome. We are in perfect accord."

"We are." And it felt wonderful. The early conversation hadn't been forgotten—how could it be? Her great sadness about never loving again meant no children, no family of her own, which was a great weight she could not ignore. But Hawk didn't press her or try to talk her out of her decision, as everyone else had done.

No, instead of pointing out that she could adopt, or go into foster care or that ten years from now, or even twenty, she could change her mind, Hawk had offered unspoken understanding and spent the rest of the day making her laugh.

Just as he was doing now. Noodles. Really. What kind of hint was that? There was an Italian restaurant not far away, on the main road. She could go for lasagna, not that she needed the calories.

He held the passenger door for her—since he had commandeered her keys and her pickup. The trailer was already unhitched, cleaned and stowed, which meant they were free to go and indulge in noodles.

"How long has it been since this truck has had any work done on it?" He settled behind the wheel and turned the key.

"The last time I could afford it." She could tease, too. "I had an appointment, which I had to cancel because I was in the hospital."

"Ah, that would explain things." It took a few tries for the starter to catch. "You could use a new clutch, too."

"It's on my list. I keep lists, too." She reached for her seat belt, but he was quick enough to take the buckle from her and fasten it. Thoughtful, since it was harder to do with her hand in a cast.

"I am well aware of your list, beautiful." He put the truck in gear and pulled into the gravel drive. Rain smeared the windshield faster than the wipers could keep up, but he drove with confidence and, apparently, eagle-eye vision. "You are keeping track of my faults. Have you made any additions?"

"Fearless driving. That's a flaw. There could be a cow in the road and you would never see it."

"I would see it." He oozed far too much confidence, but she believed him. Nor did he seem troubled by her comment. "What else?"

"You've become a good friend."

"That's a fault?"

"Well, there's a downside. You will be heading back to places unknown, like Afghanistan." She focused on the heater vent and adjusted it, although she clearly was looking for a distraction. "And then you will be an occasional e-mail, maybe a phone call now and then."

"I always come back. We can hang when I'm in town, right?"

"Sure."

"But it's not the same." He got that—he understood

a lot. Traffic was heavy and he waited at the crossroads. He wouldn't lie to himself. He was falling for her. He could try to fight with himself over it; he had more self-discipline than most. But he also knew he wasn't in control of this. These feelings were bigger and greater than anything he'd known before. There was no way to stop them.

"We can still spend time together, right?" He tossed that out after pulling into a lane of traffic.

"Sure. You probably go to a church near the post, but do you want to join me tomorrow?"

"Just try and stop me." He signaled and pulled into a puddled driveway. The modest establishment's sign flashed cheerfully in the fading daylight. "What do you think?"

"This is a Thai place."

"Right."

"Noodles." She laughed. Again. Yep, life was definitely better with Hawk around. Being with him made her world right.

Even when he was laughing, he was breaking inside. Through a shared meal and lively conversation, he stayed friendly and upbeat on the outside, but all he could think about was her confession she would never marry.

Never was a big word. One that devastated him. He refused to let her know it as he paid the bill, walked her to the truck and helped her in. The rain had paused, with dampness like vapor in the air and the black clouds above promising another shower.

This was a one-way street, he realized as he pulled out of the lot. She sat beside him, backlit by streetlights, regaling a tale of a stubborn show pony, a little girl and a huge mud puddle in one of the riding fields. September glowed—there was no other word for it. Her humor, her personality, her being dazzled him.

"Comanche shook his head through it all, as if he couldn't believe what he was seeing." Her laughter rang gently. "The pony wouldn't stop rolling. Little Hailey was covered in mud and crying—she got her new pink outfit dirty—and I comforted her while trying to get this pony to get up, which he wouldn't. It started to rain. It took three other people and two hours to get him back on his stubborn feet. I was still finding mud—under my fingernails, inside my boots—the next day."

She probably had no idea how adorable she was. How she had him all but wrapped about her little finger. She had no notion he was falling hard and fast or how much being with her hurt him. It didn't take much to see a future with her—one just like this. With her bright and lively, charming him evermore with one stable tale or horse adventure after another. Always, he would be enthralled. That future could not be. She did not want to walk down that path with him. No, she preferred to be alone.

Lord, please send me a sign. What should I do? He pulled into the park's lot and parked next to his truck. "I had fun today."

"And helped a good cause." Her hair had dried in the restaurant, into soft waves from the humidity. The spice-colored locks framed her face and made her look enchanting—someone far too whimsical and sweet to be real.

"Let me help." He unsnapped her buckle for her.

"You are always doing that, always helping me."

She studied him with appreciation—a beautiful sight for him to see. At least he knew she cared. Not the way he needed her to and not anything like how he cared for her, but he would take it.

"I'm the kind of friend you can depend on." Nearly killed him to say the word *friend,* but he meant the rest of it. He would always be there for her, come what may. Beyond duty, beyond devotion, even if she would never love him.

"I'll remind you of that come the next fund-raiser." She didn't have a clue what he had meant or an inkling of what he felt.

That was all right. All that mattered was that she looked more like the woman he remembered, full of life and peaceful joy. When he handed over her truck and helped her behind the wheel, he didn't see anything more than friendship in her manner. It stung, but he knew she was giving him all she could. She thanked him again, gave him directions to the church and waved before she put the truck in gear and drove off.

She really had no idea. He watched her truck amble through the lot and hesitate on the main road. She turned left, toward home, taking his heart with her.

The rain returned as gently as if heaven had sent it. The future he saw with September was a wish that could not come true. Alone, battling defeat, he unlocked his truck and hopped behind the wheel. In some ways, it had been a tough day. He feared tomorrow having to be her friend—and nothing more—would be tougher.

Chapter Nine

The sanctuary buzzed with conversations and excitement in the moments before the organist started to play. September loved the old-fashioned church with its intricate carvings and plentiful cathedral-style stained-glass windows. Soft daylight made the colors glow as if divinely touched.

"You're looking chipper." Chessie barreled down the row from the left-hand aisle and dropped into the pew beside her. She clutched the program and her big handbag. "How many times have I told you? You put in too many hours at the stables. A little downtime has done you a world of good."

"I do feel more rested." While being off work went against her grain, she liked staying busy and keeping active. But her big sister had a point. She had poured herself into her work and stayed at the stables long after her work hours were over because that had freed her from having to face her grief. Going home knowing there would be no letter or e-mail waiting for her, or no chance Tim would call, had been too hard. It had been easier to stay occupied.

"I hope you have the good sense not to go back to work too soon." Chessie, with evidence to support her argument, forged ahead. "You should stay home until the doctor takes your cast off."

"I'm going back tomorrow."

"To riding?" Chessie frowned. "You can't do that. What about your arm?"

"I don't ride with my arm. Besides, I did just fine on the benefit ride. Which reminds me. You owe me a check to the town's food bank." She almost laughed when her sister's frown deepened. "Relax. I'm working in the office. You don't have to get so worked up."

"I'm your sister. It's my job." Chessie tucked her program aside, opened her purse and withdrew her wallet. Instead of writing a check, she stopped to glance around.

"Looking for someone?" It was so unlike Chessie, she had to ask.

"Not really." She released the pen neatly tucked into her checkbook and uncapped it. Something had changed, though. September tried to figure out where her sister had been gazing—toward the front, where a knot of people were talking at the head of the aisle. One of them was a rather handsome man in a navy suit and tie. "Were you looking at that guy?"

"Me? Don't be silly. I don't look at men. That would be too forward." Chessie's tone held just enough shock that it could have been trying to cover up something else, like vulnerability, maybe embarrassment.

"He looks familiar. Who is he?" Curious now, she couldn't let it drop. The organ finished the last refrain and started the first notes of "Amazing Grace."

"He used to live down the street from us. Jon Matthews. You might not remember him. He's back in town now. He took a job at a law firm in downtown Tacoma." Chessie sounded casual as she tore off the check and handed it over. "He saw me in the parking lot and asked me to go with him to the church's New Year's Eve dinner."

"Did you accept?"

"I told him I would think about it. I haven't seen him since his family moved away in high school, which means I hardly know him. He could have terrible habits and dreadful faults for all I know." Chessie was hiding something.

Maybe a schoolgirl crush? Was she nursing affection for this man after so many years? September folded the check in half and slipped it into her purse. Her sister might be abrupt and forceful, but she had a tender heart. Her intentions were always the best. "Maybe you should say yes."

"This, coming from you?" Chessie nearly dropped her pen. She tucked it back into the little holder inside her checkbook and zipped her purse. "The last time we had this discussion, oh, a month ago, you told me to avoid romance. It always lets a girl down."

"Well, we are both children of divorce," she pointed out, maybe a little defensively because she had a feeling where her sis was going with this. "We are more realistic than most."

"Sure, that must be it. So, why should I say yes? He might be one of those men who are controlling after they marry you. Maybe he has a gambling habit."

"I see that smirk. Maybe he's a nice guy who would appreciate some good company for a Friday meal. How about that?" She squeezed her sister's hand. "I think you should go. He was a hunk in high school, and a kind guy. I'm sure he still is."

"Okay. I will." Chessie smiled, but it was short-lived. The church was more crowded, the pews mostly full, so it was simple to spot the brawny-shouldered man hiking up the right-hand aisle.

"Hawk." Happiness swept through September, a pure streak of joy that, like a sudden flash of sunlight after being in the dark, felt almost too intense to bear. She tried to dial it down, reining in her emotions as she patted the space beside her. "Is that you? I hardly recognize you."

"It's been awhile since I've put on a shirt and tie. The post's chapel is more casual." He slipped into the row and dropped next to her. "You are lovely."

"It's just a dress." She flushed, unable to explain why his compliment affected her or why she was glad he thought she looked nice. "You remember my sister, of course."

"Hi, Chessie." He offered her his most charming smile, probably thinking that he would warm his sister's icy stare.

He would be wrong. Before September could say more the organ stilled, and their minister appeared, friendly and wise as always.

"Good morning, friends," he greeted the congregation warmly.

"You and I have to talk," Chessie whispered in her ear, and gave Hawk a pointed look.

Poor Hawk. He had to have caught it, but he remained respectfully unaware as he turned toward the altar. She wanted to say something reassuring to him and let him know how glad she was to see him again, but the minister called out to stand and join hands.

When Hawk's fingers caught hers and helped her to her feet, something happened. Life trickled into her wounded spirit like dawn after a bleak winter storm, like a promise of peace to come, of laughter and hope. He was doing this to her, drawing her out of the dark, helping her to feel.

Years ago, she and Hawk had been little more than acquaintances. Who would have guessed that the different roads they both walked would bring them here? It seemed like God's doing. She had been certain all her prayers went unanswered, but standing at Hawk's side in the sanctuary filled with light and reverence, she saw that God had been walking with her all along. She hadn't been able to feel it, but that didn't mean that God wasn't there. He was showing her that Tim's loss hadn't taken her heart. She could feel it beating again.

Thankful, she bowed her head and listened to the minister's voice lift in prayer.

"I'm glad to see that gutter is holding up." Hawk paused on the front step to inspect the work he'd done. "Wouldn't want you to get mad at me for shoddy workmanship."

"You? Shoddy? Not a chance."

She stood in the doorway, beautiful even in the T-shirt and faded jeans she had changed into. He'd thought her amazing in the simple blue dress she'd worn, but he preferred this side of her—wholesome girl-next-door sweetness.

"I have to apologize for my sister," she went on to say. "She isn't happy about our friendship the way I am."

"I'm not out to break your heart."

"Oh, I know." She waved his concern away, as if she had no idea there was a deeper meaning to his comment. "She knows what I went through. She doesn't want me to hurt like that again."

"Neither do I." He understood what Chessie meant. He had been there, too. Twice—as a kid growing up, and the first time he'd spotted September on that dark mountain. No way could he tell her that Chessie was right on target. The older sister had been able to see what the younger could not. As hard as he tried to hide his affection, it had to show. When he smiled at her, his defenses were down, his soul on display.

He stepped inside, toolbox in hand. The mistletoe hung overhead like a beacon flashing, Remember the Kisses. As if he could possibly forget. That had been a special moment for him, but what had it been for September? The way she blushed and hurried by him suggested she remembered, too, and she wasn't eager for kiss number three.

He followed her into the kitchen. He'd been pretty devastated yesterday, up some of the night feeling too frustrated to sleep. But in church this morning her face had brightened when she'd spied him in the aisle. He had to wonder. Was he entirely alone in his affections? Was there a chance her feelings could change?

"I made you a sandwich in case you didn't grab lunch at your apartment." She opened the refrigerator. "There's soda, butterscotch pudding, leftover Thai food from last night."

He resisted the urge to pull her into his arms. He wanted to know what it would be like to hold her against his chest, she who was so very dear to him. He shook his head. "Later. I want to get going in the garage. What do you usually do on a Sunday afternoon?"

"After I've changed out of my church clothes, you mean?" She closed the fridge and leaned against it. She'd drawn her hair back into a ponytail, leaving wispy curls to tumble around her face and emphasizing the delicate cut of her high cheekbones. "You know what I do. I spend time with Comanche. I realize you don't have a lot of free time. So why are you doing this? You need to have some fun while you can."

"Tinkering with cars is fun."

She frowned at him playfully, as if she refused to believe him. "When is your next deployment?"

"Mid-January." He pushed open what had to be the garage door—sure enough, it was—and searched for the light switch. The last thing he wanted to see was the look on her face. "I'll be gone for six months. It's a limited thing, we think. I'll be back sometime in June."

"So in other words, you are spending one of your last weekend afternoons replacing my truck's starter?"

"Like I said. Fun." Light tumbled down on her pickup and her otherwise empty garage. This was, like everything, neat as a pin. That appealed to the Ranger in him. He set down the heavy box. "I'll be perfectly happy. If you trust me to stay here alone, why don't you head over to the stables? Give Comanche a howdy from me."

"Oh, I cannot abandon you here. That's not right—"

"It is, if I say so." He drew his keys from his pocket and pressed them into her hand. He was getting used to the sweep of affection that hit him like an undertow every time he was around her. "Take my truck. Go ahead."

"I'm supposed to play while you work?"

"Like I said. Fun. Besides, won't Comanche be expecting you?" Overwhelmed by a richer tone of caring, he brushed back a silken curl from her face. Surprise flashed across her features, whether from his touch or his words, he didn't know. "You don't want to let him down."

"No, but I don't want to let you down, either."

That mattered to him. A lot. Maybe she cared more than he'd thought, more than she realized. "I'll be happier knowing you are doing what makes you happiest. Go on, get outta here. I want you to."

She couldn't miss the tenderness in his tone. He probably should have tried harder to hide it, but that wasn't his forte. He couldn't be sure, but she looked a little dazed as she nodded, his keys in hand.

"I'll be back later, then." She retreated, walking backward through the kitchen. "I'll have my cell on me, so call if you need to."

"Sure thing." He fought images threatening to take over his brain—glimpses of a future with her hurrying off to the stables to ride or work. With him working on the trucks or on a honey-do list around the town house. Maybe even getting a horse of his own so they could spend Sunday afternoons riding the mountain foothills.

I want it so much, Lord. Is it possible? Or am I chasing after a dream I can't have? The front door opened and closed. A few moments later his truck started outside on the driveway and powered away.

He popped the hood and got right to work sorting through the tools and getting out the ones he would need. He had to consider September's side of things. She wasn't ready to let anyone close, much less open her heart. Sure, he understood that. He was guilty of the same thing himself. It was why he'd spent most of his adult life alone, and his few girlfriends hadn't been around for long. He blamed his job, and that was part of it. It was tough to build a relationship when you were almost always apart and with half the globe separating you. But he had been at fault, too. He'd never let anyone close, not as he'd let September.

He'd opened himself up, and it had to be to the one woman who couldn't do the same. He grabbed the droplight and hung it on the upraised hood. He uncoiled the power cord as he went, and knelt in front of the outlet. September had shut herself down to survive—surviving was something he knew about. In the heat of battle when a mission went south, you focused on shoring up your defenses, protecting your six and getting your men out alive. Losing wasn't an option, so that meant that you fought with all you had.

He figured that was how September did it. She had gotten this far in survival mode, but that was only good for so long. When the battle was over, when the turmoil was past, you had to deal and figure out a way to move on with what you learned along the way. He grabbed the drop cloth and gave it a shake to unfold it. He had learned long ago that it was his choices that defined a man, and what he fought for and stood for every step of the way.

He spread the cloth over the polished fender and chrome-accented grille. Remembering the change that widened September's expressive eyes when he'd taken her hand, he had to believe there was a possibility. Maybe a small one, maybe bigger, he didn't know. He had to let her know how he felt. Life was too short to waste the chance for something great.

* * *

"I should have known." Chessie strode out of the main aisle, dressed to ride. "You couldn't stay away, could you?"

"No lectures, please." She had enough on her mind without trying to convince her sister that she wasn't going to break into pieces. "Did you just get here, or are you finishing up?"

"I've got Princess saddled for the arena, but we haven't started yet. It's pretty crowded." Chessie didn't seem too concerned about it. "We could take a trail ride, if you want. They opened the lower trail, so it's safe."

"That's a relief. I'm glad to know that won't happen to anyone again." She stopped by her cubicle, set up in one of the forward stalls. Her desk was tidy, although a huge stack of mail and another of messages had built up. "I need to call Mrs. Toppins and check on Crystal today. Make sure she's still getting better."

"I'm surprised you aren't spending the afternoon with that Hawkins guy."

"There's plenty of the afternoon left for that." She knew a comment like that would drive her sister nuts, and so she smiled as she flipped through the address file on her desk. She found the Toppins' card with their home info and slipped it into her jean pocket. She would call from home later. "How did it go with Jon Matthews?"

"And that's your business, why?" Chessie didn't sound as harsh as usual, although she was sure trying to.

September wasn't fooled. "Because you're my sister, as you are so fond of telling me."

"That much is true." She ambled up to the desk and took Tim's picture from the hutch shelf. "I'm going to the dinner with him. It's been awhile since I've had a date."

"That's because you try to keep everyone at a comfortable distance." September sidled up to look at Tim's picture, too. Even years later it continued to hurt to see what she had lost, but not as much, she realized. She could study Tim in his army dress uniform without feeling as if she were crumbling into pieces. When he had died, much of her had died, too. So much that it didn't seem possible that she would go on living.

His dark hair, his kind brown eyes, his dependable presence pulled at her, true, but not in the same way. She thought of all the good times they'd had together—bowling, because he had been so fond of it, going on church outings, picnics in the rain. Those memories were delightfully hazy, like something good out of her past, images she would always smile over.

But images she no longer pined for. Times she had loved, but were gone now. That future was forever gone, but she could go on living. She understood that now. She began to realize how lost she'd become and how much of her had died with Tim. Sadness filled her. She still loved him, except that love had inexplicably changed. It had grown like the memories—dear and forever sweet, but no longer possible.

She could not spend the rest of the days the Lord had given her living for the past.

September set the picture on the shelf and let go. "I'm glad you agreed to go out with Jon."

"Me, too." Chessie led the way to the aisle, waving to a few fellow riders as they passed by. "Since we've talked about my love life, it's only fair we talk about yours."

"*Mine?* I don't have a love life." What on earth could

her sister be talking about? She whipped down the aisle, vaguely realizing she was moving faster than usual. "Don't tell me you want me to start dating again?"

"I thought you already were."

Had Chessie lost her mind? Comanche nickered a welcome and pressed his nose into her hands. She took a moment to greet him, wondering what her sister could possibly be thinking. Then it struck her. "I'm not dating Hawk."

"Aren't you?"

"This is me you're talking to. Me." She couldn't imagine anything so preposterous. Her pulse thundered so hard, it was like thunder in her ears. "We are friends. Trust me, there's nothing romantic going on."

"Fine, okay, no need to get so defensive. That's *my* personality defect." Chessie crossed her arms over her chest. "I was just asking, that's all."

"You have to know Hawk and I can't be more than friends." Since Comanche was teething her zipper, she helped him out and unwrapped a couple of the candies from the peppermint supply she always kept in her coat pocket. "It's totally casual."

"Fine. I believe you."

I wish I did, September thought as she watched Comanche crunch happily on his treats. Something had happened in the house today when Hawk had given her his keys, some indefinable spark of emotion that made her see him not as a friend, but as a man. A wonderful and charming man who had rescued her from her sorrow as surely as he had carried her out of the mine shaft.

You cannot care about Hawk, she ordered herself as she led Comanche down the aisle. *You must not care for him like that.*

Colleen strolled into the tack room, changing the track of the conversation. After a brief chat and saddling up, she and Chessie hit the trail. The mountainside smelled crisp from the cold and the pine scent of the forest was a perfect complement to the time of year. With Christmas a little more than a week away, she and Chessie tossed around ideas on gifts for Dad and Estelle, their stepmom, who was especially hard to shop for. They talked about last-minute gifts and donations to the church's charity tree.

September couldn't remember the last time the foothills had looked so beautiful. The crystal-blue sky stretched from emerald mountainsides to the sparkling blue-gray water of the Puget Sound, and the sun shone with a brilliance she hadn't seen in years. By the time their ride was over, the temperature had fallen and the winds had risen. Shivering, they hurried their horses into the barns and talked while they rubbed them down, stabled them and headed back to their vehicles.

Chessie raised an eyebrow at Hawk's truck. "I'm only going to say this once, and then I'll leave it be."

"I know you, sister dear. That's impossible." Since she knew what was coming, she wanted to keep it light, so she hit the remote, which unlocked the doors, and tossed Chessie a troublesome grin.

"No, it isn't, and do you know why?" She unlocked her sensible conservative beige sedan. "Because you are like your old self again. I have my sister back. But what I have to say is for your own good."

"It always is." She couldn't help it. She wrapped Chessie in a big hug, because she loved her. No one could ask for a better champion or a better sister. "You don't have to worry about me anymore."

"That won't stop me." She was smiling as she opened her car door. "Hawk isn't just a soldier, he's a Ranger. He does dangerous things in dangerous places all over the world. Just like Tim did."

"I know."

Chessie's words stayed with her on the short drive home, a warning she could not ignore. Just as she could not ignore the comforting warmth of his friendship, the way she could depend on him and how alive she felt because of him. Maybe it was simply the basic connection to another person, something she had been avoiding for too long, that had done that. Maybe that was why he was a balm to her wounds—she didn't know— but she was glad Hawk was in her world. Very glad.

She parked the truck in her driveway, shut off the lights and locked the doors. Sunset was settling in to the western sky, brushing bold streaks of violet and rose, and burnishing treetops with a heavenly golden glow.

"Welcome home." Hawk appeared on the front step, a welcoming friend, a cherished buddy and more. "Perfect timing. I just took dinner out of the oven."

"Dinner? Did you warm up the Thai leftovers?"

"Not a chance, gorgeous. I made my famous tuna and noodle casserole just for you." He strolled closer, bringing the sunset with him.

A connection bound them, she couldn't deny it. Her spirit brightened and her world came into perfect focus all because he took her hand.

Chapter Ten

"Hawk, I can't believe you did all this."

The joy layering her voice was all the reward he needed. He'd worked the entire afternoon, first in her garage and then her kitchen. He wanted her to know the man he was. He was glad he'd taken the time to set the table with the china he'd found in the upper cabinets and candles standing in crystal holders. He shrugged. "It's nothing fancy, but I thought it might hit the spot."

"It smells amazing." She took off her coat, and he was there to help her with it. The floral scent of her hair, the winter wind on her clothes, the healthy glow to her cheeks made him want to memorize the moment. If only he could slow down time and make this evening last forever.

"Where did you learn to cook like that?" She took the coat from him and hung it over the back of one of the breakfast bar chairs.

"My mom." He took matches out of his pocket and broke one from the book. "She was a firm believer a boy should know his way around the kitchen."

"Smart woman." September nodded approvingly, and he didn't miss the appreciation in her gaze.

"She is a chef." He struck the match and touched the flame to the first taper. "I was one lucky kid. Mac and cheese took on a whole new meaning at my house. I'll have to make that for you, too, sometime. The best on the planet."

"I won't argue."

"Good. Then it's a date." Why that word popped out, he couldn't say. Probably his subconscious at work, already well aware of what his conscious mind wasn't quite ready to admit, even to himself. The candles lit, he shook out the match and set it in the sink. "I ought to have you over to my place, maybe after Christmas. I'll do the works. A fancy salad, garlic bread and some sparkling grape juice."

"I'll bring dessert. I make a pretty good chocolate cheesecake."

"Great. We could do it for New Year's Eve, unless you have plans."

"Not me. Chessie was going to drag me over to her house, but now she's going out with this guy she's had a crush on forever." She was talking a little fast as he pulled out a chair at the table for her. "So that leaves me free."

"Good for her. Good for us." He helped her scoot in her chair, trying hard to sound casual. She needed that security, he understood. She wasn't ready for serious yet. For a Ranger trained to successfully face, execute and complete every mission, he was out of his depth. His training did no good. There wasn't a force strong enough on this earth to stop the tides of his heart. He had no defense against it. He could only do his best to be what she needed—a friend and nothing more. He circled around to his chair and dropped into it. "I'll rent a movie and we can make a real evening of it."

"Perfect, since we both would be home alone otherwise." She draped the cloth napkin over her lap, dainty as could be. "Part of the mountain trails are open again. It's safe."

"Funny, it's been so long ago that this area was mined for silver. Everyone's forgotten those old days. You have to wonder how many mine heads were covered over with boards, and time and the forest did the rest." He held out his hands, thinking that time changed all things. Looking at the amazing woman across the table, he had to wish that her decision never to love again might be left behind and forgotten, too. "Do you want to say the blessing, or should I?"

"Are you kidding? You *are* the guest and the cook."

Was it his imagination, or did her fingers tighten on his? Was the warmth in her voice of a deeper tone? Profound tenderness welled up within him, refreshing to a part of him that he didn't know was wrung out and worn. With hope, he bowed his head in prayer. "Dear Lord, thank You for these blessings we are about to receive and for strengthening our friendship. Please guide us in being your helpful servants in all ways, amen."

"Amen."

He liked the way her sincere alto blended with his voice. He adored the reverent way she bobbed her head, a little end to her praying, and flashed him a megawatt smile. Full of life and dazzlingly wholesome. Not the September he remembered from long ago or the sad woman who had lost her true love, but a new woman, more beautiful than she had been before.

"How was your ride?" Since he'd been the cook, he grabbed her plate and dished up a serving of casserole. He did his best to keep it casual. "At least it didn't rain for you."

"Unlike yesterday when we were riding." She sparkled with amusement as she took the plate he offered. "Chessie was there."

"I didn't know your sister still rode." He scooped up a helping for himself.

"Oh, she loves to ride, she just stopped being horse crazy in her teens. Something I have never successfully been able to do." She spooned out a few pieces of buttered carrots and asparagus, lifted the vegetable bowl and passed it to him. "Otherwise I would have gone to college and become a librarian like my sister."

"You, a librarian? I can't see it. That would put you indoors all day." He dished up a heap of vegetables. "Although I'm sure you would make a fantastic one, if that's what you decided you wanted."

"I can't see myself boxed in all day. I love working with horses and with kids. Even the barn work puts me in a good mood. The horses always do something funny, even Mel."

"Who's Mel?"

"He's this incredibly obstinate horse. He belongs to the stable. Colleen, my boss, heard from the vet about this gelding who was terribly neglected and needed a home. That's how we get a lot of our rental horses, sadly enough. People either come on hard times and can't pay for the substantial cost of keeping a horse or they are abusive."

"So the horse I rode yesterday had been rescued?"

"Yep. He was put in my section of the barn, so I

got to befriend him and I was in charge of his care. That was five years ago now." She poked the tines of her fork into the casserole. "General was grateful for the care and kindness he received. It took him a good while to trust again, but when he did it was with his entire heart. That happens most of the time, but not with Mel. No, Mel has a mind of his own."

"In a good way, or a bad way?" He leaned toward her as if he really wanted to know.

"It's sort of mixed." She took a bite, shocked by the amazing explosion of taste on her tongue. "This is really good. As in, great. This was all in my pantry?"

"I ran to the grocery store in your truck." His confession came quietly, almost sheepishly. "I had to test it out. Make sure the starter worked."

"Sure. So you planned this all along?"

"I had hoped to help you out, that's all, like friends do for one another all the time."

"I can't argue with that. This is amazing." She took another bite.

"Back to Mel," he prompted, although he looked pleased with her compliment. "You can't leave me in suspense."

"Mel likes to amuse himself at our expense. He's figured out that he isn't going to be hit or beat or abused no matter what he does. As if. Anyway, at first, I thought he was just testing. When I had him tied in the aisle while I cleaned his stall, he would unlatch other stalls with his teeth. I would look up and a horse would be loose—a serious thing—and he would be in their stall eating their grain."

"Sounds like a little ingenuity to me."

"I finally figured out he could untie his lead, so I

had to use one with a metal hatch. Then he started nipping me when I had my back to him. When I turned around, he always stood there so innocently. So I had to tie him farther down the row, and he would practically incite a riot with the other horses while I mucked out his stall. I would have to put down my pitchfork and go see why a half dozen horses were rearing and neighing in their stalls like fire had broken out."

"He wanted your attention."

"It took me longer than you to figure that out. He was such a handful. Always knocking over any bucket he came across, making sure I got as wet as he did at bath time. I would take him out for a ride to stretch his legs and he'd take the bit between his teeth, ignore me completely and charge like a lunatic over the nearest fence. Then he would walk around, still ignoring me, arrive at the gate to be let in only to do it all over again. This was all with his good-old-boy attitude. I couldn't stay mad at him."

"He ought to jump those obstacle things. Like in competitions."

"I finally figured that out, too. He's blissfully happy carrying little students on his back over the jumps in the arena. He's a character."

"I'm not surprised you helped him to be happy again."

"I think it was his indomitable spirit." She was blushing as she speared an asparagus tip. She stared at her fork, because it was easier. If she saw the regard on Hawk's handsome face, it would affect her. She wasn't ready for that.

"Either way, it's a good story. I suppose those stables are full of them."

"Every horse, every rider." She wasn't about to bore him with a hundred horse tales. "Your turn. Tell me something about Mark Hawkins. Something that no one else knows."

"I *am* a walking mystery," he quipped, showing off that sense of humor she was fond of. The candlelight softened the hard planes of his rugged face, making him twice as striking. It was easy to imagine him in a tux and equally simple to see him suited and booted for a mission. He took a swig from his juice glass. "I want to trek through Nepal. I want to learn to play the guitar. I want to marry the love of my life and grow old with her."

"You're a romantic." The words caught in her throat. His confession moved through her, and a strong and new image tried to wedge its way into her brain, but she could not let it. She absolutely could not allow it. She reached for her juice glass to wash away all traces of emotion. "I can see you sitting on the porch with a pretty woman, both of you gray and wearing spectacles."

"I'm glad you can see it. That makes one of us. Hoping is different than believing."

Her grip slipped on her glass. The contents splashed dangerously, but she was able to set it on the table without incident. Whew. For a moment there, she thought he was talking about the two of them. But no, that was her mind at work, not his. "I'm sure it will happen for you. One day you will meet the right woman and you will know she's meant to be on that porch with you."

"I pray that you are right." He looked forlorn for a moment, as if he were afraid he would never find that right woman. As if he would never be loved. "If I can let any woman close, that is."

Sympathy rushed through her. She knew exactly how it felt to look at the future and see nothing of what once had been her deepest desire. No loving marriage, no children, no happily ever after. Life would be good and wonderful, of course, but it wouldn't be as rich without a lifetime of love and family. She didn't want that for him. "I'll keep you on my prayer list. I'm sure God has the right woman for you all picked out. It's just a matter of when."

"I'm sure that's true." He pasted on a smile, but it was only a superficial one. She was surprised love meant so much to him.

Hard not to like him more for that. She swirled her fork and spooled pasta in slow twirls. "I tell you what. Until you find that special someone, I will be your date every New Year's Eve to come, unless you're away on a deployment, of course."

"I would like that." His grin widened, but his eyes continued to look sad, as if doubt were weighing him down. Maybe a little loneliness, too.

She knew what that was like. Her feelings took a dangerous dip. *I do not care about Hawk,* she told herself, but it was no longer the truth. She did care.

Far too much.

"I am looking forward to going back home." Hawk gave the nonstick pan a good swipe with the dish towel and pronounced it dry. He hiked over to the cabinet next to the stove and piled it into place on the shelf. "I'm especially psyched to see Pierce get married."

"You get a kick out of that, don't you?"

"I do. It's the real thing. This will work out for them. Pierce will be happy." He rejoined her at the sink and waited for the strainer she was in the middle of rinsing.

"How do you know?" She was curious. She'd only met Tim's brother twice, but he seemed like a nice guy.

"Pierce lives for his fiancée." He took the pot lid and gave it a good rubbing. "You would like her. Her name is Lexie and she's into horses, too. She grew up with them, or something. I'll have to pay more attention next time I hear her talking about it."

He liked that his comment was met with an amused shake of her head. September smiling was what he lived for.

"I'll have to introduce you." He squinted at the lid— dry—and stowed it in the cabinet. "She's transferring from a university in Montana to go to school in Tacoma, after they get back from their Hawaiian honeymoon."

"I would love to meet her." She bent over the sink to give it a good cleaning with the dishcloth. "We could go riding together."

"See? You two will be fast friends." He hung the towel to dry on the oven handle, watching September at the sink. He grabbed the dry-erase pen hanging from the board hung by magnets on the fridge and scribbled down the right digits.

Tonight had been nice. It was as simple as pie to see how life with her would be: easygoing evenings sharing the cooking, a meal and the cleanup. They had an amicable accord, as if their personalities fit together without effort or pretense. He couldn't ever remember being this happy and centered. He had never felt so sure.

She is what I want, Lord. If it's possible. If it's Your will. The power of the prayer left him reeling. Emotion hit him harder every time he looked at her. Every time he heard her voice.

"When do you leave?"

"Tuesday." In two days. It didn't seem possible that he could tear himself away. He hated to think of it. "Hey, you wouldn't want to help me find them a wedding gift?"

"I suppose." She looked up from scrubbing. "I promised Colleen I would help out in the office, but I could meet you in the afternoon."

"Great. I could come pick you up and drag you around town."

"As long as you don't mind me doing a little shopping, too." She turned on the faucet to rinse the edges of the sink. "I've left way too much to the last minute."

"So have I."

They walked together into the living room where the Christmas tree blazed. She had added more decorations, making the scraggly tree look noble and majestic. Garlands reflected the colorful tones of the twinkle lights. A tree skirt draped over the planter added the perfect background for the small stack of wrapped gifts on the floor beneath. He had already hid his gift—a necklace of diamonds and gold in the shape of a horse—in that pile for her to discover come Christmas Day.

"I'll walk you out." She had snagged her coat from the back of the chair, and he helped her into it. Tenderness deepened again as he did this small thing for her, holding the garment, slipping it over her shoulders, gently gathering her hair to free it from the coat's collar. He wanted to always be there for her, doing what he could to make her life better.

He grabbed his coat from the entry closet where he'd hung it earlier after coming home from the grocery store, and shrugged into it. They walked out into the chilly shadows together. Walking along beneath the glow of the porch lights, he decided nothing could be nicer than to be at her side. She wasn't ready to love again, and he had a deployment scheduled in less than a month. How would this work out? He only knew one thing—he was committed to her, heart and soul, and always would be.

"I better hand over these." She scooped his keys out of her pocket. "Tell your mom when you see her that she did a good job raising you. I'm impressed."

"You really liked the tuna casserole." He chuckled, a comforting sound on a cold night. "Maybe I'll show you how to make it one day and let you discover the secret ingredients."

"What's so top secret?"

"I'm not telling you yet. You'll have to stick around to find out." He rested against the side of the truck, as if in no hurry to leave. "Look at the street. I should have asked if you wanted me to put up house lights for you."

"I don't have any. I didn't buy any last year, and this is only my second Christmas in my town house." She joined him, leaning against the pickup to gaze down the long stretch of the cul-de-sac.

Bright, colorful bulbs rimmed the rooflines of houses, dangled like icicles from porch eaves and draped over bushes and shrubs. Shining reindeer grazed and holy stars hung in front windows. A tasteful, poignant manger scene gleamed from the front lawn across the street. How had she not noticed the beauty? On some of the shortest and darkest days of winter, there was one day of perfect light.

"When I'm gone, you'll write me, won't you?" He shifted a little closer until their elbows bumped. "I noticed a computer in your family room. Hard not to notice it on the desk."

"You mean on your deployment."

"If that's not too much to ask." He cleared his throat, as if he were a little unsure. "I don't want to make you uncomfortable. I don't want to bring up anything painful for you."

"You mean all the corresponding Tim and I did when he was overseas?"

"Yep." He appeared vulnerable, something she would have thought impossible given his tough-guy character.

"No worries. I would miss you if I couldn't keep in touch. I've grown strangely fond of you."

"Strangely?" That made him laugh.

"Maybe the better word is unexpected." A little warning buzz sounded within her, but did she listen?

No. She charged right on, saying what rose on the tide of her emotions instead of sensibly censoring it. "You've changed my world, Hawk."

"The best friendships do that." His arm stayed pressed against hers, an innocent touch and a powerful connection. One that made her feel as if her heart were threatening to open wide.

She could not let that happen. Staring off down the street, she searched for something to say that would draw back the moment, but not end it entirely. Except the silence between them felt companionable and comfortable. Maybe it would be best not to say anything more. Hawk understood they could only be friends, so why weren't her feelings agreeing?

A minivan ambled down the road and pulled into a driveway two houses down. Doors opened and a family tumbled out, the excited voices of the children ringing like carillon bells. The mom went ahead to open the front door while the dad untied the tree tied to the top of the van.

"At least you aren't the last person on your block to get a tree," he quipped, leaning a little closer. "When I get back from Wyoming, how about I help you plant it?"

"I'm pretty good with a shovel, but not so much with this cast, so I accept your offer." She couldn't help leaning into him in return.

Careful, September, she told herself, *or you will start to depend on him. And then the next thing you know, you will start needing him with every fiber of your being.*

"Look at the stars. It's a perfect night to see them, clear from horizon to horizon." Hawk gazed upward like a man comfortable with watching the heavens. She remembered that knowing how to use the stars as reference points was part of his job requirements. He turned to her, not the heavens. "It sure is beautiful tonight."

He could not be talking about her, although it felt as if he were. His caring opened her up, and she was as vulnerable as an exposed nerve. Open and tingling, overwhelmed by the emotions she could not hold back.

It is the stars, she told herself, and not this moment. Not Hawk. Not new wishes rising from the winter of the old. She simply hadn't stood out beneath the skies on a December night like this, feeling all the shades of starlight. The black sky had never looked so rich, like the perfect hue of ebony. The platinum sprinkle of stars scattered across the zenith. If she watched long enough, absorbing the brightness, she could see hints of color—of yellow, red, blue.

The kiss of the moonlight spilled from a nearly full moon, casting a shimmering path through the nearby forest and onto the blacktopped street. She felt every beauty of the mountains ragged against the sky. The beauty of the night scraped against her raw senses, blissfully welcome. She remembered the girl she used to be, who believed in dreams and happily ever afters.

That girl might be worse for the wear, but she was still here, still alive, that the essential, truest part of her had not perished. She had survived the loss of a true, deep love. And while loving wasn't something she would ever risk again, she was thankful to be here beneath the magnificent sky and to have an understanding friend like Hawk. His endless kindness, his sense of humor and every good thing he had done for her made it impossible not to care about him in return. But what could come of that?

Nothing more than this moment beneath the stars. Hawk was a Ranger, as Tim had been. She could not believe her heart would ever be truly whole again. And even if by the grace of God that miracle did happen, then she would never fall for a soldier. No, not ever again.

She eased away from him, breaking their connection, shattering the moment. The stars went on burning bright anyway, and so did Hawk's friendship for her.

"I'd best get on my way and leave you to your evening." He opened his door, but his voice was no longer casual, his tone no longer easygoing. "I'll see you tomorrow."

"Tomorrow," she mumbled, stumbling up the walk. She did not wait to wave him away from her porch step. Instead, she hurried inside to close the door on what she had seen in his star-blue eyes—honest and unmistakable love for her.

Chapter Eleven

"We were lucky she's a fast healer," Patty Toppins said as she accepted a cup of tea and sat down on one of the chairs facing Colleen's desk. "She's already complaining about being stuck in the house, so I thought a little outing might perk her up."

"Good idea. I've been keeping her in my prayers, Patty." September swiveled the office chair around to face the happy mom. "You have to be incredibly relieved. I can't imagine how terrified you must have been."

"I'm better now that she's up and around. For a while there, I feared the worst. It doesn't help with the well-meaning doctors letting you know everything that can go wrong. I was a nervous wreck, but God has been watching over my girl."

"Proof prayer makes a difference." Colleen slipped into her desk chair. "The rest of the mountain is still closed. The inspection company believes there are no more covered-over mine shafts, but I'm having a second company come in just to be sure. It's not worth risking anyone's life."

"I don't know if I've thanked you for all you two have done. Colleen, covering the hospital bills like that, and you, September. I hate to think what would have happened if Crystal had been down there alone. I'll never be able to thank you for taking such good care of her in a bad situation, although I'm sorry you got injured, too."

"I only wish I could have done more." She took a sip of hot tea, wondering how events worked out the way they had. Maybe Hawk's arrival into her life hadn't been a coincidence. God was present in her life, and He had brought them together. Why? She might argue that Hawk needed her friendship as much as she needed his, but after what she'd glimpsed last night, she was pretty sure he felt more than friendship for her.

After more well-wishes, Patty left to check on her daughter, who was spending time saying hello to her beloved mare. Colleen made a call, talking seriously to the feed suppliers about price changes on their upcoming order. September signed out of the computer, one eye on the clock. Three minutes to three. Panic zinged through her veins at the thought of seeing him again.

Should she call Hawk and cancel? Pretend she hadn't noticed what looked like love in his eyes? Hope there was some other explanation for it? These questions had kept her up much of the night and plagued her all the day through. She felt torn, not knowing what to do.

She felt his presence before she saw him loping up the front steps. He gave an impressive appearance in a heather-gray army sweatshirt, jeans and combat boots and with the wind ruffling his short, dark hair. His incredible baby blues blazed a welcome as he pulled open the door. Casual, easygoing, friendly as always Hawk. Definitely not the same look as last night.

Whew. Talk about relief. She would have stood up, but her knees wouldn't work. Tension rolled through her, a sign she had been more worried than she'd realized. It must have been a trick of the moonlight, she decided. Everything looked more romantic and fanciful beneath starry skies.

"Hey, there." He ambled over to her desk. "Sergeant Hawkins reporting for duty."

"Duty?" She turned off the monitor and grabbed her purse. Funny how her knees were still quaky. "I thought we were going to the mall."

"Think of the traffic."

"True." She shuddered remembering the long lines to get in and out. She pushed out of the chair. Her knees felt tricky, but they held her weight. Odd. "This time of year, the place is packed."

"I'm a Ranger, remember?"

"As if I could forget."

"I go where all men fear to tread." He held the door for her.

Macho. She shook her head, waved goodbye to Colleen, who was still busy on the phone, and walked past him through the door. She definitely had been starstruck last night to think Mark Hawkins would fall in love with her, or with anyone. Look at him, tough as iron, undaunted and mission-focused. Hadn't he admitted last night that he had trouble letting others close?

Maybe the problem was with her, she thought. It troubled her through the drive to the freeway and the perilous ride on I-5. Hawk drove like a NASCAR racer, fast, sure and steady, competently zipping between cars, changing lanes. When the traffic slowed to a crawl near the mall, he made one final switch and she could catch her breath.

"You don't like my driving?" Amusement tugged at the corners of his mouth. "I wasn't going more than a few miles an hour over the speed limit. Gotta keep up with traffic."

"Let's just say I would rather be on a horse. I would love to drive to the store in a horse-drawn wagon."

"It would take a whole lot longer."

"Sure, but your truck is just a machine."

"Hey, it's a very nice machine." His dimples deepened, far too attractive for the man's good.

He could stop the earth with those dimples. She shook her head, hoping to dislodge the effects of his smile. What had they been talking about? Her brain seemed to have turned to fog for some inexplicable reason. Oh yes—horses versus vehicles. "I didn't say your truck wasn't nice, just that it was a machine."

Even as the sound of the words hit her ears, she blushed. Great. Now she wasn't making any sense. She sounded like an idiot. What was wrong with her today?

Lack of sleep, she decided stubbornly. "Your truck doesn't miss you when you're gone. It doesn't snuggle with you and make you laugh. It's not your best friend. It can't love you."

"No, but I do love it." Trouble, that's what he was, and he knew it. "My truck doesn't kick me, doesn't decide to roll over in a mud puddle with me and it always does what I tell it to."

"You're using my funny stories against me." She laughed. How could she not? The man was definitely trouble of the best kind. "So you are saying convenience and control are more important than relationships."

"Do you think I'm going to say yes to that?" He kept one eye on the creeping traffic. "That is an ambush waiting to happen. I'm not about to step into that argument."

"Then that is what you think?" She could tease, too.

"If we are talking about cars, yes. I liked riding with you the other day, I won't say that wasn't one of the best days in recent times, but it would take hours to get to the mall if we decided to ride the horses."

"And you are an impatient man?"

"I can be as patient as Job if I need to be." She had no idea that was what he was determined to be. He would wait for her if it took all the days of his life. "But I'm not a fan of shopping."

"I could have guessed that. Hence, the mission talk. We get in, get out, objective accomplished."

"And no man left behind." He winked to make her laugh again, and to hide the deeper meaning, the one he could not let her guess. He would wait forever for her, he would never leave her behind. Doing his best to ignore the ever-expanding depth of his tenderness for her, he turned up an aisle of parking. "Keep a sharp eye out. Phase one in progress."

"Phase one?"

"Secure parking, then proceed to the mall."

"Phase one might take longer than the actual shopping mission." She had no idea how adorable she looked, leaning back in the seat, her hair tumbling everywhere, wearing boot-cut jeans and a Save the Whales T-shirt. "There isn't a spot anywhere."

"And a lot of competition looking." He wheeled

around the end of an aisle and drove straight down the far lot. "We have an advantage."

"Oh, sure we do." She laughed at that, a musical trill that he wanted to hear forever. She twisted to get a look up the jammed aisles. "I suppose you are the advantage?"

"I was talking about being in a truck, which puts us up high so we have a better view, but sure. If you want to think of me as an advantage, I won't argue."

"You, an advantage? If I had a snowball, I would throw it at you."

"I don't think that would teach me a lesson. It would only encourage me."

"You're an incorrigible kind of guy?"

"I try to be." He caught a set of taillights flashing to life way down the row and he wheeled into the aisle. "Looks like we've got a live one."

"Could you have found a spot farther away from the mall?" Adorable how she was teasing him. You could even call it bantering. And bantering implied a certain emotional intimacy, didn't it?

A good sign, he decided as he idled in the row. The sedan inched out of the spot, the driver peering out carefully and her view probably impeded by the enormous pile of shopping bags in the backseat, and motored off. Other cars lined up, some of them oncoming, trying to beat him to the punch. He charged into the spot, beating the competition. Victory.

September shook her head as if she couldn't believe him. "I am putting that on my faults list."

"Why? What did I do?" He cut the engine and helped her with her seat belt. "I got us a spot, that's what."

"You are a barracuda, dude. I'm keeping my eye on you."

"I was here first." He could banter, too. "I didn't cut anyone off. I didn't try to steal the spot like that sports car guy. And yet you are objecting to my methods?"

"Not objecting. Just keeping watch. I think there's more than meets the eye when it comes to you."

"You have no idea." More than meets the eye? That was the truth.

He hopped down, circled around the truck, pleased to find her waiting for him. She was an independent lady, but she was letting him be her gentleman. In time, she would want more from him. He felt it all the way to his soul. He loved her. More than there were stars in the universe. Truer than there were words to say.

He hated the moment her boots touched the ground, because she let go of him.

It wouldn't always be like this. He stayed at her side as they made the trek through the parking lot, laughing all the way.

Spending time with Hawk melted her resistance. What she thought she might have seen on his face last night was forgotten. Being with Hawk in the mall was not what she expected. He was like a big kid pointing out the mall decorations lining the walkways and stopping to look in all the store displays. They'd admired endless numbers of Christmas trees, mangers, *Nutcracker* scenes, piles of beautifully wrapped gifts and hand-painted windows.

"This ought to add to our Christmas cheer." Hawk sauntered over from a coffee kiosk with two reindeer-decorated paper cups in hand. "I got an eggnog latte and a peppermint mocha. Your choice."

"There's no contest. Peppermint mocha."

"Then this is yours."

He handed her the cup with a manly flourish, and if her knees went weak again, she refused to notice. She neatly avoided contact with his fingers—just in case the strange knee reaction happened again—and took a sip of the steaming drink.

"Whipped cream. You know how to celebrate, Hawk."

"That's something I'm proud of." He joined her at the store window.

"I think that goes on the list, too."

"Not the list!" He pretended to smack the heel of his hand against his forehead. "If you keep this up, you're going to know my every shortcoming."

"True, but if you're lucky I won't hold them against you."

"Good, because I would like to stick around for a while instead of getting kicked to the curb."

No woman in her right mind would give Hawk the boot. No, certainly not judging by many appreciative looks she'd noticed other women giving him as they cruised the mall's corridors. In fact, there was another one from a woman leaving the bookstore. September sympathized. It was very hard not to notice a man who exuded honor instead of conceit, kindness instead of brashness. He studied the colorful children's books paraded up and down a stairway display. Covers of many beloved classics brought back memories.

"My dad used to read to us." He must have been feeling the same way. "He was a logger, but I think if he could have afforded college he would have been a great literature professor. Every weekend afternoon he could manage, he would be in his chair with a classic open in hand. As far back as I can remember, he would read me to sleep. He would start the Christmas stories on the first of December, my birthday. It was our tradition. Our favorite was *How the Grinch Stole Christmas.*"

"One of my faves, too." It had to be the memories spearing sharp and sweetly. Overwhelmed by the intensity, she wanted to step away, put distance between them and tuck old memories back in the safe compartment she had stored them in. Surely Hawk wasn't having this effect on her emotions. "Chessie would always do the out-loud reading. She insisted. To this day, *The Night Before Christmas* does not sound right to me unless my sister is reading it."

"After my dad died, Christmas sort of fizzled in my house. Mom stopped baking and cooking. There was no Christmas candy. Liz and I had to make our own holiday. Of course, living next door to the Grangers helped."

"Tim's family." It didn't hurt to talk about them now. She meandered over to the wide breezeway where rows of books beckoned. "Tell me about your Christmases with them."

"Two Christmas trees in the house. Garland everywhere. The Grangers hang twinkle lights like you do, except on every available surface. The house smells like fresh-cut pine, baking bread and molasses cookies. Christmas music is constantly playing. Then there is the old upright piano. Everyone gathers around it on Christmas Eve and we sing until it's time to head off to the candlelight service."

"You've become part of the family."

"I needed one and they were there."

She thought of Hawk as a little boy, devastated by loss and a broken home. Her eyes burned for him. Caring spiraled within her, growing with every turn, affection she could not control. "I'm glad you have them."

"Me, too. I'm lucky they put up with me. They could take objection and put me out on the street."

"Very tempting, I'm sure."

"Hey!"

She loved how he could make her smile, how he could touch her deeply. She felt as hopeful as the stars twinkling from the overhead skylights. A mom ambled by with two small children in tow. Shopping bags crinkled, the baby clapped her hands and shouted, and the brown-haired boys toddled by, talking excitedly about Santa Claus. Want ribboned through her. She tore her gaze away and studied a book display without seeing it.

"I think I'm going to look for a home design book Chessie wants. I haven't gotten all of her gifts yet." She didn't know why she felt maudlin. Being alone was what she wanted. It was safer. She never wanted to go through the wreckage of loss again. Safer was better, even if it meant no children to fuss over and adore. Even if it meant no wonderful husband with Hawk's sense of humor and stalwart gentleness.

"Great. I'm going to need something to read for my flight." He browsed the bestsellers and chose a paperback to browse through.

She sidled over to the hardcover bestseller rack and spotted the book her sister had been salivating for. She grabbed a copy, but when she looked at the cover it was the wrong book. How had she done that?

Easy. Her gaze had glued to Hawk and refused to move. She replaced the volume, chose the right one this time and moved into the aisle toward him.

"Victory." He held up a book in triumph. "Now I won't be bored on the flight. Hey, that looks like something my mom would like. Where did you get it?"

She pointed, not quite able to make her brain find the words. Maybe it was a delayed problem from her mild concussion. It was the only reason she could think of for her sudden aphasia. She had lost motor skills, too, since juggling the coffee, her purse and the book took all her concentration. She found her credit card and handed it to the kid behind the counter. An aisle away, Hawk grabbed a book, studied it with an unassuming nod and paced her way.

Something broke apart inside her, a barrier she had constructed a long time ago. The last fortification fell. The speakers overhead sang "We Wish You a Merry Christmas," and as the clerk shoved a credit card slip at her to sign, she felt her world shift. A quiet, sacred emotion ebbed to life within her—an intense, singular brand of affection she refused to name.

Shock rocked through her. When she signed her name, the letters were squiggly and didn't look like her writing. Hawk approached the counter and stood next to her, handing over his merchandise to a second clerk, who greeted him and began tallying his purchases.

I do not love him, she argued with herself as she shoved the pen and receipt across the counter. It was impossible for her to love him. She simply would not allow it.

"Have a nice day." Her clerk smiled at her, but his glance fell behind her shoulder, where another customer was waiting. She fumbled with the bag, the cup and her purse again, managing somehow to move out of the way.

"Great. One down, two more to go." He joined her outside the entrance. "I still haven't found the right thing for Pierce and Lexie. But we'll trek on. Our spirits are high."

What would life with Hawk be like? she wondered as they strolled to the next store. Unexpected. Joyful. Intrepid. She could not let herself picture her future with him. They were friends, nothing more. She would tell herself that until it was totally, entirely true.

"You're looking a little pale. Are you feeling okay?"

"F-fine." She *was*. There was no other alternative. "Where to next?"

"Look. A Christmas tree." Hawk turned to the banister, gazing at the floor below where Santa sat in a red velvet chair and a long line of kids and parents waited to see him. In the middle of the plaza winked an enormous tree, dazzling with cheer and cuteness. But that wasn't the tree Hawk pointed toward.

Across the way, in a nearly bare storefront, was a wishing tree, decorated with slips of paper hung by colorful ribbons. Most shoppers hurried by, without giving it a second glance. "Let's go shopping for some kids. Want to?"

The words disappeared again. She nodded, struggling not to feel. She had to resist whatever this was threatening to take her over.

"Great. Mom always included gifts for the church's charity tree in our Christmas traditions. After she lost interest in celebrating, my sis and I kept it up." He laid a hand on her shoulder, gently guiding her through an oncoming throng of teenagers. "It's something I do whenever I'm Stateside in December."

"You know me. I think it's a great idea. Chessie and I do the same thing for our church tree." Her head rang but she was able to speak and walk at the same time. A major accomplishment considering the intensity of these new feelings. She was only slightly preoccupied as they searched through the names hanging on the charity tree. She watched him through the thick, fragrant boughs, concentrating as he read several requests, his amused reactions and the excitement on his rugged face.

"Here's one. I'm taking it." He unhooked a paper slip. "This kid would like a big yellow dump truck. As I'm especially fond of dump trucks, I know just what he wants."

"I can see you as a little boy playing on a mound of dirt with your construction trucks." Not hard at all to picture how cute he would have been, his dark hair longer and wind tousled, that cowlick at the crown of his head more pronounced. And those big blue eyes probably made his mom melt every time he trained them on her to ask for something. How could anyone say no to a face like that?

"What do you have there?" He sidled around the tree, sneaking dangerously close so that he could read the paper she held. "Oh, baby dolls. I have no experience there."

"You had a sister. Didn't she have dolls?"

"Well, let me rephrase that. I wasn't exactly honest. My sole experience with dolls is very limited. Mostly hostage taking, kidnapping, ransom demanding-type missions." He looked sheepish. "And before you say it, yes, I got into trouble big-time. Mom said a corner in the house is worn out because I spent so much time in it."

"You? Getting in trouble? I can't picture it." They laughed together.

"It's true. One corner of the living room is really dingy from me leaning against it all those years. I'm guessing you never got into trouble."

"I never got very far being troublesome." This man could make her laugh as nobody could. "Chessie was on the case. She was a very watchful big sister. The minute I stepped a toe out of line she was off to tell Mom about it."

"Got to keep those younger siblings in line." They laughed harder.

She pocketed the child's name and searched for another. She didn't know how it had happened, or the exact moment her soul had healed, but she was living again and laughing. If she was happy, that meant she could be hurt, too. She plucked another name off the tree blindly, her hand trembling. She didn't want any more pain in life. She did not want to risk falling in love before she realized it.

Next to her Hawk chuckled at something he read. "This kid wants a big package of candy all to himself so his big brother can't steal it from him. I'm surprised they wrote that on the request card. I'm going to find the best selection of chocolate and box it up for this fella. As penance for all the times I stole things from my little sister."

She shook her head, liking him more by the minute. He would be a tough man not to fall for, and she refused to do it. Whatever happened, she would not surrender her heart to him.

Chapter Twelve

"I'm going to put this up right now." Hawk tugged the store bag from his truck's backseat. September's street was alive tonight, with a caroling group serenading at the far end of the cul-de-sac. "Every other house has got at least one outside decoration up."

"It's late, Hawk. I'll go plug in my tree lights and it will be festive enough. You don't have to go to the trouble." Cute. She really thought he would opt out?

"It'll be fun." He intended to stay until the job was done. There was more decorating to do. He was no quitter. "Hey, there. What do you think you're doing?"

"Uh, getting my shopping bags."

"No, you aren't." He couldn't believe her. He grabbed her bags before she could. "Please go turn on the porch light so I don't trip over my own feet."

"That's something an Army Ranger does a lot? Trip in the dark?"

"If I did, I wouldn't be very good at my job."

"So why did you say that?" She searched through her keys, but he caught her watching him.

Nice. Maybe things were progressing better than he thought. "I just wanted to make you laugh, sunshine."

"And why is that?"

"Because when you're happy, I'm happy." He followed her up the steps and into the house. "Where do you want these?"

"Just put them anywhere." She dropped her purse on the coffee table and hit the switch. Merry lights blazed on the little tree, chasing away the dark. She whirled to face him, more beautiful to him by the moment.

Yep, he was definitely in big trouble here. With every passing second, he loved her more. He didn't know love could do that, increase exponentially until it felt too big to hold and too impossible to believe. But standing here with her *was* real.

"Look." He pointed to the ceiling. "Mistletoe."

"How convenient. You decided to stand there on purpose."

"True, but that doesn't change the fact. We have to kiss." He hauled her into his arms while the tree lights blinked as if in agreement. "Tradition."

"And you think I'm a traditional girl?"

"I know you are." The evening had been the best of his life. Being in her company, talking and laughing, had been priceless. Infinitely tender, he lowered his lips to hers. Just one brush of a kiss, that was all he meant, because he didn't want to pressure her to feel something too soon. That might frighten her. He would die before he hurt her or scared her in any way.

Yep, he meant the kiss to be one light tender caress. Chalk it up to good intentions. But her fingers curled around his as if she were holding on, as if she were swept away, too, by the incredible evening and the closeness they'd shared.

When he broke the kiss, he thought he saw an answering affection on her dear face, but then she spun away and her hair hid her expression like a curtain, shielding him.

I love her so much, Lord. His heart opened wide with prayer and thanksgiving. *Thank You for this time with her.* Loving her was the sweetest thing he'd ever known.

All his life he had worked at keeping a safe distance between him and everyone else. His best buds and lifelong friends, Pierce and Tim, had gotten the closest. But that was friendship. This—his chest swelled, his soul expanded—this was something else entirely. Wonderful. Scary. Amazing. She *had* to love him back—in time. She was his future, his beloved, his everything. He knew it beyond all doubt.

"I'm going to go put up your new yard decorations." His cheerful step knelled in the shadows. "Now you won't be the Scrooge of the neighborhood."

"I didn't know I was." Chuckling, she followed him to the door, but he was already hiking down the walkway, at one with the dark. She flipped on the porch light, realizing she'd forgotten that earlier. Probably because Mark Hawkins scrambled her brains. He short-circuited her system. His kiss was such perfection, it erased the memory of all other kisses that had come before and made her want to dream about a future with him—not that she was going to.

No, there would be no dreaming allowed.

"Where do you want 'em?" He kept just out of reach

of the light like an intruder clinging to the shadows, like a thief come to steal her heart.

He was talking about decorations, and she was trying to hold on to her careful emotional balance. The foundation on which she had built the last two years of her life. She rubbed her forehead, fighting to think.

"I'll try it along the walkway first, yeah?" Unaware of her struggle, he ripped open the box, the cracking sound of hard plastic ricocheted in the quiet. He extracted a stack of stars and their long white connecting cord. "If I march them across the lawn, they might compete with the tree. I have to say, that tree does look good from here. You know how to pick 'em."

Could she banter back with him? No, because she couldn't think of a single thing to say. Her brain had ground to a halt out of sheer panic. Neither could she move out of the doorway. She stood half in, half out. The cool night air danced over her and she shivered.

"That doesn't look half bad." The shadow in her yard stopped to study his work. One white star rose up out of her flower bed. Hawk gave it an adjustment, as if it wasn't standing straight enough for him.

You would think being unable to see him in the dark would make it easier. But no, her mind—the one that couldn't think of a single word in the English language—remembered every line and hollow of his face, every curve and edge. She didn't need light to know that with the angle of his jaw, he was frowning. And because he was thinking something through, a handsome crinkle would dig into his forehead.

That man could make her forget. He could make her want to believe. For a few hours tonight, he had. She had been like Cinderella at the ball, feeling beautiful as if she were in a gown and slippers, princess quality with a real live prince on her arm. Sure, they were only shopping, not dancing at a fancy ball, but the feeling was the same. The kiss had sealed it.

She didn't want to stop believing—not yet. She wanted this evening with him to go on forever. Laughing in his truck, shopping on his arm, choosing dolls and trucks in the toy store with Hawk at her side had made her happy and alive and full of hopeful joy. Hawk's kiss made her whole, even in the places she thought would always be scarred. New and powerful feelings beat against her defenses, wanting to be set free. Hawk had done this. He had walked into her life and made her love him.

No, she thought. *I do not love him. I will not love him. I am in control of my heart.*

"Hey, beautiful. What do you think?" He stood on the lawn, graced by the jewel tones of the Christmas tree winking through the window. He looked like a gift. He was everything she thought she would never find. Everything she was terrified of losing again.

"Just need to plug these in." Like the athlete he was, he stalked through the flower beds, hurdled the porch rail and snaked the cord through the railing posts. Red, gold, blue and green light dappled him as he knelt in front of the big picture window. The stars on the lawn burst into majestic white, glowing with steady promise. He bounded to his feet. "Mission accomplished."

"You were right. Those look great in the yard." The decorations shone like hope in the dark, light chasing away the clutches of an endless night.

"Sure you don't want any house lights?" He strolled toward her, fully illuminated, everything revealed—

the crease in his forehead, the affection in his eyes and the memory of their kiss on his lips. "I could come back with a ladder."

Why couldn't she stop thinking about that kiss? Because it hadn't been a friendly kiss. It had nothing to do with mistletoe and tradition and everything to do with what was budding between them. A romance.

She wanted to deny it. Friendship was not necessarily romance. Going Christmas shopping wasn't specifically dating. But that kiss, that *had* been romantic. Sweetly, softly romantic.

"I could come back with dinner. Maybe I could grab some takeout." Hawk leaned against the railing, appearing casual. But he wasn't. He was asking her out on a date. On *another* date.

Just as today had been. Fear raked through her. She stumbled and grabbed the door frame for support. Her mind raced over all the times she and Hawk had been together—he'd brought flowers to the hospital, pizza to her house and flowers to dinner. He'd taken her out to eat, gone riding with her, told her about what he wanted from life—marriage and a family one day. That was not only dating behavior, but courting talk.

"September, are you all right?" Concerned, he came to her, his hands curling around the curve of her shoulder, his tall shadow falling across her, obliterating the light.

All right? She thought he needed her friendship. She certainly needed his. But that had been a fool's path. From the moment he took her hand in the mine shaft, she had never been the same.

"Hawk, you are asking to come over with dinner out of friendship, right?" Her hands came up to land on his chest of their own volition. She ignored the secure feeling of being in his arms and the reliable thump of his heartbeat beneath her palms. "It's not a date?"

"Well, that depends." His baritone dipped deep and low, infinitely tender. So tender it made every part of her soul want to dream of him. His grip on her tightened slightly, as if he wanted to draw her closer, but held back. "It can be a date if you want it to be."

"What does that mean?" Confusion ripped through her. "Either it's a date or it isn't. Either we have a friendship or we don't."

"It doesn't have to be that black and white. Couldn't we just hang out and see where this goes? I don't think we need to worry about labeling or examining it."

"Then basically you are saying yes. It is a date. You just don't want to call it that." She started to shake, feeling vulnerable as if a ledge at her feet had given way and she was falling. The painful crash was only a matter of time. A painful, shattering strike of bone to earth and rock that would destroy her all over again. Love hurt. It was as simple as that. Life was uncertain at best, and she did not have the strength to hurt like that again.

"It's a friendly date." Ever gentle, Hawk didn't push. Calm, he didn't move toward her to pull her closer into his arms. Nor did he let go of her. "I want to see you again, September. I want to hang with you."

"You're trying to make this casual, but it's not." She could see it now. A plea resonated in the cool air around them, a silent emotion she could feel from his spirit to hers. She could not deny the connection between them. A mysterious bond she had never had with Tim or anyone. A tie she had to break. "I agreed to being friends. You know that."

"Have I ever asked anything of you other than friendship?"

No, she answered truthfully. But there was one thing that had not been friendship for her. "That kiss. That was not friendly. It might have started out that way, but it wasn't how I ended up feeling."

"I didn't intend for things to go from friendly to serious in five seconds flat." Sincere, ever honest, that was Hawk. "I'm sorry if it was too fast. We can hit the brakes. Keep it casual."

"Go back to being friends?"

"Whatever you want, September. As long as you please let me stay in your life." He didn't falter, he didn't back down. "That's all I'm asking for."

"You mean that's all you're asking for right now?"

"Yes." He winced, as if telling the truth cost him. "I'm here as a friend, September. Nothing more."

"But you feel more?"

"I can't say that I don't." Tension corded in his neck. That had to hurt, too. "Can you say the same?"

No, she couldn't. The truth lodged in her throat, refusing to budge. This was only going to end in sorrow. She knew that for a fact. He should know what he was asking of her. He towered before her, everything she wanted, everything she was afraid to lose.

No, she couldn't hurt like that again. She couldn't take that risk. It hurt too much. She could not go back to worrying through every deployment and expecting the worst to happen again. And what if it did? What if she gave in, fell in love only to lose him? How could she pick up those pieces a second time? She was not that strong. She wanted to be.

She wasn't.

"I wish I could be who you need me to be." Her voice wobbled dangerously. She willed down every feeling, every affection until she was a part of the shadows. She felt the star shine fade, every bit of bright light and every twinkle until only darkness remained. She had to be honest. She had to do the right thing. "But I can't be. You know what I've lost. We can only be friends."

"Only?" No emotion passed across his face. "Maybe we can agree to keep things friendly. We don't have to put time limits or constraints on it."

"I need them, Hawk. Don't you see? I can't let myself care for you more than that." She pulled away from him as if being near to him tortured her. As if he had hurt her beyond repair.

"But friendships can deepen." At least he prayed it would. *This is in Your hands, Lord, but please, if it's Your will, let this work out. Let her love me.*

All he wanted was the chance to win her heart. Just the chance.

But even he could see it was too late.

"I didn't want you as anything more than a friend." Terribly gentle came her words, laced with genuine affection. "You knew this from the start. I'm sorry, but I am never going to love you. It's not a possibility."

"Wow." A puff of air escaped him, otherwise he couldn't move, couldn't breathe. He felt frozen from the impact of her words. That happened in a serious injury, he knew from firsthand experience. The pain was too much for the body to tolerate, the shock too great for the nervous system. First came a vast, stunning stillness, which he was experiencing. Proof that he'd come to love her more than he'd realized. Then pain crashed through him like a bomb strike—a polite bomb strike. Apology was etched into her beautiful face, along with concern for him.

But there was more. He could feel her agony. This was hurting her. *He* was hurting her. The devastation felt like a death blow. He steeled his spine and pretended he was fine. This was no big deal. She didn't need to feel sorry; she'd been honest. A man couldn't ask for more than that. He pasted what he hoped was a good-natured look on his face. "I heard you loud and clear, September. Message received."

"I'm sorry to be so blunt." More than apology crinkled adorably around her pretty mouth and luminous eyes. "I don't mean to be. This isn't easy."

"You're hurting. I'm hurting. This is not what I want. It's not why I'm here. If I'm not making you happy—"

"You should leave," she finished his thought, completed his sentence and looked as broken up as he felt.

Everything inside him screamed to go to her, to draw her into his arms, cradle her to his chest and comfort her. Make this better for her. But how could he go against her wishes? No, he had to turn away. He had to walk off, knowing his love caused her pain.

His boots rang on the porch boards—a hollow sound. The tree lights blazed through the window, as if nothing catastrophic had happened. A car rolled down the street behind them. The carolers' tune grew louder as they stopped at the house next door, singing about rockin' around the Christmas tree. And September backed through her doorway, standing there like the other times she had wished him good-night. One horrible thing was different—the way she looked at him with utter misery.

It wasn't good-night this time. It was goodbye.

"Thanks for the good day." His steps drummed on the stairs. "I will remember it for a long time."

"Me, too." She didn't move from the doorway. She couldn't. "Thanks for everything you've done for me. I want you to know that it mattered."

"I'm glad. Then it was all worth it." He raised his hand in one sweeping wave for goodbye. Maybe he couldn't say the words, either. He pivoted on his heel and strode away, straight shouldered, noble, infinitely strong.

She hated seeing him go. It was killing her. She gripped the door, unable to close it, unable to deprive herself of the last look she would have of him. Watching him walk away was the hardest thing she had done since burying Tim. She felt broken all over again. There was no way to shield herself from the truth. She was not the same woman she'd been when she'd tumbled down that forgotten mine shaft. She was someone healed, someone hopeful, someone who longed to dream again.

She longed to love him, truly and deeply for the rest of her life, but he was a Ranger, in and out of danger. She could not do it. She could not face that again. Not even for him. No one, especially not she, was strong enough for that.

She heard his truck door close and the engine roar to life. She watched him drive away, her every cell, her every neuron, her very essence shrieking at her to go after him.

She didn't. He disappeared into the night, gone forever from her life. As the carolers harmonized "We Wish You a Merry Christmas," she bowed her head, overwhelmed with misery.

Black clouds rolled in from the coast, grabbing the starlight and stealing it like a thief in the dark. Hawk grabbed the shopping bags from the backseat and shouldered the door shut. The parking lot was still and silent; a few lights blazed in the base apartments. A faint drone of voices and music rose as he hoofed it up the front steps. The complex's Christmas party. He'd totally forgotten.

Not that he was in a social mood. No, he was pretty much toast. September didn't want him. She'd told him so. She was never going to love him. That would never be a possibility.

Never was a harsh word. With every step he took down the hall, the pain set in deeper. With every crinkle and rustle of the bags came a reminder of their evening together: September's blazing joy in front of the Christmas books, the prowl for a parking spot and all the fun little things they had shared, his hunt for change through his pockets for the Salvation Army donation pot. Dinner at the food court where he ate ten tacos—she'd counted in disbelief. How she'd tuned his truck radio—and he let no one mess with his radio—to some frilly station where Christmas music played 24/7 and they sang along with the carols to while away the time trying to get out of the mall parking.

Yeah, good job at not remembering, Hawk. He took the stairs at the far end of the hall, so he could avoid the loud common room where, judging by the sound of things, the party was in full swing. A singing competition of "The Twelve Days of Christmas" rang along the empty corridor as he hit the stairwell. Laughter and merriment followed him like a dog on a trail.

Never, she'd said. She would never love him. She might as well have taken a knife to his soul.

He charged into his place and shut the door. Darkness met him. The bags gave a final rustle as he dropped them to the floor. He didn't bother with the light. Finding his way by memory, he headed straight to the fridge, cracked open a can of soda and hiked out onto the balcony. Cold met him, and he welcomed it. With any luck, it would numb the agony threatening to overtake him. He could freeze his emotions enough so he would never feel the pain of September's rejection.

He eased into a frosty deck chair, planted his elbows on his knees and stared off into the night. Only a few stars remained, the rest of the sky loomed inky-black, heavy with a coming storm. Faint sounds from the party down below drifted up to him like a carol. He took a swig of soda and tuned out the music, too. Did it work? No, because the music looped him back to standing on September's yard getting the new decorations just right. Why had he let her so far in? It was a doomed mission—he could have seen it rationally. He was always going to get hurt.

"Hawk, you in here?"

He squeezed his eyes shut for a moment, drawing up his reserves, burying his hurt. By the time Reno found him, he'd been able to wipe the grief from his face.

"Why aren't you at the party?" Reno leaned against the frame of the slider door. "I came to fetch you earlier, but you were out."

"Christmas shopping. I head home tomorrow morning."

"I know. I'm your ride to the airport, remember? You look like you could use some cheering up. Some of the new recruits are going to put on some kind of Christmas skit. It's supposed to be a riot. You don't want to miss that."

"Right." He took another slurp of cola. "I'll be down in a bit."

"Something wrong, buddy?"

"Nothing I can't handle." It was true. He would face the pain. He was a Ranger; he didn't go around, he went through. He didn't give up and he didn't give in. Right now, he couldn't see there was any other alternative. September didn't want him. He had moved too fast too soon.

"Okay. I'll come fetch you for the skit." Reno sounded unsure, as if he were starting to figure out something wasn't right.

"I'm good," he assured his buddy. "Go back to the party."

"I'll see you there, then. Did you hear? Word is, our deployment's been moved up."

Hawk managed to nod. As Reno headed for the exit, he took another swallow of soda. So much for being alone. He couldn't miss the obligatory production by the newbies, but he didn't feel like being around a lot of people, either. All he wanted was September.

He'd scared her with that final kiss and he lost his only chance with her. She was his light in the dark and always would be. Grief grabbed at him, shadowed and all-consuming. She had been the one he'd let too close. Funny how he hadn't even realized it. It just happened. And now look at the result. He was sitting alone in the night without her.

She watched the last stars wink out, and she felt hopeless. She'd cried until there were no more tears, and that made no sense. She didn't love Hawk. Losing him shouldn't hurt like this.

She shifted on the window seat, the house dark and quiet around her. The entire world had gone still, as if the earth had stopped spinning. The sweet memory of their kiss remained like a treasure she could not relinquish.

She leaned her forehead against the cold glass, wishing she could turn back time and bury herself in ice. If she were numb, she wouldn't have to feel the keen-edged pain of breaking Hawk's heart. She wrapped her arms around her middle, trying to comfort herself, but the pain remained.

She relaxed into the window-seat cushions, the rustling movements echoing in her solitary family room. She had gotten carried away tonight. Caught up in a rare happiness, she had forgotten to hold back, to keep Hawk at a distance. She hadn't realized her emotions were threatening to get away from her.

Good thing she caught it when she did before she started dreaming of Hawk as her husband one day, of the happy marriage and the kids they would have. Two little boys—her rebellious, foolish mind could almost see them—and a little girl who loved horses. Dreams she could not give in to, but it was too late. Their seeds had already taken hold, and she would be haunted by their promise for the rest of her life.

Raindrops struck the window and slid down the dark glass. More followed behind them, tapping a lonely melody. A few moments later water gurgled in the gutters and the lilac bushes began to sway, their branches whispering against the siding. She couldn't help wondering if Hawk was watching the rain fall and if he were thinking of her, too. She thought so. It was as if emotion connected them across the miles, and she could sense his hurt, as bleak as her own.

Don't think of him, September. She rose from the cushions, walking through the dark room to the kitchen, where the faint blink of colored lights grew stronger with every step. The dear little tree with its nonproportional branches and lopsided trunk stood proudly at the window, limbs raised toward heaven. With the star topper blazing, the fir looked like grace itself, transformed by the light, a symbol of grace.

I cannot love him. She touched a featherlike needle and drew in the tree's comforting pine scent. Hawk was a soldier. As a Ranger, he put himself in harm's way every time he went on a mission. The thought of losing Hawk fractured her in pieces. Proof that it was too late for friendship. Her affections ran too deep. Life for a soldier was too uncertain and her heart too fragile. She had to let him go.

Help me to be strong, Lord, and to do the right thing. She gazed skyward, but heaven felt far away on this desolate night.

Chapter Thirteen

"You look terrible." Chessie marched across the cathedral's parking lot, her heels tapping a no-nonsense rhythm. They came every year for the seasonal performance. "Did you sleep at all last night? It's your arm. It's hurting you."

"Stop, my arm is fine." September wasn't about to admit why she had tossed and turned all night. "It was just one of those nights. You look gorgeous. Is that a new dress?"

"An impulse buy when I was shopping for Evelyn." Chessie gave a flourish, showing off the flowing silk garment beneath her equally tasteful wool coat. "You know how I am about sticking to budgets, but it was on sale and I fell in love with it."

"Do you know what that would be great for? Your New Year's Eve date." They followed the sidewalk to the church's wide steps.

"That's what I thought, too." Chessie paused to take two programs from the stand in the vestibule and handed one over. "So, how did your shopping expedition with Hawk turn out?"

"How did you—?"

"Ha! Colleen told me. I stopped by to see Princess. I don't think she meant to tell. She assumed I knew all about the new man in your life."

"He's not in my life." Especially after last night. Battling regret, she forged ahead down the aisle, ignoring the beautiful glasswork and the discordant notes of the orchestra warming up. She pointed to an available pew toward the middle. At Chessie's nod, she eased into the row, praying that her sister would drop the subject and knowing she would not.

"I thought things were going well." Her sister looked chagrined as she settled onto the bench. "You were spending a lot of time together."

"*Were* being the operative word. He left for Wyoming this morning."

"Well, it's still early. You can call him before you get home. It's what, only an hour ahead in Wyoming? It won't be too late."

"You want me to call him? I thought you didn't like him." She unbuttoned her coat, paying a lot of attention to each button. The one thing she could not do was to think about Hawk's laugh, or his undying optimism, or his kiss. What she especially could not afford to do was to imagine the dreams lost, pictures of a future with him.

"I told you. I don't like what he does, but look at you. If this is how much you miss him when he leaves, it's too late for my opinion. Your heart has already decided. You are in love with him."

"I am not." That came out defensively. Out of the corner of her eye she saw people two pews away turn to look at her. She lowered her voice. "Hawk and I aren't a couple, trust me."

"But you want to be?"

"No." *But we could have been.* Regret battered her. Everything inside her shouted out for him. She stowed her purse on the floor beneath the pew, doing her best not to look at Chessie. She did not want her sister to guess what had happened. "I can't fall for another Ranger. I knew it all along. You do, too, remember? You told me from the start. But—"

She hung her head, unable to admit it was already too late. She felt her sister's concern like the draft from the wide-open doors. Rustling started as the choir filed onto the bleachers at the head of the church. Soon the program would start and that would put an end to this discussion.

But not to her misery. Why couldn't she forget what it had been like to be cared for by him? If only she could forget the time they had spent together—picking out the tree, doing dishes, sipping hot coffee. It wasn't as if he had whisked her off to Paris. He had simply taken her to the mall. So why was she hung up on him? Why couldn't she bear to let a single memory of him go?

The conductor tapped his baton against the podium, and the cathedral quieted in anticipation. She tried to silence the whisperings in her mind. She tried to quiet her unmistakable sadness. The first majestic notes of Handel's *Messiah* blasted into the sanctuary, but the music didn't touch her. "Hallelujah," the choir belted out in perfect harmony, but it might as well have been silence. The beautiful, inspiring music did not touch her. It did not uplift her. It did not make her want to believe.

I'm grieving him, she realized. She hadn't imagined that love could come again into her heart. She had mistaken friendship for something more. She had ignored her deepening feelings when she should have been honest enough to examine them. As the music crescendoed and the joy of the music reverberated in the acoustic glory of the cathedral, she was in silence. The only music she heard was longing within her soul for a lifetime with Hawk. For one brief second, she saw what could be—frequent laughter and quiet moments, a lifetime spent with his companionship and his stalwart, ever-caring love. Children and birthdays and celebrations. Grandchildren and retirement. Evenings spent on a porch. A love that strengthened day by day.

A wish was all it could be, a daydream and nothing more.

Chessie leaned close to whisper, "Are you all right?"

"I will be." She set her chin, fixed her eyes on the choir and tried to let the music carry her away. She had to be practical. She might want that future with Hawk, but she was not a woman who could afford to dream. End of story. The fall that followed love lost was not worth it.

Wait a minute. Did that mean she would rather have never met Tim? That she would have been better off never loving him? No. Her life was richer—she was richer—because the sweet, enthusiastic idealistic Tim Granger had come into her life. So that made her wonder. What would she miss with Hawk?

She hung her head, realizing that was one question

she would not have answered. Remembering the look on his face, it was over. She was too late.

Sorrow hit her with a bleak punch, unfair on an evening so beautiful in a sanctuary fraught with light and glorious in song.

"You've been awfully quiet tonight." Frank Granger, Pierce's uncle, drew up a chair and hunkered down beside him at the cloth-covered table. The extended family had moved into the living room to pour over old wedding albums.

Hawk didn't have the will to join them. All through the wedding talk, rehearsal and rehearsal dinner, he couldn't help wondering about his future—the one he wanted more than air to breathe. An impossible future. He should have known that all along. He could have saved himself a passel of disappointment.

"Just got a lot on my mind." He grabbed the can of root beer he'd been working on and upended it. Drained the last of the soda in three gulps.

"When a man looks like you do, it's always woman trouble." There was no pulling the wool over Uncle Frank's eyes. He was a widower who ran a successful ranch north of Jackson Hole. It was hard not to like Frank. He was the sort of man who looked you in the eye when he talked to you, a man who always did the right thing. Hawk had known him since he was a boy and respected him more with each passing year.

"If I tell you you're right, that I've got some major woman trouble, then you will want to know about it." He set down the can and pushed back his chair.

"We don't have to talk about it." Frank reached across the table to steal a carrot stick left on the vegetable plate from dinner. "Sometimes it's best to let things simmer. If you think on it long enough, the right answer will come to you."

"I appreciate that. But I doubt there's a right answer."

"There's always a right answer, son."

"No, it's definitely over." Miserable, Hawk snatched a carrot stick, too, and crunched on it. "She dumped me."

"That hangdog look on your face can only mean one thing." Frank looked as if he had seen it all. "I was a married man for a long time. I know what a woman can do to a man's heart."

"It's my fault. Not hers." That was the worst part. He'd known how she felt and yet he went charging ahead like a good Ranger. But he forgot sometimes you got further by sitting tight. "I fell in love with Tim's ex-fiancée."

"You sure know how to find trouble, don't you?" Frank finished off his carrot stick and stole a radish off the platter. "It takes time to get over a loss like that. The more the girl loved him, the longer it's gonna take and the harder it is."

"I know. I moved too fast. I thought she felt the same way, or close enough." His guts twisted and he tossed the carrot stick onto his abandoned dinner plate.

"The thing about women is that you can never tell what they're thinkin'. They will surprise us men every time. I can see this girl means something real to you."

"As real as it gets." The conversation in the living room crescendoed into a roar. Laughter, playful shouting and Mrs. Granger's drill sergeant voice echoed through the house. Even Roger, the old sheepdog, added a *woof! woof!* as if cheering someone on. Pierce and his brother were probably wrestling in the house—something crashed to the floor. Yep, and now they were getting into trouble.

"That's no way for you boys to behave on the night before a wedding. *Your* wedding, Pierce. I'm not sure you are mature enough to get married after this." Beneath the firm layer of stern in Mrs. Granger's tone was suppressed laughter. "Sean, I can't believe you. Get off the floor and pick that up. You're lucky nothing broke. Now straighten up, both of you."

"Yes, ma'am," two voices answered in unison, stuttering laughter.

Hawk shook his head. Time passed, one year blurring into the next, but some things stayed the same. The Granger family would always be just like this, even without Tim. It heartened him to know love went on, and that families could survive. Maybe if he gave her enough time—

"This girl you're in love with. You want to marry her?" Frank broke into his thoughts.

"More than anything on this earth."

"You're the man. It's up to you to convince her of that." He leaned back in his chair, nibbling on the radish. He nodded in the direction of the kitchen doorway. "Hello there, Giselle."

"I didn't mean to interrupt." Pierce's little sister padded into the room. The dark-haired college-age sweetheart was going to break a lot of hearts one day. "I wanted to get a start on the dishes. Mom and Lexie did all this cooking and baking. Mom's tired, and Lexie is getting married tomorrow. They should not have to do the dishes."

"I agree. Let me pitch in. Make myself useful for a change." Wry-humored, Frank pushed out of his chair. "Hawk, listen. I've thought this through. You are a Ranger. Tim was a Ranger. Is that the problem?"

"It sure is." His guts coiled tighter. "Plus, I think she's afraid to love anyone again."

"Most of us don't want to walk a path that we're afraid of alone." He grabbed a few plates to stack. "Maybe she needs you more than you think."

"Maybe." Stoneware clinked and clattered as Giselle rinsed dishes and stacked them in the dishwasher. He pushed away from the table, scooped up as many glasses as he could carry and followed Frank to the sink. Music vibrated from the front room—Mrs. Granger was playing the piano. The simple melody of "Silver Bells" was drowned out by the Granger family's singing.

He wished September were here. Regret choked him. He wished he had held back on that kiss. He wished he could change her fear. He didn't know how to fix it. Uncle Frank had to be right—he was always right. What was the solution? How was he going to try to win back a woman who'd admitted she would never love him?

He missed her so much, it was a physical pain. A blade-sharp incision digging into his guts. An emptiness in his soul he couldn't heal. She touched him deeply, where no one ever had before. She turned him inside out and upside down, and yet her softest touch made peace settle within him. She was the reason he drew breath. This was no ordinary love. Not for him.

This was a divine gift. The chance for a truly special love. How could he walk away from that?

"Hey, Frank, get in here!" Mr. Granger called out to his brother, when the song ended. "You and Carol can play duets, and we'll all sing along."

"Oh boy, I knew this was gonna happen." Pretending to grumble, Frank carried one last load to the sink. "You look like a man who needs a dose of Christmas spirit. C'mon, Giselle, Hawk. We'll do these later."

Looked as though he wasn't going to be able to avoid the family—usually the one thing he looked forward to the most when he came home. Mom was sitting on the couch, cradling a cup of tea, the fireplace crackling merrily in the hearth nearby. She smiled at him and patted the cushion at her side. As Mrs. Granger made room on the piano bench and Frank gave the ivories a tickle, he gave the sheepdog a head pat and dropped down next to his mom.

"You've been awfully quiet tonight," she observed. "You aren't coming down with something, are you?"

"Nothing a good night's sleep won't cure." That was true enough. He'd hardly slept a wink last night. He feared tonight he would be doing the same. Twisted up over September, unable to fix what was wrong, looking at his future without her.

The piano burst into life, cheerfully banging out the first notes to "Jingle Bells," and everyone in the room sang along with the melody. The room was crowded— besides Pierce's family, all of Frank's grown kids circled around the piano. The younger cousins from the other uncle had settled on the floor. The fire crackled, the Christmas tree glistened and snow gusted against the big bay window.

In the center of the room sat the happy couple. Pierce, looking pretty satisfied, had his arm around his bride. Tomorrow at two o'clock in the century-old church in town, they would join their lives as one. They were going to be happy. He was happy for them. Couldn't happen to a better couple, but all this true love and happily ever after made him think of what he had lost.

September. Somehow he would go on without her, not that it would be easy. She hadn't lost her heart, the way he had. He still loved her. It was as if his heart could not help feeling hers, and his caring unstoppable. What was the right thing to do? Did he turn away from her or help her?

He lifted his voice in song with the others, but his spirit wasn't in it.

Chapter Fourteen

Rain pinged off the windshield of September's truck as she pulled into the riding stable's graveled lot. It was still early on Christmas Eve morning and the place was quiet. She eased to a stop next to Colleen's SUV. Sitting in this truck was a constant reminder of Hawk. Every time she started the engine and it turned over without a hitch, she had him to thank.

It wasn't only the truck. Every time she walked beneath the gutter, it didn't leak. Every time she turned on her Christmas tree lights. Every time she saw those stars lighting up her front yard at night. She thought of him, the man she had sent away. He'd gone home to his family. Soon he would be deploying to a war zone. He was out of her life for good.

That was what she wanted, right? She didn't know anymore. The thought of never seeing him again killed her. An iron band had cinched around her ribs, squeezing tighter and tighter with every memory he'd left her.

Pain she had not been able to drive from her heart. She had sent him away thinking it was the one way to protect herself from pain, but she had been wrong.

She yearned to see his rugged face, to hear the deep notes of his voice, to feel safe and protected and whole again whenever he towered at her side.

Stop thinking of him, September. She launched out of the truck and closed the door with a bang that echoed like a gunshot in the nearly empty lot. A few vehicles were parked near the barn's entrance. The car and SUV she recognized as belonging to owners dropping by to ride their horses, but the white pickup sure looked like Hawk's.

Don't be silly, she told herself. All she could see was the top of the cab and the truck's bed. Plenty of people drove white trucks. It wasn't his. Hawk wouldn't come back to Fort Lewis until after Christmas and his trek in the backcountry. Gravel crunched beneath her boots, and she swiped rain from her face. Disappointment sank through her. Proof how badly she cared for him.

Be honest, September. You don't just care for him.

A movement caught her eye, a flash of red in the gray rain. A man's shadowed form swaggered out of the barn. Her palms went damp. Her knees turned to gelatin. Only one man had ever had that effect on her—one wonderful man.

Hawk. Joy exploded through her at the mere sight of him shouldering out into the rain. She drank in the sight of his cherished face, his blue eyes. His stalwart, noble presence made her feel alive.

"Figured I would find you here." He jammed his fists into his pockets. He didn't look like a man who was glad to see her.

No, he wouldn't be, she reminded herself. *You broke his heart, remember? You hurt him to save yourself.* She wasn't proud of it, but she could see now that she was still letting fear rule her. She might as well be back in that mine shaft, trapped in a grave of fear and darkness. That was no way to live. She squared her shoulders, steeled her spine and tapped down the concrete walkway, splashing in his direction.

"Hawk, what brings you here?" She was pleased with how normal she sounded, not at all like a woman who had been battling regrets or another lost chance at love. She hiked her chin higher, digging deep for every scrap of courage. Facing him was like seeing the littered remains of another lost future, more impossible dreams. She was stronger than loss, tougher than sorrow.

"I came to say goodbye to Comanche." No hint of emotion on his face. No warmth in his words. No welcoming smile softening his granite face.

"Comanche?" Her footstep faltered, her knees went weaker. She froze in place on the walkway, halfway between Hawk and the barn. The wind swirled rain and stirred the grass near her feet and the trees lining the walkway moaned with the wind.

He hadn't come to see her at all, she realized. Disappointment turned to torture. She wanted to dart straight for the office door. After all, work was waiting. But she would not use an excuse to avoid him or anything, not any longer. She fisted her hands, determined to see this through the right way. "I hope you two had a good chat."

"He seemed glad to see me. I'm short three peppermints." Hawk did her the courtesy of not smiling—of not reminding her of the dimples she loved and the tiny crinkles that dug handsomely into the corners of his eyes.

Whatever she did, she refused to acknowledge the memories trying to flood her brain. She would not remember him offering her his heart. She would not remember riding horses with him, or standing in front of a Christmas tree's glow or how her hand fit perfectly within his. The one thing she could not do—that she could never do—was remember the bliss of his kiss, the gentleness, the sweetness. Or her strength would falter. He looked all warrior, not like a man who had come to hope for a second chance at love.

"Seems I'll be shipping out earlier than expected." He sounded impersonal, as if they had never been more than passing acquaintances. As if the last few weeks hadn't happened and she hadn't obliterated his feelings.

"But you were on leave."

"I'm probably going to cut it short."

"Probably?" Realization dawned across her face. "Oh, you've decided to head out."

"I haven't made it official yet, but that's my plan." He stopped, unable to bridge the rest of the distance between them. Raindrops danced on the concrete he could not make himself cross. "I'm just tying up loose ends. Saying goodbye to friends."

"I hope you have a good tour." The wind blew a shock of hair into her face and she brushed it back. "Just come back safe and sound."

"I'll do my best." Being here hurt him something fierce, but he had come to say something, and he wouldn't leave until the job was done. "How's the truck running?"

"As good as when it was brand-new."

"I'm glad. An afternoon's job well worth it." Seeing

her forlorn and hurting was like a bullet to his chest. He didn't want to make this harder for her. If he put in his paperwork, then he had to head off to Afghanistan knowing there were no second chances. No maybes. That he wasn't destroying a remote chance with her because of it. He wanted more for his life, and he was not afraid to fight for it.

"Thank you for all you have done for me. I can't begin to tell you." She hesitated.

For a moment he thought he saw something change on her face, the quietest wish, the deepest longing for him. But then it was gone, and he couldn't be sure. Then he wasn't sure at all.

He was standing like an idiot in the rain, praying for a sign—any sign, the smallest sign—that he hadn't been wrong. That he hadn't mistaken friendship and gratitude for something grander. Everything within him wanted to ask her if there was a way they could make this work, if he had a chance of capturing her heart. But he could not do it yet. He could not risk frightening her away a second time. He had to tread carefully.

"It was nothing." He shrugged off her thanks for the few odds and ends he'd done. "A few nails here, an adjustment there, a new part to install. It was my pleasure."

"I wasn't talking about things. You helped *me*." She laid a hand over her heart. "I will never forget what you gave me."

At her words, everything went still. Even the rain seemed to stop falling. "What did I do?"

"You reminded me that there are precious gifts in this life and they are worth the cost."

For a moment—just a split second—he thought he saw a question in her beautiful brown eyes. A silent plea that settled in his soul. Hope resonated throughout his entire being. "How did I do that, sunshine?"

"I don't know. It's as if I came back to life the moment you first took my hand." She took a step closer. "I'm sorry for what I said. I hurt you, and I regret that more than you know. Please forgive me."

"Done. Don't worry about it. It's already forgotten." The shadows had slipped away from him, along with the tension of pain on his face. He stood straight and tall, invincible and every last bit of her only dream.

If he was anything less of a man, then she wouldn't be hurting like this. She wouldn't be falling apart over having lost him. She wouldn't be prepared to risk her heart again. But how did she tell him? She didn't have the words. All she had was emotion carrying her toward him. "I never wanted to see you again. I wanted to mean it, but you made me love again."

"I *made* you?"

"I couldn't stop myself." She fought to hold back her feelings. She told herself to be sensible. She couldn't afford to love him. He would go off on mission after mission, risking life and limb and her heart. She'd done it once and lost. Losing like that again would be too much. She knew the cost. She knew how much it would hurt. "I didn't want to love anyone again. I couldn't help loving you."

"You don't know how good that is to hear." He closed his eyes briefly, as if giving thanks. When he opened them, she could read his devotion. "The moment I looked down into that mine and saw your precious face, I was a goner. I love you, September, with all I am and all I will ever be. I was miserable back home facing the dreams I'd lost."

"What dreams?"

"The ones with you at my side every step of the way. Starting family traditions, singing around the piano, family get-togethers and our wedding." He cleared his throat, as if overcome by emotion. "I stood up for my best man. I was happy for him. Don't get me wrong. I want him and Lexie to live happily ever after. But I want one of those, too. I want forever with you, September."

Forever. Panic lashed at her. If she wanted to start believing in fairy tales again and in the kind of love that remained true and everlasting, then she shouldn't fall in love with a Ranger. But her heart refused to listen.

"I need to know if you want that, too." Hawk's plea warmed the rain and chased the sting from the wind. "If there's any possibility, any at all. I have to know."

She was breaking apart, the reasons why she couldn't love Hawk crumbling into dust. She had no shields left, no safeguards, no way to stop loving him. Love was a risk, for anyone, anytime. She knew the cost of loving a soldier. The endless worry. The sacrifice. The hardship. But was Hawk worth it?

The answer stood in front of her, a man of noble strength she could not live without. One word filled her mind, without doubt, without condition. "Yes."

"Yes?" Uncertainty turned to joy. His eyes twinkled, his grin flashed, dimples dug deep as instead of hugging her, which she expected, or doing something like punching his fist into the air, he went down on one knee. "Then I have another question for you.

It's one I've been rehearsing most of the night, on the flight and during the drive here. September, will you marry me?"

"Marry you?" She went weak. The blood drained from her face. Her legs turned to rubber.

He rose, taking her into his arms, offering her the security of his chest and the shelter of his arms. His lips brushed her temple in light, tender kisses. Each one a silent promise, a promise no words could do justice to.

"I love you so much, Hawk." It was terrifying to think of opening her heart fully again, but a smart woman learned from the lessons in her life. "Yes. I would love to be your wife. On one condition."

"What? Name it."

"That we don't waste a moment of the time we have together." She adored Hawk. The power of her feelings terrified her, but she was certain of her choice. "No long engagements. No big wedding to plan. No putting off what we want to do."

"I like the sound of that." He pulled a ring from his pocket and cradled her left hand in his. The platinum band glided over her finger. The square-cut sapphire surrounded by diamonds glowed. "Maybe we can start planning on our next date."

"Date?" She felt full to the brim and overflowing with love and hope. She couldn't think what he was talking about. "You just said you were being deployed—"

"I'm dropping out of the Rangers for you."

"No, Hawk. I'm not asking you to give up the job you love."

"I love you more, sunshine." He brushed the damp

hair away from her face, his touch affectionate and comforting. "You have been hurt enough. I don't want to put you through that again. I talked to my commanding officer and since you've agreed to marry me, I'm going to stay. I will be helping with training right here at Fort Lewis."

"And that would make you happy?"

"Happier than I can imagine. That's what I want to do for you, September. To live for you. I promise you this. I will do my best for you every day of my life. You are my light."

"And you are mine." Never had she felt so blessed. She had received the best Christmas gift—one of true, everlasting love. She was a girl who could believe in dreams again, because she was holding one in her arms. Her amazing husband-to-be drew her tightly against him and covered her mouth with his. Their kiss was triumphant. As if heaven thought so, too, the wind gusted and the rain turned to snow.

Epilogue

❧

One year later

The lights of the Christmas tree blinked cheerfully in front of the big picture window. September Hawkins, with her arms wrapped around a gigantic bowl of popcorn, froze in the middle of the kitchen. Every once in a while it still hit her. The wonderful man sitting on her couch was her husband. They were looking forward to their first anniversary next month, and she still couldn't believe it was real. Her life was a dream come true.

"Hey, sunshine." Hawk looked up from his half-finished string of popcorn. "Good thing you've got a fresh batch there. My bowl is mysteriously empty."

"I wonder how that could have happened." She was crossing the room without realizing it, drawn closer to him with a love that would never end. Bing Crosby was serenading them in the background, a pile of presents gleamed and glinted beneath the live Christmas tree and outside the window the lit stars were joined by a small family of lighted reindeer. "You eat everything that isn't nailed down."

"It's a fault of mine. Just add it to the list." Grinning, he set down his work and rose to help her. "You should not be carrying anything."

"As if the popcorn bowl is too heavy. Really. You are overprotective, Hawk." She didn't mind that when he took the bowl from her, he took the time to give her a kiss. His hand settled on her gently swollen midsection. "I'm fine. You are just using this as an excuse to come snuggle me."

"I'll use any excuse I can get." To prove it, he dispensed with the bowl and wrapped both arms around her. "We have to take advantage of the time we have left. Three more months and we won't be alone anymore."

"I can't wait to hold Little Timothy Frank Hawkins for the first time."

"Neither can I."

Happy, September wrapped her arms around Hawk's neck. Hawk had kept his promise to her. His vow to make her happy. To live his life for her. Her world was one of light and love, of joy and fulfillment. What a beautiful year she'd had first as his fiancée, as his bride and then his wife. Soon, they would be starting a new chapter of their marriage together—parenthood. Already their nursery was taking shape. Good thing the town house had three bedrooms. It would accommodate them for several more years before they had to upsize. For now, this place was just right. Full of love, filled with happiness and hope.

To think she had almost missed this opportunity, this life. It was hard to believe now she had once been too afraid to love him. She would have missed out on the greatest year of her life. And the best, she knew, was yet to come.

"Mistletoe." Hawk's lips grazed her cheek. "I felt it was my duty and obligation to hang it up while you were making the popcorn. After all, we have to start our own traditions."

"Yes, we do," she agreed. "Traditions are very important."

His kiss was sweet perfection, as their every kiss had been and always would be.

Life is beautiful, she thought, grateful to God for her blessings. The Lord's gentle grace had brought her through the darkness of her grief to this beautiful new beginning.

* * * * *

HIS HOLIDAY MATCHMAKER

Kat Brookes

In memory of my mother-in-law,
who went home to the Lord this past Christmas.
You were more than a mother-in-law to me.
You were my second mother. I thank you
for giving me the wonderful man I am married to.
You will be missed more than you could ever know.

And God is able to bless you abundantly,
so that in all things at all times, having all that
you need, you will abound in every good work.
—*2 Corinthians* 9:8

Chapter One

"Daddy! Daddy!"

"Cupcake!" Nathan Cooper replied with a grin as he swung his six-year-old daughter, Katie, up into the air.

She burst into a fit of girlish giggles. "I'm not a cupcake."

"Sure you are," he said as he lowered her to the ground. Reaching out, he ruffled her unruly curls. "Look at all this chocolate frosting."

"That's my hair," she said with another giggle, flashing him a smile that reminded him so much of her mother it hurt. So much of Isabel lived on in their daughter. Her dark eyes. Those long brown curls. That determined chin.

Nathan tamped down the memories of his late wife that threatened to surface. Forcing his focus solely on the tiny heart-shaped face looking up at him so adoringly, he playfully pinched his daughter's lightly freckled cheek. "And I suppose these aren't sprinkles?"

"No, silly. They're freckles!" She pulled away with another giggle and ran back to the porch. "Watch what I can do, Daddy."

He smiled as she dipped a large bubble wand into the bright yellow tray that sat on the sun-warmed porch steps and then spun in a slow circle, her motion creating a long, iridescent bubble. *To be so carefree*, he thought with an inner sigh.

The door to the small, ranch-style house creaked open, drawing his gaze that way.

"Nathan," Mildred Timmons greeted with a warm smile. A smiling, robust woman in her midsixties, Mildred had been a Godsend to him after losing both his wife and his parents in the storm two years before.

He'd been a couple of towns away, working on a construction project with his brothers, when the F4 tornado touched down, leaving a path of destruction across several Texas counties. The near mile-wide twister had swept across the northernmost part of Braxton, ripping down power lines, damaging buildings and taking the lives of those he loved in a few short minutes.

"You're done early," she said, wiping her hands on the apron she had tied about her rounded waist.

"Not really. I have a break before I have to get back to the site. Thought I'd take Katie into town for a hot dog. That is, unless she's already eaten dinner."

"You're in luck. She hasn't. We were gonna make some fish sticks and fries, but I'm sure she'd rather be having dinner with her daddy. You two haven't gotten to share many meals together lately."

He nodded with a frown. As co-owner of Cooper Construction, a business he'd started with his brother Carter five years earlier, he'd had his hands full dealing with the reconstruction needs left behind in the area by the tornado that struck two Decembers ago.

"We're working overtime to get the recreation center finished before Christmas Eve, but a few unexpected setbacks are pushing us down to the wire." With so many people counting on him and his brothers to get the job done in time, the pressure was on. He couldn't let the town down. Couldn't let Isabel down. Not only did the town council plan to hold their annual community holiday festivities in the newly erected building, they had decided to dedicate the new rec center to the townsfolk that were lost in the storm. So while he hadn't been there for Isabel when she'd needed him most, he was determined to do whatever it took to see to it the dedication took place as planned. That her memory lived on.

"I have faith in you boys," Millie said. "You'll make it in time."

Faith—it was something he used to hold dear to his heart. That was before he'd lost those he loved in a violent, senseless storm.

"Just don't stretch yourself too thin," she warned, drawing Nathan from his troubled thoughts. "Katie needs you."

And he needed her, too. But it was during this particular time of year he needed to bury himself in his work. Needed to forget about the future that had been so unfairly taken from him. From Katie.

"I might be a little late tonight," he said, avoiding the issue of his demanding work schedule. "Will that be a problem?"

"Oh, goodness, no," the older woman replied as her gaze followed the energetic six-year-old around the yard. "I love having Katie here with me. She's such a breath of fresh air for an old woman like me."

"You're far from old," he told her.

"Old enough," Millie countered.

"You know, Millie, I don't know what we would've done without you these past two years."

"I could say the same thing about all of you," she said, her voice catching. Her husband had been the only other tornado-related fatality in Braxton. He'd been out doing a check of the property's fence line when the storm struck and he hadn't been able to make it to shelter. "You boys, little Katie here, and Carter's lovely wife and children have become my family. I just wish…" She looked his way, her expression doleful.

"Wish what?"

"That you would open yourself up to love again."

He sighed. "Millie…"

"I know we've discussed this before," she admitted. "But I can't help it. I wanna see you meet a nice young lady like Carter did. Be happy again. You're too young to spend the rest of your life alone."

His brother was happy. No doubt about it. Audra and her two young children meant the world to Carter. But what if something happened to that perfect world he'd walked so willingly into? Like it had to his and Isabel's?

"I'm not alone," he said, fighting a frown. "I have Katie." Though he'd nearly lost her, too, when his own perfect world came crashing down around him. Isabel had taken their young daughter out to his parents' ranch to help put up their Christmas tree when the twister struck. Katie and his father had been pulled from the rubble and taken to the hospital. Katie survived. His father hadn't, dying a day after his beloved wife and daughter-in-law.

"Have faith," his father had said during his final moments in the hospital. "There is always hope beyond the storm."

But was there really?

"Yes, you do," Millie agreed with an empathetic smile. "All the more reason for you to start living again. Besides, Katie needs a woman in her life."

"She already does. Two, in fact. She has you and Audra." Turning, he whistled to get his daughter's attention. "Park your bubble wand, Cupcake. Daddy's taking you to Big Dog's for dinner."

"Big Dog's!" she squealed in delight. "Yay!"

He turned back to Mildred. "Would you like to join us?"

"Thank you for the offer, but I have a hankering for fish sticks for dinner," she told him with a kind smile. "You go spend some special time with your little girl."

He nodded. "We'll be back in an hour or so." That said, he stepped from the porch. Scooping up his daughter, he carried the giggling little girl out to his truck.

He and Katie were fine just the way they were.

"Well, if it isn't my two favorite customers."

"Hey, Lizzie!" Katie said with a toothy grin.

"Hey, Katie," the young waitress replied. "I see you roped your daddy into taking you out for dinner again."

"She's pretty good at wrangling me into doing her bidding," Nathan admitted with a chuckle. Lizzie was a sweetheart who was loved by all. She had been waitressing at Big Dog's ever since graduating from high school. "How's school going?"

"It's going," she said. "A little challenging juggling work and my online classes, but I'm determined to get that degree before I'm too old to do anything with it."

"You're only twenty-four," he reminded her.

"Sometimes it feels like I'm twice that."

"You'll manage," he assured her with a nod.

"I wish I could be as certain as you are," she replied. "It won't be long before I'm working, taking online classes and squeezing in the required classes that have to be taken at school. My head is bound to be spinning soon."

"Keep your eye on the goal," he told her. "That meteorology degree you're working toward will help save lives down the road."

The worry left her face, replaced by a bright smile. "Thanks for the pep talk. Why don't you go grab yourselves a table while I fetch a couple of menus?"

He looked to his daughter. "Where are we sitting today, Cupcake?" His daughter liked to pick a different one each time they came in.

"Over here," she exclaimed, skipping to an empty table halfway across the room.

He followed, sitting on one of the chairs with its bright red padded vinyl seat. The bell over the restaurant's front door jingled, drawing Nathan's gaze in that direction. Two young women he'd never seen before stepped inside. Both looked to be in their midtwenties. The first had straight, dark hair that stopped at her shoulders. The one walking in behind her had long, red-gold hair that shimmered like flames under the fluorescent lighting of the diner as she moved toward him.

He tipped his cowboy hat with a polite nod as they

walked by. "Ladies." Then he removed it, placing it on the seat of the empty chair beside him.

Both offered up warm smiles, but where the first woman remained focused on finding a table, the fiery-haired woman slowed, her topaz gaze lingering in his direction for a long moment before she continued on to where her friend had slid into an empty booth.

The way the woman had studied him had Nathan wondering if they hadn't crossed paths somewhere before. Surely, he would have remembered a face like hers if he had. Especially, those eyes. He'd never seen any quite that color. Like warmed honey with flecks of gold mixed in.

Lizzie returned with their menus and two glasses of ice water. "I'll give you a couple of minutes to look the menu over."

"Appreciate it," he told her, opening one of the menus as she walked away. Try as he might, Nathan couldn't keep his gaze from sliding over to the booth the two women were seated in. The one with the darker hair sat with her back to his and Katie's table. The other, the one whose searching gaze had come to rest on him for the briefest of moments, faced his way. Her attention, however, was now focused solely on her friend and the conversation they had immediately fallen into, giving him plenty of opportunity to study her more closely.

Delicate features made up her face with the exception of her boldly lashed amber eyes. Bow-shaped lips pursed together as she cast a glance out the window beside her. A second later, perfectly straight, white teeth were sinking into her bottom lip as if she were deeply troubled by something.

It was none of his business, but Nathan found himself wondering what she was worried about.

"Daddy," his daughter whined from across the table, drawing his attention back to the task at hand.

"Have you decided?" he asked her with a smile.

"Strawberry! Strawberry! Strawberry!"

Nathan chuckled as his daughter bounced up and down on the padded booth seat, excitement lighting her face. "I thought chocolate was your favorite milk shake flavor."

She stopped bouncing and looked up at him from across the table. "Daddy, it's a girl's peroggertiv to change her mind."

His eyes widened at the unexpected response. "Prerogative?"

Katie rolled her eyes. "That's what I said."

"So you did," he chuckled. "You know, that's a mighty big word for a six-year-old."

"Almost seven," she reminded him. "And Granny Timmons says it every time she breaks her one-cookie-before-supper rule and gives me another one."

Nathan couldn't help but smile. Suddenly, Lizzie hurried back to the table. "Sorry to keep you waiting. I had to handle a carryout order." She flipped open the order pad in her hand and poised her pen over it. "What can I get for the two of you?"

Dragging his focus back to the menu, he said, "Hmm…let's see. We'll take three super dogs, ketchup on one, mustard on the other two, a large order of fries and a strawberry milk shake."

"Will that be all?"

He cast a glance at his daughter over the top of his menu. "How about we make that *two* strawberry shakes? But we'd like those *after* my little Cupcake here eats all her dinner."

"You've got it, Mr. Cooper." Shoving her pencil behind her ear, Lizzie went to place their order.

"Daddy, do you got to go back to work?" his daughter asked, her tiny lips forming a soft pout.

He nodded. "For a little while, honey."

Her small shoulders sagged at his response.

Guilt tugged at him. "Tell you what. I'll see what I can do about taking the whole weekend off so you and I can do something special. How's that sound?"

Her face lit up. "Can we go Christmas shopping?"

An all-too-familiar twinge moved through his heart. One that came every year during the holidays. He didn't want to shop for presents or put up endless strings of Christmas lights to make his house festive. If it were up to him, he'd bypass the season altogether. But he couldn't do that to Katie.

"How about we take a walk over to The Toy Box after dinner and start putting together your wish list? Then maybe we can see a movie this weekend."

"I already know what I want," she replied with a toothy smile.

He leaned forward, arms folded atop the table in front of him. "Let me guess. You want a new swing set?"

She shook her head, sending her head full of dark brown curls bouncing. "Nope."

"A doll?"

"Uncle Logan just bought me a new dolly. Guess again," his daughter urged with youthful impatience.

Rubbing his chin as if in deep thought, he hemmed

and hawed for several seconds before saying, "I know. You want a giant pink pony?"

Katie giggled. "That's silly, Daddy."

"Okay, I give up. What do you really want for Christmas?"

She leaned forward, folding her arms just like his were and said determinedly, "I want a mommy."

Nathan was speechless. She'd had a mommy. And he'd had a wife. How could he make Katie understand that no other woman could ever fill the void left behind when Isabel died?

"You have your daddy," he pointed out, trying to sound unaffected by the turn in their conversation, when in truth he was anything but.

"I know, but Bettina's mommy braids her hair every morning before school."

"I can braid your hair." He'd done so for three of the birthday parties Katie had been invited to that past year and had done a pretty good job of it if he did say so himself.

"But her mommy makes a French braid."

He hated feeling like he had somehow failed his daughter. Something he never wanted to do. "I'll see what I can do."

Her eyes lit up. "About getting me a mommy?"

"About learning how to French braid your hair."

She sank back against the padded seat, crossing her tiny arms. "But I want a mommy."

"That's not gonna happen, Cupcake," he told her, fighting to keep the turmoil going on inside him from his voice.

Her stubbornness kicking in, his daughter lifted her chin and pouted.

"Katie," he began, only to be saved from saying anything else as Lizzie came back with their orders, instantly distracting his daughter from her mommy quest. Thankfully. Marrying again was not an option for him.

And it never would be.

December first had finally arrived. Alyssa McCall walked her best friend back to her SUV, a tight ball of anxiety in her stomach.

"Are you sure you wanna do this?" Erica asked.

She nodded. "Yes." Despite her fears and reservations, Alyssa truly felt that this was where she needed to be. Where the Lord wanted her to be. Not only would she be helping to reconstruct a part of the town that had been destroyed by the tornado, she would be proving herself to the interior design firm she worked for.

Since the car accident that had nearly taken her life three years before, she'd gone from being a highly sought after interior designer working full-time to being placed on the back burner with her firm, only being given small, mostly part-time jobs.

Pure Perfection Designs, the firm she'd been working for since college, felt that her visual disability, damage done specifically to the visual cortex of her brain in the accident that left her medically diagnosed as "legally blind," left her incapable of handling the more intricate design planning and extensive hands-on attention their customers were seeking. While the pathway sending visual messages from her eyes to her brain didn't always function as it should, she could still manage to perform the tasks required of her job. So this opportunity in Braxton was her chance to prove herself. To her firm and to herself.

"Isn't there some other way you can contribute to the cause without having to stay so long?" Erica asked with a frown as they stopped beside her friend's shiny new silver Ford Explorer. "We're talking about spending most of December in a town where you don't know anyone."

Alyssa laughed softly. "Hey! Weren't you the one giving me the you-can-do-this pep talk back at Big Dog's when I went into that teeny tiny panic attack?"

"Sorry," her friend apologized. "I have all the faith in the world you can do this. Really I do. It's just the mom in me coming out. It can't be helped."

"It's okay," Alyssa said with a grateful smile. "It's nice to know I have someone in my life that truly cares about me."

"The right man is gonna come along," her friend assured her, knowing that Alyssa longed to have the kind of family Erica had.

"Not if I keep dating Mr. Not-So-Rights." Not that she had dated much since the accident. As soon as her dates found out she was legally blind, they bailed. She supposed she couldn't blame them. A relationship with her would involve some major adjustments. But at least her visual impairment wouldn't get any worse than it was now. She could live with that, even if the men she had dated couldn't.

"Don't give up on love," Erica beseeched her. "Mr. Right is out there."

Reaching out, Alyssa opened the back passenger door to collect her suitcase. "I suppose I'll just have to take your word for it."

She leaned into the vehicle and grabbed her suitcase. Lowering the black spinner onto the sidewalk beside her, she stepped away from the SUV and turned to her friend. "I guess I'll see you in a few weeks. Maybe sooner."

Erica gave her a hug. "If you change your mind about doing this—"

"I know," she said, cutting her off with a grin. "You're only a phone call away."

"I'll miss you," Erica called out as she made her way around to the driver's side door.

"Same here," she replied, lifting her hand in a wave as her friend drove away. Then she stood watching as the blurred image of her friend's SUV disappeared from sight. A sudden surge of panic had her entire body tensing.

Her hand moved over the soft leather of the purse she had draped across her as she fought the urge to dig inside it for her cell phone. No, she thought determinedly, she would not call Erica to come back for her. Fear would not control her. She could do this. Closing her eyes, she prayed for the Lord to give her the strength to do what she had come to do. As she did so, a sense of calm slowly settled over her.

Opening her eyes, she let her gaze drift down what she knew to be the main street of town. Braxton, much smaller than San Antonio according to the information she'd found on the town's website, stretched out before her in a distortion of shapes and colors. The closer buildings she could almost make out, just not the fine details. Never since the damage done to her vision from the accident had she felt the loss of her perfect eyesight more. She was far from familiar surroundings in a town where she knew no one. At the same time, she was grateful that her impaired vision would get no worse when so many others were forced to live their lives in total darkness.

"Hurry up, Daddy!" a tiny voice squealed behind her.

Alyssa turned just as a flash of red whooshed by, bumping into her with enough force to knock her off-balance.

"Sorry!" the little girl called back over her shoulder as she raced away.

A strong hand closed around Alyssa's arm to steady her. "Sorry about that," a deep, very male voice apologized. "I'm afraid my daughter had a little too much sugar at dinner."

Her gaze climbed up the giant of a man standing before her. He had broad shoulders, a black cowboy hat shading a charming smile as he towered over her five-foot-two-inch frame. As their gazes met, Alyssa was startled by the intensity of the man's blue eyes. "It's all right," she managed.

He released the grasp he had on her arm and held out his hand. "Nathan Cooper."

"Alyssa McCall," she said, smiling as she placed her much smaller hand into his. "You were in the restaurant."

He nodded. "It's one of my daughter's favorite places," he explained with a warm smile. "Best milk shakes around if you find you have a hankering for one."

She laughed softly. "I'll be sure to keep that in mind."

"Daddy, come on!" The excited cry was followed by

the sound of bells tinkling as the store's door swung open.

Releasing her hand, his gaze shifted toward the store. "I'd best get in there before my hyperactive little bull takes out the entire china shop."

"This is a china shop?" she replied in confusion.

"What?" he asked with a chuckle.

Alyssa's brow creased with worry. "I'm supposed to be at The Toy Box."

He studied her for a long moment before pointing to the sign that hung over the storefront. One that was little more than a blur to her. "You're in the right place. Largest mom and pop toy store in the county."

She let out a sigh of relief. "You had me worried for a minute." She reached for the handle of her suitcase, but he was faster.

"Allow me."

"There's no need—"

He held up his other hand, effectively cutting off her refusal of his help. "It's the least I can do after my daughter practically ran you over."

She relented, allowing him to carry her suitcase for her. And he didn't stop there. He opened the door and held it, motioning her inside.

"Thank you," she said as she moved past him into the store. If everyone in Braxton was as kind as Nathan Cooper, her stay would be far easier than she'd prayed it would be.

Chapter Two

"You aren't by any chance a traveling Slinky sales rep, are you?" Nathan Cooper asked as he followed Alyssa inside.

"Excuse me?"

"The suitcase," he said, with a charming grin. "I'm guessing you're in toy sales of some sort."

She laughed softly at his teasing. "Not even close. I'm here to see Mr. Clark."

He nodded.

"Look, Daddy!" his daughter exclaimed as she pointed to the collection of animated figurines strategically placed in the storefront window. "It's Rudolph."

Alyssa stepped closer to watch the musical display. "You know, Rudolph's story was first told by Robert L. May in 1939 in a booklet he created for a department store called Montgomery Ward. That was over seventy years ago."

The little girl tipped her tiny face upward in wide-eyed amazement. "Rudolph's that old?"

"The story is that old," Alyssa explained with a smile. "But Rudolph is a very special reindeer," Alyssa said. "He doesn't get old. In fact, none of Santa's reindeer do."

"Because they're special, too!" Katie exclaimed.

Alyssa nodded. "That's right."

Nathan called out to his daughter. "We don't have much time, Cupcake. You'd best get started on that list."

His daughter, needing no more coaxing, scurried away to disappear between the aisles. Alyssa had spent enough time in physical therapy not to miss the slight limp to the little girl's gait. Probably nothing more than a bruised knee, but it brought Alyssa back to a time in her life she'd just as soon forget.

She turned to the girl's father. "I'm sorry. I didn't mean to distract her."

His gaze shifted in the direction his daughter had gone. "It's all right. Katie tends to get sidetracked easily and we don't have much time. I have to get back to work soon."

"Daddy, look at this!" His daughter hopped across the wood floor on a white stick pony.

Nathan Cooper smiled at her lovingly. "You're a regular cowgirl."

"Can I have it?"

"Not today, Cupcake, but we'll put it on the list."

"We can't put it on the list until you try it," she told him, worry creasing her tiny face.

"Me?" he replied, clearly confused by her request. "Why would I need to try it?"

"To know if it's a good horse or not."

"Honey…"

"Please, Daddy. You know everything about horses."

He glanced in Alyssa's direction. "I'm keeping you from your appointment."

"I'm a few minutes early, actually."

"You'll probably find Rusty in the back room, watching The Weather Channel."

Her smile faded. "Why? Are you expecting bad weather?" That would make getting around on foot so much harder.

He shook his head. "Nothing more than a light, though undoubtedly cold rain. And not until later this evening. Rusty just likes keeping up-to-date when it comes to the weather." That said, he reached for the toy pony his daughter was holding out to him.

Completely understandable, she thought, considering what the town had gone through. Reaching out, she retrieved the handle of her suitcase from his grasp. "Thank you so much for your help."

"My pleasure," he told her with a tip of his coal-black cowboy hat. One just as dark as the five-o'clock shadow on his firm jaw and midnight hair.

She parked her suitcase up against the wall next to the opening that led to the store's back room. A glance back over her shoulder found Nathan Cooper straddling the painted stick. His large frame making the toy appear even smaller.

He raised the horse's head with an impressively realistic whinny, eliciting laughter from his little girl and a smile from Alyssa. Turning away, she stepped into the smaller room in search of Mr. Clark.

Having seen the playful, loving interaction between Nathan Cooper and his young daughter, she now knew what a true knight on a white horse was. Even if this particular knight was dressed in blue jeans and a flannel shirt and the horse had mop strings for hair.

"Mr. Clark?"

The leather chair creaked in protest as it spun away from the paper-strewn desk. A compact television with The Weather Channel playing on it sat atop a smaller table next to the desk.

"Forgive me," the older man apologized as he pushed his portly form out of the chair. "I didn't hear the front bell ring. Then again my hearing hasn't been the same since the tornado."

"It's quite all right," Alyssa replied with an empathetic smile, speaking slightly louder than she had been. She stepped forward, extending her hand. "I'm Alyssa McCall. We spoke on the phone."

"Ah, yes," he replied with a nod as he shook her hand in greeting. "So glad to have you here."

"I'm thrilled to be a part of this." More than he could ever know.

He stepped past her to a small table by the window to pour himself some coffee. "Would you care for some?"

"No, thank you." It was too late in the day for caffeine. She'd be up all night. And after the keyed-up day she'd had so far, she was going to require a good night's sleep in order to give her all to the job the next morning.

"Your firm's offer to help out with the finishing touches on the recreation center was quite generous, Mrs. McCall. On behalf of the town council, we are truly grateful."

"It's Miss," she gently corrected. "And my company

was more than glad to be of part of such a positive undertaking for your community."

"I have to admit," he began as he took a sip of the coffee he'd just poured himself, "that we never expected to have a professional interior designer join us on this project. I'm beyond thrilled."

She just hoped he wouldn't be disappointed. While she wanted to believe her skills were still sharp, not having as much opportunity to make use of those skills as she once had meant there was a possibility that her expertise might have diminished somewhat.

"Miss McCall?"

Alyssa snapped out of her thoughts with an apologetic smile. "Yes?"

"I was just saying that Myrna and Doris have a room for you over at The Cat's Cradle."

"The Cat's Cradle?"

"It's the boardinghouse they run at the far end of town. I'm sure you're aware the town agreed to take care of your accommodations during your stay here. The Wilson sisters have very generously offered to provide your lodgings at no cost to the town."

"That's so kind of them, but isn't renting rooms at the boardinghouse their livelihood? I'm more than willing to pay for my stay there."

"Nonsense." He waved the suggestion off. "In fact, the council already offered to pay them, but they refused to accept any money. This is their contribution to the rebuilding of our town. Besides, those two run the boardinghouse because they rarely venture away from The Cat's Cradle and welcome any and all company that comes their way. Neither one of them is in need of money. Trust me."

So far every person she had met or heard about in Braxton was unbelievably kind and giving. That eased her worries about being in a town where she knew no one. "I look forward to meeting them."

"I'm sure that goes both ways." The words had barely left his mouth when his smile faded, replaced by a worried frown. "You aren't allergic to cats are you?"

She shook her head. "Not that I know of. Why?"

"Because Doris has a real soft spot for felines." He started back to his desk. "I'll call and let them know you're on your way. You can stop by the rec center in the morning to see how things are coming along and decide on its finishing touches. Light fixtures, paint, trim and furniture of some sort."

"I'd like that. Is the boardinghouse within walking distance?"

"Maybe when the sun's shining. But there's the possibility of rain moving in. You'd be better off driving there."

"I'm afraid I don't own a car."

"Then how on earth did you get here?"

"A friend of mine drove me here," she explained. "She'll be back to pick me up once the job is finished."

"Which should be just in time for our annual Christmas Eve celebration. You and your friend are welcome to join us for it if you have the time. And while I'm at it, I would highly recommend seeing the reenactment of our Savior's birth the local church here puts on Christmas Eve afternoon. Brings tears to a grown man's eyes I tell you."

"It sounds wonderful. But Erica has family in San Antonio she'll be spending time with over the holidays. She's not scheduled to pick me up until the day after Christmas. But even if she can't make it for the church's program, I'll be certain not to miss it."

He sipped at the steaming coffee, studying her curiously. "No holiday plans for you?"

She lowered her gaze to the papers on his desk. "No."

"Well, we're glad to have you join us here in Braxton for the holidays."

"Thank you, Mr. Clark. I really appreciate that," she told him with a smile. "Now, can you tell me how to get to The Cat's Cradle?"

Rusty Clark's gaze shifted past her and a smile moved across his weathered face. "This here young man can take you there."

She turned to find Nathan Cooper's broad shoulders filling the open doorway.

"Take her where?" the cowboy replied, his gaze meeting hers.

"To The Cat's Cradle," the elderly store owner said. "Now that the sun's gone down, it's sure to be too cold for our town's guest to be walking that far."

Nathan nodded. "You'll get no argument from me there."

"I don't mind the cold," she insisted. "Besides, I'd rather not impose."

"It's no imposition" came his husky reply.

"*Miss* McCall," Rusty said, "I'd like you to meet Nathan Cooper."

"We've already met," she said, her gaze fixed on the man in the doorway. His face wasn't as clear as it had been when she'd looked up at him out on the sidewalk outside, but that didn't matter. She recalled every chiseled contour of his handsome face. The startling blue of his eyes. The slightly crooked hitch of his smile.

Rusty Clark clapped his hands together. "Wonderful. It saves me the time of making introductions. Something tells me the two of you are gonna work real good together."

"We'll what?" Both Nathan and Alyssa replied in unison.

"I assumed you already knew, seeing as how the two of you are already acquainted. Nathan and his brother's company is in charge of construction for the rec center."

She looked his way. "I had no idea. I'm looking forward to seeing what you've done so far. I can't wait to start on the design plans for it."

Nathan Cooper held up a hand. "Hold up. Design plans?" He shot a questioning look in the older man's direction.

"Miss McCall's design firm has ever so generously offered to donate their services for the project and have sent us one of their top designers to do the job."

"I thought I was handling the project through to completion," he replied as he moved farther into the room to join them. "Does the council have some sort of problem with the work I've done so far?"

Mr. Clark shook his head. "Goodness, no. Your work, as usual, has been top-notch."

Alyssa bit at her bottom lip. She hadn't meant to step on anyone's toes when she'd accepted her firm's offer to send her to Braxton for this project. "If my helping out is gonna be a problem..."

"Nonsense," the councilman assured her. "Your assistance is more than welcome here. Nathan has already given this town so much of his time when it comes to the rebuilding efforts, accepting your offer was the least I could do for him."

"You might have let me know sooner," the glowering cowboy replied stiffly, his entire demeanor changing.

"Her firm only contacted me a few days ago with their very kind offer," Mr. Clark explained. "I had hoped to surprise you."

"Well, you succeeded." Some of the harshness in Nathan Cooper's expression faded as he looked her way. "Welcome to the team."

"Thank you."

"Now that we have that settled, what brings you here?" Mr. Clark inquired of Nathan. "Problem at the site?"

Nathan shook his head. "No. We're moving right along, all things considered. I just stopped by with Katie so she could add a few dozen more things to her Christmas list."

The older man chuckled. "Just like her moth…" His words trailed off.

A deafening silence fell in the room.

Alyssa looked between the two men, unsure of what had just happened. The tension in the air was palpable.

"I really should be getting back to work," Nathan said, breaking the uncomfortable silence. He turned to her. "Miss McCall?"

"Alyssa, please," she replied. "And I'm ready to leave whenever you are."

"We'll talk more tomorrow," Mr. Clark told her as he walked them out to the front of the store.

"I look forward to it." She reached for the handle of

her suitcase only to find a much larger hand already wrapped around it—again. The warmth of his skin soothed her chilled fingers. Glancing up, she found Nathan Cooper staring down at her.

"Allow me."

"Thank you, but I think I'll walk to the boarding-house after all. The crisp air will do me good."

He shrugged his broad shoulders, looking almost relieved. "Suit yourself."

Releasing his hold on her suitcase, Nathan tipped his hat, then turned toward the aisles of toys. "Let's go, Cupcake," he hollered. "Daddy's gotta get back to work."

A tiny whine floated through the air somewhere in the vicinity of the doll aisle. "But I'm not done yet," his daughter said as she stepped into view.

"We'll come back another time," he assured her. Right now he just had to get out of there. Away from the festive holiday music and mechanical Christmas characters. Away from the woman who was going to invade his life and stir up memories he'd just as soon forget.

He flexed his hand. The one she'd touched briefly. A light, gentle touch. Accidental. But it had been so long since he'd had any sort of physical contact with anyone other than his daughter it had taken him completely off guard.

"Daddy, what's this?" his daughter inquired as she skipped up to him.

He stared at the sprig of green tied with a red bow, which she held pinched between her fingers. "It's mistletoe."

"Whose toe?"

Alyssa McCall's soft laughter filled the room. "It's called mistletoe. Back in eighteenth-century England, if a young woman stood under some mistletoe, brightly trimmed with ribbons, she couldn't refuse to be kissed. In many cases, that special kiss under the mistletoe led to love and marriage."

Nathan stared at her in disbelief. Was the woman a walking encyclopedia on holiday traditions?

"It can make people fall in love?" Katie repeated in awe.

Miss McCall nodded. "So they say. Apparently, there's something very special and romantic about mistletoe."

"Can we buy some, Daddy?"

"Not today." *Or ever.* "Now go put that back where you found it and let's get going."

She scowled as she returned the sprig of mistletoe to its hook on the aisle's end cap display.

"I'd reconsider taking that ride with Nathan to the boardinghouse," Mr. Clark advised Alyssa as she neared the door, pulling her suitcase behind her. "It's gonna be a mighty cold walk to the other end of town."

"In the rain," Katie added as she bounced over to press her nose against the store's front window.

"It's raining?" the woman who had so unsettled Nathan gasped.

"Big fat drops!" his daughter exclaimed.

Alyssa looked his way.

Nathan shrugged. "Looks like they were wrong about the rain not moving in until later."

"Oh, no."

"My offer still stands."

"If you don't mind," she replied, looking less than thrilled.

"We don't mind a bit," Katie answered for him as she opened the door, letting a gust of wind-blown rain inside. "Daddy's got a real big truck with a real big seat."

Rusty's hearty chuckle followed them out the door.

Nathan swept Katie up in his arms, carrying her out to the truck. The last thing they needed was for her to slip on the wet sidewalk and reinjure her bad leg.

"How old are you?" his daughter asked Miss McCall as they settled into the truck's roomy cab.

"Katie," Nathan admonished. Was there ever a more inquisitive child?

"It's okay," Alyssa McCall replied with a smile. "I'm used to dealing with children's questions. I teach art at a recreational center back in San Antonio."

Her reply took him off guard. "I must have misunderstood. I thought Rusty said you were an interior designer."

"I am. I have my degree as well as plenty of work experience in the field. However, I'm only working part-time in interior design at the present." She glanced down at Katie. "And to answer your question, I'm twenty-seven."

"Are you married?"

"Katie Marie!" he gently reprimanded, staring down at his too-curious-for-her-own-good little girl who was seated on the bench seat between them.

The question didn't seem to daunt Miss McCall who answered with a simple, "No, Katie, I'm not."

"My daddy's—"

"Here we are," Nathan announced, effectively cutting off his daughter's reply. The large wooden sign welcoming guests to The Cat's Cradle swung in the cold, wet, winter wind. It was a welcome sight as he turned into the half-circle drive. A second later, he was pulling up in front of the old Victorian boardinghouse.

Katie squirmed in the seat. "It's the kitty house!"

"She has a thing for cats," he explained.

Miss McCall looked down at his daughter. "Me, too."

"Do you have a kitty of your own?" Katie asked, curiosity lighting her eyes.

"I'm afraid not. No pets are allowed in the town house I rent back in San Antonio."

"I don't have a pet either," his daughter said with a sigh. "Daddy's afraid—"

Nathan cleared his throat, cutting in. "I really do have to get back to work." He had to make certain the rec center was completed in time. Not so much for the Christmas Eve party that was to be held there, but for the dedication ceremony that would open the festivities, honoring those lost in the storm. He hadn't been there for Isabel that day, but he would be there to see the project through and his wife's memory honored.

"Of course," Miss McCall said apologetically. "I'm so sorry for throwing you off schedule."

"It's not a problem," he replied as he swung open the driver's side door. "Wait here, Cupcake. I'm gonna get Miss McCall's suitcase and then see her to the door."

"I wanna see the kitties."

"Another time, honey," he said, ruffling her hair. "Uncle Carter is waiting for Daddy to come help him with the rec center."

She let out an exaggerated sigh. "Okay."

"You don't have to see me to the door," Miss McCall told him. "I'll just grab my suitcase and you can go."

"Daddy doesn't mind helping you," his daughter cut in before he had a chance to reply. "He has really big muscles."

Miss McCall met his gaze, the corners of her mouth twitching as if trying very hard to suppress a grin. "Well, then, I guess I should let your daddy help me."

"Will I get to see you again?" his daughter asked, a little too eagerly for Nathan's comfort.

Alyssa offered her a warm smile. "You can pretty much count on it."

Not if he could help it. Not with Katie in mommy search mode. Nathan stepped out into the rain and rounded the truck. Opening the tailgate, he pulled her suitcase out from beneath the covered bed.

"Thank you for the ride," she said as she stepped up beside him, attempting to shield the both of them from the rain with the floral print umbrella she held clutched in her hand.

"Thank you for handling my daughter's meddling questions so well," he said as he walked her up the wet porch steps. Reaching out, he knocked on the door.

"Children are naturally curious. I didn't mind," she assured him as she lowered the umbrella to shake the excess rain from it. "You're blessed to have such an adorable little girl, curiosity and all."

"I tend to think so, but then my opinion might be a bit biased when it comes to my daughter."

She turned to look up at him. "About my helping out with the recreation center..."

A slight frown pulled at his mouth, try as he might to fight it. "Yes?"

"My intention in coming here was to do something to help your town," she said, closing the umbrella. "If that is gonna be a problem for you…"

"Don't trouble yourself any over that," he told her. "I'll deal with it."

Chapter Three

He'd deal with it. Not a very promising start to their working relationship. The door swung open before Alyssa had a chance to reply and a tall, slender woman with a beehive of silver hair waved them inside.

"Come on in out of the weather, you two. I'll heat some water up for tea. Something to take the chill off."

"Appreciate the offer, Doris," Nathan Cooper replied with a smile, "but I can't stay. I'm just dropping Miss McCall here off."

The older woman looked to Alyssa. "Myrna and I have been expecting you. Rusty called to let us know you were on your way. Welcome to The Cat's Cradle."

"Thank you for having me," she said, propping her wet umbrella against the porch wall next to the door before stepping inside.

"It's our pleasure," Doris said, her gaze shifting to Nathan. "Are you sure you can't stay for tea?"

Nathan set her suitcase down in the front foyer. "Katie's waiting for me in the truck. I have to run her out to Mildred's place before I head back to work."

"Just be careful on those roads," Doris warned. "It's really coming down hard out there."

"You can count on it." His gaze shifted to Alyssa. "Guess I'll be seeing you tomorrow."

She nodded, then stood watching as the blurred outline of Nathan Cooper faded away behind a curtain of rain.

"A fine-looking young man, that one," Doris muttered behind her.

She turned from the window. "I was watching the rain."

"Of course you were, dear." She turned toward the winding oak staircase and cupped her hands to her mouth. "Myrna! Our guest is here."

Maybe she had been admiring the way Nathan Cooper carried himself, but that was it. She was there to do a job. Not to start something up with a man on the divorce rebound. Katie would just have to look elsewhere for someone for her daddy.

An elderly woman wearing a bright floral housecoat and fuzzy pink slippers came scurrying down the stairs. "Miss McCall!"

"Call me Alyssa, please."

Myrna stood before Alyssa, a welcoming smile parting her wrinkled cheeks. Her blue-gray hair hung in a single braid over one shoulder. "We're so happy to have you staying here with us."

"Indeed," Doris agreed with a nod. "Braxton isn't exactly the tourist capital of Texas."

A fluffy white ball shot down the stairs and past their legs, disappearing into an adjoining room.

Myrna laughed. "That blur of white is the newest addition to our family, Bluebell."

"You like cats, don't you?" Doris asked.

Alyssa nodded. "Yes, I do." Although she'd never had one of her own.

"Good, because our dear little ones tend to crave affection."

She could relate to their need.

"You have the prettiest eyes," Doris observed, then leaned closer in her inspection of them.

Too bad they didn't work. That wasn't exactly true. Her eyes were perfect. The visual cortex part of her brain, which had been damaged in the accident, was the reason for her visual impairment.

Myrna leaned closer, as well, inspecting Alyssa's eyes through her glasses. "She does. They're just like topaz under the sun."

"Goes well with her hair color."

Doris nodded. "I always thought green eyes complimented auburn hair the best, but I do believe I was wrong."

Alyssa blushed at their compliments and their close scrutiny. "You're both too sweet."

Just then two kittens with calico markings scampered into the entryway. Doris bent to pick them up. "This is Rhett and his favorite girl, Scarlett."

"Well, hello there," Alyssa said, scratching each of them behind their ears.

"Come on, dear," Doris said. "Let me give you a quick tour of the downstairs. Then I'll show you to your room."

"I'd like that."

"I'll go put some water on for tea," Myrna called out as Doris led her into the parlor.

The house was purely Victorian, from the striped

damask curtains to the countless gilded picture frames that lined the walls. Taking a walk through the rooms helped Alyssa familiarize herself with the house's layout. Like Alyssa's town house, the women's home was filled with warm, white lights and holiday decor.

When the tour ended, Doris led her upstairs to the room she'd be staying in. Alyssa stepped inside and looked around, her gaze drawn to the off-white, antique cast-iron bed. She walked over to it, running her fingers over the faded beige ribbon-threaded quilt.

"Our mother made it," the older woman announced behind her.

"It's beautiful."

"She loved quilting. Unfortunately, neither Myrna nor I inherited our mother's sewing abilities," she said, a hint of sadness in her voice.

Alyssa turned to face her. "We all have our own special abilities. You and Myrna run a boardinghouse, and yet you still find time to take in strays and love them unconditionally. It's more than some children can say about their own parents." The second the words left her mouth, Alyssa wished she could take them back.

"Your parents didn't show you love?"

"I was simply making a reference," Alyssa replied with a nervous laugh.

"Of course you were," Doris said from the open doorway. "If you ever need to talk, dear, Myrna and I are very good listeners. Now you go get settled in and then come down to the kitchen and join us for a cup of tea."

"I'll do that. Thank you." Tears pricked at the backs of her eyes as the older woman stepped from the room, closing the door behind her. No, she would not think about her mother and the love she'd never been able to show Alyssa. That was something that would never change. Her mother was gone now, so there was no use wishing for what could never be.

Instead, she would strive to focus on only the good things God had blessed her with in Braxton. Like the kindhearted sisters who had so generously opened their home to her. Like the adorably inquisitive Katie Cooper and her stick-pony-riding father.

Nathan glanced toward his daughter, who appeared to be thoroughly captivated by the rain outside. As long as it wasn't storming with gusting winds, she was fine. Let the wind pick up and Katie became panicked. Understandable, all things considered.

He thought back to what she'd said earlier. Since losing her mother, Katie had never once voiced her discontent with the way things were. He'd assumed that Mildred's presence in her life, and then that of Audra's, satisfied any need his daughter might have for a mother figure. And maybe it had in the past, but something had changed. His little girl was looking for a mom.

That tugged at his heart. He would give his daughter the world if he could, but giving her another mother was asking for more than he was ready to do. And what if he did remarry again, for Katie's sake, and things didn't work out? Where would that leave his daughter? Motherless again. Heartbroken. Emotionally withdrawn. No, it wasn't worth the risk.

So how was he supposed to handle this situation? Ignore it? Tell Katie to stop wishing for what she could never have? It was moments like this that he missed Isabel the most. She always knew the right thing to say.

He pulled up to Mildred's place and shifted the truck into Park.

"Daddy, look how big the puddles are outside," Katie exclaimed, her lightly freckled nose pressed against the passenger window.

"It's coming down in bucketfuls," he acknowledged with a nod. Crazy weather patterns. High sixties and sunshine that afternoon. Cold rain that evening.

"I wanna jump in them."

At least his daughter's thoughts had moved on to something other than Alyssa McCall's marital status. He tossed his partially soaked cowboy hat onto the backseat to dry, then stepped out into the rain. As he rounded the back of the truck, he shrugged out of his coat. Then, opening the passenger door, he gathered his daughter up in his arms, wrapping her up in his coat to shield her from the rain's onslaught. "The winds are picking up. We don't want you blowing away."

Katie stiffened in his arms with a muffled gasp. "I don't wanna be blown away," she cried out, her arms clutching his neck.

He mentally chastised himself for his careless choice of words. He tightened his hold on her with a sigh. "Don't you worry, honey, Daddy would never let that happen to you."

"But it happened to Mommy."

And there wasn't a day that went by that he didn't blame himself for Isabel's death. He'd been off with his brothers working on a job site. He hadn't been there when his family had needed him the most.

Before he had a chance to reply, the front door swung open and Mildred walked out. "There you two are. I was beginning to worry."

He set Katie on her feet. "We had to swing by The Cat's Cradle first."

"Yeah," Katie joined in, her mood shifting back to its normal carefree state. "We had to give Alyssa a ride there."

"*Miss* McCall," Nathan corrected as he shoved a hand back through his wet hair.

"Miss McCall?"

He nodded. "Apparently, she's gonna be helping out with the decorative touches to the rec center."

"She's real pretty," his daughter added with a glance in his direction.

The older woman smiled, her gaze shifting to Nathan, as well. "Oh, is she now?"

He shrugged. "I didn't pay that much attention." But he had. Enough to know that Alyssa's hair was an unusual shade of red-gold that seemed to come to life under the light. Enough to know that her thick lashes framed eyes the color of warm honey.

"I see," the older woman said, but her expression said that she didn't quite believe him. "Come on in out of that rain and you can tell me all about this Miss McCall."

"I'm soaked clean through," he said, nudging his daughter into the warmth of Mildred's house. "I need to swing by the house and pick up some dry clothes before I head back to work." What he failed to add was that Miss McCall was the last person he wanted to talk about. She was invading his thoughts with those honey-colored eyes and disarming smile, and was taking over part of the job he should have been oversee-ing and making his daughter want things, like a new mother, even more, which she couldn't have. Reaching out, he ruffled his daughter's hair. "I should be back to pick Katie up around nine thirty."

"Why don't you just leave Katie here for the night? No sense traveling on these roads any more than you have to on an evening like this."

Katie clapped her hands together. "Can I stay, Daddy? Please! Please!"

Mildred was right. The rain coming down as hard and fast as it was could make for unexpected flash floods. Better safe than sorry. "All right, Cupcake. I'll swing by at lunch tomorrow to check on you."

"Yippee!"

He bent to kiss the top of her baby-fine hair and then straightened, turning to Mildred. "Call my cell if you need me."

"We'll be fine. You just concentrate on getting the rec center done. The town is counting on you."

He nodded. "I'm doing my best."

He was the kind of man who put his heart into every job, but this time was different. Every minute, no every second he spent working toward finishing the rec center in time for the town's Christmas Eve party was a painful reminder of what he and Katie had lost. Of the Christmases they would no longer share as a complete and happy family.

Despite the turmoil that filled him, he had commit-ted himself to seeing the job through. At least, as far as the building's structure was concerned. Rusty had procured help putting up the holiday trimmings from the church's Bible group as well as the local ladies' bingo club. Katie would go to the party with Nathan's brother Carter and Audra and their kids, allowing him to avoid all that holiday cheer. Then afterward, they'd drop Katie off at home and the two of them would have a quiet Christmas Eve at home, just the two of them.

Pushing all thoughts of Christmas aside, Nathan turned his focus back to the road ahead. Water covering the pavement made hydroplaning a possibility. He eased up on the gas as he drove down the wet road. Leaving Katie at Mildred's for the night had definitely been a wise decision.

As soon as he arrived at his place, Nathan called Carter, leaving a message on his brother's cell phone that he was on his way. Then he hurried upstairs to his room to change out of his wet clothes.

When he finally arrived at the rec center, nearly half an hour later, Nathan slid out of the warmth of his truck and back into the cold, wet rain. Raising the collar of the dry coat he'd switched over to, he hurried across the rain-soaked parking area to the newly erected building. One that housed an indoor swimming pool, a TV and game room, an arts and craft room as well as several other recreation-devoted rooms. In the spring, once the weather cleared, an outdoor basketball court, a couple of shuffleboard courts and several picnic tables would be added.

He swung open the front door of the newly constructed building and stepped inside. Removing his jacket, he hung it over a nearby sawhorse, set his still-damp cowboy hat atop it and then moved farther into the room, spotting his brother atop a ladder. "Sorry I'm late."

"Don't apologize," Carter called down from his

perch where he stood working on the wiring for one of the overhead lights. "You've been working day and night to get this job done. Katie needs you, too."

No, what Katie needs is a mommy, Nathan thought, his daughter's words having burrowed themselves under his skin like a thorn.

"How is my little Katydid?" his brother asked as he moved down the ladder.

"Lively as usual," he muttered, looking around. "Where's the crew?"

"In the arts and crafts room, finishing the trim on the windows."

Nathan nodded distractedly.

"Something troubling you?" Carter asked as he walked over to join him. Just a year younger than Nathan, Carter had always been able to read his moods. Their momma used to tell them they were meant to be twins, only Carter decided to hold out a year longer before making his own grand entrance into the world.

"No," he muttered. "Why?"

His brother snorted. "You always were a poor liar. What's going on?"

Nathan stepped past him to collect his tool belt from the eight-foot folding table that held an array of power tools along with several boxes of nails and drywall screws. "Katie wants a new mother," he said with a sigh as he slung the leather belt around his waist and buckled it.

"What?" his brother choked, sounding every bit as surprised as he'd been.

He turned with a frown. "That's what my daughter wants for Christmas. A mother. She even went so far as to give her own little 'mommy interview' to this woman who just arrived in town."

His brother shook his head with a sigh. "Tough one. Not that I don't understand Katie's wanting a mother in her life. I reckon a girl needs that."

"She has Mildred and Audra. That's as close as she's gonna get to having a mother figure in her life. Speaking of which, how is Audra doing?"

His brother's face beamed at the question. "She's holding up. The morning sickness tends to get the better of her, but knowing the wondrous gift we're gonna have soon helps get her through the day. The doctor says the nausea should only last another month or so."

"Glad to hear it. You couldn't have chosen a better mother for your child." Audra had given up everything she'd known to move to Braxton with her children after her husband divorced her, abandoning his children in the process. She was determined to give them a better life. Then she met his brother and they fell in love, giving her children the true family they had always wanted.

"Agreed," Carter said, a hint of heartfelt emotion pulling at his voice. "Getting back to Katie's request for a momma. She's too young to understand what you went through when you lost Isabel. But I do. I remember praying for you every day. Wishing I could do something to bring back the brother I knew. One who used to live life to its fullest. Who smiled often. And loved completely."

"Carter—"

His brother held up a hand, cutting him off. "I don't blame you for being afraid of letting someone else into your heart." Reaching out, he clasped a hand atop his brother's shoulder. "I saw what losing Isabel did to you. I had no intention of ever putting myself in that position. But then the Lord brought Audra into my life and I couldn't keep myself from loving her. Our daddy was right. We have to have faith. In ourselves. In our love. And, more importantly, in the Lord's plan for us."

Their father had told them from his deathbed in the hospital, *Have faith. There is always hope beyond the storm.* Despite those weakly uttered last words, all three of Caldwell Cooper's sons had decided that day that faith wasn't enough. If it had been, their loved ones would still be there. They'd made a pact that none of them would ever take the risk of loving and losing again. Katie was the only exception to their rule. She was already a part of their lives and needed all the love they could give her. Then Carter had to go and let his heart get in the way of common sense. But Nathan understood. Audra was a woman worth loving and she had given her heart completely to his brother.

"So tell me about this woman our little Katie interrogated," his brother said, lifting an arm to wipe the sweat from his brow with the sleeve of his flannel shirt.

"She's from San Antonio," Nathan told him. "Apparently, she's an interior designer. Her company offered to send her here pro bono to help with the finishing touches to the rec center."

His brother arched a questioning brow. "Rusty accepted that without consulting us?"

He nodded.

"I thought we were supposed to be handling the entire project," Carter muttered, clearly ruffled by Rusty's lack of communication with them on the matter.

"So did I."

His brother shrugged. "Reckon we can use all the help we can get if we wanna get the rec center completely finished in time. I just wish Rusty had given us some notice."

"From what I understand, this was a last-minute offer." His frown deepened. "Apparently Alyssa has a degree and several years experience, and the board jumped at the chance to have her join in on the project—"

"Alyssa?" his brother cut in, his dark brow arching even further.

"Alyssa McCall. That's her name," Nathan stated matter-of-factly. "As I was saying, she has expertise in interior design and Rusty jumped at the opportunity to have her handle that part of the project."

His brother stroked his whisker-stubbled chin in thought, then let his hand fall away with a casual shrug. "I suppose it's all for the same cause and she does have a degree..."

"We don't need her help," Nathan muttered in irritation. Making decisions on the final touches for a lot of their jobs had once been Isabel's responsibility. She hadn't needed some fancy degree to make everything come together. She was a natural. Now he and Carter, along with whoever was contracting their construction services, made those decisions.

"Look at it this way," his brother said, understanding in his eyes. "It'll free up a little more time for you to spend with Katie instead of spending it all here."

Nathan scoffed. "You're beginning to sound like Mildred."

"She must be rubbing off on me," his brother said with a grin. "So, is she pretty?"

"Mildred?"

Carter rolled his eyes. "I already know what a pretty gal Millie is. I was referring to Miss McCall. More important, is she single?"

Nathan groaned. "I've just figured out where Katie gets her nosy nature from."

"I wasn't asking for you. I was asking for Logan."

"Our brother happens to be a confirmed bachelor," he replied with a frown.

His brother eyed him curiously.

"What?" Nathan demanded.

"The little lady caught your eye," Carter accused, his grin widening. "That's why you're so bristly about her being here. She must be a pretty one."

Nathan's patience with the conversation ended. "I don't care how pretty she is. The only woman I ever loved is gone. I'm not looking to replace her. So stop—" his words were cut off by the ringing of his cell phone.

Pulling it from his jeans pocket, he glanced down at the caller ID and then back at his brother. "It's Millie," he said.

His brother nodded, stepping away while he took the call.

"Hello?"

"Nathan," Mildred said, her voice quivering. "I'm sorry to bother you at work."

The tremor in her voice had his heart dropping like a lead weight. "What's wrong?"

"I'm afraid there's been an emergency," she told him.

Despite their strength, his muscular legs threatened

to give way beneath him. He struggled to take a breath. *Please, God, not again.*

Carter was beside him in an instant. "What is it, Nathan?"

He waved his brother off and forced the dreaded question from his suddenly bone-dry mouth. "Is it Katie?"

"Oh, goodness, no. She's right as rain," Millie assured him. "It's my sister."

Relief swept through him with gale force. "Your sister," he repeated as he dragged a hand back through his hair. Then his thoughts shifted to concern for Millie, who had been through enough after losing her husband. "Is she all right?"

"From what I understand, Eleanor lost her balance coming down the stairs this evening and broke her ankle. It's bad enough to require immediate surgery, which they've scheduled for tomorrow."

"Ah, Millie," he said, shaking his head, "I hate to hear that. Is there anything I can do?"

"That's why I'm calling. Eleanor's all by herself. I really need to be there with her."

"Of course, you do," he said without even a moment's hesitation. "I'll come get Katie."

"No need to pick her up right now," Millie assured him. "She can sleep here tonight like we planned and you can pick her up in the morning. I'm not about to drive up to Laredo tonight. Not with the weather being what it is."

"I can drive you there," he offered. How could he not? Millie had done so much for him the past two years.

"I appreciate the offer," she said, "but Eleanor really needs to get some rest before her surgery tomorrow."

"Are you sure?"

"I'm sure. You just keep on working to get that rec center done in time for the party. I'll make a few calls and see if I can round up someone to watch Katie until I get back. I'm not sure how long I'll be needed in Laredo."

"Don't trouble yourself any," he told her. "I'll just bring Katie into work with me tomorrow. There's no school. Some sort of teacher in-service day, which will be followed right after by Christmas break. I'm sure Audra would be willing to help out if I need her while you're away."

"Of course," she said. "Thank you for being so understanding about my leaving."

"Eleanor's your sister," he told her. "You need to be there for her. Now you be sure to get some rest yourself. I'll be by first thing tomorrow morning to pick Katie up."

"I'll have her ready."

"And, Millie…"

"Yes?"

"Give Katie a kiss good-night for me."

"I'll do that."

He turned the phone off and found Carter standing there staring at him.

"What happened?" his brother asked, his brows furrowed in concern.

"Millie's sister in Laredo busted her ankle pretty bad. She's having surgery tomorrow and Millie's gonna head on up there to be with her. Sounds like she'll be staying with her sister for a while afterward to help out."

"I have to admit, when you first answered her call and I saw the color drain from your face, I thought something had happened to Katie."

"You and me both," Nathan admitted. His baby girl was his world. If anything ever happened to her...

He forced the thought from his mind and pulled the hammer from its loop on his tool belt. "What are we standing around for? We've got us a rec center to finish."

Chapter Four

The morning sun shone brightly through the multipaned windows of the dining room as Alyssa hurried downstairs, eager to start her day's work at the rec center.

"Good morning, dear," Doris greeted from the dining room, giving Alyssa a start.

"You're up early," she said. "I hope I didn't wake you."

"Not at all. I rise with the sun."

Just then, Myrna entered through a door on the far side of the room, a warm smile moving across her face. "Perfect timing," she said as she moved toward the antique pedestal table in the center of the room. In one hand, she held a bowl filled with what Alyssa guessed to be scrambled eggs. In the other, a plate of crispy bacon, which had Alyssa's mouth watering. "Come on in and have a seat, dear. We'll see to it you're fed before you start your busy workday."

Alyssa stepped into the room and settled into one of the balloon-backed Victorian chairs. "You didn't have to make me breakfast. I could have grabbed something on my way through town."

"Honey, this is a bed-and-breakfast," Doris reminded her as she and Myrna took their places at the table. "You can't have one without the other."

Myrna set the filled dishes in the center of the table and then reached for the vintage rose-print teapot. "Tea?"

Alyssa nodded. "Yes, please."

Lifting the delicate old teapot gingerly, she filled Alyssa's teacup with steaming water and then pushed a doily-lined wicker basket filled with assorted teas across the table to her.

"You were so tired last night," Myrna said as she dipped her tea bag up in down in her tea water, "that we decided not to bombard you with questions about yourself."

"There's not much to tell," Alyssa said as she perused her choices, selecting an apple-cinnamon tea. "I was born and raised by a single mother in Waco. No brothers or sisters. I never knew my father."

"I'm so sorry to hear that," Doris said with an empathetic frown.

Alyssa forced a smile. "Can't miss what you never had," she said. "After graduating from Baylor, I was offered a job with a large interior design firm down in San Antonio. So I packed up and moved south to begin my new life."

"Have you ever been on TV?" Doris asked as she spooned two heaping teaspoons of sugar into her cup.

Alyssa was thrown by the unexpected question. "TV?"

"You know," Myrna joined in. "On one of those

home makeover shows you see all over television these days. You're sure pretty enough to be a TV star. Isn't she, Doris?"

Her sister nodded, the beehive of hair piled atop her head shifting to and fro. "I could see her starring in one of those cooking shows, looking all pretty in her ruffled apron."

Alyssa laughed softly. These two women were so endearing. "I'm afraid cooking is not my forte."

"All you really need to know how to make is sweets," Doris noted as she sipped at her tea. "My beloved Henry, God rest his soul, was especially fond of my sister's county-fair-winning apple-pecan cobbler." Her gaze drifted off and a soft smile lit her face. "That man had quite the sweet tooth."

"Most men do," Myrna said. "Nathan Cooper included. Just ask Millie."

"She's a close family friend," Myrna explained. "Always baking up sweets for those Cooper boys."

"Nathan… I mean Mr. Cooper," Alyssa quickly corrected, "has sons, too?"

"No, only Katie," Myrna clarified. "My sister was referring to Nathan and his two younger brothers, Carter and Logan. Big and strong, those boys. Some of the heartiest stock Texas produces."

"Like three peas in a pod," Myrna told her. "All with that same dark, wavy hair and bright blue eyes. Just like their daddy had. Real lookers, those Cooper boys."

If his brothers had even a smidgen of Nathan Cooper's good looks and charm, she could understand why even women old enough to be the men's grandmothers were smitten with them.

* * *

Huddled beneath the hood of her jacket, Alyssa quickened her step. The previous night's rain had left the earth damp and the air chilled. She should have thought to bring gloves with her when she packed for the trip. It would have made the long walk from the boardinghouse to the opposite end of town far more tolerable.

The moment she saw the large Cooper Construction sign flanking the front sidewalk of what had to be the town's new rec center, relief swept through her.

Picking up her step, she hurried toward the entrance. The warmth that greeted her when she stepped inside was a welcome respite from the chill outside. Pulling the door closed behind her, she brought her hands to her mouth, breathing warmth onto her very cold, very stiff fingers.

"You walked here?" a deep, familiar voice demanded behind her.

Startled, she turned to find Nathan Cooper watching her from a nearby doorway. Frown still intact. "How else was I supposed to get here?" she asked in her own defense. "Taxis don't exactly line the streets of Braxton."

"I could have given you a ride."

"The walk wasn't that bad."

"I suppose the tinge of blue in your lips is some sort of newfangled lipstick color?"

"They're blue?" she gasped, her chilled fingers flying to her lips.

"Close enough," he said as he joined her in what would, once finished, be the lobby area. His narrowed gaze traveled over her, then with a shake of his head he said, "Come on," motioning for her to follow him down a long hallway.

"Where are we going?" she asked as she unzipped her jacket.

"There's a space heater in the next room. You can warm up some before you get started doing whatever it is you do."

"That would be nice," she said, following him. It was all she could do to keep up with his long strides.

He pointed to an open doorway. "You can warm up in there." That said, he disappeared into another of the rooms that lined the hallway.

"Thank you," she called out after him. Then she stepped into the room he'd directed her to where several men were busily at work. One by one the sounds of hammers and drills stopped and she felt more than saw their gazes shift her way. Lifting her hand, she offered a nervous smile, hoping their dispositions would be a tad more welcoming than Nathan Cooper's had been. "Hello."

A man who had been running a nearby table saw walked over to where she stood by the door. He was wearing safety goggles, his dark, wavy hair brushing over the top of them. His height caused her to crane her neck as he stopped in front of her.

"Can I help you?"

"I'm Alyssa McCall."

Shoving the safety goggles off his face and onto his head, he studied her with a widening grin. "The interior designer?"

"That's what I have my degree in, but I also teach art classes to children at a recreation center in San

Antonio, which is where I'm from. It's a job I enjoy immensely."

His gaze moved over her in an assessing manner. "When my brother told me you'd be joining us sometime this morning, he conveniently left off the part about your being…"

"My being what?"

He glanced toward the other workers before saying, his voice low, "Not old."

She stiffened at his response. "I can assure you I have plenty of design experience."

"I'm not doubting your skill," he said apologetically. "Let's try this again." Pulling off his leather work gloves, he extended a hand. "Carter Cooper. Co-owner of Cooper Construction. Welcome to the crew."

She took the offered hand. "Thank you."

His dark brow lifted. "Your hand's as cold as ice."

"I know. The walk here was a little chillier than I expected," she admitted.

"You walked here from the boardinghouse? It's clear on the other side of town."

She resisted the urge to roll her eyes at his stunned reaction. The walk hadn't been all that far. Not for someone who was used to walking nearly everywhere she went. The problem was having been underdressed for the inclement weather.

"I did," she replied. "Your brother sent me in here to warm up by the space heater."

"And here I am talking your ear off," he muttered with a frown. "Back to work," he hollered to the other workers. "Come on," he told her. "The space heater's over here."

She trailed after him, grateful when she felt the

warmth from the portable heater start to curl around her. "So what exactly did your brother tell you about my being here?" she asked as she leaned in, shoving her hands closer to the heat.

He smiled. "He mentioned you'd be stopping by today."

"Much to his dismay, I'm sure," she murmured as the chill began to ease from her shivering limbs.

His husky chuckle filled the air. "Try not to take it personally, Miss McCall."

"It's a little hard not to," she said. "Your brother was all smiles and politeness when we first met, but the second he found out I was gonna be helping with the interior design portion of the recreation center, his demeanor toward me did a complete one-eighty."

"I'll talk to him," he assured her with a kind smile.

"I'd appreciate it. I truly do want the same thing you all do," Alyssa said. "To help give this town back some of what it lost in that storm."

"Miss McCall!" The high-pitched shriek echoed off the unpainted walls.

Alyssa glanced back over her shoulder to see Katie Cooper hurrying in her direction, the little girl's limp slightly more pronounced than it had been the evening before. "Katie," she said with a smile. "What a surprise finding you here this morning."

"Daddy just told me you were here. He had to bring me to work with him today."

"He did?" she said in surprise. "Is your mommy sick?"

"No," she replied, her beautiful smile sagging. "She went to Heaven with Grammy and Pappy."

Alyssa's heart wrenched. She'd assumed the day before that her father was divorced. Not for a second had she ever considered the possibility that he was widowed. Not at his age. She couldn't manage any kind of response. How could she when she had no idea what to say? Instead, she offered up a silent prayer for the Lord to watch over this dear, sweet, motherless child. And her father, as well.

"Hey, Katydid," Carter said from behind Alyssa, breaking the uncomfortable silence. "How would you like to give Miss McCall here a tour around the rec center?"

The little girl's face lit up once again. "Sure!"

Alyssa flashed him a grateful smile for saving the moment. Her heart ached for Katie. So very young to have lost her mother.

"You can hang your coat over there," Katie said. Her earlier bright smile back in place.

Pulled from her sympathetic musings, she looked to where Katie was pointing, but she could only make out shadowy outlines on the far side of the room.

"I think Miss McCall might wanna keep her coat on," the little girl's uncle cut in. "She's a little cold from outside."

"Actually, I'm feeling warmer already." Removing her coat, Alyssa crossed the room, stepping cautiously around worktables and over electrical cords. She scanned the area, relieved to spot several empty coat hooks on the wall by the door. She was still slightly chilled, but the building was decently heated.

"Come on," Katie said excitedly, holding out her hand.

Clasping her hand around Katie's, she smiled down at her. "Lead the way, my little tour guide."

She couldn't get Katie's sorrowful admission out of her mind. How unbearably tragic to think she'd had a mother who would have given the world to be there to guide her child. To raise her. To love her. Unlike Alyssa's own mother who'd thrown away that same chance.

"This is the ball room," Katie announced at their first stop.

Alyssa looked around as she withdrew her notepad from her purse. "You could fit a lot of dancers in here."

Katie giggled. "You're not supposed to be dancing while you're playing ball."

It took a moment for Katie's words to sink in. What had she been thinking? This was a rec center. A ball room in a recreation center would not be a ballroom. She needed to get her mind on her work instead of on things she couldn't change. But it wouldn't be easy. This little girl touched something deep inside her.

"There's gonna be basketball and volleyball and maybe even kickball in here," Katie continued on excitedly.

"Sounds like you're gonna have so much fun."

Her little smile sagged ever so slightly. "Not me."

"Why not?"

"'Cause I can't play ball," she answered with a frown.

"I'm sure your daddy could teach you."

She shook her head, her dark brown ponytails bouncing atop her slender shoulders. "He won't 'cause of my leg."

Alyssa didn't want to pry, but it seemed like Katie wanted to talk about it. "I noticed you were limping a little bit. Did you hurt your leg?"

"It got broken real bad."

That explained the slightly awkward gait. "Maybe when it's all better you can play kickball?"

"It is all better. As better as it's gonna be," she said. "I have a special piece in my leg. I have to be careful."

Katie must have had either had a rod or plate of some kind put in her leg. She recalled Nathan carrying Katie out of the store to the truck the night before. No doubt making sure she didn't slip and fall and possibly reinjure her leg. No wonder she felt a connection to this sweet, little girl.

"I have a special piece, too," she told her.

Katie's dark eyes widened. "You do?"

Alyssa nodded with a smile. "I sure do."

"In your leg?"

"No," she said. "Mine's in my head."

"Do people make fun of you for it?" the little girl asked timidly.

"Not many people know about it. Has someone said something to you about your leg that hurt your feelings?"

She hesitated, looking down at the floor. "Sometimes other kids say things…"

Alyssa knelt in front of her. "You know, Katie, sometimes people are scared of things they don't understand. They don't have special pieces inside them like we do, so they aren't sure how to react. Unfortunately, there are times when their reactions hurt our feelings."

"I suppose so," she mumbled.

Alyssa offered a comforting smile. "You know, sweetie, it's up to us to be strong when others get scared of our being special. We have to find ways to make them understand. To feel comfortable about our differences."

"I don't wanna be different," Katie whined, her mouth forming a tiny pout.

"You aren't different," Alyssa assured her. "You are wonderfully special."

"I am?"

She nodded emphatically. "Absolutely. Tell you what, how about you and I be strong together?"

"Forever?" she asked. The dark eyes looking up at Alyssa hopeful.

A part of her wanted to say yes, but she wouldn't be there forever. Only a few weeks. Less than that, if Nathan Cooper had his way. "I have to go home to San Antonio once I'm done helping your daddy with the rec center. But if you're ever having one of those days when you're sad because someone hurt your feelings, don't be afraid to talk to your daddy about it."

"But he might not understand 'cause he doesn't have any special parts."

"He'll understand. I promise," she said without hesitation. Having seen Nathan Cooper with his daughter, she had no doubt he would be able to give Katie the emotional support she needed. "Besides, I believe it was you who pointed out just how strong your daddy is. Isn't that right?"

Katie nodded.

"Then who better to help you to be strong than your daddy? Someone who loves you with all his heart." Unlike her own father, who'd chosen to go on with his own life without Alyssa ever being allowed in it.

* * *

Nathan stood in the doorway, taking in the scene before him. Katie and Alyssa's conversation had drifted out into the hall along with the sounds of construction being done in the room next to this one. It wasn't surprising that sound traveled so easily inside the newly erected building. Not with the flooring having yet to be laid, walls to be painted and doors to be hung.

His first instinct had been to go to his daughter and soothe her emotional hurts, but Alyssa McCall had done that for him. Surprisingly well, he had to admit. If what she'd told Katie about having her own special piece were true, then she truly understood what his daughter was going through.

He studied the woman comforting his daughter. She wasn't as tall as Isabel had been. And her hair was red. Not a bright red like the town's new fire truck. But a deeper, warmer red with hints of gold in it. He preferred dark hair like his wife's had been. But he had to admit the color seemed to suit Miss McCall. Warm. Soothing. Just as her words had been to his daughter.

"Thatta girl," Miss McCall said, giving his daughter's ponytail a playful tug. He watched as she rose up from the crouch she'd been in to smile down at Katie. "I can't wait to see everything your daddy's done so far. I understand he's been working very hard on the rec center."

"Granny Timmons says he's gonna work himself to the bone. I don't want my daddy to be a skeleton. They're scary."

Alyssa laughed softly. "I don't think that's what your granny meant by that. When people say someone is working themselves to the bone, what they're really trying to say is that the person is giving everything they have in them to do the best job they can. Your daddy is giving his all to have this place finished in time for the Christmas Eve festivities."

A smile pulled at his lips. He didn't want to be drawn to the woman who had been thrown into his life, into his neatly laid-out plans for the rec center, but watching her with his little girl, hearing her kind, reassuring words, did just that. Alyssa McCall affected him in a way no other woman had since Isabel.

"I wish Daddy didn't work so much," his daughter admitted with a sigh. "I miss him sometimes."

His daughter's words tugged at his heart. His attempt to bury himself in his work to forget the past had clearly left Katie feeling neglected. He'd never meant for that to happen.

"I'm sure he misses you, too," Miss McCall said, drawing him from his troubled thoughts. She still hadn't noticed him standing there. Probably a good thing, seeing as how he needed a moment to collect himself before making his presence known. She reached out, gently ruffling Katie's ever-wild mane of curls. "Just think of how happy your daddy's gonna make the people in town when they finally have their recreation center back. Now how about giving me a few minutes to take a peek around the room and then we can continue on with our tour?"

"Okay," Katie chirped. Leaving Alyssa to her work, his daughter set off across the expansive gymnasium floor, arms out wide, giggling as she twirled about in slow circles.

Alyssa McCall was something else. Despite his initial reservations, he felt himself softening toward her.

That thought lasted all of about ten seconds as Miss McCall began her peek around the room, which appeared to be more of a thorough scrutiny of his work. Bristling, he watched as she moved about the room, running her fingertips over the recently sanded drywall sheets, pausing to examine each and every one of the multipaned windows and unstained door frames that lined the unfinished walls. Isabel had never questioned his ability.

"You can leave the drywall inspection to me," he said as he stepped up behind her.

Startled, she swung around to face him. "Mr. Cooper. I didn't see you come in."

"I'm not surprised," he grumbled. His gaze shifted to his daughter, who was at the far side of the unfinished gymnasium, and then back to Miss McCall. "Let's get one thing straight," he said, keeping his voice low. "Your job is to pick out paint colors and fixtures. Not to inspect my work."

"Inspect your work?" she replied, her expression one of confusion. Then her gaze fell to the drywall dust coating the tips of her fingers. "I…" She lifted her gaze to his.

"I'll do my job," he said brusquely. "You do yours."

"For your information," she began in a tone of forced patience, "I wasn't *inspecting* anything. I happen to be a very tactile person when I work. At least, I have been since—"

"Hi, Daddy!" Katie called out as she skipped over to join them.

His attention shifted to his daughter. "Hey, Cupcake."

"I got a job."

He arched a dark brow. "You do?"

"Uncle Carter asked me to give Miss McCall a tour," she said with a bright smile. "We're gonna go see the cafeteria next. Wanna come with us?"

Alyssa didn't give him a chance to reply. "I'm sure your daddy is far too busy to tag along."

He met her gaze, seeing a hint of hurt in her eyes. Why did the thought of that bother him? Maybe because he had been less than the gentleman his momma had raised him to be when setting her straight moments before. It wasn't her fault the firm she worked for had sent her there to do the job. The same job Isabel would have been handling if she were still alive.

"Daddy?"

Feeling as if the walls were closing in on him, he forced his attention back to his daughter. "Honey, I'd like to, but right now I have to—"

"*Please*, Daddy." Katie looked up at him with pleading brown eyes.

Get it together, Cooper. Your daughter needs you. And according to the conversation he'd overheard a few minutes ago, he hadn't been there enough for Katie during the past few months. "I suppose I could spare a few extra minutes for my favorite girl," he said, bringing a delighted smile to his daughter's face.

"Yay!" she exclaimed, and then she turned to Miss McCall. "Follow me! It's right next door."

"Careful!" he called after her with a worried frown. "I don't want you tripping on any power cords!"

"I won't!" she called back before disappearing through the open doorway.

"I wish I had half her energy," Miss McCall said as they started after her.

Do the right thing, his conscience told him. "Miss McCall," he said, stopping her just before they reached the framed-in doorway.

She turned to look up at him. "Look, I'm not here to step on your toes. Really I'm not. I can do most of my work from the boardinghouse on my computer if you'll email me a copy of the rec center's layout and measurements. Then you won't need to worry about having to cross paths w—"

He reached out to touch her arm, needing to explain that the problem wasn't her. It was him. "I'm sorry for making you feel like you aren't welcome here. It's just that I haven't worked with another woman since…" His words trailed off.

She reached up to curl her fingers around his hand, easing it away from her arm. "Since your wife passed away?" she asked softly.

His surprise must have shown on his face, because she added, "Katie told me."

"My daughter's a regular little chatterbox," he said, his voice tight with the emotion he fought to keep inside.

"I'm sorry for your loss."

He nodded, closing his eyes for a long moment before opening them to meet her softened gaze. "Isabel was in charge of the interior design portion of my company. She didn't have a fancy degree, but she knew how to make things work."

She didn't release his hand. Instead, she gave it a comforting squeeze. Eyes the color of amber searched his own. "I promise I'm not trying to replace her. I'm just here to do my job. But if my doing so is gonna be this hard on you, I'll pull out. The firm I work for can send a replacement. They have two men on their interior design staff. If one of them is free over the holidays…"

"No," he said, the words thick with emotion. "You need to stay."

She released his hand with a warm smile. "Okay."

Nathan cleared his throat, glancing around uneasily. Other than the overwhelming love he had for his daughter, this was the first time he'd really felt anything in the way of true emotion in two years.

"We should go," she said. "Katie will be wondering what happened to us."

"Before we go…" he said as he collected himself. "I wanna thank you."

"For what?"

"For being so kind to my daughter. I overheard the two of you discussing her leg."

"Mr. Cooper—" she began.

"Nathan," he cut in. "We're gonna be working together. No need for formalities between us."

She nodded. Her beautiful smile widening. "Agreed. Call me Alyssa, please. And you don't have to thank me for being kind to Katie. She's precious and endearing. And I understand what she's going through more than most people."

"Because of the plate you have in your head?" he said, wanting her to know that he'd been listening to their conversation longer than he should have before making his presence known. Another thing his momma would have taken him to task for.

"That's part of it," she said, biting at her bottom lip as if wanting to say more.

What more could there be? And then it occurred to him. "You lost your mother at a young age, as well?"

"Although my mother has been lost to me for most of my life, she only recently passed away," she explained. "She was an alcoholic."

"I'm sorry."

"Don't be. God has a plan for my life," she explained with a conviction he found himself wishing he still had when it came to the Lord. "In fact, what I've gone through has made me a much stronger person." She laughed softly. "'Stubbornly resilient' as my best friend, Erica, is fond of telling me."

He wanted to ask her why she wasn't angry with the Lord instead of being so accepting. How could she smile when all he wanted to do was grit his teeth at all the injustices he'd suffered?

"And the other reason I understand what Katie is going through," she continued, "is because I'm legally blind."

Chapter Five

Blind?

Nathan watched Alyssa go, his feet frozen in place. Her admission ringing in his ears. How was that possible? He would have known if she was visually impaired. Wouldn't he? His mind played back their first meeting. Alyssa hadn't seen Katie charging toward her until it was too late. And then when he'd joked about his daughter being a bull in the china shop, Alyssa's expression had grown troubled. She'd told him she'd been looking for The Toy Box, which, of course, she'd been standing right in front of. And it would make sense as to why her friend had driven her to Braxton, leaving Alyssa without any means of transportation for what could amount to several weeks. She couldn't drive.

He had so many questions he wanted to ask Alyssa about her unexpected revelation, but he would wait until they had some modicum of privacy. He loved his daughter dearly, but Katie was like a little mynah bird and there might be things Alyssa would prefer his daughter not announce to all and sundry.

"Daddy!" His daughter's voice carried down the hallway, no doubt from the cafeteria where she'd gone to give Alyssa McCall a tour.

He forced his feet to move in that direction, once more stopping just inside the open doorway. Leaning against the unfinished door frame, he casually crossed one booted foot over the other, planted his thumbs into the front pockets of his jeans, and watched as his daughter did the job her uncle had given her to do.

"This is where the tables are gonna go," she told Alyssa with a wave of her arm.

"I can see them there already," Alyssa replied with a nod.

"You can? How?" Katie looked around, a bit bewildered by the statement.

Alyssa laughed softly. "Like this." Her long lashes shut against cheeks lightly dusted with freckles like Katie's. "Close your eyes."

His daughter did as she was told. "All I see is dark."

"The dark is your mind's eye."

"I have three eyes?"

More of Alyssa's soft laughter filled the air. "Not exactly. Think of the darkness you see as an empty chalkboard. Imagine the room as you'd like to see it and create it on your blackboard."

"Mine has round tables," she chirped excitedly.

"The best kind. Now add some color to the walls."

"What color?" Katie asked, her eyes squeezed tight.

"Whatever color you'd like," Alyssa told her. "Make it polka-dotted if it pleases you."

"Polka dots?" Nathan cut in, drawing both their gazes his way. "We're building a rec center, not doing some fancy home makeover show."

"Your daughter is designing her own version of what she imagines this room should look like," Alyssa explained, with admirable patience. "You'll be happy to know, however, that polka dots are not part of my plans for this room."

"That's a relief," he muttered.

"I'm leaning more toward painting a line of dancing carrots across the back wall."

His brow shot up. "Dancing carrots?"

"To promote healthy eating," she said, attempting to muffle a snort of laughter.

She was teasing him. Two could play that game. "Might wanna throw in a couple of juicy, red apples to remind folks that an apple a day keeps the doctor away."

"Daddy," his daughter groaned, her eyes once again closed. "I'm trying to draw and all your talking is making me mess up."

At his daughter's admonishment, a smile tugged at Alyssa's mouth, the sight of which distracted him thoroughly. He shouldn't be noticing her smile. He should be focused on the work he had to do. But how could he not notice it with her standing so close? Truth was, he hadn't even looked twice at another woman since Isabel's passing. Why now? Why her?

"You ladies go ahead and work on your drawings," he told them. "I need to go see how things are coming along with the indoor pool." His gaze shifted back to Alyssa. Thick lashes lowered once again, she returned to the game she was playing with his daughter. The gentle smile on her pretty face had his own mouth pulling upward.

He flattened his mouth as soon as he realized what

he had done. He wasn't supposed to be thinking of someone he was going to be working with in that way. Then again, other than Isabel he'd only ever worked with men. Straightening, he pushed away from the door frame and slipped out into the hallway, trying to clear the image of Alyssa McCall's bright smile from his mind.

He strode toward the room that held the yet-to-be-filled Olympic-sized swimming pool. Alyssa McCall might get under his skin in an unwanted way, but he couldn't deny the positive effect she had on his daughter. He just hoped Katie wouldn't become too attached, seeing as how Alyssa was only there until the project was finished. And if things progressed the way he hoped they would, her stay in Braxton would be even shorter than planned.

"Something wrong, big brother?" Carter asked the second Nathan entered the swimming pool room.

"No," he replied. "Why?"

"The grimace you had on your face when you came in had me wondering," his brother replied as he slid the handle of the hammer he'd been holding into the oversize loop at the side of his tool belt.

"That wasn't a grimace," he said with a frown as he walked around to do a visual inspection of the tile work that had just been laid along the top inside edge of the pool walls. He wasn't getting into what was bothering him with his brother. He preferred to work things out on his own. "I just have a lot on my mind right now."

"Ah, so that would explain why you forgot to mention that Miss McCall was both young and pretty," his brother said as he accompanied him around the pool. "Wait until Logan catches a glimpse of her."

He shot his brother a scowl. "Alyssa is off-limits to Logan and the rest of the crew. And would you mind keeping your voice down? Sound carries in this place, remember?"

"Off-limits, huh?" his brother repeated with an all-too-knowing grin as he continued on around the pool ahead of Nathan. "That include you?"

"Don't make me take a staple gun to your big mouth," he warned as he knelt to inspect a section of the tile where a little more grout needed to be added.

Carter chuckled, not the least bit intimidated by Nathan's empty threats. "Thought so," he murmured as he moved from window to window along the far wall, inspecting their crew's work.

Nathan's frown deepened. He wasn't looking for a replacement for Isabel. Katie and Carter were going to have to accept that. Just because Carter had managed to push aside everything they'd been through to find happiness with Audra didn't mean that was what he and Logan wanted.

"Good to see you're giving my question some real thought. Definitely a step in the right direction." Carter walked away, making his way back around the pool to the door.

Nathan's gaze drilled into his brother's departing form. "I hardly know the woman," he called after him. That was the best he could come up with? What happened to "mind your own business, Carter" or "don't you have a life of your own to pay mind to?"

Before he could change his response, Alyssa stepped into the room.

"Don't tell me your tour guide gave you the slip," Carter said with a smile.

She laughed. "No. Katie sent me in here to wait while she ran to the water fountain for a drink. Truth be told, your niece is an excellent tour giver."

"Trained her myself," he boasted with a grin.

Nathan found himself waiting for her gaze to shift to where he still knelt on the far side of the pool. Waiting to be on the receiving end of one of those smiles she so freely seemed to give.

"Don't believe a word he says," Nathan called out when her attention failed to shift in his direction. "He's always trying to take credit for everything that goes right."

"Nathan?" Alyssa's gaze searched the far side of the room. For him.

How could he have forgotten? She couldn't see him from where she stood. Up close she seemed to do better. Or was she that good at making herself fit in? Just as he did when it came to church. Sure, he went every Sunday. But he never prayed. Not anymore. Not since the Lord had seen fit to take Isabel away in the prime of her life. He only went for his daughter's sake. Isabel had wanted their daughter to be strong in her faith. He would see her wishes carried through. Even if going to church tended to be an emotional challenge for him.

"Over here," he replied as he got to his feet, his voice echoing in the vast room. "Far right corner."

Carter chuckled. "I doubt she needs directions, big brother. You're standing right here in the same room."

Even from where he stood, Nathan could see the unease move through Alyssa. But it wasn't his place to tell Carter why he'd made his whereabouts known.

"I didn't realize you were in here," she confessed, looking Nathan's way.

Carter's expression slid from playfully grinning to utterly and thoroughly confused. "I seem to be missing something here."

"We can talk about it later," Nathan told him. Once he'd had a chance to discuss things with Alyssa. He needed to know just how much she wanted others to know about what she'd admitted to him.

"It's all right," she said, sending him that smile he'd been hoping for. "It was foolish of me to think no one would find out."

"Find out what?" Carter inquired, his gaze shifting back and forth between the two of them.

"I didn't realize your brother was standing on the other side of the room," she admitted, "because I'm visually impaired." She bit into her bottom lip as if expecting some sort of negative response from his brother.

Was that how the world reacted to her disability? Had she had her feelings hurt by others because of it? The thought of anyone being intentionally cruel to Alyssa had him clenching his fists.

His gaze shifted to Carter, who studied Alyssa closely. No doubt trying to read the sincerity in her words. A habit that came from having a younger brother who was always trying to pull the wool over their eyes. But unlike Logan, Alyssa wasn't playing around and Nathan knew the moment his brother recognized it for the truth it was.

Carter nodded, offering her an accepting smile. "Reckon that'll spare you from seeing my brother's ugly mug on a daily basis."

Nathan stiffened. What could his brother have been thinking making a remark like that? Couldn't he tell how uncomfortable Alyssa had been just admitting... Before he could finish the thought, her sweet laughter filled the air.

"I'm not *completely* blind," Alyssa clarified as she reined in her laughter. "Just enough for doctors to give me the life-altering label of legally blind. That being the case, I'm fully aware that your brother's mug is nowhere near as bad as you're trying to make me believe it is."

Carter looked his way, one lone, dark brow raised.

She'd noticed his face, Nathan thought with a hint of satisfaction he shouldn't be feeling. But it was hard not to appreciate the compliment. Especially when it served to put his brother in his place for his teasing remarks.

"I've gotta admit I had no idea," Carter said, shaking his head. "So do you wear corrective contacts?"

"Carter," Nathan grumbled as he finally walked around the pool to join them.

"I don't mind answering," she assured him, turning her attention back to his brother. "I don't wear contacts, because the problem isn't with my eyes. They're perfect. This issue is with the part of my brain responsible for processing the images my eyes see. The result of head trauma I suffered in a car accident a few years ago. It won't get any worse, but it's not reparable either."

Carter frowned. "I'm real sorry to hear that."

"Before you let my visual impairment worry you, know this. I'm very good at what I do. I have a degree. I have several years of hands-on experience. I can still get an accurate layout of the places I'm designing for and then am able to give the customer what it is they are looking for."

"You don't have to sell yourself to me," Carter cut in, beating Nathan to it. "You were sent here to do the job by a highly respectable interior design firm. You're giving up your personal time over the holidays to stay here and help see our project through to completion. That tells me all I need to know." His brother looked Nathan's way. "You got any issues with her doing this job?"

He met her gaze from where she stood just a few feet away. "I'd be lying if I said I didn't have any issues with it. At least, at first. Not because of her visual limitations, but because of my own emotional ones."

Surprise lit his brother's face at the heartfelt admission. Understandably so. He wasn't a man who openly admitted his vulnerability. But when Alyssa had so openly shared hers, he felt the pressing need to join her.

Nathan went on before he lost the nerve. "I seem to have a problem letting go of the past. I know that. And Miss McCall—"

"Alyssa," she reminded him, her tone kind.

"Alyssa," he repeated, unable to take his gaze off the comforting smile she aimed his way, "understands my reasons for it and, I hope, knows that I'm gonna work on turning my mind-set around."

Her smile lifted even higher. "Not an easy task, but it can be done. I'm living proof that we can wish things could be the way they were, but still accept God's will."

Nathan's jaw clenched, despite the smile pasted on

his face. He was just about to voice his opinion on God's will when his brother cut him off.

"My wife's been craving dill pickle spears with a side of chocolate milk!"

The blurted-out words had both him and Alyssa casting questioning glances in Carter's direction.

His brother shrugged with a grin. "Figured since everyone else was doing it, I ought to make a confession, too."

No, what his brother had been doing was attempting to avoid a debate over being so accepting of God's will, knowing where Nathan's feelings lay in that regard. It worked. It was hard to focus on his anger toward God when his brother was discussing dill pickles and chocolate milk.

Nathan rolled his eyes. "That's not a confession."

Laughing once again, Alyssa nodded in agreement. "Not even close."

"How about if I find myself craving it, too?"

"I'm thinking that's one confession you ought to have kept to yourself," he told his brother. Just as he would his stirring interest in Alyssa's pretty smile. Because his focus needed to be on completing this project on time.

"You looked like you could use a Big Dog's double-thick double-chocolate shake."

Alyssa glanced up from the notes she'd been making on her laptop to find the waitress who had served her lunch holding a lidded cup out to her with a friendly smile.

"It's the perfect fix for anything that's troubling you." She nodded toward the open laptop.

Alyssa sat back with a sigh. "That obvious, huh?"

"Only a little," the young woman replied, her kind smile widening. "And only to a waitress who prides herself on having the ability to know when her customers are in need of something."

She looked up at the other woman. "You know, a chocolate shake is exactly what I need to clear my head. I seem to be having trouble focusing on my work at the moment." Her thoughts were too preoccupied with what she'd learned that day about Nathan Cooper and his precious little girl.

"Well, I hope it helps. I can't imagine how hard it must be to leave your own life for weeks to work in a town where you don't know anyone," the young woman added. "Speaking of which, consider that milk shake a token of my appreciation for offering your services to our town's effort to rebuild what we lost in the tornado."

Her kind words touched Alyssa. "Thank you," she said, taking the offered cup. "I'm happy to be even a small part of it all. But how did you know who I was?"

"Word travels fast in a small town. I'm just sorry I didn't know who you were when you were here the other day or I would've thanked you then." She held out her hand. "I'm Lizzie Parker. Waitress by day. Student by night. Takes one to pay for the other."

Accepting the offered hand, Alyssa said, "Alyssa McCall. Been there. Done that. I worked my way through college, too. What are you studying?"

"Meteorology."

"Admirable field. You must be really good with math and science."

"Fortunately, I am." Pushing her long, strawberry

blonde ponytail back over her shoulder, she sighed. "But that doesn't keep me from wondering sometimes if I'll ever get my degree. I'm twenty-four and not even halfway through with my course work."

"You'll get there," Alyssa assured her. "You just have to keep your eye on the goal."

Lizzie laughed softly. "You and Nathan should work well together. That's the very same advice he gave me."

Alyssa certainly hoped they would. Their working relationship hadn't exactly started off on a positive note. Only now she understood why Nathan had reacted to the news of her working with him on the project the way he had. Leaning in, she took a sip of the shake and moaned softly. "He and I seem to have the same opinion of the shakes here, as well. This truly is the best shake I've ever had."

"Nathan should know," Lizzie said with a smile. "Katie drags him in here nearly every week to get one. Not that he complains. That man has a sweet tooth to match his daughter's."

Alyssa's thoughts went back to her conversation with Doris and Myrna. It appeared that men, even big, rough and tough men like Nathan Cooper, had a thing for sweets. Growing up without a father and having dated very little left her embarrassingly ignorant of these little tidbits of information.

"I had better let you get back to work."

Alyssa's gaze shifted to the notes she'd been making on her laptop and then back up at Lizzie. "Maybe we can talk again sometime."

"I'd like that. I miss having the chance for girl talk. Most of my close friends went off to college and moved to other parts of the country."

Alyssa could relate. She was already missing Erica, even though her best friend was only a phone call away. Reaching into her purse, she pulled out a business card, handing it to Lizzie. "My number's on here. Call me when you have some free time and we can meet up. I'd love to know more about the town and the people who live here."

Lizzie eyed the card and then slid it down into the front pocket of her apron. "I look forward to it." Just then an elderly couple stepped inside the restaurant. "Back to work," she said with a grin. "Let me know if I can get you anything else."

"I think I'm good," Alyssa said. "Thanks again."

With a nod, Lizzie hurried off to greet the couple. Smiling, Alyssa sipped at her shake. Maybe her stay in Braxton wouldn't be quite as solitary as she'd feared it might be.

Chapter Six

Katie sprang out into the hallway of the rec center as Nathan was passing by. As usual, she was all smiles and sunshine, which had his own smile widening.

"Daddy, guess what!" she exclaimed as she raced toward him. His daughter never did anything at an unhurried pace. At times, he fretted over it, concerned she would reinjure her leg. But her doctor had assured him that she could do almost anything other children her age did, so he fought the instinct to tell her to slow down.

"What?" he replied as he caught her up in his arms, spinning them both in a slow circle.

"I decorated the new art room all in my head," she answered with a happy giggle.

He loved seeing his daughter so enthusiastic about life. There had been a time shortly after Isabel's death that he'd feared she'd never know joy again. But his baby girl was made of tough stock. She'd grieved the loss of her mother and grandparents, and then like a hardy little wildflower she'd bloomed again.

"You did?" he said, easing her down until her tiny feet rested on the cement floor. "Keep that up and

I might just have to hire you on to work for Uncle Carter and me."

"And Alyssa."

"*Miss* McCall," he corrected.

"It's all right," Alyssa said as she joined them in the hallway, notebook in hand. "I asked Katie to call me by my first name."

"'Cause we're friends and that's what friends do," his daughter explained with a bright smile. "Alyssa said I could help her decorate the rec center while I'm here."

His gaze shifted. "She did, did she?" As glad as he was to see his daughter so happy, he couldn't help but be concerned that Katie was forming an attachment that was going to leave her heartbroken once Alyssa went back home to San Antonio.

Alyssa nodded. "We were going through some of the paint color strips I picked up at the hardware store this morning and I have to say her choice of both the main and the accent colors was spot on." She smiled down at Katie. "Your daughter has a real knack for artistic design."

Something else she'd inherited from her mother, he thought with a sad smile. "I know," he replied, his gaze fixed on his little girl. "We have a wall at home that displays my daughter's artistic ability." He ruffled Katie's hair playfully.

"Daddy," she groaned. "I was only three when I did that. Why can't we paint over it?"

"Because your mother loved it." Lingering grief edged his voice.

"Little Miss Katydid," Carter said as he stepped

into the hallway from the lobby. "Look who came to see you."

"Uncle Logan!" she shrieked.

Logan knelt, arms extended. "I was outside working on the landscaping and decided I needed to come inside and get myself a Katie fix," he told her as she wrapped her arms around his neck in a loving embrace. His gaze moved past the head of dark curls beneath his chin to settle on Alyssa. "I heard a rumor there were two pretty girls hanging around this place, but it's plain to see some rumors sell the truth short. You two are beyond pretty."

A faint blush moved across Alyssa's cheeks.

Pressing a kiss to Katie's brow, he eased from her hold and straightened, extending his hand to Alyssa. "Logan Cooper."

She slid her hand into Nathan's brother's with a warm smile. "Alyssa McCall."

"Pleasure to meet you," his brother replied with a crooked grin. "A real pleasure."

"Don't you have some more trees to plant?" Nathan grumbled.

"Nope," Logan replied, holding on to Alyssa's hand longer than necessary. "All planted."

"It was nice to meet you," Alyssa said, retrieving her hand from his brother's eager grasp. "I hate to run off, but I need to take another run through the swimming pool room and finish up my notes."

"Mind if I—"

"I'll go with you," Nathan said, cutting off Logan's offer of joining her for the walk-through.

Carter snorted, muttering something under his breath about being glad he was already hitched. Then he scooped Katie up, draping her over his shoulder like a sack of potatoes. "Katydid and I are gonna take a run into town to the hardware store to pick up some flooring samples for Miss McCall to look over tonight."

"But I got work to do," Katie proclaimed.

"This is work," his brother assured her. "As Miss McCall's helper, it's your duty to see she has the supplies she needs to do her job. And she's gonna need to choose the flooring right quick so we can get it ordered and put down as soon as the painting is done."

"Reckon I best go," Katie agreed, looking up at her uncle. "You might pick out the wrong thing."

"My thoughts exactly," Carter teased. Then he turned to Logan. "You wanna ride along?"

"Thanks, but I've gotta run by the nursery to talk to Jack. I'm gonna need a few more flats of pansies and white and purple violets."

Jack Dillan owned the local nursery Logan used for his landscaping company. He was also the father of the only woman his youngest brother had ever truly loved. Hope Dillan. Even though they'd only been teenagers at the time, Nathan had believed the two would eventually marry. But he'd been wrong, and his brother had spent the past nine years putting on a happy front when both he and Carter knew it to be a cover for the deep hurt that lingered just below the surface.

"Send him our regards," Nathan said.

"Will do."

"You might wanna take a look at some of those Virginia pines Jack's got in the back field while you're there," Carter suggested. "We're gonna be needing one for the rec center's Christmas party."

Logan nodded. "I'll be sure to do that."

"I wanna help pick it out!" Katie exclaimed. "Can I please, Uncle Logan?"

He chuckled. "I promise to let you help me when it comes time to chop one down. And after the holidays, we'll turn it into mulch and add it to the landscaping outside." Logan turned to Alyssa. "You free for dinner? I could pick you up after work. Maybe show you around town."

"She's already got plans." Nathan scowled as he answered for her.

"I do?" Alyssa couldn't keep the surprise from her voice.

Nathan's gaze stayed fixed on his younger brother. "She's having dinner with me and Katie tonight."

"She is?" Katie squawked excitedly from her perch atop Carter's broad shoulder.

A grin slid across Logan's face as he turned to Carter. "You're right."

Carter nodded. "Told you so."

Logan nodded with a chuckle, then tipped his cowboy hat to Alyssa. "Pleasure meeting you." He looked to Carter. "Walk me out?"

Their brother nodded. "Right behind you."

Alyssa watched them go, Katie's giggles trailing behind them as they disappeared from sight.

"You have any brothers?" Nathan asked.

She turned to him. "No. I was an only child."

"Consider yourself lucky," he said, shaking his head.

"Oh, I don't know," she said. "I think having brothers like yours would have made my life so much more interesting."

He chuckled. "That's because you haven't spent any

real stretch of time with them." Then he inclined his head. "Come on. I'll walk with you to the swimming pool room."

"I like your brothers," she admitted as they moved down the hallway.

"I do, too," he agreed. "At least, most of the time."

They stepped into the oversize room that housed the Olympic-sized swimming pool. Alyssa opened her notebook and slid the pen free of the spiral binding. "What would you think of my going with a rich, warm sand color on the walls with a twelve inch strip of dark blue going around the room at chair-rail height? I was thinking about hand painting small sections of waves in a bright white paint inside the blue accent stripe."

His gaze scanned the room as if envisioning her plans. Then he nodded. "I like it." He glanced her way. "But it's a big room. That's a lot of wave painting."

"I don't mind. I'd rather work than sit around doing nothing."

He nodded in understanding. "I feel the same way. We've got painters who can take care of the basic painting of the walls. Just give me a list of what colors go where."

"Will do."

"My men can paint walls, but adding decorative murals or designs will have to fall to you."

"Perfect." She started around the pool only to have him join her.

"Watch your step," he said, placing himself between her and the still-empty pool.

She smiled up at him as they walked. "Have you always been so protective of others?"

He looked away, falling silent.

What had she said? "Nathan?"

He heaved a heavy sigh. "I wasn't there for my wife when the storm hit. I should've been there to protect her."

Reaching out, she placed a hand on his arm. "She wouldn't blame you for that."

He stopped, turning to face her. "But I do."

Her heart went out to him. For all he'd gone through. For the undeserved guilt he'd taken upon himself. For the pain she saw in his eyes. She gave his arm a gentle squeeze before letting her hand fall away. "It was a tornado. They're sudden and unpredictable. You had no way of knowing. If you had, you would have moved Heaven and earth to be there for her and for Katie. Your wife knew that."

His expression changed. Softened. "Do you always know the right thing to say?"

"Hardly," she said with a smile. "I just have a tendency to be honest and speak from the heart."

"You say that as if it's a bad thing."

"It can be," she admitted softly. "When people find out about my condition…" Her words trailed off.

"It shouldn't make a difference."

"But it does," she said, looking up into caring blue eyes. "I'm a realist. I've simply had to learn how to work around the prejudices and hold strong to the belief that God has a plan for me."

"You're a remarkable woman, Alyssa McCall," he told her with a smile that bordered on tender.

They stood unmoving for several long moments before Alyssa forced her gaze away from his handsome face. "I should let you get back to work," she said, trying to focus on the notes she'd been making in her notebook.

"You sure you're okay in here?"

She glanced up at him. "I'm fine. Though I do appreciate your concern."

He nodded. "Um…about dinner tonight…"

She looked up at him questioningly. "Dinner?"

"When I told my brother you already had plans, I was sorta putting the cart before the horse. Would you like to join Katie and me for dinner this evening?"

Other than being invited over to Erica's for family dinners, she'd never had anyone offer to make dinner for her. "I'd love to."

His smile widened. "How do you feel about creamed chicken and biscuits?"

"It's one of my favorites."

"Katie's, too," he admitted. "She likes to help me make it. But I have to warn you. The biscuits are gonna come from a can."

She laughed softly. "Is there any other kind?"

Before he had a chance to respond, his cell rang. "Excuse me," he said, pulling his phone from the front pocket of his jeans. "Nathan Cooper speaking."

Alyssa stepped away, to give him some privacy for his call.

"Millie," he said, his deep voice echoing in the open room. "How's your sister doing? Sorry to hear that." There was a long pause before he said, "Take all the time you need. I'll figure things out with Katie."

Alyssa didn't mean to eavesdrop, but the large, empty room amplified everything. "Everything okay?" she asked when he disconnected the call and stepped over to join her.

"The woman who usually takes care of Katie for me while I'm at work had to go to Laredo for a family emergency. Apparently Millie's sister has had some complications following surgery, so she's gonna have to stay out there with her longer than expected."

"Is her sister gonna be okay?"

He nodded. "Thankfully, yes."

"That's why you've been bringing Katie into work with you?" she asked. At least he had for the two days Alyssa had been working at the rec center.

"I don't really have a backup," he said with a frown. "My brother's wife, Audra, just found out she's expecting and is having a rough time of it with morning sickness and all. I didn't feel right asking her to watch Katie for me. Not when she's already got two little ones of her own to watch over."

"Understandable. And Katie seems to love coming here."

"You've made her feel very special, allowing her to help you out. I want you to know that I really appreciate it."

"I don't mind. I enjoy spending time with her."

"But when you told her she could help you with the interior design plans, you had no idea Katie would be coming to work with me every day now that she's on Christmas break. Possibly until this project is done. I intend to make sure my daughter understands that she's not to make a pest of herself."

"Please don't," she implored. "I want her to feel free to ask questions and offer suggestions."

"Even if those suggestions entail dancing carrots?" he asked with a chuckle.

"The dancing carrots were my idea," she reminded him with a smile. "But, yes, even then. I love helping children discover their creative abilities."

"Fine. I'll hold off on having a talk with my daughter. But if she gets to be too much, I want your promise that you'll let me know."

"You have it," she said warmly.

He glanced toward the door and then back down at her. "I'll be in the women's locker room if you need me."

"Excuse me?"

He chuckled again, a sound she found herself being drawn to more and more. It was warm and soothing and had her own smile widening. "We're installing the wall lockers today."

"Oh, of course." She walked him to the open doorway. "What time should I be at your house tonight?"

"Katie and I will drop you off at the boardinghouse after work and then come back for you around six. Does that work?"

"Yes, but I—"

"Can walk," he finished for her. "I think we've already established that you've got a thing for walking. Even in the cold. But my momma raised us boys to be gentlemen. That means picking up a lady we've invited to dinner. Not having her find her own way there." That said, he stepped from the room, leaving Alyssa watching after him.

His momma sounded like a wonderfully caring woman. But then it only stood to reason, considering the kind of men she'd raised. And that night she'd be having dinner with one of them. A man who had become both father and mother to his young daughter after the tragic loss of his wife. One whose love for that little girl shone so brightly it couldn't be missed whenever they were together. A man who worked hard.

And if all of that didn't make Nathan Cooper special in her eyes, he was the first man since her accident that hadn't been put off by her visual impairment. He'd not only accepted her for who she was, he trusted in her ability to do the job she was there for. That meant the world to her because she had to succeed in the job she'd been sent there to do. Doing so, she prayed, would help convince her firm that she truly was capable of more than they were allocating to her. And before that could happen, she would have to prove to Nathan and his brothers that she was capable of the task she'd been given. Their feedback could make or break her career as far as Pure Perfection Designs was concerned. She could not fail.

He had his brother to blame for his temporary insanity. If Logan hadn't come into the rec center all smiles and charm and asked Alyssa out, he would never have blurted out that she already had plans—with him.

He'd done it to protect her. His little brother was a fun-loving flirt who didn't have any intentions of settling down. While Logan would never deliberately set out to hurt Alyssa, his brother didn't know what she'd gone through. Yep, that was why he'd done what he'd done.

Son, a half-truth's the same as an untruth. He could almost hear his momma speaking those words. And she'd be right. If he were being completely honest with himself, he'd admit that he'd cut his brother off at the pass because *he* wanted to be the one to take Alyssa to dinner. Or, as was the case, invite her over for dinner. He wanted to get to know more about her. Wanted to spend time with her outside of work.

A wave of guilt swept over him. He shouldn't be wanting anything. It felt like a betrayal of what he'd had with Isabel. His focus needed to be on finishing the rec center, not on a tenderhearted female who would be gone in a few short weeks.

"Is it time yet?" Katie hollered from where she stood looking out the front window, shoes and coat already on.

His gaze shifted to the clock on the kitchen wall. Ten minutes to six. "It's time," he acknowledged with a frown.

"Yay!" his daughter exclaimed, racing for the door. "Hurry up, Daddy!"

Turning off the burner, Nathan moved the pan of creamed chicken to the back of the stove top and dropped the lid onto it to keep it warm. Then he grabbed his coat from the back of the kitchen chair, shoving his arms into the sleeves as he followed his daughter outside.

"You know Miss McCall will be leaving in a few weeks, maybe less," he told his daughter as he leaned over to buckle her into her seat. Something he appeared to need reminding of himself.

"Not if she likes it here," Katie countered. "Then maybe she'll stay."

"She has a life somewhere else, Cupcake." Settling back against the driver's seat, he fastened his seat belt and started the engine. "A job. Friends. A place of her own." He pulled out and started down the gravel road.

"But if I had some mistletoe, I'd have a new mommy and she'd have you."

His daughter was persistent if anything. "Alyssa is a very special lady. And as nice as she is, chances are she already has someone special in her life. Now no more talk about her staying here in Braxton. Just enjoy the time we have to spend with her while she's here." How did he make his daughter understand that he was incapable of loving another woman ever again? That his heart had broken irreparably when he'd lost Isabel.

A tiny frown of disappointment pulled at his daughter's lips as she replied with a sigh, "Okay, Daddy."

Her response left him feeling both relieved and guilty, the second an emotion he seemed to be experiencing more of the past few days.

Katie, as resilient as a Texas Tea Bush, turned her attention to the bag of crayons and paper she'd brought with her from home, her "work" supplies, and began singing softly to herself as she sifted through the various colored crayons in the box.

A few minutes later, they pulled up in front of the boardinghouse. His daughter sprang from the truck and raced for the house before Nathan could call her back. Shaking his head, he let himself out and strode toward the deep-set traditional porch with its assortment of antique rockers. His daughter had already disappeared inside by the time he reached it, no doubt eager to see the kittens before returning home.

The front screen door swung open just as he started up the steps and Alyssa stepped outside. The sight of her nearly had him stopping midstep. Instead of the jeans and sweater she had worn when working today, she was wearing a simple knee-length floral dress with a short-waisted jean jacket. Only there was nothing simple about it. The pale peach flowers with their dark green leaves complemented the golden highlights of her red-gold hair. His gaze slid down to the fawn-colored boots she wore.

"Hello."

Her voice drew his gaze upward. Her smile caught

and held it. "Hello," he replied, feeling oddly off-balance.

"Doris took Katie back to the kitchen to see Blue-bell, Rhett and Scarlett, who are busy feasting on a plate of tuna. Would you like to come in?"

He shook his head. "We'd best get going. I've got dinner waiting on the stove. Would you mind just giving Katie a holler?"

"Sure thing," she said. "Be right back."

The second she slipped back inside, he pulled out his cell and dialed his brother.

Carter answered on the second ring. "What's up, big brother?"

"I need you to come over for dinner."

"When?" his brother asked.

"Tonight," he replied. "In five minutes."

"You want me to come over for dinner in *five* minutes?"

"Bring Audra and the kids, of course. We should be home by then."

"We?"

"Alyssa, Katie and me."

"Why?"

Because he didn't trust himself where Alyssa was concerned. He didn't want to notice she was pretty. Didn't want to sit across the table from that beautiful smile and yearn for it to be aimed at him. But he settled for "Because that's what family does. They get together and have dinner."

"Maybe so, but I'm afraid that won't be happening tonight," Carter said. "Audra just took the kids upstairs for their baths. Besides, we already ate."

"You could come. You don't have to eat."

His brother laughed. "If I didn't know better, I'd think you were afraid to be alone with Alyssa."

"She's wearing a dress," Nathan said with a frown.

"As women sometimes do," Carter pointed out with another chuckle, enjoying Nathan's discomfort a little too much. "Besides, you'll have Katie there to keep you from drooling too much."

Why had he ever thought calling Carter was a good idea?

Alyssa's gaze swept over the wraparound porch that made up the front and one side of Nathan Cooper's house. Unfortunately, it was one of those times when her vision wasn't at its best, so she couldn't make out much more than the shape of the porch and the color of the house—white trimmed in a steel blue.

"Farmhouse?" she asked, knowing Nathan would understand.

"Yes, but not an old one," he explained. "I built it the year before Katie was born."

"What I wouldn't give to have a porch even half this size at the town house I live in," she admitted.

He shrugged. "A porch is a porch."

But it was so much more than that. It was a place for family and friends to sit and share special moments. A place for couples to watch the stars from at night. A place it suddenly struck her that neither of them could enjoy to its fullest. Because she didn't have family to share those special moments with. And Nathan had lost the woman he loved.

The screen door creaked open and Katie popped her head out. "Are you guys coming?"

"On our way." Nathan reached for the door and then, holding it open, motioned her inside.

The house was clean with very little clutter she noted as he walked her through the spacious living room, which was open to a large dining room area. She tried to make out the pictures on the walls, but the images in them were nothing more than darkened blurs. Were there pictures of Isabel hanging there? Something told her the woman had been quite beautiful. And perfect. A wife without flaws.

Why did it matter? It wasn't as if this was a date. It was simply Nathan and Katie being kind. She forced her gaze down to the table in front of her and the floral-edged china that had been set out for the meal. "The table looks lovely."

"Katie insisted we bring out the good china," Nathan said. "The plastic silverware was her idea, as well," he added with a grin.

"My favorite kind of silverware," Alyssa replied, appreciating the effort Katie had put into making dinner special.

Katie beamed at Alyssa's approval of her hostessing skills. "It's good on picnics, too."

"I'll bet it would be."

Nathan chuckled. "You make it sound as though you've never used plastic silverware when you've gone on picnics. They must do things a bit more fancified in San Antonio than they do here."

She kept her gaze fixed on the table. "I don't know how they do it in San Antonio or anywhere else. I've never been on a picnic."

"Ever?" Katie gasped.

She shook her head, forcing her gaze upward. "Afraid not."

"Not even when you were little?"

"Katie," Nathan said, his tone gentle. "Not everyone goes on picnics."

"They should," she insisted. "Can we have an inside picnic, Daddy? Like we do sometimes when it rains?"

"I doubt Miss McCall wants to eat her dinner on the living room floor."

Katie looked up at her. "Do you wanna have a picnic with us?"

Alyssa exchanged glances with Nathan, whose expression was nothing less than apologetic. She smiled, then looked down at Katie. "I would love to have a picnic with you and your daddy. Do I need to watch out for ants?"

Katie giggled. "No, silly. Ants live in the grass. We're gonna be sitting on the rug in front of the fireplace."

"Well, then," she said, feeling nearly as excited as Katie was, "do you have paper plates? I'd hate to use your father's good china on the floor."

"We'll use the china," Nathan said as he moved past her to collect the dinner plates and salad bowls from the table. "Alyssa, would you mind grabbing the silverware? Katie, you're in charge of finding us a blanket to have our picnic on."

His daughter raced off to fetch it.

"I'm sorry this isn't gonna be the dinner you expected," he said over his shoulder the moment Katie was gone.

"No," she agreed. "It's not. It's gonna be even better."

He turned to face her. "You really don't mind?"

She shook her head. "Not at all." Her gaze fell to the

dishes he held. "I just feel bad you have to go through all this trouble because of me. The table looked so nice."

He shrugged. "It's no trouble. Besides, my daughter's right. Everyone should experience a picnic at least once in their life. Or as close to a real picnic as we can offer," he added with a grin, "seeing as how it's too cold outside to have one out in the yard."

Don't cry, she told herself as the sting of tears in her eyes threatened to have her doing just that. No one had ever done anything so special for her. Ever. Embarrassed by her inability to control her emotions, Alyssa kept her back to him as she gathered up the plastic silverware. A tear slid down her cheek and she closed her eyes, willing the rest not to fall.

"Alyssa?" Nathan's caring voice wrapped around her. "You okay?"

"Fine," she said, her voice breaking.

"Are you crying?"

"One tear doesn't constitute crying," she assured him, her lips trembling as she turned to face him with a reassuring smile.

"Was it something I said?" he asked with a worried frown.

"Yes," she answered honestly. "But not in a bad way."

"How can my making you cry not be a bad thing?" Confusion lit his blue eyes.

"I've never had anyone do this for me," she said, waving her hand over the stack of delicate china he held in his large, work-roughened hands. "Make dinner for me. Invite me on a picnic."

Understanding filled his eyes and his mouth quirked up on one side. "An inside picnic."

"I know," she said with a soft sniffle. "Don't mind me. I'm just being silly."

"Not at all," he said. "I'm glad that I...that is, Katie and I could give you this. It's the least we could do for all you are doing for our town."

"Katie is so lucky to have a father like you," she said softly. "So kind and caring. So strong in your love for your family and in your faith—"

"Got it!" Katie exclaimed as she dashed back into the room, carrying a faded blue blanket.

Thankfully, Katie's return saved Alyssa from saying any more. She stepped away from Nathan to help Katie spread the blanket out before the fireplace.

Nathan joined them, the three of them working together to set their new table.

Alyssa glanced up to find him watching her, the amber glow of the fireplace lighting his smiling face. She smiled back, wishing there were more men like Nathan Cooper in the world. But experience had shown her his kind was a rare find.

"If you two can finish setting up for our picnic," Nathan said, "I'll head into the kitchen and warm up the biscuits so we can eat." His tall form straightened until he towered over them as they knelt on the blanket. "Can I fix you ladies something to drink while I'm in there?"

"I made lemonade," Katie announced with a proud tilt of her tiny chin. "With real lemons."

"Lemonade sounds like the perfect drink for a picnic," Alyssa said excitedly, making Katie's smile widen even more.

"Two lemonades coming right up." Turning, Nathan disappeared into the kitchen.

Katie settled cross-legged onto the blanket. "Do you like my tree?" she asked, pointing to the small, spindly tree standing next to the fireplace. One probably no taller than Katie herself.

Alyssa took in the hazy glow of the miniature white Christmas lights. Tilting her head slightly to bring the sparsely decorated tree into better focus amid the shadowy spots that hampered her vision that evening, she took in the smattering of colorful bulbs that hung from several of the slender branches. A garland made of popcorn wound its way around the tree, while a piece of burlap snugly surrounded its base. It reminded her of the tree in *A Charlie Brown Christmas.*

"It's the perfect size," she told Katie.

"I picked it out myself," she said with a glance toward the kitchen. "Daddy cut it down for me."

"Where will your big tree go?" she asked, looking around.

"We won't have one. Daddy says he's not good at decorating," she explained. "But I think it's 'cause he's too busy."

Her heart went out to Katie, knowing what it felt like to spend Christmas in a home void of holiday spirit. Only in Katie's case it wasn't because her daddy didn't care. It was because he was a single father, trying to run a company while raising a young daughter. He was probably too tired after a long day's work to feel like stringing up Christmas lights or putting out holiday decorations. Maybe she could help. After all, decorating for the holidays was a favorite pastime of hers. And she'd love nothing more than to give Katie the sort of Christmas she had always longed for as a little girl.

Chapter Seven

"I have to admit I was surprised to see Alyssa arrive with you and Katie this morning," Carter said as he and Nathan stood watching Alyssa and Audra talking outside of Braxton's only church.

"Katie invited her to join us today," Nathan grumbled. Going to church always left him feeling torn. There was a part of him that used to believe in God's good grace, in what it meant to have unyielding faith. He supposed that part of him still lingered somewhere deep inside, having been a part of him since childhood. But he'd long since locked that part of himself away.

Besides, if they hadn't given Alyssa a ride there, she would have walked. Doris and Myrna, though devout Christians, almost never left their boardinghouse. After Doris's husband passed away, she'd developed an aversion to going out, and Myrna chose to remain at her sister's side. They even had their groceries delivered. He understood the urge to lock yourself away after losing someone you love, but he didn't have that option. Not with Katie in his life. He simply carried on.

"She's wearing a dress," his brother said with a

chuckle, distracting Nathan from his troubled thoughts. "Is that why you're in a mood?"

She was. A long, almost to her ankles, light blue dress that fluttered in the breeze. Covered by the fitted, camel-colored jacket she wore. He looked Carter's way with a scowl. "Worry about your own wife's dress."

Carter chuckled. "Just trying to figure out why you're acting like you got a burr stuck in your britches, and I remembered how her wearing a dress to dinner last week had you all in a fluster."

"It doesn't have anything to do with her dress," he said. Even if she did look right pretty in them.

His brother grew more serious. "Care to let me in on what's really eating at you? You haven't been yourself for days."

Nathan's frown deepened as he glanced Alyssa's way again. "I'm not the man she believes me to be."

"How so?"

His gaze shifted, locking with his brother's. "She's a good woman."

"You won't get any argument from me there."

"Honest."

His brother nodded. "A definite plus."

"I've never known a woman stronger in her faith."

His brother studied him with a critical eye. "Okay. I've got all that. What I'm trying to figure out is how her having all those positive qualities fits in with her not knowing who you really are."

So strong in your love for your family and in your faith. Her words had stuck with him, forcing him to take a look at the man he'd become. A man lost. A man pretending to be something he wasn't. A man undeserving of someone like Alyssa but failing in his attempts to fight the pull she seemed to have on him.

Nathan sighed deeply, his gaze settling on his booted feet. "Alyssa thinks that because I'm a good father and take Katie to church every Sunday, I'm a man who's strong in his faith."

"And you're not?"

He looked to his brother. "You know I'm not."

"I know your faith has been tested," his brother replied matter-of-factly. "And that you're angry with God. But I also know that you'll find your way back. Just as I did."

Could he? He wasn't so sure. Nathan's gaze was drawn in the direction of the church. Alyssa, with her beautiful smile, was laughing at something Audra had said. Sunlight glinted off her hair and lit her face. It felt like that same sun was seeping into his chest, warming him. But he knew it wasn't the sun melting the part of his heart that had been frozen for two years. It was Alyssa. And he found himself wanting to be a better man. The man she thought him to be. The man he once was. Problem was, wanting to do so and being able to do so were two vastly different things.

"Frowning like that isn't the best way to win a woman over," Logan said as he joined his brothers where they were standing at the edge of the church's parking lot, waiting patiently while the women visited and the children played. "Females tend to prefer warm, friendly smiles," he said, directing his words toward Nathan. "I could show you how it's done if you like."

"Not the best time to poke fun at him," Carter warned. "Big brother here's got himself all tied up in knots."

Logan's gaze shifted back to Nathan and he sobered instantly. "You really like her," he said, the surprise clear on his tanned face.

Not that Nathan could blame him. He and Logan had held firm to their decision to remain confirmed bachelors. Or at least they both had until now.

"He *really* likes her," Carter said, answering for him.

"I never said that," Nathan said, his attention drawn once again to the woman he'd made cry—in a good way.

His brother snorted. "As if you had to. It's as plain as the longing we see written on your face. You like her, but you're determined not to."

"I loved my wife."

"We all did," Logan said.

"But she's gone," Carter said as if Nathan needed to be reminded of that fact. "It's been two years. No one is gonna think badly of you for wanting to find happiness again."

His jaw clenched as emotion roiled in his gut. "I can't."

"You can," Logan countered. "Isabel would have wanted you to be happy again."

The about-face his youngest brother had just done had Nathan's tossing a questioning glance his way.

"Don't go looking at me like that," Logan grumbled. "I know what we decided, but you have Katie to think about."

Carter nodded.

"It doesn't matter how I feel," he told them. "Alyssa's only here for a couple more weeks before she returns to her life in San Antonio. The best thing I can do for my daughter—and for Alyssa—is to remember that."

"Nathan…" Carter said, his tone pleading.

He held up a hand. "No. For the next couple of weeks, I'm gonna focus on getting the rec center done, which means keeping things between Alyssa and me strictly professional. Nothing more."

"Can't you do both?"

"My attention has to be directed toward seeing that the dedication to those lost in the storm happens as planned. I can't afford to be sidetracked."

"Nathan—"

"Uncle Nathan!" Audra's seven-year-old son, Mason, hollered out as he and Katie raced out to the parking lot, putting an end to his brothers' determined attempt to convince him otherwise.

He cast a smile their way. Mason and his baby sister, Lily, had been abandoned by their birth father, Audra's ex-husband, both emotionally and physically. How any man could do that to his child was beyond Nathan. However, Carter was in the process of legally adopting them. They already considered him their father, just as his brother considered them every bit as much his children as the baby Audra now carried inside her.

"Daddy, guess what!" Katie exclaimed as she did her best to keep up with her cousin in spite of her slight limp.

"What?" he asked with a grin as they came to a stop in front of him, their little cheeks pink from their sprint across the churchyard.

"You're gonna help Miss McCall with the manger," Mason told him.

"I'm what?" he said, looking in Alyssa's direction.

She mouthed *I'm sorry* before turning her attention back to whatever it was Audra had been saying to Reverend Johns' wife, Rachel, and several other women who had gathered around them.

Sorry about what? His gaze dropping back down to the two smiling children in front of him, he said, "What are you two talking about?"

"Mrs. Gillis was asking if anyone had time to help work on the manger," Mason explained.

"Alyssa said she'd be happy to," Katie said excitedly. "I told Mrs. Gillis that you'd be happy to help, too, 'cause you're a team. And you have to drive her here."

"Looks like someone's gonna have to focus on more than just the rec center," Logan said with a grin.

Carter snorted.

Nathan growled, then immediately regretted doing so. Thirty-year-old men did not growl. Especially with two children standing within hearing range.

"I'm not doing it alone," he told his brothers. "You two are volunteering, too."

"Think he needs us there to keep his focus where it ought to be?" Logan asked Carter with a grin.

His brother nodded. "Might be a good idea. He won't be much help if he's constantly hammering his thumb instead of the nails he's supposed to be pounding in."

Audra and her five-year-old daughter, Lily, came over to join them before Nathan could defend himself.

"Darlin'," Carter greeted her with a loving smile. Then he reached out, curling his arm around his wife's slightly expanded waist. "Enjoy your visit with Alyssa?"

"Very much so," she answered with a smile. "She's so easy to talk to. I feel like I've known her forever."

Nathan understood what Audra meant about Alyssa being so easy to talk to. She had a way of making people feel at ease around her. He nodded in agreement.

"I'm looking forward to spending more time with her," his sister-in-law said. "We're going to get together for some girl time with Lizzie one of these days. Mrs. Johns offered to watch the children for a few hours so we could."

"Sounds like fun," Carter agreed, despite his happy expression drooping ever-so-lightly. "But you have me to watch the children. Why would you need the reverend's wife to help out?"

Her expression grew tender. "Because as much as I love it when you spend time with my—" she caught herself, her warm smile deepening "—*our* children, you have a very important job to get done. You never know how late you're going to be working. Especially during the next couple of weeks. So I was grateful for Rachel's kind offer. Unfortunately, Alyssa won't be in town for much longer, so we can't wait until after the rec center is finished."

At the mention of Alyssa's imminent departure from Braxton, Nathan's searching gaze moved once more in the direction of the church's front walkway. Those who had milled about after that morning's service were now gone. Alyssa included. Had she forgotten something, and gone back inside to fetch it? No, he definitely recalled her holding her purse when they'd walked out. Maybe she'd gone around to the other side of the church to see where the nativity scene would be set up.

"If you're looking for Alyssa," his sister-in-law said behind him, "she asked me to let you know that since it's such a beautiful day, she's going to walk back to the boardinghouse."

While the day was pleasantly warm, despite it being a week into December, it was still a long walk. And she would be doing it in heels. "Katie, get in the truck," he said, his gaze now fixed in the direction Alyssa was headed.

"Why don't you leave Katie with us?" Carter suggested, drawing Nathan's attention his way. "The kids have been wanting to have some real playtime together with their new cousin."

Audra nodded. "Katie can stay for dinner and you can pick her up later this evening."

"Please, Daddy!" his daughter implored, working him over with her big brown eyes.

He hesitated only a moment before giving his consent. "Mind your manners."

"I will!"

He watched as she scampered off to Carter's truck with an equally excited Mason and Lily.

"Katie will be fine," Audra assured him before she and Carter took their leave.

"You best get a move on or Alyssa will be at the boardinghouse before you even start your truck."

He turned to find Logan watching him with a knowing grin.

"Traitor," Nathan grumbled as he started for his truck.

"Call it a change of heart," his brother called out. "At least where your remaining a bachelor is concerned."

Nathan yanked open his truck door and slid into the cab. One of these days, his little brother was gonna get what was coming to him. Hopefully in the form of a female who made Logan every bit as unsettled as Alyssa made him.

Unsettled didn't even come close to describing how he felt after he'd driven all the way to the boardinghouse only to be told by Myrna that Alyssa hadn't gotten home yet. How was that possible?

Unease moved through him as he pulled away from the boardinghouse. Had Alyssa gotten lost? Or had she stopped somewhere in town to pick something up before heading back.

A flash of baby blue through the trees where the walking bridge crossed over the Blue Falls Creek caught his eye. Pulling off the road, he cut the engine and jumped out of the truck.

Taking the dirt path through the woods, he stepped from the trees to see Alyssa standing on the narrow bridge. Relief swept through him at finding her safe and sound.

Her head was tipped back, her eyes closed, every inch of her awash in sunlight. A gentle breeze had the hem of her dress fluttering lazily around her legs. She looked right pretty standing there, taking in the sweet sounds of nature, feeling the warm caress of sun on her face, the whisper of the wind.

All of those things he hadn't allowed himself to fully appreciate for so long. But Alyssa had a way of making him feel things. Even when he fought hard not to. Carter had once told him he needed to come back to the land of the living. Those words came rushing back to him now as he moved toward the bridge. That was exactly how he felt. Alive.

The sound of a twigs cracking under quickened footsteps had Alyssa turning.

"There you are."

"Nathan," she breathed, her heart thumping. "You startled me."

"Reckon that makes us even then," he drawled as he moved to stand beside her on the narrow wooden bridge. "I went looking for you when I left church and you were nowhere to be found. I was afraid... Well, I thought maybe you had gotten lost."

Her first thought was to inform him that she was perfectly capable of taking care of herself. But the fact that he cared enough to worry about her well-being had her apologizing instead.

"I was on my way back to the boardinghouse when I heard the rippling of the creek beyond the trees. I couldn't resist taking a few minutes to appreciate it." She looked up into his handsome face, concern and something more filling those deep blue eyes. "I never meant to worry you. I asked Audra to let you know that I was gonna be walking back to the boardinghouse."

"She passed your message on," he said with a frown. "What I don't understand is why you didn't wait for Katie and me to give you a ride home."

Turning, she looked out over the rail, her gaze fixed on the gently flowing water below. "You were busy with your family and I didn't wanna take you away from that." It sounded better than *Because you've shown me what my life's been missing and being around you and your wonderful family only makes me want more.*

"Alyssa," he said, "if I made you feel like you weren't welcome to join us…"

The last thing she wanted was for him to feel as though he'd done something wrong. She lifted her gaze to his. "You didn't do anything."

"Then it was something someone else said?" he asked with a frown.

"No," she answered honestly. "Everyone has been more than welcoming. It's just that I'm used to watching others with their families, not partaking in it." With the exception of Erica's family. But even then she only saw them all together a few times a year.

"Then it appears we'll have to work on that," he said, his words tender. "You don't have to be family to take part in our conversations."

"Thank you," she said, lowering her gaze. "I'll keep that in mind."

"You do that. It appears I'm not the only one in my family who enjoys your company," he added with a grin.

She looked up at him in surprise. "I thought you were counting down the days before you were rid of me."

His expression grew serious. "In the beginning, yes. But it didn't take long before I realized what a positive addition you were—are—to the team."

"Tell that to my employers," she mumbled. "They don't think I'm capable of doing my job any longer."

"They'd be dead wrong," he said firmly. "But that's not why I want you to stick around. Truth is, I like having you around, and I know for a fact my daughter does, as well. At the risk of crossing some unspoken professional line, I'd really like to get to know you better. Outside of work."

Her eyes widened in surprise. "You wanna spend personal time with me?"

His devastatingly handsome smile returned. "I'd like the opportunity. Why do you seem so surprised?"

"Because…" What if Nathan found her lacking as other men had? The thought he might be disappointed kept her silent.

"Alyssa…" he prodded gently.

She sighed deeply. "Because I'm not perfect."

"And you think I am?" he replied with a husky laugh. "Far from it," he admitted. "Just ask my brothers."

That made her smile. "You know what I mean. There are things I can't do because of my vision."

"There are plenty of things I can't do and I have twenty-twenty vision."

"It's not that simple," she said, wanting him to know the full extent of what he was getting into.

"Nothing in life is simple," he told her. "I've learned that the hard way." Turning, he clasped his hands atop the railing. "When Isabel died, I forgot how to breathe. How to feel. I put on a brave face for my daughter, but inside I was numb." He glanced her way. "And then you came into our life. I can't explain it, but when I'm around you, I feel like I can breathe again."

Unshed tears stung her eyes. "That's the nicest thing anyone's ever said to me," she said, her words catching on a choked sob.

"All I'm asking for is a chance to get to know the

woman you are beneath the hard-working, incredibly focused interior designer I see at work every day. The woman who was so deeply touched by something as simple as a picnic on my living room floor. A chance to become…friends."

Emotion clogged her throat. "I'd really enjoy spending more time with you and Katie outside of work." Nathan Cooper truly was a man worth holding on to. If only as a good friend. He hadn't run the other way the moment he'd learned she was legally blind. Yet she knew better than to expect anything more than the friendship he spoke of, despite the comfort she felt working alongside him at the rec center and sitting beside him and Katie in church.

His smile widened. "Are you in a hurry to get back to the boardinghouse?" She didn't miss the hint of eagerness in his voice.

"No," she said, wondering what he could be up to. "Why?"

"There's something I'd like to show you." His gaze dropped down to the sling-back heels she'd worn to church, and his mouth twisted into a thoughtful frown. "Reckon I'm gonna have to carry you there."

"Carry me?" she said, letting out a little shriek as Nathan scooped her up in his arms.

"Can't have you twisting an ankle," he said as he carried her across the bridge to the other side, and then onto another wooded trail that ran along the curving creek bed.

"Just how far are you gonna carry me?" Not that he showed the least bit of strain at having to do so. The man was incredibly strong, both inside and out.

He grinned down at her as they moved along the well-worn trail. "I'd carry you all the way to the boardinghouse if the situation called for it. But the waterfall is only about another hundred feet or so ahead."

"Waterfall?"

"Not a large one," he was quick to explain. "But it's right pretty, nestled in a vee of rocks where it cascades down into the creek below."

He seemed so excited that she didn't have the heart to tell him she probably wouldn't be able to see the beauty of what he was describing. It was the thought that counted. And that he'd thought to share something so beautiful with her touched Alyssa deeply.

The trail opened up onto a small grassy bank, beyond which was a wider expanse of the creek and what, though blurred, appeared to be a rocky hillside. Nathan set her on her feet and then said in a hushed voice, "Shh...just listen."

She heard birds chirping happily in the trees above them. The creek gurgling a few feet away from where they stood. And the sweetest sound of all, the rhythmic fall of water into the creek below. Like a gentle rain, but centered in one place.

It suddenly struck her that Nathan hadn't brought her there to *see* the waterfall. He'd taken her there to *hear* it. At that moment, she felt like the luckiest woman in the world.

"It's beautiful," she said, her words tight with emotion. "Thank you for bringing me here."

"Maybe you can come back to Braxton for a visit this summer when the creek is warmer and we can wade in to see the falls close up."

"I would love that," she said, looking up at him. "Katie, too?"

His smile widened, seemingly pleased by her question. "And Katie, too."

"Nathan had you over for dinner?" Erica gasped on the other end of the line. "Are we talking about Nathan the incredibly hunky construction worker you've been working with on the rec center? The one who wasn't exactly thrilled to have you there?"

Alyssa smiled. "One and the same."

"So am I to assume he's gotten over any issues he had about working with you?"

"He has." She went on to tell Erica all about the special picnic she'd shared with Nathan and Katie that past week and how he'd taken her to church with them. "That was so incredibly sweet of them to take you on a picnic," her friend said. "And then to invite you to go with them to church, I know that had to mean a lot to you."

"It did," Alyssa admitted. To find a man who valued faith as much as she did meant the world to her. And then what he'd done for her at the waterfall. She grew misty-eyed just thinking about it. "And there's more."

"The man already sounds perfect. What more could there be?"

"He told me that he'd like to see me outside of work."

Another gasp. "As in dating?"

"As in building a friendship," she clarified.

"Some of the best relationships have begun with friendship."

She couldn't bring herself to get her hopes up. "I

don't think Nathan's looking for that kind of relationship. But I'm willing to take things one day at a time and see where things go between us."

"Don't even think about it!" her friend blurted out, her words followed by the phone clattering on the other end of the line.

Alyssa blinked. She certainly hadn't expected that reaction from her friend. Erica had been trying to convince her that her Mr. Right was out there. And now that she found a man who came close to being her image of Mr. Right, her friend was demanding she not let it happen?

"But I really like him."

The sound at the other end of the line was muffled. Alyssa stepped over to her bedroom window at the boardinghouse, hoping it might improve the connection, which had suddenly gone from good to bad.

She was just about to hang up and call Erica back when her friend came back on the line.

"Sorry about that. I was in my closet hanging up some of Michael's shirts and my darling daughter decided to use our bed as a trampoline. I dropped my cell into the laundry basket on my mad dash out of the closet to grab her."

Relief swept through her. "So you weren't speaking to me when you said 'Don't you dare'?"

Her friend laughed. "Are you kidding me? I am beyond thrilled for you. There's no one I know more deserving of finding true happiness. And if your friendship with Nathan leads to more? Well, then I'll be more than happy for you."

"I know you would be." Alyssa glanced toward the clock on the nightstand. "I hate to cut our call short, but I need to head downstairs. Myrna and Doris fixed Texas chili and homemade cornbread for dinner."

"Then I'd better let you go. Munchkin here is due for her bath anyway," her friend said. "Aren't you, munchkin?" Whatever Erica did elicited squeals from her daughter. "Have fun, Alyssa."

"You, too." Alyssa disconnected the call, a smile stretched wide across her face. Maybe, just maybe, her friendship with Nathan would lead to more, and she would have her very own happily-ever-after someday, too.

Chapter Eight

"**Y**ou have no idea how excited I am for our girls' night out," Lizzie announced as Alyssa slid into the backseat of Audra's minivan. "Monday was crazy busy at work. Thankfully today was a little slower. But then I only work half days on Tuesdays unless Verna needs me to stay on longer."

"You aren't the only one looking forward to tonight," Audra said from the front seat. "By the time my third child arrives, there won't be anyone willing to watch that many kids all at once."

"If I lived around here, I'd be more than happy to help you out," Alyssa told her, meaning every word of it. Audra's children were adorable and well mannered.

Lizzie sighed. "If I didn't have a full schedule with work and school, I'd volunteer, as well."

"It's not as if I mind spending most of my time with my children. They truly are blessings from God. As is my supportive and loving husband."

Alyssa smiled, but inside she ached for all those things. To be a mother. A wife. Loved. Shaking the dismal thoughts away, she said cheerily, "So where are we going?"

"Ryan's Pies and Pins," Lizzie replied excitedly. She had volunteered to choose their entertainment for that evening and Alyssa and Audra had happily agreed. "I reserved us a lane. We can enjoy some of Ryan's hand-tossed pizza while we bowl a few games."

"Bowling?" Alyssa said worriedly.

The two women looked her way.

"If you'd rather not bowl," Lizzie said, "we can do something else. I should have asked if the two of you liked bowling before making definite plans."

"It's not that." Alyssa wasted no time assuring her. "I actually love bowling. Although I haven't done so since…"

"Since?" Audra pressed worriedly.

Alyssa sighed. They would have figured it out sooner or later anyway. "I'm visually impaired. Legally blind is the actual medical diagnosis I've been given."

"I had no idea," Lizzie gasped.

"Alyssa," Audra breathed.

"It's all right," she told them, pasting on a bright smile. "Most people don't know. A few years ago, I was involved in a serious car accident. By God's grace I survived, but the head trauma I suffered left me visually impaired."

"I'm so sorry," Audra said.

"Don't be," she told her. "God gave me a second chance at life. I refuse to waste one precious moment of it feeling sorry for myself. Instead, I wanna live as normal a life as I possibly can. And that includes bowling with my two new friends."

"Then that's exactly what you'll do," Lizzie announced, her youthful smile returning.

A few minutes later, they were walking through the entrance of the bowling alley and pizzeria.

"There's a single step down about five feet in front of you," Audra announced as she closed the door behind them.

"Thanks for the warning," Alyssa said with a grateful smile. She might not have noticed in the dimly lit entryway. Thankfully the much larger bowling alley area farther inside was abundantly lit.

"Well, well, if it isn't my long-lost little Lizzie Parker," a man with wavy blond hair and a neatly trimmed goatee greeted from behind the counter when they stepped into the bowling area.

She approached him. "We have a lane reserved for six thirty."

"I know you do," he said, his charming smile widening. "Saw your name on the book when I came in." His gaze slid to Audra and he nodded. "Mrs. Cooper."

"Audra, please."

His attention shifted to Alyssa and he let out a low whistle. "The pretty ladies in this town just keep on multiplying."

Lizzie rolled her eyes with a groan. "Reckon I should've warned you both before we got here that Ryan fancies himself a bit of a smooth-talking ladies' man."

He chuckled. "Can't change something that's a pure fact." The ladies rattled off their shoe sizes to Ryan and he pulled three pairs out from under the counter. "Here you go. You ladies are on lane eighteen. Can I get you anything else?"

"A menu please," Alyssa said.

"Thank you," Lizzie said as he held one out to her. "And for the record, I'm not little and I haven't been lost. Just busy with work and school. If you'd ever stop by Big Dog's, you'd have known that."

"And give my competition the business?" he said with a teasing grin.

Alyssa took in the playful banter between the bowling alley owner and Lizzie, and couldn't help but wonder if there was something more going on between them. Not that it was any of her business if there was. Turning her focus elsewhere, she listened to the sound of bowling balls being dropped onto the wooden lanes before rolling down the alleys. In the distance, she heard the crack of pins. The familiar sounds took her back to a more carefree time in her life. Oh, how she had missed this.

"Okay, spill," Carter said as Nathan drove them to the bowling alley across town.

"Spill what?" Nathan said.

"What's got you so out to sorts that you've called us all together for an evening out," his brother replied.

Nathan frowned. "Does something have to be wrong for me to wanna spend time with my brothers outside of work?"

"Yep," Logan muttered. "Something's definitely troubling him."

Nathan released a long-drawn-out sigh. "It's nothing."

Logan leaned forward from the backseat of Nathan's truck. "Nothing, as in Alyssa?"

"I asked her to be friends," he said with a frown as

he turned into the parking lot outside of Ryan's Pies and Pins.

Logan laughed. "As opposed to being her enemy?"

Parking in one of the empty spaces, Nathan turned to glower at his brother.

"Logan's right," Carter said. "So you asked Alyssa to be friends. Why do you think that's such a bad thing? We happen to like her."

So did he, Nathan thought with a frown. More than he ought to.

Carter clapped a hand atop Nathan's shoulder. "What do you say we go get our game on? Loser springs for the pizza."

"I'm in," Logan said. "Prepare to buy me dinner, boys."

Win or lose, it didn't matter to Nathan. He needed this night out. A night where his thoughts could be centered on something other than his pretty coworker, Alyssa McCall.

No sooner had they stepped into the place than soft laughter caught Nathan's attention. Sure enough, the very woman he'd gone to the bowling alley to escape thinking about for one evening was laughing with his sister-in-law and Lizzie at the far end of the bowling alley over a ball Audra had just rolled.

His gaze snapped to Carter. "Did you know they would be here?"

His brother shook his head. "Nope. I don't think Audra knew where they were going tonight. Lizzie was in charge of planning tonight's festivities."

His brother frowned as he stared across the room at his wife. "Do you think she ought to be lifting that ball in her condition?"

Logan shrugged. "I'm no expert, but I've seen pregnant women picking up their other children with no problem. They've gotta weigh more than a bowling ball."

Nathan's attention was centered on Alyssa, his brothers' conversation becoming nothing more than a hum of chatter behind him. The girls were clearly enjoying their night out. He watched in surprise as Alyssa stepped up to take a turn. He worried over her twisting an ankle in the gutter if she misjudged where she needed to be standing.

Logan stepped up beside him, giving him a nudge. "You wanna go somewhere else?"

Nathan shook his head, his gaze fixed on Alyssa. "She's bowling," he stated worriedly.

"And doing quite well," Carter stated. "She just took down nine pins."

"Well, well, this must be family night."

They turned to see Ryan, a smile lighting his face.

"Appears that way," Logan agreed.

Ryan extended his hand, greeting each one of them. He and Logan had gone to school together and still managed to get together on occasion in spite of their demanding businesses.

"Carter?"

All heads pivoted toward the sound of Audra's voice.

"Hey, darlin'," he greeted with a loving smile.

Her smile wavered, concern lighting her eyes. "Are the children all right?"

He looked confused for a moment before promptly setting her mind at ease. "Right as rain and in good hands with the reverend and his wife."

"Then why are you here?" she asked, looking every bit as confused as his brother had been moments before.

"I invited him," Nathan told her.

Carter nodded. "We had no idea you'd be here."

"Didn't you see the minivan outside?"

Actually they hadn't, Nathan thought. They'd all been too distracted by his moment of emotional panic. "We can go somewhere else," he suggested.

She laughed. "Why ever would you do that? Come join us." She looked to Ryan. "Is the lane next to ours reserved?"

He shook his head. "It's all yours if you want it."

"I don't think—" Carter began only to have Nathan cut him off.

"We'll take it."

"Are the children okay?" Alyssa asked when Audra returned alone.

"They're fine," she said, her relief evident. "The men decided to enjoy a night of bowling after work and had no idea we'd be here. I hope you don't mind, but I invited them to join us."

"The more the merrier," Lizzie chirped.

"I don't mind," Alyssa said. She welcomed any chance to spend time with Nathan and build on their growing friendship.

"Something told me you wouldn't have an issue with it," Audra teased, her words making Alyssa blush. "As soon as Ryan can find shoes large enough to fit their big feet, they'll be right over."

A few minutes later, three big strapping men moved

toward them. Alyssa's gaze was drawn immediately to Nathan.

"Ladies," they greeted in unison as they walked over to place their balls in the ball return tray.

Nathan turned to face her with a smile. "Fancy meeting you here."

She returned his smile. "Where's Katie?"

"The reverend and his wife are babysitting," he answered with a smile. "The kids are working on decorations for the rec center's Christmas party."

"Sounds like fun."

"Speaking of fun," Lizzie said with a cheery smile. "Why don't we share the lanes and keep all the scores on one sheet?"

"I'm not so sure that's a good idea," Nathan told her. "We Coopers tend to get very competitive."

"So do I," Alyssa countered with a playful smile. "But if you men are afraid you might be outbowled by us women..."

"It's not that," he said worriedly.

"If you're afraid her vision's going to hold her back," Audra said, guessing the cause of his hesitation, "think again."

Lizzie nodded in agreement.

Nathan's dark brow lifted in surprise. "They know?"

Alyssa smiled, her gaze moving to the two women who had befriended her. "Friends should always be honest with each other."

"What do you say we get this game on the road?" Logan announced. "I'm starving and loser buys the pizza tonight."

"We'll play for pizza another time," Nathan told his brother with a frown.

"Why?" Alyssa asked. "I'm game if the other girls are."

"I'm in," Audra said.

Lizzie dropped down onto the scorekeeper's chair. "Me, too."

"Alyssa," Nathan said worriedly.

"Don't you dare count me out, Nathan Cooper."

A slow smile moved across his handsome face. "I'd never count you out. You forget, I've seen firsthand what you're capable of once you've set your mind to something."

Alyssa smiled at the compliment. Things were going well with the rec center. Both Nathan and Carter were supportive of her ideas and suggestions, even making a few of their own.

"Well, now that we have that settled, you two are up," Lizzie announced as she began adding names to the electronic scoring screen.

Without a moment's hesitation, Alyssa stepped up to the tray of bowling balls and reached for the one she'd chosen to bowl with that night.

Nathan joined her. "I was surprised to find you here. But I'm glad I did."

She smiled up at him. "I'm gonna remind you of that after the final scores are tallied."

An amused grin moved across his face and a dark brow lifted. "Someone counting their chickens before they're hatched?"

"Maybe," she said with a giggle, and then she started over to her lane. "Oh, and, Nathan…"

"Yes?"

"I may have forgotten to mention that I was captain of my college bowling team for two years straight. Division champs both times."

"Watch out, Nathan," Carter called out, "I think she's their ringer."

He gave a husky chuckle. "I think you might be right."

She adored this playful, easygoing side of him. He'd been working himself so hard to get the rec center done that it was nice to see him taking some time for himself.

"How about I bowl left-handed instead?" she suggested with a grin as she lifted her ball.

"You're ambidextrous, aren't you?"

She giggled. "Maybe."

With a groan, he said, "Something tells me dinner's gonna be on me tonight."

This could be her life. Sharing special moments with Nathan, no matter how silly they might be. Working with him. Laughing with him. Loving him. *Loving*. She pushed that thought away. Nathan wanted to be friends. Nothing more. She couldn't allow wishful thinking to make her believe otherwise.

At the end of the evening, Alyssa and Nathan sat at the bottom of the score rankings with only one throw remaining for each of them. "Looks like one of us is buying," he said as they reached for their balls.

"Hope you brought your wallet," she said with more confidence than she felt. Bowling wasn't nearly as easy as it had been when she had perfect vision. But she'd had fun anyway.

It was Nathan's turn so he stepped forward in the

lane. Then, with perfect form, he sent the ball spiraling toward the pins, then sent the pins scattering.

"A split," Lizzie announced, no doubt for Alyssa's benefit for which she was extremely grateful. All evening the others had found ways to let her know where things stood without making her feel like she was a hindrance to their game.

"Go ahead," he told Alyssa.

"You might as well finish first," she told him.

"Alrighty," he said, reaching for the ball that had just shot up the ball return. Wasting no time, Nathan walked over, aimed and threw.

"Field goals only count as a score in football," Carter said with a husky laugh.

"Bummer," Logan snickered.

Nathan motioned for her to go. "Your turn."

She needed at least seven pins to beat him. In college, that would have been a done deal. Tonight, however, odds weren't in her favor. But she'd give it the old college try. Easing her ball up into the air in front of her, she prepared to send it spiraling down the lane.

"Hey, darlin'," Nathan called out the second she drew back to roll the ball down the aisle.

The weighted ball slipped from her grasp and onto the floor with a loud *kerthunk*, rolling at what could only be described as a turtle's pace up the long alley. She spun around to face her handsome opponent with a disapproving frown. "What?"

"I was gonna offer to fetch you a lighter ball if you thought the one you're using was too weighty," he said with feigned innocence. "Reckon it doesn't matter now."

"You distracted me on purpose!"

Grinning, he shrugged. "What can I say? A man will do almost anything to save his pride from taking a complete thrashing."

"Nathan Cooper, you're a cheater!"

"He is that," Logan agreed from the bench.

"Just goes to prove that the saying 'cheaters never win' is true," Carter remarked from where he sat on the bench, arm curled around his wife. He motioned in the direction her ball had gone.

Nathan turned, a deep sigh passing through his parted lips. "Serves me right, I suppose."

"What are you talking about?" Alyssa said as she followed their gazes.

"You just rolled a strike," Lizzie told her.

"I did?" she gasped.

"You did," Nathan confirmed. "Roll again, darlin', while I dig my wallet out. Looks like I'll be buying tonight."

"That's the most fun I've had in a long time," Lizzie exclaimed as they pulled out of the bowling alley's parking lot.

"Me, too," Alyssa said, smiling.

"Despite losing and having to buy pizza for everyone tonight, something tells me Nathan enjoyed himself even more than we did," Audra said. "Then again, we know why that is."

Alyssa knew they were referring to her. "Nathan and I are just friends." And if she told herself that enough times, maybe she'd be able to accept it.

"I don't know," Lizzie said. "Sure felt like more than that to me. Every time he looked at you, his expression softened. I don't ever remember him smiling as much as he did tonight."

"Alyssa wasn't the only one holding a man's attention this evening," Audra said with a grin.

Lizzie looked to her questioningly. "Someone was watching me?"

"Logan?" Alyssa guessed. Not that she'd noticed, but then she'd been slightly distracted by another Cooper brother.

"Nope," Audra said.

"Then who…" Lizzie began and then stopped. "Please tell me you are not referring to *him*."

"Him who?" Alyssa blurted out.

"Ryan," both women replied. Only Lizzie's response was far less enthusiastic.

Alyssa smiled. So she wasn't the only one who'd noticed something in the air between them. "He seems very nice."

Lizzie snorted. "He's the most frustrating man ever born. 'Little Lizzie,'" she said, repeating his earlier remark. "The man is determined to think of me as his little sister's childhood playmate instead of the woman I've become. Not that it matters anyway. I'm no longer the young girl who followed him around like some lovesick puppy. I've grown up. And in doing so, I've come to accept that life doesn't always go the way we'd like it to."

Alyssa nodded. "I understand completely."

"Oh, Alyssa," Lizzie gasped. "I'm so sorry. Here I am rattling off my frustrations when they're so minor compared to what you and Audra have been through."

She offered a reassuring smile. "We've all been through things in our lives we'd rather not have had to go through. But here we are today, stronger women because of it. God is good."

Lizzie nodded. "So true."

"Amen," Audra said as she pulled up in front of the old farmhouse where Lizzie lived with her elderly parents.

"Thanks again for such a fun evening," Lizzie said as she gathered up her purse. Reaching out, she opened the sliding door and stepped from the minivan.

"Maybe we can do it again sometime," Audra said hopefully.

"I would like that. Night, girls." Closing the door, Lizzie stepped away from the van, waving as they pulled away.

Alyssa waved back, wishing with all her heart she could be there to join them for another girls' night out, but she would be returning to San Antonio as soon as her work there was done, leaving behind her new friends, dear sweet Katie and the man who was quickly stealing her heart. Lizzie had the right of it. Life didn't always go the way one hoped it would.

Chapter Nine

"Thank you so much for agreeing to help us out this evening," Reverend Johns said as he and Nathan carried more lumber around the side of the church to where the nativity scene was being set up next to a large, sprawling oak. "I know you already have a lot on your plate."

"Glad to lend a hand," Nathan replied. A part of him hoped that giving something back to the church would ease some of the guilt he felt every Sunday when he sat determinedly tuning out whatever sermon the reverend was giving to the congregation. There had been a time he used to soak up those sermons and leave feeling good about his life. But since losing Isabel and his parents, all he felt was empty. Until his daughter had invited Alyssa to join them for church the Sunday prior. That morning had changed something inside him.

Alyssa's presence beside him in church had soothed him, giving him a feeling of peace he hadn't known for a very long time. And, much to his surprise, he found himself really listening to the reverend's sermon. He had spoken of forgiveness. Would he ever be able to do that? Let the anger and resentment he felt toward God wash away and start his relationship with the Lord anew?

He caught sight of Alyssa as they rounded the corner of the church. She sat alone at the folding table that had been set up a short distance away from where the manger was being constructed. Her head was bent, her focus solely on painting wood cutouts Carter had made of sheep both standing and lying down that would be staked into the grass near the manger. The sight of her hard at work made him smile. Alyssa dedicated herself fully to any project she committed herself to. He admired that in her.

After depositing the two-by-fours onto the stack by the manger, he walked over to see the one woman he couldn't seem to get off his mind.

He stepped up behind her, taking in the perfectly detailed sheep drying atop the table. She was good. "Is there anything you can't do well?" he asked with a grin.

Her head lifted, the brush stilling in her hand as she glanced back over her shoulder at him. A sweet smile moved over her pretty face. "A few things."

"Somehow I find that hard to believe," he teased. "I've yet to see it."

Setting the paint brush down, she turned in the chair to look up at him. "For starters, you probably wouldn't want me driving around in your truck."

The playful smile she had on her face while talking about something that had to be painful for her made him admire her all the more.

"And," she continued, her smile edging up even higher, "I think I'd hesitate just a bit before asking me to operate a chain saw."

Laughter rumbled in his chest and then spilled out. "I'll keep that in mind," he said, paying no mind to the looks the sound of his laughter had drawn their way. His attention was centered on her. A living, breathing ray of sunshine.

She glanced past him toward the partially built nativity scene. "How are things going?"

He followed her gaze. "We're moving right along. Carter should be back soon with the plywood for the roofing and Logan's picking up straw to spread out across the roof and over the stable floor."

"I know your helping out here this evening wasn't exactly your choice."

Her apologetic tone drew his gaze back to her pretty, fretting face. No, it hadn't been his choice. If he'd had his way, he would have steered clear of the whole thing. But now that he was there, he was grateful Katie had volunteered his services. It felt good to be a part of this again.

"How could I not be here? We're a team, remember?" he told her with a grin, repeating Katie's description of his and Alyssa's relationship.

Her smile returned. One that had proved infectious with his little girl.

More often than not since losing her mother and her grandparents, Katie had been withdrawn and quiet around anyone not close to her. But since Alyssa's arrival, there had been a change in Katie. An inner spark that came out in a constant deluge of bright smiles, excitement and laughter. Alyssa had somehow managed to bring his daughter out of her emotional shell, something even the therapist he'd taken Katie to after the tornado hadn't been able to do.

Forcing himself back from his wandering thoughts, he said, "I should let you get back to painting."

"I suppose," she said with an exaggerated sigh. "These sheep won't paint themselves."

"And the stable won't build itself either," he agreed. "I'd best get back over there."

"Will you be able to finish it tonight?"

"The framing will be done," he replied. "After that, the ladies of the church will take over, adding the finishing touches."

"I wish I could be here to see everything all put together."

"Why wouldn't you be?"

She looked his way. "At the rate things are going here, the rec center will be finished before Christmas Eve and I'll be back in San Antonio."

"Then stay."

"What?"

"Stay here in Braxton, Alyssa. At least through the holidays like you planned. For Katie," he said, and then he added, "And for me."

She opened her mouth to tell him she couldn't, but nothing came out. How could she refuse him? She didn't want to leave, despite knowing she had to. But there was no reason she couldn't stay on a few extra days. It would give them more time to see what might develop between them. And they'd be together for Christmas. Excitement filled her at that thought. While she would miss visiting with Erica and her family, she would be spending the holidays with a man who truly cared about her and his adorable little girl.

"I'd like nothing more than to spend the holidays with you and Katie. We can go to the church's Christmas program together. You were planning on going to it, weren't you?"

"You can count on it."

"Looking good."

Alyssa turned with a smile at the sound of Nathan's voice. "You think?" she said fretfully. "I'm starting to question my decision to add the waves."

"I like them," he said as he crossed the room to stand beside her. He studied the wall, his gaze fixed on the strip of dark blue she'd been hand painting waves across. "Much better than dancing bananas."

She elbowed him playfully in the ribs. "Be serious."

"I am," he said, shooting a teasing glance her way. Then he moved along the wall, admiring her work. "I was wondering if you had any plans for this evening."

"You didn't see enough of me last evening when we were working on the nativity?" she teased. "Actually, I was gonna go online and do some Christmas shopping," she said as she went back to painting. "It's how I do most of my shopping nowadays."

"Because you can't drive," he said, more a comment than a question.

She nodded.

"Why don't Katie and I take you shopping after work this evening? We could grab a bite to eat on the way."

Lowering her brush, she turned to him with a smile. "I'd like that. Speaking of Katie, I haven't seen her for a while. I think she got bored watching me paint squiggles on the wall."

"That's my daughter," he said with a chuckle. "Always has to be doing something. Last I saw her she was in the gym with Carter. He's hanging the netting from the hoops we put up yesterday and has appointed Katie his official basket tester."

"I'll bet she's loving that."

"Let me put it this way. My daughter's arms are gonna feel like limp noodles tonight." He glanced at his watch. "I'd best get back to work. Quitting time in one hour."

"So soon?" she gasped, her gaze shifting to the unfinished stripe that ran along the center of the wall. She still had half the length of that wall to finish adding waves to.

"Not soon enough," he said with a grin as he walked away whistling.

Smiling, she turned back to the section of waves she'd been working on.

"Am I mistaken or was that my brother who just came out of this room whistling a happy tune?" a deep voice asked.

She glanced back over her shoulder, watching as Carter's blurred form came into view. "It was."

He shook his head. "Thought maybe I was dreaming. Nice waves, by the way."

"Thanks," she replied with a smile. "Why would you think you were dreaming just because Nathan was whistling?"

"My brother never whistles," he replied. "At least, he hasn't since…" His words trailed off.

"Since Isabel died," she said in understanding.

"Yes." He leaned against a section of the wall she hadn't gotten to yet and crossed his arms. "Can I be honest with you, Alyssa?"

This sounded serious. She lowered the paintbrush she was holding. "I would hope you would be."

He smiled tenderly. "Because of you, Logan and I might actually get our brother back."

"I don't understand," she replied, confused by his words.

"Plain and simple, you've managed to knock down some of that emotional wall Nathan put up after Isabel's death, something no one else has been able to do for the past two years. And for that, Logan and I will be forever grateful. If there's ever anything we can do for you, all you have to do is ask." Pushing away from the wall, he started from the room.

"Carter," she called out.

His retreating footsteps ceased.

"He's taken down some of my walls, too."

He walked back over to her. "If things work out between the two of you the way I think they could, know that you'll be welcomed into our family with open arms." That said, he walked away, whistling the very same tune his brother had.

A family of her very own. It was something she had longed for all her life. Oh, how she wished she could hope for her and Nathan's relationship to grow in that direction. But how could she ever compete with the memory of his beloved wife? A woman Nathan had loved with all his heart. A woman who had been perfect in every way.

Unlike her.

Dressed and ready for her outing with Nathan and Katie that evening, Alyssa headed downstairs to wait. The twinkling lights of the Christmas tree drew her into the living room where it stood tucked away in the far corner. She moved toward it, drawn in by its warm, welcoming glow. It was the first evening since she'd been there that the tree had been lit.

The shining star at the top of the massive pine was only a few inches shy of the twelve-foot ceiling. Delicate glass ornaments dripped from nearly every branch, adding a wealth of color.

She thought about the tiny tinsel tree she'd bought with money she'd earned babysitting for a neighbor when she was thirteen. It had sat in her living room without lights and with only a few homemade paper ornaments because anything more would surely have weighed its frail, wiry branches down, possibly even broken them. How had she ever thought her tree beautiful?

Reaching out, she gingerly touched one of the tree's delicate ornaments. A deep burgundy heart trimmed in tiny gold flowers.

"Henry bought me that our first Christmas together."

Alyssa let her hand fall back to her side, embarrassed to have been caught so wistfully admiring the tree. "It's lovely." She glanced over as Doris came to stand next to her. "I hope you don't mind my…"

"Oh, don't fret, dear," the older woman said, her gaze moving up the beautifully decorated tree. "This room is intended to be a place for our guests to relax and enjoy. This lovely tree included."

"I didn't realize how beautiful it was," she admitted in awe.

"Perhaps because tonight is the first night we've had it lit since you've been here. We turn the tree lights on for the first time on this day every December in memory of our parents who were married on this date."

"That's such a touching way to honor your parents." Alyssa looked to the tree. "There are so many ornaments. And none of them are alike. Wherever did you find them all?"

"Each and every ornament on that tree is a tiny memory of the blessings our Lord has bestowed upon us over the years." She went on to point out ones that held particular meaning to her. "Nathan and his brothers gave me this one," she said, pointing toward the basket of kittens suspended by a bright red ribbon.

Alyssa felt a tug at her heart. "How wonderful it must be to have such meaningful ornaments to reminisce over."

"There's nothing quite like a tree filled with sentimental old ornaments to make a Christmas more special," Doris said with a wistful sigh. Then she glanced her way. "You don't have any special ones of your own you've collected?"

Alyssa shook her head.

The older woman smiled. "Well, it's never too late to start." Reaching up into the tree, she freed a crystal gift box and handed it to Alyssa.

She stared down at the ornament in her hand. "I can't accept this."

"Sure you can," Doris insisted. "'Tis the season for giving and this is my gift to you. In years to come, when you look back at it, know that it represents the selfless gift you gave to the folks of Braxton. Putting your own life on hold to come here and help give us back something we lost in that awful storm."

Tears filled Alyssa's eyes as she held the delicate, sparkling piece. "I'll treasure it forever. Thank you so very much."

"Oh, dear, I didn't mean to get you all misty-eyed right before your date with Nathan. Myrna is bound to cluck her tongue at me if I take you into the parlor all choked up."

She laughed softly, wiping a single tear from her face. "I'm fine. Really I am." How had a woman she'd known for a little over a week touch her more deeply than her own mother ever had? "And it's not a date. We're just friends."

"Whatever they're calling it these days, dear," the older woman said with a smile. "Now come on into the parlor for some tea before you go."

"But Nathan and Katie will be here any minute."

"If they get here before we're finished, we'll simply invite them in to join us for a cup."

It was hard to imagine Nathan Cooper, in all his big, strong manliness, sitting down for a cup of tea served in antique china. Then again, the man did have a soft side that never failed to warm her heart.

With a nod, Alyssa followed her into the parlor where Myrna was setting out a plate of what she could only assume, thanks to her limited vision, were cookies.

"Perfect timing," Myrna said with a warm smile.

"Alyssa was admiring our tree."

"It's beautiful," Alyssa told her. "Your sister gave me this lovely ornament for my tree back home." She gingerly laid the crystal ornament on the table next to her teacup.

"We're helping her start her very own ornament collection," Doris explained. "Ours is her very first."

Myrna looked her way. "Really?" she asked, surprise in her tone.

"My mother was never one for decorating during the holidays. So there were no special keepsakes to pass down when she passed away." Truth was, any spare money her mother had left after paying bills went to buying more liquor and cigarettes. At least her mother had managed to keep a roof over their heads despite her addiction to alcohol, and for that she was grateful.

Looking across the table at the empathetic expressions that had fallen over her hostesses' once beaming faces, she forced a bright smile. "I'll be sure to put this gift to good use. I love decorating my place in San Antonio for the holidays."

The doorbell rang and Alyssa's heart sped up. She started to rise, but Doris motioned for her to stay seated.

"You haven't finished your tea. I'll go bring your young man and his little girl inside."

"Tell Nathan we have cookies," Myrna called after her.

Her sister glanced back over her slightly stooped shoulder. "I think Alyssa's being here is all we need to entice the young man in."

Warmth filled her cheeks and it was still there when Doris led a grinning Nathan into the parlor.

"Ladies," he said with a polite nod. Then his gaze sought her out and his smile widened.

She returned his smile, then looked past him. "Where's Katie?"

"With Logan," he replied. "My brother called to tell her he was gonna go see some Disney movie and asked if she wanted to join him, then do a little Christmas shopping of their own."

"Logan was going to a Disney movie?" she repeated suspiciously. Nathan's brother going to watch an animated children's movie wasn't something she could quite picture in her mind.

"Oh, my," Doris said worriedly. "Your brother went

to all that trouble to give the two of you some alone time and here we are keeping you from it."

Myrna looked at Nathan. "You two had best get going. We'll do tea another time."

"And just when I was eyeing that plate of cookies," Nathan said, feigning disappointment.

"We can take care of that," Doris said, scurrying off into the kitchen. A few seconds later, she returned carrying a small, plastic baggie, which she began filling up with cookies.

Smiling, Alyssa pushed away from the table and collected her precious gift. "I'll be right back down. Doris and Myrna gave me this lovely tree ornament to start my own special collection. I need to put it in my room and then we can go."

"That was kind of you," Nathan said to the sisters as they walked him out onto the porch to wait for Alyssa.

"We adore her," Myrna said.

Doris nodded. "She deserves a whole tree filled with special memories. Not just one from two eccentric old women."

"That she does," he agreed, turning as the screen door swung open behind him. "All set?"

Alyssa nodded happily. "Ready when you are."

"We'll leave the porch light on for you," Doris called out as he walked her out to the truck.

"Thank you," Alyssa hollered back, attempting to smother a giggle. Then she added in a hushed voice as he helped her up into the cab, "They are too cute."

"They are that," Nathan agreed, the cookie-filled sandwich bag Doris had given him dangling from his hand. Closing the passenger door, he rounded the truck, feeling like a teenager on his first date.

"Baby steps," he said to himself, knowing he needed to slow down, to rein in his growing feelings for Alyssa. But she'd breathed life into him and he didn't want to go back to just existing. For the first time in two years, she had him rethinking the way he'd been living his life. Especially when it came to his relationship with the Lord and the anger he'd been harboring toward Him. She even had him willingly doing something he would have avoided altogether if not for his daughter—going Christmas shopping.

Venturing out to a busy mall in the middle of December of all things. One he knew would be festively decorated for the Christmas holiday. A time that held some very painful memories for him. But like Katie, Alyssa deserved to experience those things. The holiday shopping trips. Picnics under the sun. The beauty of a waterfall. And so much more.

Smiling, he started the truck, shifted into gear and pulled away from the boardinghouse. "Would you like to grab something to eat first?"

"I think that might be a good idea. We need to talk and I doubt that's something we'll be able to do in private while walking through a crowded mall."

"We need to talk," he repeated with a sinking feeling. "Sounds serious." He glanced her way.

"To me, it is," she said, glancing his way. "If I'm being completely honest with you, I'm scared."

He certainly hadn't expected that. The last thing he wanted Alyssa to be was scared about anything. "I'm pulling over so we can talk this out."

"It can wait," she said, nibbling on her lower lip.

"We're on a back road with little or no traffic. It doesn't get any more private than this." Pulling off the road, he shut off the engine, undid his seat belt and then turned to face her. "Talk to me, Alyssa," he said, reaching for her hand. "What is it you're afraid of?"

She glanced down at his hand over hers. "Of anything beyond friendship." A frown immediately followed. "Not that you've implied you want more."

His searching eyes met hers. "And what if I do?"

"Nathan…"

"What if I do?" he repeated. "I've tried to focus on work. On Katie. On having a friendship with you and not wanting more. But my thoughts continually drift back to you. To us."

"Don't," she warned in a soft whisper, her gaze fixed on their joined hands.

"Is it the long-distance thing that worries you?" he said, his thumb caressing her hand. "Because I'm willing to find a way to make it work."

"It's so much more than that," she confessed with a sigh. "It's knowing that I'm not really what you're looking for. It's my fear of not being able to give Katie everything she needs. It's—"

"Shh…" he said, squeezing her hand. "I'm gonna stop you right there. First of all, I wasn't looking for anyone. Just ask my brothers. They know what my thoughts were on ever letting another woman into my life again. Then you came to town and everything changed. I find myself counting the hours until I see you at the rec center each morning, when I should be focused solely on the job I've been hired to do."

Her smile returned. "I could say the same thing."

He offered a tender smile. "Glad to hear it. And as

far as my daughter's concerned, you are exactly what she needs in her life. You're smart. You're talented. You're strong in the face of adversity."

"Nathan," she said, blushing.

"I'm not done. You have one of the most giving hearts I have ever known. You're as beautiful inside as you are on the outside. I know we've talked about building our friendship, but I find myself wanting to give a relationship between us a chance."

She grew misty-eyed. "I want that, too. And since honesty is so important to me, there's one more admission I need to make."

"You're already married?" he teased.

"Not even close," she said, looking up at him. A tiny smile teased the corners of her mouth.

"Then there's nothing you can say that'll change my mind about wanting to date you."

"I can't remember the last time I dated. I'm not even sure I remember how to date." She lowered her gaze as if embarrassed by the fact.

She thought that was a bad thing? He was relieved there was no one in her recent past to compete with for her affection. "I haven't dated anyone since Isabel," he admitted. "Looks like we'll be learning how to date again together."

And since honesty is so important to me...

Nathan sighed as he recalled her words. That honesty should go both ways. Had to go both ways for things between them to have any chance of working out long term. "While we're laying everything out on the table, I reckon it's only fair that you know what you're getting into with me. I'm not the man you think I am."

She looked up at him questioningly.

"I'm not the devout Christian I once was."

"I don't understand. You go to church every Sunday. You're helping to build the nativity scene for the church's Christmas program."

He frowned. "For Katie's sake."

She fell silent, contemplating his words. Then, she said softly, "You said *used to*. What changed things for you?"

He looked away, jaw tightening as he recalled the storm. The loss. The pain that followed. "Having Isabel and my parents taken from me, from Katie, in such a horrific way. How could my God, the one I'd put my trust in above all others, allow something like that to happen?"

She gave his hand a gentle squeeze. "I can't even begin to imagine what you went through. I only lost my vision."

"Only?" he said with a hollow chuckle. "It's still a loss. My family. Your eyesight. It all cuts deep."

"Maybe so, but I don't hold God responsible for what happened to me. And as awful as what happened to your family was, you need to know that He loves them. You need to *believe*."

"I don't know if I can," he muttered, hating that this one truth could change everything between them. "Can you accept me, knowing that I might never find my way back?"

She smiled softly. "I accept you. Not in spite of the possibility you might never find your way back to Him, but because I have faith that you will."

Chapter Ten

"Daddy," Katie groaned, "I don't feel so well."

Nathan stopped what he was doing and crossed the room to where his daughter sat shivering in her coat on a makeshift bench. Placing a hand on her forehead, he frowned. She was warm to the touch.

"You feel feverish," he said, immediately worried that his baby girl was ill.

"But I don't want a fever," she whined. "I have work to do."

"Work can wait," he told her with a frown. "Were you feeling bad this morning when I woke you up?"

She nodded her reply.

"Honey, why didn't you say something?" He would have kept her at home. Not dragged her into the rec center.

"I already told you why, Daddy. I gotta be here to help Alyssa."

"Not if you're sick," he told her, yet couldn't help but feel proud at her determination to see a job she'd been given through to the end. "You should be home, tucked snugly in your bed."

Katie had spent the past several days tagging along after Alyssa and loving every minute of it. While he'd worried at first about his daughter getting too attached, especially knowing she was looking for something he wasn't prepared to give her, everything had changed. He loved watching the two of them "working" and playing together. His daughter was happier than he'd seen her in a very long time.

Carter stepped up beside him. "She okay?"

"I think she has a fever."

"Let me see, kiddo." He bent to place a hand to her brow. "Yep, she feels pretty warm."

The front door opened and Alyssa stepped inside with her usual cheery smile. He'd offered to give her a ride to work when they'd talked on the phone earlier that morning, but she'd insisted on walking to work because it was such a nice day. "Good morning!"

"Morning, yes," Nathan muttered. "The good part is questionable."

"Why? What's the matter?"

"Katie's not feeling so well," Carter answered for him.

Setting her work tote on the floor by the door, she hurried over to them. "Ah, sweetie, what's wrong?"

"My tummy hurts."

"She's feverish," Nathan said as he studied his daughter's flushed cheeks and glazed eyes.

Alyssa knelt in front of her, pressing the back of her hand to Katie's cheek. "You poor baby. You must have picked up a bug somewhere." She looked up at him. "Why on earth did you bring her in today if she wasn't feeling well?"

"I didn't know," he replied, feeling as though he

had failed Katie as a father. How had he not noticed the telltale flush in her cheeks?

"Where does your tummy hurt?" Alyssa asked her.

"Right here," his daughter replied, pointing at her stomach. "And I'm itchy."

"Itchy?" all three adults repeated in unison.

Katie nodded, her tiny bottom lip pouting.

Alyssa looked up at Nathan. "Is she on any medication? Something she might be having a reaction to?"

"No."

"Can I take a look at your tummy, sweetie?" Alyssa asked calmly.

Katie lifted the bottom of her shirt to display several red spots. Alyssa leaned in to inspect the raised red flesh more closely.

A rush of panic moved through Nathan as he eyed the angry red welts. "I need to get her to the hospital."

"The hospital?" Katie exclaimed, her bottom lip trembling. "Why, Daddy? I don't wanna go there again."

"I know, honey, but you've got spider bites we need to have looked at."

Alyssa sat back and reached out, placing a calming hand on his arm. "I don't think they're spider bites."

"Then what are they?" Nathan insisted with a worried frown.

"Look closer," Alyssa said softly. "Tell me if you think they look more like little blisters than bites. Any puncture holes?"

"No puncture holes," he said, his voice tight with worry.

"Watery blisters?" she repeated.

He frowned, worry creasing his brow. "Yes."

She offered him a reassuring smile. "I'd say Katie has all the symptoms of chicken pox."

"Chicken pox?" he exclaimed, eyes widening as he stared down at his daughter's polka-dotted tummy.

She nodded. "We had several cases of it at the rec center last year in San Antonio. Turn around, sweetie," she said to Katie, lifting her shirt to reveal more of the telltale red specks on his daughter's lower torso. "More watery blisters?"

"Yes." He lifted his gaze to meet hers. "But how did she get the chicken pox?" Nathan asked. "She hasn't been around anyone that has them."

"Jennalynn had polka dots on her when she came over to draw chalk pictures on Granny Timmons' sidewalk with me," Katie said sleepily.

Surely she would have been sick before now if that's really what this was. "Honey, that was over two weeks ago," Nathan pointed out.

"And probably when she contracted them," Alyssa said knowingly. "If I remember right, the incubation period is between ten to twenty-one days."

"I should have known something was wrong," Nathan said with a frown.

"You're not a doctor," Carter said. "Now that we know she's sick, we need to get her home and in bed."

"I'll take her home," Nathan said.

"I'd have Audra come get her, but I don't know if Mason and Lily have had the chicken pox yet. Or her for that matter," he added with a frown.

"She's pregnant," Alyssa said. "Better off not taking the chance either way." She stood and turned to Nathan. "Chicken pox is fairly contagious. I suggest making sure your crew has all had it."

"I will. Carter and I have already had it. And you?" he asked worriedly.

"I've had it, too."

Relief swept through him. Katie being sick already had him turned inside out. If Alyssa were to get sick, too, he didn't know what he'd do.

"I'll let the guys know," Carter announced.

"I'm taking Katie home," Nathan said, scooping his daughter up in his arms.

"Take care of Katie. I'll hold the fort down here until you're able to come back to work."

"I'd be happy to stay with Katie at your place while you work," Alyssa offered, her gaze fixed on Katie's shivering form.

"Can she, Daddy?" his fevered daughter asked hopefully.

"I can't ask you to do that," Nathan said, shaking his head in refusal.

"I don't mind at all," she told him. "I've already had the virus, so that won't be an issue." She offered a sympathetic smile to Katie who looked ready to fall asleep at any moment. "And I can work on my computer while she sleeps, which will probably be most of the day once we get some medicine in her for that fever. If you don't already have some at your place, we should pick up some oatmeal bath on our way there. It'll help to soothe her discomfort. And you should call Katie's doctor to see what antihistamine he recommends we give her for the itching."

She looked up to find Nathan and Carter staring at her. "I'm sorry," she quickly apologized. "I wasn't trying to overstep. You—"

"Should take her up on her offer," Carter said, cutting her off. "Sounds to me like Katie would be in excellent hands with Alyssa."

Nathan looked at her as if in awe. "I couldn't agree more."

"I'll go talk to the men," Carter said. "You'd best get my little Katydid home."

"Going right now." He started for the door, his daughter held so lovingly in his arms.

Alyssa grabbed her work tote and hurried after his departing form. "What about your coat?" she called after him. Thankfully, Katie had been wearing hers.

"Don't need it," he replied, his steps not faltering.

Was the man crazy? It was freezing outside. However, she managed to keep her protests to herself. Nathan was under enough stress as it was. His focus at that moment was on getting his sick daughter home and into her bed. So she grabbed his jacket on the way out, determined to have him put it on as soon as he had Katie settled in the truck's cab.

After stopping at the local drugstore where Alyssa ran in to pick up the items they needed for Katie's care, they headed out of town. Katie had fallen fast asleep beside Alyssa in her booster seat.

Alyssa glanced down at the head resting against her. Sun shining in through the passenger window glinted off the sleeping child's dark curls. "I would give anything for hair like hers," she said softly, gently stroking the silken strands.

"She has her mother's hair," Nathan said, his gaze shifting to his sleeping daughter. "Her eyes, too."

"Your wife must have been beautiful."

He hesitated in answering, his attention shifting back to the road ahead.

"It's okay," she told him. "Isabel was a very important part of your lives. Always will be, if only in memory. I want you to be able to talk about her. For your sake and for Katie's."

"Yes," he said. "She was beautiful." Then he glanced her way with a sincere smile. "She would have liked you."

"Thank you for saying that," she said, touched more deeply than he could ever know. "That means a lot to me."

They fell into a comfortable silence for the remainder of the drive home.

When they arrived, Nathan came around to the passenger side of the truck. Together they lifted Katie out until she was once again in her daddy's arms.

Alyssa followed them inside.

"There's bottled water in the fridge," he told her. "Would you mind grabbing one for Katie so we can get her medicine into her?"

He said *we*, not I. She smiled softly. "Not at all. Get Katie to bed and I'll be right in."

She grabbed a bottle of water from the fridge, and then went in search of Katie's bedroom.

She found it at the end of the upstairs hallway. The room, definitely a little girl's room, was filled with brightly colored stuffed animals. A large dollhouse stood in the far corner. Beside it sat a basket filled with dolls to play with inside the miniature house. A cotton-candy-pink ruffled valance hung over a small bay window that overlooked the tree-lined backyard.

"I've got the water," she said.

"Honey," he said against Katie's ear, "you need to wake up. Daddy's got to get you ready for bed."

She stirred with a sleepy grumble.

"Here," Alyssa said, setting the bottle of water down on the nightstand. "Let me help you." She slid Katie's boots from her feet and set them on the floor near the foot of the bed. Then she moved to help Nathan with Katie's coat.

Once they had changed her into her nightgown, had gotten the medicine into her and had settled her into bed, Nathan drew the sheet up over Katie. Then he grabbed for the Disney Princesses comforter folded neatly across the foot of the twin bed, but Alyssa stilled his hand.

"She's got a fever," she whispered. "You don't want her getting overheated. Do you have a lighter blanket?"

He nodded. "In the hall closet."

"I'll get it."

When she returned, Alyssa paused in the doorway, her heart melting as Nathan bent to place a tender kiss on his daughter's fevered brow. "You're gonna be fine, Cupcake." His hands smoothed the sheet covering her, his muscular shoulders flexing beneath the flannel work shirt he wore. His physical strength a stark contradiction to his gentleness.

Smiling, she stepped into the room, unfolding the blanket as she went. "How is she?" she whispered.

"Sleeping." He backed away and stood for a long moment watching over his daughter.

Alyssa placed a comforting hand on his arm. "She's gonna be okay, just a little uncomfortable for the next week or so."

"I know," he said with a nod. "It's just so hard seeing her sick."

"I can imagine, considering all she's been through."

He turned to look at her. "You've been really good for her."

"I care about her," she said softly. *I care about you.*

"Did you eat before coming in to work?"

She hesitated before shaking her head, not wanting him to have something else to concern himself over. "No."

"Come on," he said, taking her hand. "Let's go fix a couple of sandwiches and have an early lunch before I head back to the rec center."

"Do you have time?"

He smiled. "Carter can handle things until I get back."

They went downstairs to the kitchen, where Nathan released her hand and went to open the fridge. "Turkey or ham?"

"Turkey's fine. Can I do something to help?"

"Paper plates are in the cupboard to the left of the window," he said as he reached into the fridge for a package of lunch meat. "Tomato?"

"Sounds good." She lifted two plates off the stack and set them onto the counter.

Nathan stepped past her, pulling a loaf of bread from a nearby drawer. "I'll give Mildred a call this afternoon and see if she has any idea when she might be coming home."

"You don't have to do that," she assured him as he moved to the counter to start making their sandwiches. "I have the layout for all the rooms, so I can do most of my work on my laptop from here. I'd hate for Mildred to feel like she needs to rush back to Braxton when she's already promised her sister that she'll be there to help her out until she's back on her feet."

"I suppose you're right."

"I just know how much it means to have someone there with you when you're recovering. To offer you support both physically and emotionally."

He glanced her way. "I wish I could have been there for you."

That touched her. "I had Erica."

"I'm glad." With a smile, he went back to making their sandwiches. "And you're right. If she knew about Katie being sick, Mildred would drop everything to race home and be with her. And that wouldn't be fair to her sister. I just wish…" His words trailed off.

"Are you concerned that I won't be able to take care of Katie?" she heard herself asking in a tone that bordered on hurt. But she couldn't help it. It wouldn't be the first time someone thought she was less capable of doing something because of her visual impairment.

His gaze shot up to meet hers. "Not for a second," he said in all sincerity. "I saw how you responded at the rec center when you knew she was sick. I panicked. You remained calm. You had a fairly good idea of what was going on with my daughter, while I was imagining all sorts of things that could be wrong with her. I just wish I was better at handling this sort of thing. But I promise there is no doubt in my mind, whatsoever, that my daughter will be well cared for and safe in your hands."

Tears pooled in her eyes. "That means so much to me."

He drew her to him. "And *you* mean the world to

me. I'm so glad you came into our lives." His gaze fell to her lips and her pulse began to race. She was certain he'd been about to kiss her when his cell phone rang. Releasing her, he pulled his cell from the front pocket of his jeans and then looked up at her, saying, "It's Logan."

She nodded.

"She's sleeping," Nathan told his brother. Then he glanced Alyssa's way. "Thanks for the offer, but Katie's in capable hands. Besides, we might need you to help out with some of the finishing touches to the rec center." He nodded. "Okay, see you in a few." He disconnected. "Carter called Logan to tell him about Katie, so he was calling to offer himself up as Katie's temporary caretaker."

"Carter didn't tell him I was gonna to be staying with her?"

"He did," he said as he walked over to the pantry to grab a half-empty bag of potato chips. "But Logan thought you might be needed at the rec center."

"That was thoughtful of him, considering he has his own business to run, as well."

Nathan shook a small pile of chips out onto each plate. "Contrary to the flirt you've come to know, my brother does have a responsible side." He motioned toward the fridge. "If you wanna grab a couple of bottles of water for us, I'll carry our plates out to the table."

"Sounds good." She walked over to get their drinks. When she stepped out into the dining room area, Nathan was nowhere to be found. Her gaze shifted to the plates on the table and then toward the open living room. Had Katie cried out?

She set the bottles down and had just started for

the stairs when Nathan came down the steps. "Is she okay?"

"She's fine," he said as he walked her back to the table and their awaiting lunch. "Still fast asleep."

Alyssa understood his need to check on his daughter. Katie was all he had left of Isabel. "God will watch over her."

He looked as if he wanted to say something in response. Instead, he pulled a chair out from under the table and motioned for her to have seat. "Let's eat."

She smiled up at him as he walked to the chair kitty-corner from hers. At least, he hadn't dismissed the likelihood of God watching over Katie. Even if she'd seen the doubt on his face for a fleeting moment. It was a start, no matter how small, of his finding his way back to the Lord. The thought warmed her.

They sat in silence for several minutes as they ate. Or maybe as she ate. The turkey sandwich and potato chips on Nathan's plate remained mostly untouched.

Alyssa reached out, covering his hand with her own much smaller one. "Are you okay?"

His worried frown deepened. "I shouldn't be going back to work. My place is here with Katie."

"If you feel that strongly about it, then call Carter and tell him you won't be coming back today," she said, fully understanding his need to be with his daughter.

"It'll put us behind schedule."

"Then it puts us behind," she said. "You have to follow your heart."

"Katie is so excited for the Christmas Eve party," he said with a frown. "If we get behind, there's a chance that might not happen. And then there's the dedication…" He glanced in the direction of the hallway. "You really think she'll sleep for a while?"

"Most of the day, I would guess," she assured him.

His jaw clenched as he struggled with what to do. Finally, he looked her way. "You have my cell number?"

She smiled. "I do."

"And you'll call me if you need anything?"

"I will."

"Then I'll go back to the rec center and see that we get the job done—for Katie." He pushed away from the table and stood.

"You haven't finished your lunch."

"I'm not very hungry," he replied. "I'll eat it when I get home this evening."

"I'll walk you out." Together they started for the front door, his hand laced through hers. The slight tension she felt in his grasp was that of a man torn between what he needed to do and what he wanted to do.

"There's apple juice and iced tea in the fridge," he said when they reached the door. "And chicken noodle soup and snacks in the pantry. Help yourself to whatever you need for you or Katie." His worried frown had deepened, no doubt brought about by the thought of leaving his sick little girl. He pulled open the door and stood there. "I'll try to come home early."

She reached up to touch his cheek, smiling softly. "Katie and I will be fine. Do what you need to do. We'll see you this evening."

"You'll call if her fever gets any worse?"

"Of course."

Hand on the doorknob, he paused. "Alyssa…"

"Yes?"

He bent to kiss her cheek. "Thank you." And then he was gone.

Hand pressed to her cheek, Alyssa walked over to the window, watching as the blur she knew to be Nathan climbed into his truck and drove away. A slow smile spread across her face as she turned away and remained there as she moved toward the stairs to check on Katie.

She was still fast asleep. Alyssa stood at her bedside, watching her for a long while, relieved to see that the little girl's shivering had eased. Like Nathan, she hated seeing Katie ill. She'd come to adore her. No, she'd come to love her.

I could be her new mother.

The thought settled in, filling her with both elation and trepidation. She would never try to replace Isabel. But if things worked out between her and Nathan down the road, she would become a very important part of Katie's life. She would be responsible for helping to guide her in both life and in faith as she grew into a young woman, for nurturing her, for doing all the wonderful things Erica did with her children. Mother things.

But she wasn't Erica. There were so many things she couldn't do that other mothers could. Like drive Katie to birthday parties for her friends. Like riding bikes any farther than the driveway because she might not see a car coming until it was too late. Even playing hide and seek would be a real challenge. What if what she had to offer Katie wasn't enough? She didn't think she could bear failing Katie. Or Nathan.

The elation that had filled her only moments before faded, leaving behind a growing sense of panic. She needed to talk to Erica. Her best friend was a straight shooter who told it like it was. She also understood the insecurities Alyssa had worked so hard to get past since her accident.

Stepping from the room, she drew the door shut, leaving it slightly ajar in case Katie awoke and needed something. Then she went out to the kitchen where she'd left her tote and purse. Pulling out her cell, she dialed her friend's number and then began searching through the kitchen drawers for some plastic wrap to cover Nathan's nearly untouched meal with.

Erica answered on the second ring. "Hey you!"

"Hey."

"Uh-oh. Do I detect a hint of unhappiness in your voice?"

"Only because I'm worried about Katie. She's come down with chicken pox."

"The poor baby."

"I offered to take care of her while Nathan goes back to work on the rec center. "

"What about your work?"

"The flooring that Nathan, Carter and I decided on has already been ordered and should be in the day after tomorrow. His crew has been busy painting the rooms with the colors I chose. Tables are picked out for the cafeteria and the art room. All I need to do is order the light fixtures for the lobby, rec center office and for above the mirror-backed counters in the locker rooms. I can do that from here."

"Sounds like you have everything under control on your end."

"I do," she said proudly. If only she were as in control of her emotions.

"Excuse me one moment," her friend said. "Huck Benson, if that hamster gets loose again, he's gonna have to find himself a new place to live!"

Alyssa couldn't help but smile. "Hamster troubles?"

"Sorry," her friend apologized. "Things have been in a bit of an uproar here."

"Why? What happened?"

"When I got home from the grocery store this morning everyone, my husband included, was in a panic because Huck's hamster had gone missing. We went on a mad search to find it before our cat did."

"Apparently, you found it," she said, her own concerns temporarily pushed aside. She knew how much Huck loved his furry, little pet.

"Thankfully, yes. He was in Cecilia's bedroom, dining on Cheerios."

"What?"

"My daughter decided Mr. Cuddles was too cramped in his hamster cage and moved him into her doll house where she fed him the rest of the cereal she'd been snacking on."

"Oh, the joys of motherhood," she said with a snort of laughter.

"Laugh all you want now, my friend, but one of these days I'm gonna be the one laughing at the mischief your children get into."

Her children. The reminder of why she'd called her friend to begin with had her frowning once more.

"Hello? Alyssa?"

"I'm here," she said with a sigh. "And funny you should mention children. I was having a moment of panic over the possibility of being someone's mother someday."

"Are you referring to Katie?"

"Her or any other children I might have." And she would willingly take however many God chose to bless her with. "But I can't help but wonder if I won't be able to give them everything they deserve."

"Like a mother who loves them with her whole heart?" her friend asked. "One who would protect them, guide them and teach them. One who would show them what it means to stay strong and hold on to their faith, even in the face of adversity."

"Erica…"

"Don't 'Erica' me," she said. "You are all of those things. And any child will be more than blessed to have you in their life."

Oh, how she prayed her friend was right. Because she never wanted to fail someone she loved as her mother had failed her.

Chapter Eleven

Seeing a movement out the corner of her eye, Alyssa looked up from the sketch she was working on. "Katie!" She pushed away from the kitchen table and walked over to the sleepy-eyed child. "What are you doing out of bed?"

"I'm thirsty."

Her face looked a little flushed. Then again, the tiny, red blisters that had popped up over her cheeks and forehead added to the extra color she saw in Katie's face. Alyssa placed a hand to her brow, fearing the fever she'd been without the past two days had returned. Blessedly, it hadn't.

"Why don't I walk you back to bed and then I'll fix you a glass of lemonade?"

She shook her head, adding in a tiny whine, "I don't wanna be in my bed. Not by myself."

"Why not?"

"'Cause I had a bad dream."

"What about, sweetie?" she asked in a calming tone.

"The storm."

"But the rain shower has passed." It had rained most

of the day, but not hard enough to bring about night-mares.

"Not that storm," Katie said, adding in a hushed voice, "The tornado."

Alyssa didn't miss the shudder that passed through Katie's tiny form at her mention of the storm that had ripped Braxton apart two years ago. "Oh, honey," she said, dropping to her knees in front of her. She drew her into her arms and held her tight. "I wouldn't let anything happen to you. It was just a dream. It's over now."

"It'll come back," she said.

"The dream?"

"And the tornado," she replied, her bottom lip trembling. "I don't wanna be crushed again."

Alyssa ran her hand in soothing circles over her tiny back. Her first instinct had been to promise her that such a storm would never happen again, but no one had any say over where and when natural disasters would take place. Only God knew what the future held. So she settled for, "That was a rare storm. One that's not likely to happen here ever again."

Katie didn't look convinced. "Will you sit with me till I go back to sleep?"

Alyssa glanced toward the open laptop and the paper-strewn table and then back to Katie with a sympathetic smile. "Of course I will, sweetie. Have a seat on the sofa while I go get you that drink."

"Okay."

"Would you like me to fix you a snack before you lie back down?"

"No, thank you," Katie replied with a tired yawn. "I'm just thirsty."

"I'll be right back." Alyssa hurried into the kitchen, her heart heavy for the little girl whose dreams should have been filled with rainbows and butterflies, but were instead filled with memories of that terrible day.

She stepped up to the stove, leaning close to read the clock. It was just after five, which meant she'd been working on ideas and sketches for nearly three hours straight. Nathan had called sometime around four o'clock to check on Katie and to see if Alyssa minded him sticking around the site a little longer. Apparently the inspector was running behind on his appointments due to bad road conditions. Of course, it hadn't been a problem for her. She was actually getting a lot done while taking care of Katie. And when his daughter wasn't sleeping, they spent a lot of time playing board games, watching princess videos and just talking.

Yet, in all that time, Katie had never mentioned having nightmares. It sounded as if this hadn't been the first she'd had them. Did Nathan know? They were definitely something he needed to be aware of.

Alyssa filled a glass with ice and then the lemonade she and Katie had made yesterday. Then she returned to the living room where Katie sat waiting for her. "Here you go, honey."

Katie took several long swallows, then started for her room. "Where's my daddy?"

"He's still at work. But he called to check on you."

"Will he be home soon?"

"He needs to stay a little later at the rec center, but he said to tell you he was gonna stop by Big Dog's tonight to pick us up dinner and your favorite treat."

"A milk shake!" she squealed, her sleepy eyes lighting up.

Alyssa nodded with a smile, taking the glass from Katie's hand. "Now let's get you back in that bed so you'll be rested up for when your daddy comes home."

Alyssa and Katie went upstairs to her bedroom, where she climbed up onto the soft mattress and settled back onto her pillow. "You won't leave, will you?"

"I'll be right here." Setting the glass on the nightstand, she pulled Katie's covers up. Then she walked around the bed and settled onto the mattress beside her, resting her back against the headboard.

Katie snuggled up against her, once again fighting sleep.

Alyssa pushed the dark curls from her cheek. "Just close your eyes and sleep. I promise to keep the bad dreams away."

Katie looked up, her dark eyes hopeful. "Like Daddy does?"

That meant Nathan was aware of the nightmares Katie had. She smiled down at her. "How does your daddy keep them away?"

"He sings."

Alyssa's eyes widened. "He sings?"

"Uh-huh. Daddy says it'll scare all the bad dreams away."

Alyssa couldn't contain her grin. Nathan Cooper was a man of many talents. "Well, I don't think I can compete with your daddy's singing, but I can make a really mean face guaranteed to scare away any bad dreams."

"Can I see it?"

"Here goes." She scrunched up her face and pursed

her lips, the effort eliciting giggles from Katie. "What's so funny?"

"You don't look scary. You look like my daddy did when Uncle Carter dared him to eat a lemon."

Alyssa smothered a giggle. Ah, the information one could glean from a child. "Well, lucky for you bad dreams fear sour lemon faces *and* bad singing. Now close your eyes and go to sleep."

Within minutes, Katie was sound asleep, her little fingers curled into the comforter Alyssa had drawn up around her.

Caring for Katie this past week had been one of the most fulfilling experiences of her life. And she felt closer to Nathan than she'd ever dreamed possible. Life was good. Closing her eyes, she said a quick prayer of thanks to God for sending her on this path. Then her thoughts went back to Nathan, envisioning that big, strong man sitting patiently by Katie's side, singing her nightmares away as his daughter drifted off to sleep.

The rec center inspection had taken a lot longer than Nathan had expected, but at least it was done. They'd passed without a single violation. Now he could go home to his girl. *His girls.* He liked the sound of that. Liked having Alyssa there to greet him when he came home every day. Liked feeling like he had a family again.

He glanced at the clock on the dash. It was only 7:10 p.m., but it felt a lot later thanks to the early winter sunset. Beside him on the passenger seat, sat the carryout bag from Big Dog's. Alyssa had been incredible, not only taking care of his daughter, but fixing dinner for the three of them every night. Tonight, however, he was bringing dinner home to his girls. Hot dogs, fries and thick milk shakes.

Nathan turned onto the drive that led to his place. The kitchen and living room lights were on, but the rest of the house was dark. He pulled into the back garage and cut the engine. Then, grabbing the bag filled with their dinner, he went inside.

Closing the back door, he set the carryout bag on the kitchen counter, then shrugged out of his coat, hanging it from a hook by the door. So much for his family greeting him. Katie must still be asleep. Alyssa had said she'd been asleep when he'd called earlier.

After placing the shakes in the freezer, he started walking through the house in search of his girls. Alyssa's laptop and notes were spread out across the kitchen table, but she was nowhere to be seen. He made his way up to his daughter's room where the Cinderella lamp cast a soft glow across the double bed.

There they were. Katie fast asleep, her slender arm curled snugly around Alyssa's waist as she burrowed up against her. Alyssa's head tipped downward, her face covered by a curtain of coppery hair.

"Sorry I'm so late getting home," he said in a whisper.

No response.

He stepped closer. "Alyssa?"

Her soft, even breathing told him she was asleep, as well. He hated to wake them, but the hot dogs and fries wouldn't be too tasty cold. He walked around to Alyssa's side of the bed and reached out, gently pushing her hair away from her face. Then he whispered, "Dinner's here, darlin'."

She stirred, her head lifting as she slowly awakened. Her lashes fluttered open and then a startled gasp escaped her lips.

"Shh…" he said. "It's just me."

"Nathan?"

"Yes."

Coming more fully awake, she smiled up at him. "I didn't hear you come in."

"I figured as much." His gaze shifted to his sleeping daughter. "How is she?"

"No fever and the oatmeal baths seem to be helping with the itching."

He nodded, relieved to hear his daughter hadn't been suffering too much.

She looked down at his daughter with a slight frown. "Some dream chaser I am."

"Excuse me?"

Meeting his gaze once more, she said, her voice low, "Katie had a bad dream earlier. I was supposed to be watching over her and keeping the nightmares away. And what do I do? I fall asleep."

Not again. Would the nightmares ever fully go away? The therapist had told him they would eventually come with less frequency and at some point might go away altogether. But it would take time. Hard to swallow for a man wanting his daughter to feel safe always.

"Thank you for sitting with her. I'm sure you had things you needed to be doing."

"Not really," she admitted. "I managed to get a lot more done today than I had hoped to, so I had plenty of time to spare."

He frowned. "I hate to wake her. She's sleeping so soundly."

"I don't think you'd hear the end of it if you didn't," she told him. "Katie's expecting that milk shake I told her you were bringing home for her."

"I suppose we ought to get her up then. Logan will be by in a little over an hour to take you home." His brothers had been taking turns picking Alyssa up at the boardinghouse in the mornings and bringing her out to his place, where she'd stay with Katie while he went to work. Then either Carter or Logan would take Alyssa back to the boardinghouse after dinner each evening, allowing Nathan to spend more time with her than what little they were able to share during his all-too-brief afternoon lunch breaks.

Alyssa gave Katie a gentle nudge. "Katie, your daddy's home."

"Time to wake up, Cupcake," he joined in. "Dinner's waiting."

His daughter stirred, then stretched with a big yawn before opening her eyes. The minute she saw him in the lamplight, she untangled herself from Alyssa and threw back the covers. "Daddy!"

A smile pulled at his mouth. "Hey there, sleepyhead."

Katie scrambled to her feet, launching herself over Alyssa's legs and into his arms.

He caught her easily, shifting her around to rest on his hip. "How's my little chicken today?"

Hands clasped around his neck, she tipped her head back with a groan. "I told you before. I'm not a chicken. I got the chicken pox. That's different."

Alyssa slipped from the bed to join them. "I don't

know, Katie. With all those polka dots you have, I'm thinking you might be part leopard."

Laughing, they made their way downstairs to the dining room where Nathan set Katie down onto one of the chairs.

"Let me clean up my mess," Alyssa said, hurrying to scoop up the notes and sketches that were strewn about the table.

"I'll go grab the food." Nathan stepped into the kitchen, grabbed the shakes from the freezer and the carryout bag from the counter, then headed back out to the dining room.

"Which one's my shake?" Katie asked excitedly.

His gaze dropped down to the Styrofoam disposable cups. "Let's see…this one says Strawberry," he said, reading the lid where the flavor of each of the shakes had been handwritten across it.

She looked up at him. "But I wanted chocolate."

His brow lifted. "Chocolate? But I thought—"

"That's exactly what he brought you," Alyssa said. "I thought I'd give strawberry a try and see how I like it."

He looked at her questioningly. When he'd called to tell her he was bringing dinner home and to ask what flavor of shake she preferred, she'd requested chocolate.

"You'll like it," Katie assured her. "It's my second favorite."

What had his daughter said about it being a woman's prerogative to change her mind? It appeared such a thing was a common occurrence—for all women. Alyssa's kind gesture endeared her to him all the more. He would have given up his own shake to make his daughter happy, but he'd ordered a peanut butter shake for himself.

"Are you sure?" he asked Alyssa.

"I like to think of myself as the adventurous type," she told him with a smile as she reached for the cup marked Strawberry.

He handed Katie the chocolate one and then passed out the disposable containers that held their dinners in them. Then he looked to Alyssa. "Would you like to say a prayer before we eat?"

"I will! I will!" his daughter volunteered excitedly.

"That would be lovely," Alyssa told her with a smile.

Katie folded her hands together and closed her eyes. "Dear God, thank you for the yummy milk shake I'm about to drink. And for bringing Alyssa here. Amen."

Nathan met Alyssa's gaze, a grin tugging at his mouth. "Amen."

Alyssa smiled. "Amen."

Katie popped open her dinner container and dug into her fries.

Nathan had just taken a bite of his hot dog when Katie announced, "Alyssa snores."

Both he and Alyssa stopped midbite to look at her.

"What?" he managed around the mouthful of hot dog he had yet to swallow.

"Not loud like you do," his daughter explained. "Just tiny, little snores."

Alyssa's face colored. "I guess I have Rhett to blame for that."

"Rhett?" he repeated with a curious tilt of his head.

"He's Miss Myrna and Miss Doris's kitty," Katie told him with a smile.

Alyssa nodded. "He likes to play at night and one

of his favorite games is tapping your face with his paw while you're sleeping."

Katie giggled. "That's silly."

Silly wasn't what he'd call being awakened from sleep in the middle of the night by a frisky cat. "Why don't you shut him out of the room?"

"I tried, but he sits outside the door and meows. It's easier to let him in and pull a pillow over my head until he gets bored and leaves."

"No wonder you drifted off earlier," he said with a frown. "You need to be getting your rest, too."

"Please don't worry about me. I'm fine."

"I always concern myself when it comes to people I care about."

Katie nodded in agreement. "And Daddy really likes you. Don't you, Daddy?"

He smiled, meeting Alyssa's gaze. "Yes, Cupcake. I really like her. I like her a whole lot." More than he ever imagined he could care for another woman after Isabel. And for the first time since he'd begun having feelings for Alyssa, he felt no guilt. His brothers were right. Isabel would have wanted him to move on. To be happy. Alyssa had given him that and so much more.

Katie stepped from the bathroom in her plush pink princess robe. Now that she was feeling better, she had begun to bathe herself again. Alyssa would fix her special oatmeal bath and then wait for her in the hall.

She walked Katie to her room. "Let's see how that tummy is looking."

Katie raised her nightshirt, revealing her lightly speckled stomach. "They don't itch anymore."

That was a good thing. But her trunk and limbs still

needed to be monitored for any new blisters. Kneeling on the floor in front of her, she leaned in to inspect her as best she could. Most of the blisters had finally scabbed over. She glanced up at Katie with a smile. "No new blisters that I can see, but we'll have your daddy double-check when he gets home tonight."

"So I'm all better?" Katie said excitedly.

"Another day or two and you should be able to leave the house. We'd hate to risk letting you around other children too soon and maybe getting them sick."

"Another day or two?" she whined. "That's too long."

She of all people understood Katie's restlessness. Those long, seemingly endless days she'd spent in the hospital and then in rehab after her car accident had verged on unbearable. "I know how hard this is for you, sweetie. But you wouldn't wanna risk giving the chicken pox to some other little boy or girl, would you?"

Katie shook her head. "Can we go outside?"

"Sweetie, it's too chilly out today. And they're calling for rain this evening. That means the air outside is probably damp. Not good for someone who recently recovered from a fever."

Katie sighed. Her pale, dotted face held a look of both misery and longing as her gaze drifted to the large picture window and the yard outside. "I wish I had my own dog to play with like Uncle Carter got for Mason and Lily."

Poor thing. Though her fever was long gone and chances were she was no longer contagious, to be on the safe side she was still confined to the house. Another day or so and Nathan should feel comfortable bringing Katie in to work with him again. Thankfully, none of Nathan's work crew had come down with the virus and things were moving along pretty close to schedule.

"Tell you what," Alyssa said, hoping her idea would cheer Katie up. "Since your daddy is too busy to decorate for the holidays, why don't you and I surprise him and do it for him?"

Katie gasped, her eyes widening in excitement. "Really?"

Alyssa smiled, relishing in the look of pure joy that had come over Katie's little face. She nodded. "It can be our special Christmas gift to your daddy."

"Yay!"

"Do you know where your daddy keeps the Christmas decorations?"

Her little head bobbed up and down. "In the roof."

"The roof?" Then it dawned on her. "Do you mean in the attic?"

She nodded enthusiastically.

"Well, if we're gonna surprise your daddy before he gets home we had better get started." The thought of giving Nathan a warm, cheerful, festive home to come back to after a long day's work had her smiling. Part of Christmas was giving to others and this was one way for her to give back to Nathan and Katie for accepting her into their lives and making her feel needed for the first time in years. Even loved, despite Nathan's never having said as much. As far as she was concerned, words were just words. Nathan had made her feel loved in so many other ways.

Taking Katie's hand, they ventured upstairs and down the hallway to where a rectangle-shaped panel above indicated the entrance to the attic. Letting go of Katie's hand, she reached up to grab the knotted pull rope hanging from one end of the door panel.

"Step back, sweetie," she warned as she pulled on the rope, lowering the narrow door. Then she grabbed for the folded steps and carefully opened them. Then she turned to Katie. "Wait down here while I go see what I can find."

"But I wanna help," she said with that adorable little pout her father couldn't resist. Unfortunately for Katie, Alyssa could. At least, when it meant keeping her safe.

"You will," she quickly assured her. "But with the decorating, not carrying heavy boxes down these wobbly stairs. You need to save your strength." She glanced toward the opening in the ceiling above her. Hopefully, she'd be able to find what they were looking for.

Three hours later, Katie was fast asleep in her bed, exhausted from their afternoon spent decorating. It had all been worth it. The house looked beautiful. Lights had been strung across the fireplace mantel with Katie's bright pink princess stocking hung on one side and Nathan's on the other. Katie had proudly informed her that she had made her daddy's stocking for him. The crooked *N* that had been written on it in bright green glitter paint had Alyssa smiling, knowing it had been made with love.

She did one final walk-through of the house to make sure everything looked just right. Snowman placemats surrounded a centerpiece done in silver and blue ribbon with a coating of fake snow dusted over it. A porcelain nativity scene sat atop a gold table runner on the coffee table. Snowflakes she and Katie had cut out of paper Alyssa had brought with her hung in all the front windows upstairs and downstairs. A pair of holiday hand towels hung from the wooden towel bar on the downstairs half bath wall. Outside on the porch, a large wreath hung on the front door. Below it, a welcome mat designed to look like a gift with Welcome printed on its tag awaited holiday visitors.

She couldn't wait for Nathan to get home and see it all. The thought had no sooner crossed her mind than she heard his truck coming up the drive. She hurried to Katie's room, giving her a gentle shake. "Your daddy's home."

Katie shot upright in her bed. Sleep clearing quickly from her eyes, replaced by unrestrained excitement. "He is?"

"Yes," she told her. "We'll greet him at the door when he comes in."

Katie sprung out of bed.

Together, they hurried down the stairs to welcome Nathan home.

Stepping up to the front window, Alyssa peeked outside. Sure enough, his truck sat in the drive. Turning away from the window with a soft giggle, she moved to stand behind Katie, her hands clasped over her tiny shoulders.

The thump of booted footsteps sounded on the front porch.

"He's coming," Katie whispered.

"I know." Reaching out, Alyssa flipped the light switch that would turn on the outside lights that she and Katie had hung along the porch rail and around the front door. Her heart pounded with excitement as she waited for Nathan to step inside, a smile on his handsome face.

Only the door didn't open.

"Where is Daddy?" Katie said, her voice hushed.

Alyssa glanced toward the window, wondering herself what was taking him so long. Had Nathan forgotten something in his truck? No, she would have heard him move back across the porch. Maybe he'd gotten a call and was finishing it up before coming inside.

Then the doorknob rattled, the front door swinging open to reveal Nathan's tall form. Only he wasn't smiling. His face looked as if it were carved out of granite, his jaw was clenched so tight.

"Surprise!" Katie exclaimed before Alyssa had a chance to stop her. It was just as they'd planned, only something was wrong.

"Nathan?" she said, trying to get a feel for what was going on with him.

"What did you do?" he demanded, his voice tight. Not with emotion but with something else. Anger?

"Katie and I wanted to surprise you," she said, forcing a smile.

"Well, you succeeded," he said with a frown as his gaze swept the inside of the house. His expression hardened even more. "Katie, go to your room."

"But I just came down," she whined.

"Miss McCall and I need to talk. Go."

"It's okay, sweetie," Alyssa assured her. "It won't take long." As soon as she had disappeared up the stairs, she turned back to Nathan. "What is going on with you?"

"*You* had no right to do this!" he said, motioning around him.

"I thought that since you didn't have time to decorate for Christmas, Katie and I could do it for you."

"Time had nothing to do with my not putting up decorations," he said through clenched teeth. "I don't want festive lights and smiling snowmen filling my house. I don't want any reminders of what the holidays mean to me. The loss of my wife. Of Katie's mother. Of my parents. Of the life I was supposed to be living!"

She reached for him, tears in her eyes. "Oh, Nathan, I'm so sorry."

He pulled away. "Don't. I can't do this. Not right now." Turning away, he walked back out the door.

She went after him, standing in the doorway as he strode toward his truck. "Where are you going?"

"I need to clear my head," he shot back as he moved in angry strides around to the driver's side. And then, he was gone.

Chapter Twelve

"It's all my fault."

Alyssa turned to see Katie standing at the foot of the stairs, her favorite princess doll clutched to her chest, tears rolling down her cheeks. "Oh, honey, nothing is your fault."

"Yes, it is. My daddy's mad at you and it's all my fault. I showed you where the Christmas boxes were."

"He's not mad at me," she said, trying to calm Katie. "He was just…surprised." Only not in the way they'd intended him to be.

Katie shook her head with a sob. "I heard him yell at you. Now you'll never get to be my mommy, and my daddy will go back to being sad again."

Before she could respond, Katie ran off toward the kitchen. A door slammed, making Alyssa gasp. "Katie!" she hollered as she raced into the kitchen. The blinds hanging over the back door window were swinging to and fro. Katie had gone outside.

The poor thing was so upset and she couldn't blame her. Alyssa followed her outside, expecting to find her sitting on one of the porch chairs, but she was nowhere to be seen.

"Katie?" she called out, trying to remain calm despite her pounding heart. "Where are you?"

When she didn't answer, Alyssa ran back into the house to grab her cell phone and Katie's coat before hurrying back outside. Still no sign of her. She called Nathan, but his phone went straight to voice mail. So she called Audra.

"Hello?"

"Audra, it's Alyssa," she said, trying to calm her breathing. "Do you know where Nathan is by any chance?"

"No, I don't," she replied. "You sound upset. Is everything all right?"

Alyssa fought back the tears. "No, it's not. Nathan left and I can't reach him. Katie ran off somewhere and I can't find her. And it's getting dark."

"I'm sure she's fine. Just calm down and tell me what happened."

"There's no time," she replied. "I have to find Katie." Disconnecting the call, she started across the yard, calling out to Katie as she went. When she reached the pines that lined the expansive backyard, Alyssa caught sight of something shimmering in the fading light and moved toward it.

Katie's princess doll, with its sparkly gown and miniature tiara, lay face down on the bed of pine needles that covered the forest floor. She picked it up and looked around. "Katie!"

The woods were cast in shadows and would only grow darker as the sun dipped beneath the distant horizon. She stepped through the wall of pines, holding

Katie's coat up in front of her face to shield her eyes as she went. Thankfully, the woods thinned out and she was able to move more freely through them.

An owl screeched somewhere in the treetops above her, making Alyssa jump. She had grown up in cities, not somewhere wild animals roamed free. She knew about traversing sidewalks, not finding her way through thickly wooded acreage.

"Katie!" she called out louder, her desperation growing. It felt like she'd been walking forever. *Please, Lord, keep her safe in Your loving arms until I can find her.*

The cell phone she clutched in her hand rang. She'd forgotten she held it. "Hello," she said, her hand trembling as she held it to her ear.

The caller's voice on the other end was garbled, cutting in and out. She glanced down at the screen. It was Carter. "If you can hear me, I'm in the woods behind the house, searching for Katie. Please tell Nathan I need him." The call cut out before she could say anything more.

Alyssa's gaze swept the thickening shadows and a feeling of helplessness came over her. Her vision was blurred. How would she ever find Katie when she could barely see the trees in front of her? Was she even searching for her in the right area? She'd wandered so deep into the woods she wasn't even certain where she was herself or if she'd be able to find her way out. All that mattered was finding Katie. Poor, sweet, heartbroken Katie.

Why had she ever allowed herself to believe she could be the woman to make Nathan happy? And now, under her care, Katie had run off into the woods alone. She had failed Nathan. And now she was failing Katie.

She struggled onward, another spindly branch clawing at her face and snagging the sleeve of her sweater. She felt a trickle of warmth slide down her scratched cheek. Tears welled up in her eyes. She turned the screen of her phone on, hoping to try to reach Nathan again, but there was no signal now whatsoever. Distracted, she didn't see the gnarled root protruding from the forest floor. She went down hard, landing on her knees. Katie's coat cushioned the ground beneath her hands, but the impact sent her phone skittering out of her hand to disappear into the blur of the woods around her.

She struggled to find it; her hand sweeping frantically over the ground around her until she felt its familiar shape beneath her fingers. Then, clutching tightly to the phone, she shifted into a sitting position and tipped her face upward. Her gaze fixed on the blur of treetops and the fading sky above, she offered up a silent prayer.

She was still sitting there when the rain began to fall in thick, cold drops. Her tears quickly followed, turning into loud, wrenching sobs as the feeling of true helplessness overcame her.

"Alyssa?" a fearful voice called out in the distance.

Her head snapped around. "Katie!" she gasped, between sobs. Relief swept through her. Katie was safe. She scrambled to her feet. "Stay where you are," she hollered back. "I'll come to you. Just keep talking."

"I don't like the dark," Katie cried out.

"We'll be home before you know it," she called out

reassuringly as she followed the sound of Katie's voice deeper into the woods.

"I'm sorry I ran away," she heard her say.

"I know you are, sweetie." All that mattered was that she was safe. "Can you see me yet?"

"Y-yes."

She had to be close or she wouldn't have been able to make out the sound of Katie's teeth chattering. "You can come to me now, Katie." She held out her arms, desperate to hold Katie in them. To know that she truly was safe. If anything had happened to her... She couldn't even bear to think of what it would do to Nathan.

Tiny feet shuffled across the ground and then slender arms wrapped around Alyssa's waist in a fierce hold. Katie sniffled softly. "I'm so glad you came looking for me."

"Of course I came looking for you," she said as she wrapped her arms around the trembling little girl beside her. "I love you, sweetie." And she did. Every bit as much as she loved her daddy.

Katie looked up at her, drops of rain stinging her face. "I love you, too, Alyssa."

"I have something that belongs to you." She held up the dirty, wet doll.

"Is that Princess Sparkles?"

"It sure is." She handed the wet doll into Katie's safekeeping. "We took a bit of a tumble, but we can clean her up once when we get home."

"She's missing her crown," she said worriedly.

"We'll find it, sweetie. We might just have to wait until tomorrow when there's more light to see by."

"Okay." Katie shivered. "This rain is making Princess Sparkles cold."

"Then you'll have to tuck her inside your coat to keep her warm," Alyssa told her as she held the blessedly well-insulated, waterproof jacket out for Katie to slide her arms into it. Thankfully, she'd thought to grab it on her way out the door. If only she'd thought to grab her own, as well. But then she hadn't intended to venture into the woods when she'd left the house in search of Katie. She knelt on a bruised knee to zip Katie up snuggly. "Better?"

She nodded. "Princess Sparkles is happy." Then she frowned. "Where's your coat?"

Alyssa gave her a reassuring smile as she straightened, knees aching. "We'll be home long before I need it." At least, she prayed they would be. Surely, someone would find them soon. Instinct had her wanting to get Katie back to the safety of her home, but common sense reminded her that when lost in the woods, it was best to stay in one place and wait for help to arrive rather than risk getting even more lost.

Taking Katie's hand in hers, she looked around. "We need to find a dry place to wait for your daddy." *Dear Lord, please let him find us soon.* Crawling under the thick bushes beside them was their best option. It wouldn't keep out all the rain, but it was better than where they were standing now.

"We could wait in the cave."

Alyssa looked down at her. "What cave?"

"The one I found back there," she said, pointing in the direction from which she'd come. "But it's dark."

"Dark is better than cold and wet," she told her. "Do you think you can find it for us?"

She nodded, her wet curls drooping down over her damp face. "This way," she said, tugging at Alyssa's hand. Not more than thirty feet ahead the thickening of pines opened up onto a rocky hillside. Katie led her around to the far side where she pointed to a wide crevice in the rocks. "There it is."

The opening was probably a good eight feet wide and maybe five feet tall at its highest point. Inside it was dark. Who knew what else huddled in there for protection from the cold and the rain?

"Stay here a minute while I have a look inside." Pulling her cell phone from the back pocket of her jeans, she tapped on the flashlight icon. A beam of light streamed from the back of the phone, lighting the cave's entrance. She stepped closer, listening for any sound of movement. Hard to tell with the rain coming down outside, but surely if something was in there it would have tried to flee when it heard them approaching from the woods.

Movement on the floor in front of her drew her gaze down to what looked to be a very large centipede. At least eight inches in length. She took a step back with a shudder, waiting until it had disappeared from sight before venturing farther into the cave. Raising the light, she cringed when she saw a gossamer web stretched across a portion of the cave's ceiling to one side. She was quite certain the blur she saw in it was a spider waiting patiently for its next meal. Other than those two creatures, the cave appeared to be a safe haven from the elements outside.

"Come on in, sweetie," she called out.

"Are there bats in here?" Katie asked as she took a tentative step inside.

"Not that I see. Just a wonderfully creative spider adding a touch of decor to our temporary rain shelter."

Katie seemed to be satisfied with that answer, moving farther in to where Alyssa stood to admire the spider's handiwork for herself. "It's pretty."

She would have to take Katie's word for it as the finer details of the web were lost to her. "Let's have a seat while we wait."

They settled onto the dirt floor, Katie safely ensconced in Alyssa's lap. She wrapped her arms around both Katie and her beloved doll, her heart aching. She'd come so close to having a family of her own, but tonight had proved she could never be anybody's mother. A tear rolled down her cheek, the saltiness of it stinging the scratches on her face.

"What do we do now?" Katie asked.

"We say a prayer of thanks to God for providing us with shelter when we needed it," Alyssa said as her gaze fell to the cell phone she held clenched in her hand. Prayer appeared to be their only hope as a cell signal was nonexistent.

Together they bowed their heads and prayed. Then Alyssa pressed a kiss to Katie's rain-dampened hair. "Now close your eyes and try to get some sleep."

Katie curled up against her, the warmth of her tiny body helping to ease some of the cold that had seeped into Alyssa's bones as she'd walked coatless through the rain. "Will you tell me a story?"

Alyssa smiled softly, her heart so full of love for this little girl. "It would be my pleasure." Resting her chin atop Katie's head, she began, "Once upon a time there was a beautiful princess…"

* * *

Rain splattered across the windshield as the storm the weather station had predicted moved in. Having driven around the back roads of Braxton for a good hour or so, the shock and pain he'd felt when he'd first arrived home that evening had faded. In its place, guilt washed over him.

He could still see the confusion and hurt on Alyssa's face when he'd allowed his pain to loosen his tongue. She'd had only good intentions and he'd blamed her for something she had no way of knowing would upset him. He'd never told her about his aversion to all things Christmas. And if his behavior toward Alyssa hadn't been bad enough, he'd raised his voice to his daughter, something he'd never done. She'd been so excited for him to see what they'd done while he was at work. But once he'd seen that wreath hanging on the front door, the one his wife had made just days before the tornado struck, he'd been overwhelmed by emotions he didn't want to feel.

Needing just a few more moments to process his thoughts before returning home, he pulled off on the side of the road and cut the engine. Then he let his head drop back against the headrest and closed his eyes.

He owed Alyssa an apology. Now that he'd had time to recover from the shock of coming home to a house filled with holiday cheer, he knew that he'd been wrong to take the joy of Christmas away from his daughter. To take away the memories Isabel would have wanted him to share with their daughter.

Like Alyssa, his wife had taken great delight in the holidays. In the true meaning of Christmas. In the Lord. She believed Christmas was a time to receive God's tender mercy, abundant love, forgiveness and grace.

Maybe it was time for him to let go of the anger he'd been holding on to, which had left him feeling cold and empty, and step willingly back into the Lord's embrace.

A horn blasted on the road behind him. Nathan opened his eyes just as Carter pulled up alongside his truck, motioning for him to lower his window. He did despite the rain, the expression on his brother's face telling him something had happened. Nathan's gut clenched.

"Where have you been?" his brother demanded.

"Took a few back roads before parking to mull a few things over. Why? What's wrong?"

"You need to get home. Now," his brother said with an urgency that had Nathan's heart dropping.

"Is it Katie?" he asked, barely managing to get the words out.

His brother nodded. "She ran off and Alyssa is out in the woods looking for her."

"In the woods?" he exclaimed. Katie never went any farther than the end of their yard.

"That's what Alyssa told me before the call cut out," his brother replied as the rain fell harder.

"She'd have little or no signal in those woods," Nathan called out over the pounding rain. Then his brother's words hit him like a blow to the gut. "Alyssa called you?" Had he messed things up so badly between them that she'd sought help from his brother instead of him in her time of need?

"She tried to reach you," he yelled out, "but it

went straight to voice mail. So she called Audra, who called me."

"How long ago?" he said as he started his truck.

"Not quite an hour ago. I was in Uvalde picking up some supplies when Audra called to tell me what happened. That's where I'm coming from now. Logan should already be at the house."

With a nod, Nathan threw the truck into gear and hit the gas. His girls needed him. His gaze penetrated the rain outside to settle on the dense woods that covered his property. The sun, barely visible behind the thick, gray clouds, was rapidly setting behind the distant mountains for the night. The woods would be dark, cast in shadows. And, in this rain, damp and bitingly cold. Katie and Alyssa were out there alone, and it was all his fault.

Nathan knew what he had to do. Something he hadn't done for two long years. He prayed. "Lord, I humbly ask for Your forgiveness for turning my back on You during my time of loss. I was weak and I lost my way. In Your good grace, You sent Alyssa into my life. A woman strong in her faith and convictions, a woman blessed with a giving heart. Through *Your* love and her gentle patience, I am finding my way back. I pray that You will watch over my daughter and the woman I love, keeping them safe until they can be found. Amen."

Logan's truck sat in the driveway in front of the house when they arrived. Nathan parked his truck and jumped out. Carter did the same.

"We'll need flashlights," he told Nathan.

He raced into the house to grab a battery-operated

spotlight and a couple of flashlights along with a pair of two-way radios.

Carter met him out back. "Got everything?"

Nathan nodded, handing his brother a flashlight. "Let's go." They set off in a jog across the rain-slickened yard and were almost to the tree line when Logan stepped from the woods.

Hope flared inside Nathan for the briefest moment. Then his gaze moved past his brother to see that no one followed him out. He met Logan's gaze. "No sign of them?"

Logan shook his head. "I picked up a trail and was able to follow it about a hundred yards in, but it got too dark to see."

Nathan handed him the other flashlight and then turned on the battery-operated spotlight he'd brought along. "Let's go find my girls."

Logan led them back to the trail he'd been following. "What do you think happened?" he asked, his voice raised over the sound of the rain. "It's not like Katie to run off like this."

The guilt returned full force. "*I* happened," Nathan admitted. "The girls thought they'd surprise me by bringing out the Christmas decorations. Katie was so excited. Alyssa had a smile on her beautiful face." He looked to his brothers. "And I raised my voice to them both, told them they had no right to do what they'd done, then I walked out."

His brothers looked his way, concern filling their eyes.

"I need to find them," he said brokenly. "Need to tell them how sorry I am and ask for their forgiveness."

"Don't worry. We'll find them," Carter said.

Despite his brothers' assurances, they soon discovered that any trail left behind by Alyssa and his daughter was quickly being washed away by the rain. At least Alyssa was moving in the same direction that Katie had gone in. He had to wonder if God hadn't had a hand in that, considering Alyssa's limited vision. He said a silent prayer of thanks to the Lord for guiding them down the same path and asked that He continue to keep them safe from harm.

They'd gone nearly three-quarters of a mile into the woods, calling out to Katie and Alyssa in hopes of getting some sort of verbal response. But the only sound came from the rain falling through the trees to the ground below.

"How can they not hear us?" Nathan said in frustration. "Voice carries in the night."

"The rain probably isn't helping matters," Carter acknowledged as he raised the collar of his coat in an effort to keep out the pulsing rain.

"I reckon it's possible we're following the wrong trail," Logan suggested with a frown. "With all this rain and the lack of good light, it's hard to tell if the tracks we're picking up around here now are animal or human."

"They're human," Carter said from where he searched about ten feet away.

They turned their lights onto him to see their brother holding up a small, glittery crown.

Nathan closed the distance between himself and Carter and reached for the silvery piece. "That's Princess Sparkles's crown."

Logan motioned to the ground. "Looks like someone fell."

Nathan's first thought was that it had been Katie who had fallen. How else would her doll's crown have ended up on the ground? He clutched the tiny crown in the palm of his hand, his gut clenching as he looked to the spot his brother was pointing out. Sure enough there were two deep indents in the soft earth where what he assumed had to be knees had dug in. Just past the pitted ground, the bed of pine needles that made up the forest floor had been tunneled through in two long lines. Too big to have been made by Katie's hands.

"Alyssa," he said, his words barely audible. His light shone on the gnarled root sticking up only a couple feet away. Of course, she wouldn't have seen it. Not with her poor vision and the fading light of day. Had she injured herself in the fall? And was Katie with her now? She had to be, he told himself. How else would that crown have gotten there? Alyssa had found his daughter.

Carter clasped a hand over Nathan's shoulder. "There's no blood, and the fall didn't keep her from continuing on. That's a good sign."

Nathan's frown deepened. "Except that they're going in the wrong direction."

"Unless they respond soon to our hollering, we're gonna lose their trail altogether. The rain's coming down too hard," Logan said, unable to keep the urgency from his voice.

"No, we're not," Carter said, drawing both men's worried gazes his way. "Boone can find them."

Boone was the droopy-faced bloodhound mix Carter and Audra had adopted from the pound for the kids. Despite his massive size, weighing in now at close to eighty pounds, the dog still hadn't reached full maturity. He still liked to test the limits Carter set for him. But Nathan was willing to try whatever it took to find Katie and Alyssa. If they didn't find them soon, he was calling the sheriff to start a search party.

He looked to Carter and said determinedly. "Get him. Logan and I will keep looking."

With a nod, Carter took off through the woods, dodging back and forth around trees and brush until he'd disappeared behind a curtain of darkness and rain.

"Katie!" Nathan hollered again, his voice starting to show the strain of the repeated yelling he'd done.

"Alyssa!" his brother joined in, his voice sounding no better.

Still no response.

He would not allow his thoughts to travel down a negative path. He would trust in God's will and hope that *His* will was for them to bring Katie and Alyssa home safely. Nathan turned to his brother. "Before we go any farther, there's something I'd like for us to do."

"Name it," Logan said.

"I'd like for us to pray."

Something wet moved over Alyssa's cheek. She swatted at it sleepily. Then as the memory of the huge centipede she'd seen crossing the cave floor came into her groggy mind, her eyes shot open. Something warm and moist caressed her face.

Dear Lord, please don't let it be a bear.

Lifting her phone with trembling hands, her heart pounding, Alyssa turned on the flashlight. Two dark eyes surrounded by sagging folds of fur-covered skin peered into her face. Try as she might, she couldn't keep the startled shriek from escaping her lips.

Katie's head shot up, awakened from the peaceful slumber she'd fallen into. The squeal she let out put Alyssa's to shame. "Boone!"

Before Alyssa could stop her, Katie flew at the bear, throwing her arms around its neck. Horrified, Alyssa moved to pull her back and put herself between Katie and the whimpering bear.

"Oh, Boone, you found us," Katie was saying. "Good dog."

Good dog? The giant creature was a dog? Alyssa felt light-headed with relief.

"Boone!" a familiar voice called out from the darkness outside.

The dog barked in response.

"Uncle Carter!" Katie exclaimed.

"Katydid?"

"Katie!" Nathan's worried voice carried into the cave.

"We're in here!" Alyssa called out, shining the beam of light from her phone out into the night.

Footsteps pounded atop the muddied ground outside, coming closer. A moment later, three hulking figures squeezed into the opening of the cave.

"Daddy!" Katie shot out of Alyssa's lap, running toward him.

Setting the light he held down beside him, he knelt on the ground, catching Katie in his outstretched arms. He hugged her tight, pressing kisses to the top of her tiny head. "Baby girl," he said, holding her away from him to look her over. "Are you all right?"

She nodded. "I was scared, but Alyssa found me."

He looked past Katie to where Alyssa sat unmoving on the floor of the cave. "Logan," he called back over his shoulder.

"I've got her," his brother said, reaching for Katie.

"I'm gonna take Boone outside," Carter said as he clipped a leash onto the dog's collar.

"We're right behind you," Logan said, bending low as he carried Katie out of the cave.

Tears rolled down Alyssa's cheeks. *Katie was safe. Katie was safe.* That was all she could think about as she sat shivering on the ground.

Then Nathan was there, wrapping his strong arms around her. "Alyssa."

She leaned into his warmth, trembling.

He immediately pulled away, his gaze moving over her. "Where's your coat?"

"B-back at the house."

"But Katie had hers on," he said, as he hurried to remove his own coat.

"I grabbed it when I went in to get my phone," she said as he worked her chilled arms through its sleeves.

"And not your own?" he said as he bundled her up in the warmth of his coat.

"There wasn't time."

Reaching up, he pushed the tangle of her hair back from her face and gasped. "You're hurt."

"A few scratches."

Cupping her chin he tipped her face upward to inspect it. "Your beautiful face," he said, his words filled with anguish. Then, leaning forward, he pressed a tender kiss to her cheek. "Thank you for being there for my daughter and keeping her safe."

"We were there for each other," she said, her voice

cracking. "And your thanks should go to the Lord who kept us safe and gave us shelter."

"I agree," he said, his response surprising her. "God is good. He answered my prayers."

She lifted her head to look up at him. "You prayed?"

He nodded. "God and I had a long talk. Actually, I did all the talking, but that's how it needed to be. I asked for His forgiveness and then asked that He bring you and Katie home safe to me. My prayers were answered." Lifting her into his arms, he stood, leaning forward just enough to avoid the cave's low ceiling. "Time to go home."

Tears filled her eyes as he carried her out to where the others waited. Just when Nathan finally found his way back to the Lord, something she needed for their relationship to work, her own failings made it clear she could never be a part of his life the way she'd hoped to be. No matter how deeply she loved him.

Chapter Thirteen

"Gather up your things, Cupcake. We've got a few errands to run before we head to the rec center this morning."

"Okay!" Katie exclaimed, excited to be well enough to be around other people again. She scurried off to her bedroom to get her backpack full of coloring books and crayons and the handheld gaming system Nathan's brothers had bought her last Christmas.

He'd called Alyssa after Logan had taken her home the night before, needing to hear her voice. Needing to know that she was okay after all that had transpired, since they'd had little time to talk when they'd gotten back to the house the night before. All focus had been on tending to Alyssa's injuries and warming her and Katie by the fire. When Alyssa'd asked Logan to take her back to the boardinghouse, Nathan had insisted he take her. She'd refused, telling him that his place was with his daughter. But there was so much he'd wanted to say to her. Words that would just have to wait until the time was right. So he'd settled for another heartfelt thank-you and then told her to sleep in.

That he and Katie would pick her up around eleven the following morning to take her to see the newly completed rec center.

Smiling, Nathan walked into the kitchen to grab his coat from its hook by the door. He couldn't wait for Alyssa to see all her design plans in their finished state. She was as much a part of this project as he and his brothers were and she'd missed so much staying home with Katie. Everything fit so well, from the colors she'd chosen for each room to the various types of flooring that had needed to be laid. Even the furniture, a more modern style than he would have chosen, worked perfectly.

Rusty Clark, representing the town council, had stopped by the rec center the previous afternoon and had been duly impressed by the detail Alyssa had put into the project. He'd even placed a call to the design firm she worked for, putting in a word of praise for her work. Not that it mattered, Nathan thought to himself, his smile widening. If everything worked out as he hoped it would, this would be just the first of many projects he and Alyssa would be working on together. Her firm hadn't realized what a true talent Alyssa still was, but he did.

Pulling out his cell, he called Carter.

"Are you at the rec center?"

"Got here about twenty minutes ago," Carter replied. "Logan is in the gymnasium, making sure the Christmas tree is secure before it's decorated. The crew and I are packing away the rest of our tools. Then I'm sending them home to their families. You on your way in or is my little Katydid still sleeping?"

"Are you kidding? She was up hours ago. She can't wait to see the rec center."

"She'll be surprised."

"That she will." So much had changed during the time Katie had been forced to stay home while she recuperated from chicken pox. "The reason I'm calling is to ask you for a favor."

"Name it," his brother said without hesitation.

"Katie and I have a couple of special errands we need to see to in town. She wants to get Alyssa something special to thank her for what she did."

"A nice gesture," Carter agreed. "But then my niece did inherit her thoughtfulness from me. What's the other errand?"

Nathan smiled. "I wanted to get Alyssa something special, as well. She's expecting Katie and me to pick her up around eleven, but I'm not sure if we'll be done in time. Think you can run out to the boardinghouse and pick her up around that time?"

"I'd be glad to."

"Thanks, Carter. I owe you one." Disconnecting the call, he went to round up his daughter.

A little over an hour later, he and Katie pulled into the rec center parking lot. Carter hadn't returned yet from picking up Alyssa. That was good. It gave him time to collect himself and go over the words he wanted to say in his head before he actually tried to speak them.

"Everything looks so pretty," his daughter exclaimed the second they stepped through the door.

Nathan smiled, understanding her surprise over what had been done. She hadn't seen the rec center since coming down with chicken pox. "Alyssa did a fine job."

"With my help," Katie promptly reminded him.

He chuckled. "That goes without saying, Cupcake." He ruffled her dark curls playfully. "Daddy's very proud of the work you and Alyssa did here."

She looked up at him. "Do you think Alyssa is mad at us?"

Her words brought forth the same concern that had plagued him through the night. Not in regards to Alyssa being upset with Katie. He knew better. Alyssa understood why Katie had reacted the way she had. But a part of him worried that his apology hadn't taken all the sting of his words away. Hopefully, his intended surprise would stir her to forgive him and allow them to become the family he knew they could be.

"No, honey," he replied with confidence. "She's not mad at us. Why would you think that?"

She looked down at the toe of her boots. "'Cause you yelled at her and I ran away and made her get hurt."

He smiled reassuringly. "She understands that everybody has a bad day once in a while and that Daddy is very sorry for raising his voice to the both of you." At least, he hoped she did. But he left his explanation at that, since Katie wasn't quite old enough to understand the emotions that had driven him to react the way he had. "And Alyssa doesn't blame you for her getting hurt. She loves you. So much so, she went into the woods to find you, even though her eyes aren't able to see as good as most people's. That's why she fell. She didn't see the root sticking up through the fallen pine needles."

"I love her, too," his daughter said.

"That makes two of us," he told her.

Her eyes widened. "Even without the mistletoe?"

His brows furrowed in confusion. "Mistletoe?"

She nodded. "Remember what Alyssa told us in the toy store? She said mistletoe makes people kiss and fall in love. But you had to be standing under it for it to work." She looked up at him. "Is there mistletoe in our woods?"

He chuckled. "Not that I know of. Sometimes the heart just knows, even without the help of mistletoe."

The rec center door swung open and Carter stepped inside—alone.

"Where's Alyssa?" Nathan asked.

"She's not coming in," Carter said, frowning.

"What do you mean she's not coming in?"

"Does she have my chicken pox?" Katie asked worriedly.

"No, honey," Carter said. "She doesn't have your chicken pox. As far as I could tell, she wasn't sick at all. Just a little out of sorts."

"Cupcake," Nathan said, his gaze fixed on his brother, "Daddy needs to have a word in private with Uncle Carter. Why don't you take your backpack into the art room and draw Alyssa a pretty picture to give her with the flowers we picked up for her?"

Carter nodded. "I'll bet she'd like that."

"Okay," she said, walking over to grab her backpack off one of the lobby chairs.

Nathan waited until she was out of hearing before saying, "Are you certain she's not sick? They were out in that damp weather for nearly three hours last night."

"I reckon she could be, but her coloring looked good," Carter replied. "But she seemed a bit off."

"Off how?"

His brother shrugged. "Not real sure how to explain it. Withdrawn, maybe. I suppose she might just be a little skittish after all that happened yesterday. What she went through had to have worn on her mentally. Probably why she said she needed some time to sort through things today."

Concern coming over his face, Nathan pulled his phone from the front pocket of his jeans. This was not a good sign.

"I think I'd wait on calling her," his brother suggested with an empathetic smile. "When a woman asks for some time to herself, a smart man knows to steer clear. Take it from a man who was in the not-so-smart category where Audra was concerned during one of our earlier rough patches."

It took everything in him to hold off on calling Alyssa. He needed to know where her head was at. And, more importantly, where her heart was. Because he knew how he felt. He loved her. Couldn't imagine his life without her in it. But his brother was right. She'd been through an ordeal yesterday, and he needed to respect her need for some breathing room.

Until then, he needed to try to redirect his thoughts elsewhere. "Let's get this place cleaned up." All that was left to haul out to their trucks were a couple of nail guns they'd used for the trim and baseboards, a table saw, a scattering of hand tools and the plywood and sawhorses they had set up to do the final cuts on the trim.

Carter looked around the room. "Hard to believe this place is gonna be all festive and filled with townsfolk in a few days."

Nathan nodded. It was even harder to believe that he was going to be there attending the Christmas Eve gathering along with them. But he would be. Not only for Katie's sake, but for the woman he loved. Alyssa loved the holidays, something she'd never had the chance to enjoy growing up. He wanted to be the man to give her all those things she'd missed out on. A real home. A family. Love.

"I'm gonna ask Alyssa to marry me."

Carter's head snapped around, his eyes wide. "Run that by me again."

"I love her," he admitted aloud for the first time. It felt good. "And before you try to talk me out of rushing into things—"

"Hold up a moment, big brother," Carter said with a grin. "Remember who you're talking to. It's not like I took my time getting to the altar once I knew Audra was the one for me."

His brother's response lightening his mood, Nathan chuckled. "How do you think Logan's gonna react to the news?"

"After what Alyssa did for Katie last night, I wouldn't be surprised if he was thinking about marrying her himself."

That wiped the smile from Nathan's face.

This time it was Carter who was chuckling aloud. "Boy, do you have it bad. Question for you, big brother. Have you told Alyssa yet that you love her?"

"Not in those exact words," he admitted.

"Might be good to get that little tidbit in before you actually propose to her. Take it from a man who knows."

It was all Alyssa could do to force herself from bed that morning, only a few days shy of what would have been her first Christmas Eve with Nathan and Katie. Even a call from her design firm, telling her they wanted to discuss bringing her back on full-time when she returned to San Antonio hadn't lifted her spirits.

She'd dressed, her heart heavy, knowing Nathan and Katie would be by to pick her up to go tour the newly completed recreation center. Knowing she wouldn't be going with them. But Carter had shown up in their place, telling her Nathan had a few things he'd needed to take care of in town and would meet them at the rec center. Probably a blessing. She wasn't certain she was strong enough yet to do what she had to do. Instead, she had sent Carter on his way, telling him she needed some time to herself.

Her work at the recreation center was done. It was time to go. Even if her heart was pleading with her to stay. All she wanted to do was go back to bed and pull the covers up over her head and cry some more. Just as she had all night. But that wouldn't change anything. Her visual impairment had put Katie's life at risk. What if next time Katie wasn't physically able to cry out for help so Alyssa could find her? She shuddered at the thought of what that could have meant for Katie.

No, Katie deserved a mother who could protect her from harm. And Nathan deserved a woman he could trust to keep his daughter safe. She wasn't that woman.

Tears spilled down her cheeks as she pulled her suitcase from the closet and placed it atop the bed. Then she reached toward the nightstand for her cell phone and dialed Erica's number.

"Good morning!" her best friend chirped when she answered.

Oh, how she wished it were. But there was nothing good about having to walk away from the man that you loved.

"Alyssa?"

"Can you come get me?"

"I thought you were gonna be staying in Braxton through the holidays."

"Things have changed," she said, her voice catching.

"I hate that Nathan hurt you."

"I'm the one who is gonna be hurting him," she said, her heart breaking at the thought of it. "But sometimes when you truly love someone, you have to set them free."

"Did you say *love*? As in you're in *love* with Nathan?"

"And his precious little girl," Alyssa replied, tears filling her eyes.

"Alyssa," her friend said, her tone laced with a mix of compassion and concern. "You love him. Whyever would you feel the need to walk away?"

With a heavy sigh, she went on to tell her friend all that had happened the night before. Then she hung up and started packing her things. Erica had tried to convince her to rethink her decision, but Alyssa knew it would be selfish of her to stay. So she was doing the only other thing she could. She was going home.

By the time she'd finished packing, exhaustion, both mental and physical, had her crawling back atop the quilted bedspread and closing her eyes. She had a few hours before Erica could get there to pick her up and even less time before she had to face Nathan with the news of her leaving. But for now, all she wanted to do was sleep. And so she did.

A tap at the bedroom door roused Alyssa from sleep. "Come in," she said tiredly.

Doris poked her head in the door, announcing in that sweet, grandmotherly voice Alyssa recognized immediately, "You have a visitor, dear."

A visitor? Sitting up, she swung her legs off the bed. "I'll be right down," she told her as the sleep cleared from her mind.

"No need," the older woman said. "He's right here. I'll give you two a moment to talk while I go put the teapot on."

Doris scurried off and a very tall, slightly blurred form stepped in from the hallway. The second her vision adjusted enough to see her visitor somewhat clearly, she gasped. "Nathan?"

He moved toward her, a frown on his face. "Never took you for a quitter."

Her heart lurched.

"Or is Erica mistaken about your leaving town?"

"How did you—"

"She called me," he said, his hurt at what she'd intended to do clear in his voice.

She pushed off the bed and walked over to look out the window, unable to face him. "She shouldn't have."

He stepped forward, boots clicking across the hardwood floor as he closed the distance between them.

His hands came to rest on her shoulders, gently turning her to face him. "Were you really gonna leave without saying goodbye?"

She forced herself to meet his troubled gaze, guilt filling her. "No," she said in a whisper. "I would have said goodbye."

"What about Katie?" he asked. "You're gonna break her heart."

"I have to go," she said with a soft sob. "She could have died last night because of me."

"But she didn't," he said determinedly, running his hands up and down her arms in a slow, calming manner.

"I couldn't even get her back home once we found each other," she said with a soft sob.

"Grown men have gotten turned around in those woods in broad daylight. And you never gave up on finding her, despite the dark, despite the cold, despite the miserable rain."

Her bottom lip quivered as she fought to hold back the tears. "She's better off without me."

"I'm not so sure she'd agree," he replied. "I know I don't."

"Nathan…"

"Alyssa, *you* are the one we want in our lives. *You* are the one I trust to care for my daughter."

"How can you trust me to care for her after last night?"

He smiled tenderly. "You've nursed my daughter through a lengthy illness, caring for her as if she were your very own. And when my thoughtless words sent her running in tears from the house, you didn't allow your visual limitations to keep you from going after her." He reached out to gently brush his thumb over her tender cheek. "You risked and endured injury to find her. And once you did, you made certain Katie was warm and protected until we could find you both." He let his hand fall away. "How could I not trust you?"

Tears spilled down her cheeks. His kind words, his gentle touch, were weakening her already shaky resolve.

"Say you'll at least stay until the party," he pleaded. "For Katie's sake. She's expecting you to be there and she's not the only one," he reminded her. "Rusty and his wife, the reverend, my brothers, Audra and her little ones, the ladies from the church. I could go on and on."

Her gaze settled onto the hardwood floor between them. "I don't know if I can."

"Reckon that makes two of us."

She looked up at him questioningly.

"For the first time in two years, I'll be taking part in the town's Christmas Eve celebration. That means surrounding myself with all that warm, fuzzy holiday cheer I've been so determined to steer clear of. And then there's the dedication. It's not gonna be easy," he said, his words taut with emotion. "I don't wanna do this alone."

"Nathan…"

"You are my heart's light, Alyssa. Say you'll go with me and help to keep the darkness away."

"Tea's ready," Doris interrupted from the doorway. "Why don't you kids come on down to the parlor and have some? Myrna made coffee cake this morning. You can have some of it with your tea while you two sweethearts make up."

Make up? Before Alyssa could set Doris straight on her misconception that there could be anything more than friendship between her and Nathan, the older woman was gone.

Nathan released her, letting his hands fall away. "What do you say, darlin'? You willing to sit down with me and talk things through?"

"It won't change anything," she told him as she reached for her suitcase. "I'm not meant to be in your lives." No matter how desperately she wished it to be true.

Just like the first day they met, his hand beat hers to the handle of her suitcase, curling firmly around it. "I've got it."

"You don't have to—"

"Seems to me we've had this conversation before," he said as he headed toward the open door. Stopping in the doorway, he turned to her with a grin the size of Texas. "As far as things being meant to be, what do you say we leave that in God's hands?" With that, he was gone.

Alyssa stood staring at the empty doorway, joy filling her despite the heartbreak her decision to leave was causing her. Something good had come from her and Katie getting lost in the woods. Nathan had finally found his way back to the Lord.

With one final walk around the room to make certain she hadn't forgotten anything, she headed downstairs to say her goodbyes. The sight that greeted her in the parlor stopped her dead in her tracks. The small room was filled with people.

Heart pounding, she let her gaze do a slow sweep of the room, grateful that her vision had seemed to clear up from what it had been upstairs. Carter and Logan stood at each end of the mantel, propped against it in a leisurely pose. There was no mistaking their tall, hulking forms. And if she had to guess, she was sure they were both grinning. Doris and Myrna sat in the center of the room at the antique pedestal table, smiling. And to her left, Audra and the kids stood by the parlor window. Her gaze searched for the one face, with the exception of Nathan's, that she longed to see.

"I'm over here," a tiny voice called out, tugging at her heart.

She looked toward the deep burgundy Victorian love seat that sat in the far corner to see what could only be Katie seated there, waving her hand excitedly. Dear, sweet, Katie. How would she ever be able to tell her goodbye?

"Hello, Katie," she said with a teary smile. She was going to miss seeing that adorable little face every day.

"I'm here, too."

She turned to see her best friend standing next to Doris and Myrna's beloved tea cart. "Erica?" she gasped. "What are you doing here? I thought you had to work until four."

"Now what kind of best friend would I be if I stayed at work and missed this?" she said, sounding almost happy.

"Missed what?" Alyssa said in confusion.

"This," a deep voice said.

Her gaze shifted once again to find Nathan walking toward her. The look on his handsome face was one of determination. Reaching out, he took hold of her hand. "What are you doing?"

"Reckon you could say I'm putting my heart on the line," he replied, his tender gaze locking with hers.

"I don't understand," she said, searching his eyes.

"Maybe this will help," he said with a grin as he knelt in front of her.

Her soft gasp filled the parlor.

"Before you came into my life, I simply existed. Through your never-ending patience and your un-yielding faith in God, you taught me how to truly live again." His thumb caressed the back of her hand. "How to love again."

"Nathan…" she began, her legs trembling beneath her.

"Hear me out, Alyssa," he implored. "A man only gets to do this once in his life. Twice if God sees fit to bless him with a second chance. You, Alyssa Mc-Call, are my second chance."

Tears left wet trails down her cheeks, brought on by his beautiful words and the love she felt for the man kneeling before her.

"Daddy, you're making her cry," Katie said, sounding worried.

Laughing softly, she said, "They're happy tears, Katie. Very happy tears."

"I love you, Alyssa McCall," Nathan continued.

"Me, too!" Katie chimed in.

He chuckled, amending his words, "*We* love you. And we want you to be a part of our lives for as long as the good Lord sees fit. I know we've only been court-ing a short time, but you and I both know how fast life can change. I wanna spend whatever time I have left on this earth loving you. Working side by side. Laugh-ing together. Alyssa McCall, will you do me the honor of agreeing to become my wife?"

"And my mommy!" Katie blurted out, the love seat creaking as she bounced up and down in delight.

"We don't have to get married right away. But I want us to keep moving forward," he said, looking up at her with undeniable love shining in his eyes. "When you're ready, say the word and we'll set the date."

"I…" She was so shocked, she could hardly speak.

He smiled warmly. A smile she would have the chance to see every day for the rest of her life if she chose to trust in the love he was offering her.

Looking down at Nathan, she returned his smile. "I would love nothing more than to be your wife."

"And my new mommy," Katie blurted out.

Nathan knew she would never try to take Isabel's place in Katie's life. But she would give his daughter what she needed. Another mother to care for her and help guide her into adulthood. "And," she added, her voice tight with emotion, "Katie's new mommy."

"Reckon my daddy was right," Nathan said, his tender gaze never leaving hers. "He told us boys there is always hope beyond the storm. And here you are, pushing away the dark clouds in my life and filling it with never-ending sunshine."

"Best get to sealing the deal," Carter hollered from across the room. "Before she up and changes her mind."

"She might even decide she'd rather marry me," Logan said with a teasing chuckle.

"Sorry, baby brother," Nathan shot back. "This girl is mine. You're gonna have to go find your own." Reaching into his shirt pocket, he withdrew a small blue ring box. Then he raised the lid, revealing a large solitaire flanked by two smaller diamonds."

"It's beautiful," Alyssa breathed, her heart pounding.

Taking the ring from its velvet nest, he slid it onto her finger and then stood, drawing her into his arms. "No, darlin', *you're* beautiful." Then he lowered his mouth to hers in a gentle, loving kiss.

"Alyssa was right," Katie squealed, pointing to the top of the entryway.

Everyone's gaze lifted to the sprig of dark green mistletoe tied in a cheery red ribbon that hung just above the newly engaged couple's heads.

"Kissing under the mistletoe makes two people wanna get married," Katie went on to explain in a way only a six-year-old could. Then she ran over to throw her arms around Nathan and Alyssa. "Now we'll get to be a real family."

"Yes, sweetie," Alyssa said, pressing a kiss to Katie's brow. "We most certainly will."

"Only I'm gonna have to change my Christmas list," Katie said with an exaggerated sigh. "'Cause I already got what I was asking for—a mommy under the mistletoe."

Nathan chuckled. "What more could you want?"

Looking up at her daddy, she said, "I would like a dog just like Boone for Christmas…a really big picnic basket so we can go on lots of picnics together… and maybe a baby brother or sister."

With a chuckle, Nathan said, "It appears my daughter and I have the exact same Christmas list. With the exception of a brother or sister for Katie. That's gonna have to wait until next Christmas."

Laughter filled the room. And soon Alyssa found herself being embraced and congratulated, her heart overflowing with happiness. She had the love of a wonderful man, the precious gift of a child to love and someday soon she'd have a huge, loving family to call her very own.

Epilogue

"Merry Christmas, darlin'," Nathan said as he came in from the kitchen to stand behind his beautiful fiancée, wrapping his arms around her waist as they stood admiring Katie's lovingly decorated Christmas tree.

She glanced up at him over her shoulder with a warm smile. "Merry Christmas to you, too. Were you able to get Katie's special surprise?"

"Took some doing," he said with a grin. Luckily for him, Carter had heard him pull up and had come out to help him round up the rambunctious pup he had been hiding in his brother's barn for the past two days. "Boone wasn't too happy about my taking his furry little friend away, but I told him they'd have plenty of time to play together in the future. Oh, and we're supposed to be at Carter's for Christmas dinner at four."

"My first Christmas dinner with your family," she said, her face alight with excitement.

"Soon to be your family, too," he reminded her.

Days before, with Alyssa and his daughter by his side, he had attended the church's annual Christmas program. One that had moved him both spiritually and emotionally. Then on Christmas Eve they had all gone together to the rec center for the dedication which had been a beautiful way to both cherish and finally let go of Isabel. He'd even made it through the Christmas festivities that followed without the darkness he used to feel any time he so much as thought about the holidays. The painful memories of his past had been replaced by new ones. Memories filled with family and friends, laughter and love, and so much more.

"The first of many," he added, his words a promise.

"Should we go wake Katie so you can give her the gift you got for her?"

"Not yet," he said with a tender smile. "First, I have a special surprise for you."

She turned in his arms, looking up at him with a teasing smile. "I'm getting a puppy, too?"

He chuckled softly. "Sorry to disappoint you, darlin', but your gift isn't nearly as fun." Leaning past her, he hooked a finger through one of the gift bags he'd set out around the tree the night before, lifting it from the assortment of prettily wrapped presents. "But," he said as he handed the glittery snowman gift bag to her, "I think you're gonna like it all the same. Why don't we have a seat on the sofa while you open it?"

"I already like it," she said as they walked over to the sofa and sat down. "I have a thing for snowmen."

"And handsome construction workers?" he added with a grin as he settled onto the sofa next to her.

Her smile widened. "*And* handsome construction workers. Especially one in particular."

He cupped her chin and tilted her face his way. "Well, I seem to have developed a thing for beautiful redheads."

A hint of color filled her cheeks. "My hair's not red. It's auburn."

"I stand corrected," he teased, lowering his mouth to hers in a sweet kiss. Then he pulled back and nodded toward the gift on her lap. "Best get to opening your present before Katie's special surprise figures out some way to escape the temporary wall I put up across the back porch steps."

Smiling, she reached into the bag and pulled out a tissue-wrapped bundle. Opening it carefully, she discovered there were several smaller tissue wrapped gifts inside. She peeled the paper away from the first and then held up the delicate glass ornament. "A bowling pin?"

"I know how much that ornament Doris and Myrna gave you means to you," he said. "I thought I'd add to your collection with some memories of our own."

Tears filled her eyes. "I love it."

He took the glass bowling pin from her, handing her another of the tissue-wrapped bundles.

She gasped when she opened it, holding the miniature picnic basket in the palm of her upturned hand.

"This is for the inside picnic we shared," he told her. "And for all the picnics out under that big blue Texas sky we're gonna have in the years to come."

She sniffled, tears filling her eyes. "I can't wait to share those moments with you and Katie."

"One more," he said, taking the tiny basket and placing it atop the tissue it had been wrapped in.

"When did you have time to do all this?" she asked as she unrolled the wrapping from around the last piece.

"It's called online shopping with overnight shipping."

"Nathan," she gasped as she lifted from the tissue the ornament he'd made special for her.

The crystal teardrop ornament had come topped with mistletoe. He'd added a miniature hammer and paintbrush to it that he'd found in the dollhouse section of Rusty's toy store, attaching them to the mistletoe with the thinnest red ribbon he could find. "Reckon it was pretty enough without the fixings, but I thought the hammer and paintbrush made it more personal."

"It's perfect," she said, her words catching as she reached up to swipe a tear from her cheek. "I'll cherish it always." Reaching out for the gift she'd set on the end table when she'd arrived that morning, she handed it to him. "This is for you."

His smile widened as he took it. "A lump of coal?"

"Never," she replied. "Something I made special just for you."

His brow lifted as he eyed the gift with curiosity. "You made this, huh?" Peeling away the paper, he opened the top flaps of the box and pulled out a large, round, festively decorated Christmas tin. Then he lifted the lid, a wash of emotion coming over him. "You made me cookies."

"I have it on good authority that men have a thing for sweets," she explained with a smile. "And I decorated them all myself."

Inside the tin was at least two dozen iced sugar cookies. Each one had something different written across them in red or green icing. Love. Family. Forever. Yours. He lifted his gaze to Alyssa. "I love you."

"I love you, too."

"Is it Christmas yet?" a tiny voice chirped behind them.

They turned to find Katie standing in the living room entryway, attempting to suppress a sleepy yawn.

"It sure is," Alyssa said gleefully. "And wait until you see the special surprise your daddy has for you."

Katie glanced toward the lit tree and the gifts spread out beneath it, and her eyes widened.

Nathan helped Alyssa place her gifts back into the gift bag and then stood. "Settle yourself onto the floor by the tree, Cupcake, while I go get your special present."

Alyssa walked over to wait by the tree with his daughter. Unable to keep the smile of happiness from his face, he went to get Katie's surprise, returning a couple of minutes later with a very large picnic basket, a big red bow tied around one of its handles.

"You got me a picnic basket!" his daughter squealed in delight.

He set the basket onto the floor in front of her and then stepped back to stand beside his fiancée, sliding an arm around her waist.

The basket wiggled, making Katie jump. Then a tiny whimper slid through its woven cracks. His daughter wasted no time pushing the handles down and whipping open the lid. A tiny beige head popped up and Katie exclaimed in delight. "It's a dog!"

"A puppy," Nathan corrected with a grin. "Which means we'll be doing a lot of cleaning up after her until she's housebroken."

She hefted the roly-poly little Lab pup from the basket and hugged it to her as it planted wet puppy kisses across her face. "I love her!"

"What are you gonna name her?" Alyssa asked as she knelt to pet the squirming ball of fur.

"I'm gonna name her Mistletoe," Katie announced as she attempted to dodge another onslaught of eager kisses.

"That's a pretty big name for such a little pup," Nathan said as he knelt next to his girls—all *three* of them.

"How about calling her Missy for short?" Alyssa suggested.

"Missy," Katie said, sounding it out. Then she lifted the pup, looking up into its round little face. "What do you think? Should I call you Missy?"

The pup barked excitedly. More to be let down to run wild than in appreciation of the name, Nathan thought with a grin, but it was all his daughter needed to settle on it. "Welcome to our family, Missy," Katie said, planting a kiss atop one of the pup's floppy tan ears. "This is the most special Christmas ever!"

Nathan looked to Alyssa, the woman who had rescued his heart, filling it with love, and his eyes misted over. God is good. "Yes, Cupcake," he said, his gaze meeting Alyssa's. "It surely is."

* * * * *